Book Three of the Sigmar Trilogy

GOD KING

The Legend of Sigmar

Graham McNeill

BLACK LIBRARY

To Anita. For everything.

A BLACK LIBRARY PUBLICATION

First published in Great Britain in 2011 by
BL Publishing,
Games Workshop Ltd.,
Willow Road, Nottingham,
NG7 2WS, UK

10 9 8 7 6 5 4 3 2 1

Cover illustration by Jon Sullivan.
Map by Nuala Kinrade.

A CIP record for this book is available from the British Library.

UK ISBN 13: 978-1-84416-898-9
US ISBN 13: 978-1-84416-899-6

See the Black Library on the Internet at
www.blacklibrary.com

Find out more about Games Workshop
and the world of Warhammer at
www.games-workshop.com

Printed and bound in the UK.

THIS IS A dark age, a bloody age, an age of daemons and of sorcery. It is an age of battle and death, and of the world's ending. Amidst all of the fire, flame and fury it is a time, too, of mighty heroes, of bold deeds and great courage.

AT THE HEART of the Old World lie the lands of men, ruled over by the Emperor Sigmar.

Once a land divided, it has been united into the Empire, stretching from the Sea of Claws in the north to the Grey Mountains of the south. At Reikdorf dwells the Emperor, the only man with vision enough to see that if men could not overcome their differences and rally together, their demise is assured.

TO THE FROZEN north, Norsii raiders, barbarians and worshippers of Dark Gods, burn, slay and pillage. Grim spectres haunt the marshlands and monstrous beasts gather in the forests. Greenskins plague the land and will forever be the bane of men. Defeated at Black Fire Pass, they gather their strength in mountain lairs, waiting on another chance to invade the Empire.

BUT SIGMAR DOES not stand alone against his many enemies. The dwarfs of the mountains, great forge smiths and engineers, are his oath-sworn allies. As a great and terrible evil from the dawn of time arises to lay waste to the Empire, all must stand together, dwarf and man, for their mutual survival depends on it.

Our Land in the time of Sigmar

Salzenhus

FOREST OF SHADOWS

Brass Kee

Fauschlag Rock

FOREST ROAD

CH

Battle of the
Berserker King

THURINGIANS

Count Otwin's
Castle

H

JUTONES

Unter

THE GR
FORE

Jutonsryk

TEUTOGENS

GREAT NORTH ROAD

BRETONII

Marburg

Astofen

Reikdorf

ENDALS

UNBEROGENS

PALE
SISTERS

GREY MTNS.

BOOK ONE

Danse Macabre

Thus Sigmar wept not for Middenheim
Nor did he weep for his burned lands.
But he wept on seeing his brother lie dead
While all his people wept for themselves.

From that day upon the Fauschlag Rock
We did not speak boldly;
And we passed not either night or day
That we did not breathe heavy sighs.

Thus it was that Death carried off
Pendrag, whose strength and vigours had been mighty
As it will every warrior
Who shall come after him upon the earth.

✦ ONE ✦

Fire and Retribution

LORD AETULFF WAS dead, and they carried the body from his village in a long procession through the snow towards the surf-pounded shoreline. Those that had served under him, those despised few who had survived the long flight from the vengeful blades of their enemies, followed the solemn bier with their broken swords carried before them. Their lives were forfeit, but there were few enough men remaining along the coastline to put them to death for their cowardice.

The chieftain's favoured huscarls carried the body on a palanquin of broken shields, the body wrapped in a tattered flag brought from the south. The body was light; a wasting sickness had eaten the flesh from his bones upon his return from the disastrous war. Zhek Askah had said it was punishment from the gods, and none dared gainsay him.

Broken in spirit, Aetulff's wounded body had lingered six seasons after the defeat before finally succumbing. He

11

had been strong, and he took a long, painful time to die.

His sons were all dead, slain in battle as the gods decreed, and none now remained to preserve his line. He had died in the knowledge that no living creature would carry his name into the future. He would die unremembered and his bloody deeds would be forgotten in a generation.

The womenfolk did not follow the body, and his shame was complete.

The shield bearers followed a path to the water, where a fire burned in a pit hacked into the frozen ground. The waters of the ocean were dark, cold and unforgiving, and a storm-battered ship rose and fell with the surge and retreat of the tide. Sturdily built from overlapping timbers and tar, a rearing wolfshead was carved at its prow. It was a proud vessel and had carried them through the worst storms the gods could hurl from the skies. It deserved better, but if the last year and a half had taught the people of the settlement anything, it was that this world cared nothing for what was deserved.

The warriors following the body climbed aboard and turned to help lift the dead chieftain onto his ship. They were strong men and it took no effort to manoeuvre him onto a tiered pile of precious timbers and kindling. One by one, the warriors slashed their forearms with the broken blades of their swords. They spilled their blood over their dead war chief and dropped their useless weapons to the deck. Blood shed and swords surrendered, they climbed over the gunwale, which looked bare without lines of ranked-up kite shields and banks of fighting men hauling at the oars.

One warrior with a winged helm of raven's feathers waited until the others had splashed down into the sea before upending a flask of oil over the body. He doused the ship's timbers with what remained and tossed the flask to the deck. The raven-helmed warrior tugged a tied rope at the mainmast, and the black sail unfurled with a boom of hide.

He turned and dropped over the side of the ship, wading ashore to take his place with the rest of his forsaken band. Their war chief had died, yet they had lived. Their shame would be never-ending. Women would shun them, children would spit on them and they would be right to do so. The gods would curse them for all eternity until they made good on their debt.

The freezing wind caught the sail, and the ship eased away from the shore, wallowing without a steersman to guide it or rowers to power it. The tide and wind quickly dragged the ship away from the land, twisting it around like a leaf in a millpond. The treacherous currents and riptides around this region of the coast had dashed many an unwary vessel against the cliffs, yet they bore Lord Aetulff's ship out to sea with gentle swells. Gulls wheeled above its mast, adding their throaty caws to the chief's lament.

The raven-helmed warrior lifted a bow from the shingle and nocked an arrow to the string. He held the cloth-wrapped tip in the fire until it caught light and hauled back on the string. The wind dropped and he loosed the shaft, the fiery missile describing a graceful arc through the greying sky until it hammered home in the ship's mast.

Slowly, then with greater ferocity as the oil caught light, the ship burned. Flames roared to life, hungrily devouring the rotten meat of the dead man and setting to work on the oily timbers. Within moments, the ship was ablaze from bow to stern, black smoke trailing a mournful line towards the sky.

The warriors watched it until it split apart with a sound

like a heart breaking. It slid over onto its side and with a final slurp of water vanished beneath the surface.

Lord Aetulff was dead and no one mourned him.

FROM A CAVE mouth high on the cliffs above the village, a man in tattered furs and a cloak of feathers watched the last voyage of the doomed wolfship. His face was bearded and long hair hung in matted ropes from his head. Once it had been jet black, but it was now so wadded with mud and dirt that its true colour had long since been obscured. The filth of living in a cave encrusted his skin and his arms were rank with sores and rashes that burned and tingled pleasurably in equal measure.

The villagers called him Wyrtgeorn, though he could make little sense of the word. What he had bothered to learn of their language allowed him only the most basic understanding. A fetish-draped shaman had spat it at him a year and a half ago when he and the wizened immortal stepped from the wolfship that now burned to ashes. Though he did not know its meaning, it was a name to hide behind, a shield to hold before the deeds of his true name.

The immortal had left the village, imploring him to travel onwards into the northern wastes, but he had refused, climbing the cliff and making this cave his home. He knew he should have gone; his presence here would draw the hunters, but something had kept him from leaving, as though invisible shackles held him here.

He shook off such gloomy thoughts, and watched the wolfship slide beneath the waves. A rolling fogbank crept in from the south, obscuring the horizon and making the air taste of wet cloth. He watched the warriors as they trudged through the snow to the village, all too familiar with the shame they bore for their survival.

He threw a guilty look over his shoulder, wincing as the wound that would never heal flared with old pain. The immortal had given him a cloth-wrapped bundle as they fled across the ocean, and even without unwrapping it, he knew what lay within. How such a thing was possible was a mystery. He had thrown it away in the wake of defeat, yet there it was.

He kept it wedged in a cleft at the back of the cave. He knew he should hurl it into the sea, but also knew he would not.

Something moved in the fog, and he lifted a hand to shield his eyes from the winter sun.

A phantom of the mist, or something darker?

His right hand twitched with the memory of slaughter, and his gaze slid towards the settlement as old instincts and new senses prickled with danger.

From out of the fog, a dozen ships cut through the water towards village.

POWERFUL SWEEPS OF oars drove the ships onward, and their decks were crammed with armed men in gleaming iron breastplates and full-face helms of bronze. They clutched axes and swords and spears, and he sensed their anger, even from high on the cliff. He looked back into his cave, but closed his eyes and took a deep breath. He had feared this moment ever since he stepped onto the shore, but now that it was here, he found himself utterly calm.

The same calm he felt before a duel. The same calm he felt before he killed.

He watched the ships surge through the crashing breakers and slide up the shingle beach. The village's few warriors ran to meet them with axes held high over their shoulders, old men and youngsters mainly. Fifty men of sword-bearing age were all that were left to defend the village.

Nowhere near enough.

Whooping war shouts echoed from the stony beach as women and children ran towards the cliffs. There was no escape there, just a postponement of the inevitable. These warriors would leave no survivors. They never did.

Even isolated in his cave, he had heard the recent scare stories of the seaborne raiders, the killers from across the ocean who wiped out entire tribes in their vengeful slaughters. Their crimson and white sails were the terror of the coastline, a sight to drive fear into the hearts of those that had once been masters of the ocean.

A score of armed men dropped from the lead ship, led by a warrior in gleaming silver armour and a gold-crowned helm. He bore a mighty warhammer and smashed one of the village warriors from his feet with a single blow. More ships beached, and in moments a hundred warriors were ashore. Arrows leapt from the decks of the ships, serrated tips slicing into proud flesh, and flame-wrapped barbs landing amid the tinder-dry homes of the villagers.

A dozen warriors were dropping into the surf with every passing second. Though the defenders of the set-tlement were hopelessly outnumbered, they fought with the fury of warriors given one last chance to reclaim their honour in death.

Lightly armoured men with bows fanned out onto the beach, taking aim at the fleeing villagers and cutting them down with lethally accurate shafts. Iron clashed with iron on the shore as the last of the defenders were overwhelmed. He watched the raven-helmed warrior hurl himself at the leader of these reavers from the sea with his axe slashing down over his head. The warham-mer swept up, and the blade slammed down on its haft. Such a blow should have shattered any normal weapon and split the enemy's skull, but he knew that this was no ordinary warhammer. Nor was the warrior who bore it any ordinary foe.

The warhammer spun in the warrior's hand, faster than any weapon of such weight and power should move. Its head slammed into raven-helm's face, caving his skull to shards and knocking him to the red snow.

'No pyre for you,' he said as the warriors from the sea advanced into the settlement.

Its buildings were burning and its people dead, yet the raiders kicked them down, leaving nothing standing to indicate that anyone had once called this bay home. This was no raid for gold or slaves or plunder. This was an attack of destruction.

The raiders hauled the bodies of the defenders from the sea and began stripping their helmets. One by one, the warrior with the warhammer bent to look at their faces, but each time he would shake his head in disappointment.

Wyrtgeorn chuckled as the warrior shook his head and hissed, 'You won't find what you're looking for among the dead.'

He heard a noise from further down the cliff and pulled back into the shadow of the cave mouth. A slender, hard-faced woman carried a pair of children up the icy cliff paths towards the cave. Her steps were faltering, and he saw a pair of arrows jutting from her back. She saw him and tried to speak, but no words came, only a froth of bubbling blood.

She reached the ledge before his cave and collapsed onto her knees. Her eyes were frantic. Only seconds of life remained to her and she knew it.

'Wyrtgeorn,' she said in a language not her own. 'Save... my... children.'

He backed away from her, shaking his head.

'You must!' she said, thrusting the youngsters toward

him. He saw they were twins, one a boy, the other a girl. Both howled with uncontrollable sobs. The woman's eyes closed and she swayed as death reached up to claim her. The woman's daughter threw her arms around her mother's neck and the pair of them fell from the cliff, falling a hundred yards into the sea.

The warriors on the shoreline saw them fall, their eyes drawn up to the cave on the cliff. He knew he was invisible in the shadows, but the boy stood on the ledge as plain as day. Four warriors ran from the beach towards the cliff paths, and the man cursed. He felt a tugging at his fur jerkin and looked down into the coldest blue eyes he had ever seen. The boy stood with his fists bunched at his sides, and there was pleading desperation in the way he met the man's gaze.

'You are Wyrtgeorn,' said the boy in the man's own tongue. 'Why did you not come down and fight them?'

'Because I have no wish to commit suicide,' he replied.

'They have killed my tribe,' wept the boy. 'Why won't you kill them?'

'I will kill anyone who tries to kill me,' said the man.

'Good,' said the boy. 'Zhek Askah said you were a great warrior.'

'I don't know who that is.'

'The shaman who named you Wyrtgeorn. Lord Aetulff wanted you and your friend slain, but Zhek Askah said you were a killer of men and that we should let you live in the cave.'

'Did he now?' replied the man. 'I wonder why. Perhaps it was to save your life.'

Four warriors were climbing towards them, carefully picking their way along the treacherous path. They carried long knives, eschewing axes on so narrow a ledge. The man watched them come: confident, arrogant and with a swagger that didn't match their abilities. He'd watched them fight on the shore. They were competent warriors, but no more than that.

'There is a passage at the back of the cave,' said the man. 'It leads through the rock and comes out a few miles north of the village. Wait for me there. I will join you shortly.'

'I don't want to run,' said the boy, and the man saw fierce determination behind his fear.

'No,' he agreed. 'You don't, but sometimes that's all you can do.'

'What do you mean?'

'Nothing,' said the man. 'It doesn't matter. But I know now why I did not leave this cave.'

Before the boy could ask any more, the light at the mouth of the cave was blocked as two of the warriors reached his squalid dwelling place.

'Get behind me,' said the man, pushing the boy away.

The first warrior stepped cautiously into the cave, his eyes adjusting to the gloom. A second followed close behind. The blades of their knives glittered in the dim light.

'What do we have here?' he said, his voice heavily accented. 'A hermit and a shit-scared boy. Should be nice and easy, lads.'

'You should go and never come back,' said the man, his voice calm and even.

'You know that's not going to happen,' said the warrior.

'I know,' agreed the man, leaping forwards with dazzling speed. Before the warrior was even aware he was under attack, the man slammed the heel of his hand against his throat. Windpipe crushed, the warrior dropped to his knees, already choking to death.

The man caught the falling dagger and plunged it into the throat of the second warrior. The blade sliced into the gap between his iron torque and the visor of his helmet. He gave a strangled gurgle and toppled to the ground as his lifeblood squirted over his killer and the walls of the cave.

Lethal instincts returned with a vengeance as the hot stink of blood filled the man's nostrils. He leapt, feet first, towards the remaining two warriors. His booted feet slammed into a chest encased in a heavy hauberk of linked iron rings, and the warrior was pitched from the ledge, arms flailing as he fell to his death. The man landed lightly as the last warrior thrust a dagger towards his guts. He swayed aside, locking the warrior's arm beneath his own, and sent two lightning-quick stabs of his purloined dagger through the visor of his victim's helmet.

'No glorious sights in the Halls of Ulric for you,' hissed the man, letting the body fall from the ledge to dash itself on the rocks far below. He stood on the edge of the rocky spit of stone before his cave, his arms and upper body drenched in blood. His heart should be racing, yet it beat with a casual rhythm, as though he rested in a peaceful meadow beneath the clearest sky.

Looking down at the beach, he saw the raiders staring up in horror. Alone of the raiders, the warrior in the gold-crowned helm met his gaze. A dozen men ran for the cliff path with murder in their hearts. The man threw the dagger away and returned to the cave, moving with grim inevitability to the cleft in the rock.

Quickly he pulled out a pitch-blackened bundle of cloth and carefully undid the rotted length of twine that secured it. The boy looked on in wonder as he revealed a glittering sword with an ivory handle and gold-inlaid hilt. The blade was slightly curved, in the manner of the Taleuten horsemen, and it shone like fresh-minted silver.

His hands closed around the hilt like a long lost friend, and he sighed as though welcoming a midnight lover.

'Zhek Askah was right,' said the boy. 'You *are* a great warrior, Wyrtgeorn.'

'I am the *greatest* warrior,' said the man, stripping the sword belt from the first man he had killed. He slid his own blade home. It was a loose fit, the scabbard designed for an Unberogen stabbing sword. 'And do not call me Wyrtgeorn. It is not my name.'

'It isn't?'

'No. My name is Azazel,' he said, letting the name settle in his mouth, as though he hadn't really earned it until now. The boy looked up at him with a mixture of awe and wariness.

Azazel smiled and put his hand on the boy's shoulder, leading him towards the hidden passageway through the rocks. The warriors pursuing them would find the entrance, but they would never find them in the warren of tunnels that lay beyond.

The boy looked back at the slice of light at the cave mouth and hesitated.

'There is no going back,' said Azazel. 'There never is.'

THE BODIES WERE taken from the cave and carried down the narrow cliff path to the waiting ships. None of their number would be left behind on this cold land, they would be taken back to their homelands for the proper funerary rites to be observed. Their souls demanded no less. Wolfgart studied the ground and splashes of blood on the walls with eyes of cold anger, tracing the course of the fight, though it could hardly be called a fight such was the speed with which his comrades had been killed.

He ran a gloved hand through his long red hair, pushing the woven braids from his face as he shook his head. Wolfgart was no youngster, but his body had lost only a little of its youthful power since he had first swung a sword in battle.

His body was a warrior's, yet his face was that of a rogue.

'It was him, wasn't it?' said a voice behind him.

'Aye,' agreed Wolfgart. 'But then you knew that, didn't you?'

'As soon as I saw him on the ledge,' said the warrior with the gold-crowned helm.

Wolfgart gestured to the tracks and scrapes on the cave floor. 'It happened so damn quick, the poor buggers didn't have a chance. He killed Caeadda first and took his weapon. Then he cut Radulf's throat with it. You saw what he did to Paega and Earic.'

The warrior removed his helm and handed it to another behind him. His golden hair was bound in a short scalp-lock and his face was handsome with a rugged edge that made him a leader to follow in war and an Emperor to obey in peace.

Sigmar, ruler of the lands of men and Emperor of the twelve tribes.

'Only Gerreon could have killed them so quickly,' said Sigmar, his differently coloured eyes tracing the course of the fight and reaching the same conclusion as Wolfgart. 'I should have known he would be here.'

Wolfgart turned to look up at his friend and Emperor. 'Why? How could you know he would be here?'

'The burning ship,' said Sigmar. 'It is how the Norsii send their dead to the gods. To fight in the shadow of unquiet souls is an omen of ill-fortune.'

'Aye, well we've had enough of them over the last year,' grumbled Wolfgart.

Sigmar nodded and moved to the back of the cave, peering into the darkness of a rough passageway. Wolfgart's eyes were drawn to the mighty warhammer hung on Sigmar's wide leather belt. The hammer's rune-encrusted haft glittered with pale winter's light and its heavy head was unblemished by so much as a single drop of blood. This was Ghal-maraz, ancient weapon of dwarfcraft that had been gifted to Sigmar by King Kurgan of the mountain folk.

Sigmar turned and Wolfgart was struck by the change that had come upon him in this last year. Though he had just entered his fortieth summer, Sigmar carried himself with the poise and strength of a man half his age, yet it was his eyes where he bore the weight of years. The rise of his Empire had been hard won, built upon foundations of blood and sacrifice. Friends and loved ones had been lost along the way, and enemies old and new tore at the newly-birthed Empire with avaricious claws.

A full year had passed since the defeat of the Norsii invasion at the foot of the Fauschlag Rock; a year that had seen Sigmar's raiding fleets scouring the icy coast-lines of the north. Village after village was burned to the ground and its people put to the sword. Wolfgart had been as vocal in his support as any when Sigmar had announced his plan to take the fight to the lands of the Norsii, believing that such vengeance would safeguard the Empire for decades to come.

Now he wasn't so sure, for these raids were building hatred for the lands of the south that would only fester and grow stronger with every passing year. With every bloody slaughter, Wolfgart understood that Sigmar's reason for these attacks was more personal. In every ruined village, he sought signs of the swordsman Gerreon, the traitor who had killed the woman he loved and plunged a broken sword into the heart of his dearest friend.

Wolfgart rose to his feet, his height a match for Sigmar's. The wan light entering the cave only served to highlight the frustration he saw in his friend's face.

Sigmar slammed a gauntleted fist into the rock of the cave.

'He was here,' snapped Sigmar. 'He was here and we missed him. We were so close.'

'Aye, we got close, but he's gone now,' said Wolfgart.

'Gather the men,' ordered Sigmar. 'That passageway likely opens out somewhere north of the village. If we hurry we can mount a pursuit.'

Sigmar made to pass him, but Wolfgart laid a hand on the centre of the Emperor's breastplate. Though the air in the cave was cold, the ancient metal was warm to the touch, the magic bound to it sending a threatening vibration through Wolfgart's fingertips.

'He's gone,' said Wolfgart. 'You know it too. Who knows where these tunnels lead, and do you really want to go haring off into the darkness after someone like Gerreon? It's time to go home, Sigmar.'

'Really? I seem to remember you were the one who called me a fool for not going after him the last time.'

'Aye, that was me, but I was young and foolish then. I'm older now. Can't say as I'm much wiser, but I know when a quest is hopeless. The Empire needs you, my friend. It's been the hardest year for our people, and they need their Emperor to guide them. The suffering doesn't end just because the fighting stops.'

Sigmar looked set to argue, but the light of anger went out of his eyes. Wolfgart hated to be the one to tell him these truths, but there was no one else. Not any more.

'Pendrag was better at this sort of thing than me,' said Wolfgart, feeling the ache of loss once again. 'But he's not here, and I'm all you've got. Like I told you in the Brackenwalsch, you're stuck with me.'

'Aye, Pendrag was the wisest of us,' agreed Sigmar, looking over his shoulder at the darkened passageway.

Wolfgart saw him accept the truth of his words and his shoulders slumped just a little.

'The Empire needs us,' said Wolfgart. 'But more to the point, it needs you.'

'You are wiser than you know,' said Sigmar. 'It's starting to worry me.'

'Don't worry, I won't let it go to my head,' said Wolfgart. 'I live in a house of women who keep telling me how much cleverer than me they are.'

'Then let's get you back to them,' said Sigmar. 'They must be missing that.'

'Aye,' said Wolfgart with a broad smile. 'Let's do that.'

THEY WATCHED FROM a concealed ledge further along the cliffs. A rutted track twisted through the rocks and defiles behind them, leading down towards the bleak landscape of the north. Beyond the cliffs, the achingly wide vista became ever more irregular, a harsh mix of tundra, ice shelf and blasted wilderness. The horizon shimmered, and the boundary between earth and sky blurred as though the difference between them was maddeningly inconstant.

Beyond the horizon, Azazel knew the world grew stranger still, the land no longer bound by the laws of nature and man. It was a shifting realm of nightmares and Chaos, its character broken and bitter, like a land shaped by spiteful gods.

Azazel smiled, knowing that was exactly true. He could feel the breath of northern powers sweeping down from the realm of the gods, laden with ruin and aeons-old malice. He and Kar Odacen had ventured far into that forsaken wilderness, travelling paths known only to madmen or those whose lungs drew breath of the air touched by the great gods of the north.

It had changed them both, though Azazel remembered

little of the journey save the monumental tomb of an ancient warrior and a duel with its guardian. The quest into the north had reshaped him in ways beyond his comprehension. His body was faster and stronger than was humanly possible, and his senses were honed to preternatural levels.

Those senses now told him he would venture into that wilderness again.

They were silent as to whether he would ever return.

He and the boy had threaded their way through the tunnels of the cliffs, finally emerging in a sheltered defile high on the flanks of the mountain. They lay in a concealed ravine high above the soaring white cliffs that marked the boundary of this icy realm, watching as black smoke from the burning settlement pressed down on the bay like a mourning shroud. A hundred and thirty-four people had lived there, mostly women and children, with fifty men to bear swords. All were now dead, slain by a man he had once called friend.

Azazel hadn't known any of the villagers and felt nothing at their deaths. Everyone had been slain, but this one boy had survived. That had to mean something, didn't it?

Azazel looked down at the young boy. He was clean limbed and looked strong for his age, with a shock of hair so blond it was almost white. His high cheekbones were characteristic of the Norsii tribes, and Azazel saw he would grow into a strikingly handsome man.

Tears cut through the grime on his young face, his body wracked with sobs now that the adrenaline of fear had worn off. Azazel sensed a confluence of fates in their meeting, the twisted schemes of higher powers at work. Kar Odacen would have said it was the will of the gods that had brought them together, but the shaman had been raving and delusional when Azazel had seen him last.

Perhaps it *was* the will of the gods, but who could tell? Anything could be interpreted as a sign from the gods, and it was no use trying to guess their intent. All he could do was follow his instincts, and his instincts were telling him that this boy was special in ways he couldn't even begin to imagine.

He returned his attention to the south, watching as the crimson sails of the raiders from the Empire pushed out to sea, past where Lord Aetulff's wolfship had sunk beneath the waves. The ships cleared the headland, but instead of turning along the coastline to seek fresh slaughter they kept going, aiming their tapered prows to the south.

'Are they going home?' asked the boy.

Azazel nodded. 'It looks like it, yes.'

'Good,' sobbed the boy.

Azazel slapped him hard, knocking him back onto his haunches. Instantly, the boy was on his feet, his grief swamped by anger. He reached for a sword that wasn't there, and hurled himself at Azazel.

'I'll kill you!' he screamed.

Azazel sidestepped his rush and pushed the boy to the ground. Before the boy could rise, he planted a booted foot in his chest.

'Anger is not your friend, boy,' said Azazel. 'Learn to control it or I will throw you from these cliffs. Listen to me, and listen well. You are the last of your tribe. No other will take you in except as a slave, and the land will kill you if you do not start using your head. We are going to travel into the north and you will do exactly as I say or it will be the death of us both. I will teach you what you need to survive, but if you ever disobey me, even once, I will kill you. Do you understand me?'

The boy nodded. His grief and anger were gone, replaced by smouldering resentment.

That was good. It was a beginning.

He held his hand out to the boy, hauling him to his feet. An angry red weal burned on his cheek where Azazel had struck him.

'That is the first lesson I will teach you,' said Azazel. 'It won't be the last, but it will be the least painful.'

The boy regarded him coldly, rubbing his cheek and holding himself straighter.

'Look out there,' said Azazel, pointing out to the ocean. 'What do you see?'

'The raiders' ships,' said the boy.

'Yes, and they are going home to a land that hates you.'

'Will they be back?'

'I doubt it. Southerners don't do well with this cold. Even the Udose don't get winters like we do up here.'

The boy looked at him with a sneer curling his lip. 'You say "we" like you are one of us.'

'I am more part of this land than you will ever be,' Azazel promised him. He turned from the diminishing ships, setting a brisk pace along the path over the cliffs. This was the first day of their journey, and who knew how long it would last.

The boy trotted after him, throwing careful glances towards the smoke rising from the ruin of his home.

'Will we ever come back here?' he asked.

'Oh yes,' promised Azazel. 'One day we will. I promise. It will be many years from now, but we will return and we will avenge all that has befallen us.'

'Good,' said the boy, his jaw clenched and his blue eyes cold and dead.

Azazel paused in his march as a thought occurred to him.

'What is your name, boy?' he asked. 'What do they call you?'

The boy drew his shoulders back, and said, 'I am called Morkar.'

─❮ TWO ❯─

Young Minds and Old Men

EOFORTH TRIED TO keep his frustration in check, but it was hard in the face of such thick-headedness. Teon wouldn't listen; he had no interest in listening, and stared defiantly at Eoforth, daring him to press on. Eoforth perched on the edge of his desk, a finely made piece of furniture crafted by Holtwine himself, and folded his arms across his chest.

'I ask you again, Teon,' he said, pointing to the tally marks chalked on the slate. 'If you multiply the first number by the second, what do you end up with?'

Teon looked over at Gorseth, his best friend and companion in troublemaking. He winked and said, 'A sore head. It's all nonsense anyway. Who needs numbers when you can swing a sword as well as I can?'

He flexed his arm and Gorseth laughed on cue. The rest of the class nervously followed.

'Enough!' said Eoforth, lifting the birch cane from beside his desk.

'Go ahead,' said Teon, 'I dare you. My father will kill you, old man or not.'

For all his bluster, Teon was popular with the other boys. Powerfully built for his age and blessed with handsome features and an easy manner beyond the classroom. Close to his fifteenth birthday, he would soon ride out on his first war hunt. His father was Orvin, one of Alfgeir's captains of battle, and the boy saw little need to spend his days cooped up in a classroom when there were fights to be gotten into and maidens to pursue.

Eoforth stood and limped towards Teon's desk, the cane swishing the air before him like a threshing scythe.

'Every day you cheek me, Master Teon,' said Eoforth. 'Every day you test my patience, but I counselled King Björn in the time of woes when all around us threatened to destroy the Unberogen. I stood at his side when the Cherusens and Taleutens raided our lands. I brokered the peace that first united those tribes as allies, and I have spoken with the kings and queens of all the great tribes. I have done all this, and you think you can intimidate me? You are a foolish young boy with a head as thick as a greenskin skull and the manners of a forest beast.'

Teon frowned, unused to being spoken to like this. He was off balance and Eoforth smiled as he stopped by the boy's desk.

Eoforth tapped the cane on the arithmetical problem chalked on the slate surface of the desk. 'Now I am asking you again. What is the answer to the problem?'

Teon looked up at him defiantly before spitting on the slate and smearing the chalk illegible with his sleeve. 'A pox on you, old man. I spit on your sums and letters!'

'Wrong answer,' said Eoforth, slashing his birch cane down on Teon's fingers.

The youngster snatched his hand back with a howl of

pain. Tears brimmed on the curve of his eyes and Eoforth wasn't proud that he hoped they would spill out. Some shame and humility would do the boy a world of good. Teon's face flushed with anger and he rose to his full height, clutching his hand to his chest.

'My father will hear of this,' he spat, heading for the classroom door.

'Indeed he shall,' said Eoforth. 'For I will tell him, and he will give you a sound beating for disrespecting your elders. Your father knows the value of discipline, and he would thrash you within an inch of your life were he to see you behave like this.'

Eoforth wished that were true. Orvin was as brash and quick to anger as his son, yet he was a fierce warrior and had ridden with Alfgeir's knights for ten years. Though Eoforth did not like the man, he knew of his respect for the proper order of things. He just hoped his son saw that.

Teon paused and Eoforth saw the battle raging within him. To lose face by complying with Eoforth's demand or to risk a beating from his father. The lad returned to his seat, though he continued to glare fiercely at Eoforth.

'Thank you,' said Eoforth, moving between the lines of desks. A dozen boys and girls filled his classroom, a dusty room within a timber-built schoolhouse on the southern bank of the River Reik. A hundred children of Reikdorf learned their numbers and letters here, taught by women he himself had instructed. No men taught at the school, for the youngsters tended to rebel more against male teachers, and seemed more reluctant to pick fights with the matronly women Eoforth had chosen.

'I know what you are thinking,' he said. 'You are thinking that this is a waste of time, that you would much rather be practising on the Field of Swords, learning how to fight. The skills of a warrior are important, and every

Unberogen needs to know them. But consider this, without your numbers how will you know how much beef to carry in your wagons when you go to war? How much grain and fodder for the horses, and how much extra for the beasts of burden who pull those wagons? How many swords will you need? How many arrows and what size of war chest should you bring to pay your soldiers?'

Eoforth paced the length of his classroom, his limp forgotten as he warmed to his theme.

'And what of your orders? How will you read the map to deploy your warriors, or read the names of the towns your captain has sent you to? Will you be able to work out how far you must travel or where your evening campsites must be? How will you send word to your fellow warriors without knowledge of your letters?'

He paused by Teon's desk and fished a lump of chalk from the pockets of his grey scholar's robes. He scratched the problem on the slate once more.

'Now let's try again,' he said.

THE LESSON CONTINUED for another twenty frustrating minutes, with the youngsters seemingly incapable of grasping the concept of numbers and solutions that couldn't be calculated on their fingers. Eoforth pinched the bridge of his nose between his fingertips and took a deep breath. Everything was easy when you knew how it was done, and it was hard to remember what it was like not to know these things.

He was in the process of chalking a simpler problem on the board when an excited shout went up from one of the boys seated by the window. Eoforth heard the sound of metal and the whinny of horses from beyond the walls of the schoolhouse.

'Look!' shouted a girl with corn-coloured hair and petite features, pointing at something beyond the window. She bounced on her stool with excitement, clapping her hands together.

'Erline!' snapped Eoforth. 'Your attention please.'

'Sorry,' said Erline. 'But look!'

The rest of the class hurried over to the windows and an excited babble broke out as the boys cheered and the girls blushed and scolded one another at their whispered suggestions. Eoforth stooped to look through the window and knew there would be no more lessons today.

While part of him was angered at that fact, he could not deny his Unberogen heart was stirred by so formidable a display of martial power.

Fifty horsemen rode down the thoroughfare, each armoured in a heavy shirt of mail and gleaming iron breastplate. They bore crimson and white shields bearing the hammer of Sigmar, and each carried a lance supported in a Taleuten-style stirrup cup. Spitted upon each lance tip was a rotting greenskin head. A glorious banner of white silk emblazoned with a black cross and wreathed skull flew over these warriors, and Eoforth smiled as he recognised the bronze-armoured warrior who rode at the head of these horsemen.

Alfgeir, Grand Knight of the Empire.

SUNLIGHT FILTERED THROUGH the forest canopy in thin bars, leaving much of the silent spaces beneath cloaked in shadows. Cuthwin slid through the trees towards the road, a seldom-used track that ran south from Reikdorf all the way to the Grey Mountains. Hardly anyone used these roads any more; the settlements at the foot of the mountains had been destroyed by greenskins ten years ago, and the wilderness had risen up to claim them back.

But someone was using them now, someone who was in trouble.

He moved with an arrow nocked to his bow, a

magnificent weapon of yew and ash inlaid with lacquered strips of rowan. Blessed by a priest of Taal, the weapon had never once let him down and had saved his life more times than he could count. The string was loose, but could be drawn in an instant. Sounds of battle were coming from the road, the clash of iron weapons and the screams of wounded souls. Normally Cuthwin would give such sounds a wide berth, for the monstrous denizens of the deep forests were as fond of making war amongst themselves as they were on humanity.

He'd been about to carry onwards to Reikdorf when a loud bang echoed through the forest. Birds fled the tree-tops and he darted into hiding to string his bow. Another booming echo rolled through the forest. Cuthwin knew that sound, it was a dwarf weapon; one of their thunder bows. He'd seen the mountain folk use them at Black Fire Pass and knew how lethal they could be. His mind made up, he swiftly followed the sounds to their source.

Clad in hard-wearing leather and fur, Cuthwin was the colour of the forest, a ghost moving from shadow to shadow with carefully weighted footfalls. Dead leaves pressed softly into the dark earth without sound and twigs were pushed aside by his buckskin boots. His long hunting knife was sheathed in a leather scabbard, and his pack was hung from a high tree branch a hundred yards behind him. He kept his hair long, though it was pulled back over his ears and held by a leather cord around his temples. He scanned the forest to either side, his peripheral vision alert to anything moving on his flanks.

He heard the clang of swords, the howls of wounded creatures and more of the banging reports of thunder bows. The wind carried their smoke to his nostrils, acrid and reeking of hot metal, like Govannon's forge on a hot day. Beneath that there was a familiar smell of rank, unwashed bodies and rotten food.

Cuthwin knew that smell. He remembered it from the days before Black Fire Pass, when he and Svein had scouted the mountains and discovered the vast host only days from descending into the Empire.

Greenskins.

He heard malicious, squealing voices, squawking war cries and vicious wolf barks, answered by deep, rumbling voices that sounded like they came from the deepest pits of the earth. Cuthwin eased through the forest, keeping his back to the trees and altering his approach every time the wind changed.

Cuthwin was travelling alone, a dangerous pastime in the forests of the Empire, for all manner of peril lurked within their shadow-haunted depths. He knew the risks he took, but was confident enough in his skills to see such dangers as a challenge. To Cuthwin there was nothing as liberating as spending time alone in the deep forests. To survive by his skill with a bow and an innate empathy with the seasonal lore of the wilds was what made him feel alive.

The sounds of battle were growing louder, and Cuthwin pressed himself to the thick bole of a larch, easing his head around it and peering through its branches to the clearing below.

The ground sloped down to the road, a rutted track almost obscured by high grass and gorse. Bodies lay strewn around four wagons arranged in a loose circle on the road. Six dwarfs in long mail shirts fought from the backs of the wagons, armed with a mix of hammers and short-hafted axes. The mules hauling the wagons were dead, and a dozen wiry creatures with pallid green flesh wrapped in filth-encrusted rags surrounded them.

Smaller and weaker than orcs, goblins were cunning

little runts that had learned to strike from ambush and kill with the backstab and the low blow. A man or a dwarf was more than a match for a goblin in a straight contest of arms, but that wasn't how these vicious creatures fought. Half bore compact bows of horn and bone, while others swung curved blades with rusted and serrated edges. They rode emaciated wolves that howled with bloodlust, their fur matted and their jaws dripping with saliva.

Two dwarfs emptied fine black powder into the barrels of their thunder bows, while the others slashed at any goblins that came too close. As things stood, the dwarfs would be overrun, but like Sigmar before him, Cuthwin would aid the beleaguered mountain folk.

He hauled back on the string of his bow and sighted on a goblin with a skullcap of bright red leather.

EOFORTH DISMISSED HIS class, knowing there would be no more work done today. He was disappointed, but remembered the excitement he had felt when the royal brothers, Björn and Berongunden, had ridden through his village behind their father, Redmane Dregor. The king had been magnificent that day, clad in his burnished bronze armour and leading a host of Unberogen horsemen from the back of a tall dappled stallion of grey and white. His white bearskin cloak fell like a mantle of snow from his armoured shoulders and his hair was the colour of fire.

Powerful and elemental, Dregor had stopped beside him.

'You are Eoforth?' asked the king.

'I am, my lord,' he said, surprised the king knew his name.

'And this is your village?'

'I am the elder of Ingaevon, yes.'

'I have heard of you, Eoforth of Ingaevon. The other village elders say you have no taste for war. Is that true?'

'It's true I have no love of killing, but I know it is sometimes necessary. That is why I have trained men under arms quartered here. It is also why I had our carpenters construct a high palisade wall and the village's stockade. I may not carry a sword in this world, but I know how to stay alive in it.'

'Aye, they said you were a sly fox,' said the king, surveying the lines of the hilltop fort and the well-built and nigh-impregnable walls of the settlement. 'You may not swing a sword, but you wield that mind of yours like a weapon.'

The king sighed, looking him in the eye, and Eoforth had been surprised at the marrow-deep weariness he saw in his gaze. The king leaned down and lowered his voice so that only Eoforth could hear his words.

'This world is changing, but the Hag-Mother of the Brackenwalsch tells me I will not live to change with it. That will be for those that come after me. I have need of men like you, men who know that not all battles are fought by warriors, that men of peace will one day be as important as men of war.'

'I would hope that such a day is already here,' Eoforth had replied.

Dregor laughed, a rich, wholesome sound that lifted the hearts of all who heard it.

'For a clever man you are naïve, Eoforth, but I like your optimism.'

'What is it you want of me, my lord?'

'I want you to come to Reikdorf,' said the king in a tone that suggested this was not a request that could be ignored. 'My boys are good lads, but like their father, they are headstrong; all too eager to rush into battle without considering what other options may be open to them. When Berongunden is king, he will have need of a wise man at his side. I want you to be that wise man.'

'I am flattered, my lord,' said Eoforth, genuinely taken aback.

'Then you'll do it?'

'Of course. It would be an honour.'

Thus had begun his long years of service to the kings of the Unberogen. A life that had seen the Unberogen grow in strength and prominence with every passing year. Björn had readily accepted Eoforth's counsel, but Berongunden was a warrior cast too closely in his father's image to listen to anyone's voice but his own. Proud, reckless and full of Unberogen fire, Berongunden had died in the mountains to the north of the Fauschlag Rock, torn to pieces by a winged beast that haunted the highest crags. A year later King Dregor followed his son into the depths of Warrior Hill, his chest pierced by a dozen greenskin arrows, and Björn had taken the crown.

The power and influence of the Unberogen had steadily increased under Björn's leadership, with many sword oaths and trade pacts sworn with neighbouring tribes. Gold and goods from all across the land flowed into Reikdorf, and as the fame of Björn's farsightedness spread, many tribal kings came to his settlement to meet this wise ruler.

Björn honoured Eoforth for his wisdom and when Sigmar eventually took the crown after his father's death fighting the Norsii, he had continued to advise the Unberogen king. Sigmar was now Emperor and Eoforth knew his own span was coming to an end. Sigmar had proven to be a greater king than any of his ancestors, bringing all the tribes of men together under his rule, forging the Empire of men and holding it firm in the face of all enemies.

A mix of his father's keen mind and his grandfather's

hot temper, Sigmar was a ruler fit for the Empire: warlike when roused to fight, diplomatic and persuasive when called to pass judgement. Of course there had been times when Eoforth's steadying hand had been required, such as the incident with Krugar and Aloysis and the dread crown of Morath.

Thankfully, Sigmar had learned valuable lessons from those moments of weakness, a strength born from understanding that no man was infallible, that such perfection was best left to the gods. Since then Eoforth had quietly faded into the background, content to pass his teachings onto the next generation of Unberogen.

He sighed, thinking back to his treatment of Teon. The lad had been rude and arrogant, but Eoforth should have been above such retaliation. In striking the young boy, he had already lost.

'I may not be a warrior, but I am Unberogen,' he said, smiling as his good humour was restored at the recognition that no matter how cultured a man could become, there was no escaping his heritage. He gathered his books and writing tools from the desk, running a gnarled finger over the carvings around its lip.

Master Holtwine was a master craftsman and many of the pieces in the Emperor's longhouse had come from his workshop. His work was truly extraordinary, and was in demand by patrons as diverse as Count Otwin and Count Adelhard. Marius of the Jutones had several pieces, including a great bed frame carved with his heroic deeds during the battle for the Fauschlag Rock.

Eoforth made his way from the classroom and stepped out into the warm spring sunlight. Winter had broken early and the farmsteads around Reikdorf were being prepared for the sowing. The warm smell of freshly turned earth filled the air, even in the heart of the city, reminding Eoforth that it was not by swords that empires endured, but by keeping food plentiful.

He made his way along the street, meandering between the streams of youngsters as they gawped at the armoured horsemen. He saw Teon speaking to his father. Eoforth wondered if he was recounting his punishment in class. He decided that was unlikely; he knew the boy and his father were not close. Orvin was of typical Unberogen stock, broad-shouldered and powerfully built with a shock of dark hair. His bearing was confident to the point of arrogant, but unlike his son he had earned the right to walk with a swagger.

Eoforth waved as he saw Alfgeir walking his horse along the cobbled street towards him.

'Welcome home, Grand Knight of the Empire,' said Eoforth. 'I take it you were successful? The orcs are defeated?'

Alfgeir lifted his helmet's visor and scowled at Eoforth's use of his formal title. Alfgeir had many titles, Grand Knight of the Empire being but his most recently acquired. Marshal of the Reik was another, but to Eoforth he would always simply be his friend.

'That we were, High Scholar of the Empire,' replied Alfgeir, returning the favour. 'We caught them at Astofen and trapped them against the river.'

'Astofen?' said Eoforth as Alfgeir walked his horse towards a water trough. 'Strange how the greenskins always find their way back to Astofen. I wonder what draws them there?'

'Does it matter? They come and we kill them.'

'And the following year they will need killing again.'

Alfgeir nodded and looked over towards the flag flying over the longhouse to the north of the city. 'Any news of the Emperor?' he asked.

It had been nearly nine months since Sigmar had set off to the north. With ships requisitioned from Count

Marius's fleet at Jutonsryk, he'd taken the swords of the Empire across the frozen seas to the lands many were already calling Norsca. The Norsii were going to learn that there were consequences to attacking Sigmar's realm.

'There is indeed,' said Eoforth. 'Redwane sends word from the Fauschlag that Sigmar's ships have put ashore in Udose lands at a place called Haugrvik.'

'Do you think they found him?'

'Gerreon? I doubt it,' said Eoforth. 'We would have heard.'

Alfgeir nodded, having already suspected that would be the answer.

'So when is Sigmar coming back to Reikdorf?'

'Soon, I expect. If they're done with the war across the sea, then they're probably on their way now.'

'Good,' said Alfgeir. 'It's time he was back. We're not an Empire without an Emperor.'

Alfgeir had a point. In the year following the great victory against the Norsii, the Empire had weathered the storm of war in consolidation. Each of the counts had returned to their lands to regroup and refortify, but instead of returning to Reikdorf, Sigmar had gathered a force of warriors and crossed the sea to make war on the Norsii. No more would the banished tribes of the north dwell with impunity in their frozen homelands, believing themselves safe from attack. Yet without the Emperor, the people of the Unberogen grew restive, withdrawing behind their palisade walls and spears. Many traders now carried on up the coast to Marburg and Jutonsryk or headed east to Three Hills or south to Siggurdheim.

The Unberogen needed their Emperor back.

The horse lowered its head and Alfgeir patted its flanks as squires arrived from the stables to care for the knights' mounts. These were beasts bred from Wolfgart's stock, wide-chested, powerful and trained to fight. Bred for strength and musculature, not speed and height, the knights' horses were squat and pugnacious beasts. Iron plates riveted to a boiled leather harness protected the horse's flank, while segmented bands of iron and mail sheathed its neck and head.

'Maybe the greenskins keep attacking Astofen due to its historical significance?' suggested Eoforth, returning to their earlier discussion.

'I still don't see why it matters,' said Alfgeir.

'Perhaps if we knew why they came, we could do something about it,' said Eoforth as Alfgeir's squire led the horse away to be stripped of its armour, rubbed down, fed and watered. The care of a good warhorse was a thorough and expensive business.

Alfgeir sat on a stone bench at the side of the street, and Eoforth saw how tired he was. It was a long ride from Astofen and as much as the Empire was far safer than it had been in Björn's time, it still did not do to be away from the scattered pockets of civilisation for too long. Orcs were not the only dangers that lurked in the depths of the Empire's forests.

'Very well, I will indulge you, scholar, but what is there to do?' said Alfgeir, tilting his head back to allow the breeze to cool his skin. 'Orcs are savages, they are driven by their lust for blood. There is no force in this world that can change that.'

'You may be right,' said Eoforth, sitting next to him. 'It is a depressing thought.'

'That I am right or that the orcs will never change?'

Eoforth smiled. 'I was referring to the orcs, my friend. Tell me, does the dwarf bridge still stand to the south of Astofen?'

'It does,' said Alfgeir. 'And someone has erected a shrine on the north bank.'

'Oh? Dedicated to which god?'

'To no god. It is dedicated to Sigmar.'

'To Sigmar?' chuckled Eoforth. 'An understandable gesture, but let us hope it is too small for the gods to notice and take offence.'

'Indeed,' said Alfgeir, removing his helmet and pulling back the coif. He set the helmet next to him and ran a hand through his sweat-streaked hair. Eoforth noticed it was thinning at the crown, and there was more than a hint of grey to its hue.

Alfgeir saw the look and said, 'None of us are getting any younger, scholar.'

He smiled as he said it, but Eoforth saw the horror of aging in the warrior's eyes.

He forced a smile. 'There's truth in that, my friend. Even I am starting to feel old.'

They sat in companionable silence for a while, watching the youngsters fussing around the knights, offering to carry their lances, lead their horses or polish their armour. The knights shooed them away with smiles or pantomime growls, and Eoforth watched the boys following behind them, wielding sticks like swords and miming the slaying of their enemies.

'How goes the teaching?' asked Alfgeir, nodding towards the books in Eoforth's lap.

'Slowly,' admitted Eoforth. 'As you see, the boys are more interested in learning to kill than to read poetry or count.'

'We will always need warriors to defend us,' pointed out Alfgeir.

'And we will also need poets to inspire them, artists to commemorate them and tallymen to organise their armies.'

'Young men don't care for that,' said Alfgeir. 'They hunger for glory, not numbers and letters. Unberogen boys weren't made for study. I mean no offence by that, the pursuit of wisdom is an honourable one.'

'No offence taken,' said Eoforth, 'but it saddens me that we still need warriors at all. Wasn't the foundation of the Empire supposed to be an end to wars?'

'Even a rose needs thorns to defend it,' said Alfgeir.

Eoforth gave Alfgeir a sidelong look. 'Poetry?'

Alfgeir looked embarrassed. 'I read that book you loaned me. The writings of the Brigundian saga poet, what was his name…?'

'Sigenert,' said Eoforth. 'I wasn't sure you'd read it.'

'I read it,' replied Alfgeir. 'It just took me a while.'

'What did you think of it?'

Alfgeir shrugged. 'A lot of it went over my head, but I liked his words.'

Eoforth laughed and pushed himself to his feet. 'That's about all a poet can hope for, I suppose.'

—≺ THREE ≻—

Flight and Fight

CUTHWIN LOOSED BETWEEN breaths, his goose-feathered shaft thudding home at the base of the goblin's skull. It toppled from the back of the wolf with a surprised squeal. He drew another arrow from the quiver at his shoulder and sent it through the throat of a wolf-riding goblin. One of the riderless beasts leapt onto the wagons, bloody saliva dripping from its jaws.

It pounced onto one of the dwarfs armed with a thunder bow and bore him to the ground. Yellowed fangs fastened on the dwarf's neck and blood fountained as the beast bit through his throat. Cuthwin's next arrow punched though its eye socket, and the beast dropped next to its victim with a howl of agony.

The goblins either didn't realise they were under attack from a different direction or didn't care. A flurry of ragged arrows flew from the goblin bows. Most thudded harmlessly into the timber sides of the wagons, but a dwarf fell with two shafts buried in his chest. The wolf-riding goblins were quick to take advantage of the

45

situation, two of their number goading their mounts to leap onto the wagons.

Swinging his bow around, Cuthwin's arrow slashed into the flank of the first wolf, his next into the hindquarters of the other. The dwarfs fell upon the downed goblins and slew them with quick, economical blows from their axes. A shot rang out from the dwarf with the thunder bow and another goblin was punched from the saddle.

Cuthwin exhausted his quiver, emptying another four saddles and killing three wolves. He set his bow upright against the tree next to him and drew his hunting knife, a foot of cold steel that had shed more than its fair share of greenskin blood. Two more dwarfs were down, one with an arrow protruding from his neck, another with a goblin blade buried in his guts. The thunder bow spoke again and a goblin died with half its head blown off.

Cuthwin ran down to the road and leapt on the back of a wolf, plunging his blade into the goblin rider's side. The creature shrieked in agony and he hurled its corpse to the ground. He rammed his bloody blade into the wolf's back. It howled and rolled, trying to dislodge him. He landed lightly beside it and stabbed its throat as it scrambled to get upright.

Another wolf landed on him, the claws of its front paws scoring his thigh and barrelling him to the ground. Cuthwin rolled as its fangs snapped for his throat. He threw up his knife arm and hammered its jaw with the pommel. Yellow teeth snapped beneath the Empire-forged iron and the stinking beast threw back its head and roared. One of the dwarfs dropped to the road and ran towards him, but a goblin with better aim or luck than most loosed a shaft that sliced home into his rescuer's neck.

The dwarf sank to his knees, blood pumping in a flood down his mail shirt. He pitched forward as the goblin turned its bow on Cuthwin. A thunderous boom echoed across the clearing and the last goblin fell from the back of its wolf with what passed for its brains mushrooming from its skull.

Cuthwin rolled to his feet as the wolves, free of their cruel masters' spurs and goads, fled into the forest, leaving the clearing silent save for the laboured wheezes of wounded beasts. Cuthwin's leg ached, but the cuts were not deep. He scrambled over to the wagons, checking each of the dwarfs in turn. Only one still lived, the dwarf who'd fired the shot that had saved his life. An arrow was lodged in his chest, its shaft warped and crudely fletched with what looked like raven feathers.

The dwarf's beard was twisted into three heavy braids, each bound with an iron band at the end, and his cheeks were black with powder burns. The dwarf was bald, his heavy brow pulled down in pain. Blood flecked his spittle and his eyes were glassy and unfocussed.

'You're hurt,' said Cuthwin. 'Pretty badly, but if I can get you to Reikdorf you might live.'

The dwarf looked at him in pained confusion and murmured something in a strange, angular language of harshly edged words. Cuthwin didn't understand and shook his head.

'I don't know what you're saying. Do you understand me?'

The dwarf nodded slowly, grim faced and belligerent.

'My fellows?' he said.

'They're all dead.'

The dwarf nodded and Cuthwin saw a depth of pain and anger that frightened him with its intensity. He had felt sorrow at the death of friends, but this was a different order of feeling entirely.

'Were they your kin?' he asked, helping the dwarf to sit upright.

'All dwarfs are kin,' hissed the dwarf, as though he was being wilfully dense.

'Sorry I asked,' replied Cuthwin. 'Now hold still. I need to get that arrow out, and it's going to hurt.'

The dwarf looked down at the jutting shaft and said, 'Don't tell me it will hurt, manling, just do it before I die of old age.'

'Suit yourself,' said Cuthwin. 'I'm going to count to three, and then–'

He jerked the arrow out in one swift motion. The dwarf roared in agony and swung his fist at Cuthwin's head. He'd been expecting that and swayed back from the blow. Blood pumped from the wound and the dwarf's eyes rolled back as the pain threatened to overwhelm him.

'Stay with me, mountain man!' said Cuthwin, holding the dwarf upright. 'Come on, look at me! Listen to me, you have to stay awake or you're as good as dead. There's likely more of those goblins out there, and it won't take them long to get here on those wolves. So you need to come with me if you want to get back beneath the mountains.'

The dwarf gripped the edge of the wagon and it seemed as though his anger alone was sustaining him. Cuthwin turned to cut strips of cloth from one of the dead dwarfs' cloaks to bind the wounds. The dwarf watched him and said, 'What is your name, manling?'

'I'm Cuthwin of the Unberogen,' he said.

'The Heldenhammer's tribe...' said the dwarf, the hard edges of his voice softening with blood loss and fatigue.

'The very same,' said Cuthwin, binding the dwarf's wound as best he could. He would have preferred to lace the wound with healing poultices, but they were in his pack.

'And you? What's your name, mountain man?'

'Deeplock,' said the dwarf, his voice already sounding distant and faint. 'Grindan Deeplock of Zhufbar, Engineer to the Guildmasters of Varn Drazh, Keeper of the–'

The dwarf's voice faded and the ragged howling of wolves from further south told Cuthwin it was time to move on. Slinging the dwarf's arm over his shoulder, he set off towards where he'd set his bow and hoped he could put enough distance between him and the goblins before they were able to pick up his tracks.

'Wait…' said Deeplock. 'Must bring…'

'No time, mountain man,' said Cuthwin, half carrying, half dragging the wounded dwarf into the shadows of the forest. Were it only the larger greenskins behind them, Cuthwin wouldn't have been worried, they were strong but not too clever.

But goblins were cunning and would find their tracks swiftly. On his own he could evade them without trouble, but with a wounded dwarf in tow…

That was going to be a challenge.

'Hand me the tongs, son,' said Govannon, squinting in the smouldering orange light of the forge. His hand grasped air until Bysen placed the warm metal in his hands. The furnace was a blaze of light before him, the roar of its heat and the hiss of water droplets from the powered wheel that worked the bellows acting as a sounding guide for him as he thrust the tongs into the hot coals.

Govannon felt the metal and clamped it hard, drawing it out and placing it upon the anvil.

The stink of hot iron burned the air and its orange-yellow colour told him it was just right. His sight was all but destroyed, but his sense for the metal was just as strong.

'Looks good, da,' said Bysen. 'Forging heat right enough.'

'Aye, I can tell, lad,' nodded Govannon, handing his son the tongs and feeling on the workbench for his fuller. Its curved, walnut grip slipped into his hand and he hefted it to get the weight right before bringing it down in a short, powerful arc onto the iron bar. He struck several blows, swiftly establishing a working rhythm as Bysen turned the bar and drew it out, gradually lengthening the metal. They'd done the hard work earlier, working with strikers and other apprentices to work the cold lump of iron into a long bar from which to shape the blade.

It was to be the sword of the Empire's Grand Knight, for Alfgeir had earned great accolades in his defence of the realm in the Emperor's absence.

'Turn it again,' said Govannon. 'Once with each strike.'

'Aye, da,' said Bysen. 'Once each, aye, da. Like you say.'

Govannon worked the fuller along the length of the iron, working by instinct and earned skill. The bar was a blurred outline of yellow gold before him, and he could only tell Bysen was turning the bar by the sound of the hot metal scraping on the anvil. Counting his strokes, he adjudged the iron to be the right length. He had taken Alfgeir's measurements and tested the weight and balance of his currently favoured blade before laying a hammer to the metal. The Grand Knight of the Empire preferred a weapon with the weight slightly towards the tip, requiring a stronger arm to wield it, but delivering a more powerful blow when it landed. The ore that formed this sword had come from the mines of the Howling Hills, Cherusen land, which meant it was freer from impurities and should produce a blade of great brilliance.

'Look long enough?' he asked.

'Aye, da,' said Bysen. 'Just right, da.'

Govannon wiped a meaty forearm across his brow,

blinking away salty beads of sweat as they dripped into his eye. Just for a second, he could see the outline of his son clearly, a giant of a boy, nineteen summers old, but with the mind of a child.

Grief and guilt welled in the smith's heart.

It had been at Black Fire when everything had changed.

Govannon and Bysen had been fighting in the heart of the Unberogen lines, smashing greenskins down with powerful strokes of their iron-headed forge hammers. After hours of fighting, the day was almost won, and the warriors of the Emperor's army were hot and close to exhaustion. Victory was so close, they could almost touch it, and that alone kept them fighting beyond the limits of endurance.

A shadow fell over their sword band and an abominable stench rose up as a monstrous, rugose-skinned troll crashed into their flank. Taller than three men and growling with a throaty roar of idiot hunger, it swung a tree branch as thick as an oaken beam. Six men were bludgeoned to death with a single blow.

Many ran from its horror, but Govannon and Bysen stood firm, their hammers feeling woefully inadequate to face such a towering mass of muscle and fury. Warriors rallied to their side, for they were men much respected amongst the Unberogen, and together they charged the hideous creature. Its leering grin split apart in a mass of broken teeth and half-chewed flesh, but it was not in anticipation of feeding. A burbling heave spasmed through its stomach, and a caustic flood of acidic bile spewed from its wide mouth.

Govannon was one of the lucky ones. Leading the charge, he was spared the agony of being eaten alive by the deadly acid. His helmet took the brunt of the splash, but after three hours of fighting in the punishing heat, he'd pushed the visor up. Droplets of the viscous stomach bile dripped into his eyes, and the fiery agony as it burned into them was the worst pain in the world.

He remembered Bysen leaping to face the hideous beast. Its heavy club had smashed him to the ground and left him lying with his skull caved in like a broken egg. That had been the end of their battle, and the next Govannon had known was days later when he awoke in the surgeons' tents at the mouth of the pass. Bright light hurt his eyes and only the dimmest outline of shapes and contrasts were visible to him.

Though his sword brother, Orvad, had splashed water into his face moments after his wounding, the damage was done. His sight was virtually gone. Orvad died later in the battle, but with the help of one of the surgeons' runners, Govannon had sought news of his son. It took two days to find him among the thousands of wounded, and though he still lived, the lad left the better portion of his brain in the dusty sand of the pass.

Govannon could not weep, his eyes ruined by the beast's venom, but he sat with his son until they were set upon wagons for the journey back to Reikdorf.

Black Fire had taken away his sight and his son's mind, but there wasn't a day went by he wasn't glad he had stood in the line and faced the greenskin horde.

'Da?' said Bysen. 'What the matter, da?'

Govannon snapped out of his melancholy, squinting through the gloom at the blurred outline of his son. He held the sword metal in the tongs, and Govannon shook his head at his foolishness. The metal had cooled too far to work, and would need to be reheated. That was careless, for the quality of the blade would suffer after too many reheats.

'Nothing, son,' said Govannon. 'Let's get this metal heated up or this sword will be no better than a greenskin club.'

'Aye, da,' grinned Bysen. 'Heat it up, aye, heat it good.'

The metal was thrust into the fire and the process began again.

Govannon watched the seething glow, wishing for the thousandth time that he'd kept his visor lowered.

'Damn you for a fool,' he whispered, the words lost in the roaring of the furnace.

THEY WERE GETTING close now, too close. Cuthwin moved as fast as he could with the injured dwarf stumbling alongside him. He bore the bulk of Deeplock's weight, which was slowing him down and making it much harder to keep their passing secret. The forest had closed in, thick and ideal for getting lost in, but Cuthwin had travelled this way many times.

The forest was a harsh companion, a friend to those who understood its rhythms, a deadly enemy to those who didn't give it the proper respect. Cuthwin knew how to make his way in the wilderness, but the goblins were equally at home in its shadowed depths. Their pursuers were, at best, a mile behind. The wind carried the yapping barks of the wolves and though Cuthwin tried to angle his course so that it wouldn't carry his scent to them, it was proving to be impossible. He'd kept to the hard packed earth and stony ground where he could, wading through shallow streams and leaving false trails to throw their pursuers. That had bought him time, but hadn't shaken the goblins.

He'd stopped every now and then to give the wounded dwarf a rest, and had used the time to set traps on their back trail. At least one snare had caught a wolf; he'd heard its plaintive cry of pain. The breath heaved in his lungs and he knew he couldn't run much further. At some point soon he'd have to turn and fight. There hadn't been time to pluck his arrows from the goblin and wolf corpses, but his retrieved pack had a spare quiver with a dozen arrows. He didn't want to face the goblins and their wolves with only his bow and hunting knife, so any ambush would have to be planned carefully.

Cuthwin looked up through the high branches of the tangled canopy, trying to judge how far it was to the river. He could hear the distant sound of it and its cold, clear scent was a crisp tang over the mulchy greenness of the forest. If they were going to get away from these creatures, he'd need to have plotted their course correctly.

Deeplock stumbled and almost dragged Cuthwin down with him.

'Up, mountain man!' he hissed. 'Use those damn legs of yours!'

'Must… go back…' gasped the dwarf, and Cuthwin saw there was blood in his beard.

'Not if you want to live,' he said, hauling the dwarf to his feet.

Deeplock muttered something else, but Cuthwin couldn't make it out. He set off again through the trees, but the dwarf fell before they'd managed ten yards. Cuthwin fell with him, rolling to keep his bow from touching the ground.

'Damn you, but you're trouble,' he hissed.

The sound of a howling wolf drifted through the trees. It was east of him, and another answered it, this time to the west. There would be more behind him, at least four, and he knew they were racing to get ahead of him, to close the circle around him and leave him nowhere to run.

How far away were they? Listening to the echoes through the trees, he guessed they were no more than half a mile from him. He cursed and gripped the dwarf's tunic, hauling him over his shoulder.

'Ulric's balls, but you're heavy,' he told the unconscious dwarf. Though much shorter than Cuthwin, the dwarf was at least as heavy as a tall man. Bowed under the dwarf's weight, Cuthwin set off again, following the building swell of river noise, hoping that he'd emerge from the trees where he'd planned.

He ran on, sweat dripping into his eyes, losing track of time and distance as he fought to keep going. At last he saw a break in the trees and heard the rushing sound of falling water. Despite his exhaustion, he smiled, knowing the forest had steered him true. The sound of wolves was louder now. They knew they had him cornered, and were howling to get the fear pumping in his veins.

'We'll see about that,' he hissed, emerging from the trees onto the banks of a fast-flowing tributary of the Reik. Tumbling from the high peaks of the Grey Mountains, it wended its way through the uplands of the forest, gathering speed as it fed into the basin of the fertile southlands of the Empire.

Perhaps fifty yards wide, the river poured northwards in a tumbling froth of white spume and swirling black pools. The riverbed was only a yard or so down, but it would take all his strength to keep his feet against the speed of the water.

Greasy rocks slicked in moss jutted from the river as it widened towards a crashing waterfall. A glittering rainbow arced over the edge of the drop, the water falling to a wide pool of upthrust rocks far below.

Cuthwin set down his burden, leaning the dwarf against a boulder at the side of the river. His pallor was terrible, and Cuthwin doubted that even the best healers in Reikdorf could save him. To be killed rescuing a dwarf that likely wouldn't live out the day. That would be a poor way to meet his end.

Heavy tree branches drooped over the water, willows,

whip-limbed birch and young, supple saplings. Cuthwin shucked off his pack. He strung his bow and unsheathed his hunting knife, moving quickly to the treeline and testing the longest and thinnest tree branches.

A wolf howl came from the forest, and Cuthwin knew he didn't have much time.

SWEATING AND BREATHING hard, Cuthwin looped Grindan Deeplock over his shoulders and waded back into the river. Swollen with mountain water, it was bitterly cold and the breath caught in his throat. It threatened to snatch him from his feet and send him hurtling over the waterfall, but thanks to the additional ballast of the dwarf, Cuthwin was able to keep his balance. He waded out into the river, biting his lip to keep the pain of the cold at bay.

A dozen yards to his right, the waterfall boomed and roared like a hungry beast, and he tried not to think of how much it would hurt to be dashed to death on the rocks below. He reached the halfway point of the river, shuffling his feet through the mud and stones of the riverbed. Just ahead of him was a jutting boulder, its surfaces worn smooth by the passage of centuries of water. He slid Deeplock from his shoulders and propped him up against the rock, pressing his own back into the dwarf to hold him in place.

The wolves emerged from the trees, seven of them, each with a goblin perched behind the blades of their shoulders. Chittering laughter giggled from beneath the goblins' hoods, and hooked noses twitched in anticipation. They spat curses at him in their foul language, and many lifted their short horn bows from their backs.

Cuthwin pulled back on his own bowstring and let fly, sending an arrow into the mouth of a snarling wolf and dropping it instantly. The goblin fell from its back and plunged into the waters of the river. It squealed in fear before being carried over the waterfall. The roar of the water swallowed its cries. Four of the wolves entered the river, the flesh of their jaws drawn back over their fangs. A black-fletched shaft skittered off the rock and Cuthwin flinched, swinging his bow around and sighting down the length of his arrow.

He exhaled and loosed, watching the arrow as it slashed through the air to sever the thin knot of bound saplings he'd wedged in the soft earth before the bent branches of a long-limbed willow. Its branches whipped around, like the arm of a catapult laid on its side, and slashed into the wolf-riding goblins. Two of the wolves in the shallows were smashed from their feet and howled as they were swept downriver towards the falls. They and their riders vanished over the edge and as the other goblins watched in dismay Cuthwin nocked and let fly with another arrow.

It punched through the chest of the goblin whose wolf had leapt back quick enough to avoid his trap. Another goblin arrow spun up to slice the skin of his forehead. Blood streamed down Cuthwin's face, and he shook his head clear as the remaining four wolves leapt into the river, their lean bodies powering them through the water as the goblins held on for dear life.

Cuthwin waited until they were a dozen yards from him and sent his next shaft into a branch he'd wedged beneath a precariously perched boulder further upriver. His arrow thwacked into the wood, but the branch didn't move. The wolves snapped in the foaming water, and Cuthwin saw their feral hunger to tear him apart. He loosed another shaft into the wood, and this time it fell from where it was wedged into the soft mud he'd dug out of the riverbed.

The boulder toppled over, and the water breaking

behind it surged downriver with tidal force. The wave slammed into the wolves and broke against them with enormous power. They were helpless against the strength of the current and all but two were borne over the edge of the falls by the surging water. Their howls and the screeching fear of the goblins dwindled as they fell.

Before he could congratulate himself, a goblin arrow ricocheted from the rock and sliced through his bowstring. Cuthwin took hold of his now useless bow and hurled it towards the far bank. It was a good throw, and the weapon landed in the ferns at the edge of the river. He couldn't move from the rock for fear of losing Grindan Deeplock, so drew his knife and prepared to fight the last two of his pursuers.

The wolf was fighting against the current, and before it could reach him in his sheltered enclave, Cuthwin lunged forward. Keeping one hand braced against the dwarf, he slashed his blade across the wolf's snout as the goblin swung its sword at him. The beast yelped in pain and the goblin's sword went wide. Cuthwin plunged the tip of his dagger into the rider's throat. Blood spilled over his hand, and the goblin lurched back, yanking hard on the rope reins of its mount. The creature's pain outweighed its sense of danger and the power of the river eagerly snatched it away.

The last wolf had entered the river higher up and used the flow of water to its advantage. Swimming with the current, it lunged towards him. He hurled himself back against the rock and its jaws snapped shut an inch from his face. The goblin stabbed with its rusty blade. Cuthwin swayed aside and Grindan Deeplock slid away from him, his head sinking beneath the level of the rushing water.

Cuthwin punched the wolf in the face and rammed his knife into the goblin's side. Both tumbled away from him and he twisted the dagger in the greenskin's flesh, pulling it out and stabbing it down into the wolf's skull.

Its yelp of pain was abruptly cut off and the corpses spun lazily away, disappearing over the edge of the waterfall. Cuthwin let out a long breath and turned to lift the dwarf from beneath the water. His eyes were closed, and it was impossible to tell if he were alive or dead. Checking the treeline for more enemies, Cuthwin hauled Grindan Deeplock over to the far side of the river and dragged him onto the bank.

He pressed his fingertips to the dwarf's throat, and was rewarded with a pulse. Weak, but steady. Cuthwin's pack was sodden, but the oiled lining had kept the worst of the river at bay. Stripping the dwarf of his sodden clothes, he wrapped him in a woollen blanket from his pack and rubbed circulation back into his limbs.

'Just as well you're unconscious, mountain man,' said Cuthwin. 'Don't think you'd be keen on me doing this for you.'

Satisfied the dwarf wasn't about to die from the cold, Cuthwin swiftly redressed his wounds, using a healing poultice of valerian and spiderleaf and binding them with strips of vinegar-soaked linen. The dwarf grunted a few words in his harsh language. Cuthwin tied the bindings off under the dwarf's shoulder and lay back against the bole of a tree, letting the adrenaline drain from him in a series of slow breaths. There was nothing more he could do for the dwarf, and they were still some days from Reikdorf.

The dwarf would either live or die on his own terms.

Night was coming, and they needed to find shelter. Cuthwin saw foresters' marks on a nearby tree and dragged the dwarf further into the woods, following the signs towards a sheltered overhang of rock and fallen trees. A fire had been set in this hollow by its previous occupant, a fresh base of kindling and twigs ready for the next traveller to take shelter here. A stack of firewood lay bundled and tied with twine beneath the overhanging lip of a hollow tree.

Cuthwin recognised the style of fire that had been set. Though he had never met the man, he knew him to be a hunter who favoured his right hand and walked with a slight limp. He was a successful hunter, as his footprints – when Cuthwin could find them – were always deeper on the way home than on the way out. Whoever he was, he lived perhaps a day or two from here, somewhere along the high ridges of the south-east.

Cuthwin pulled out his tinderbox and got the fire going without difficulty. The hunter had built a good fire, and soon a small blaze was warming their sheltered hollow. With the fire going, he lay back and rested his eyes. He wouldn't sleep though. With only one of them able to stand guard, it didn't pay to leave their safety during the night to chance.

Grindan Deeplock grumbled in his sleep, yet amid the unintelligible words of his strange language, Cuthwin heard a few heavily accented words in Reikspiel.

One was *buried*, and he thought the other was *organ*.

That didn't make any sense. Were these dwarfs selling musical instruments?

Putting the dwarf's ramblings from his head, Cuthwin set about restringing his bow and settled down for the night.

⤙ FOUR ⤚

New Friends and Old Enemies

THE EMPEROR'S ARMY returned to Reikdorf in triumph, his black steed flanked by a dozen others, and trailed by two thousand marching warriors. Since arriving back on Empire soil, his forces had swollen with followers, farm boys eager to take up a life of the sword and warriors from distant lands wishing to serve under the Imperial banner.

Though Gerreon had escaped them, the stated purpose of the campaign had been to strike terror into the hearts of the Norsii, to let them know that they were not safe in their desolate realm of ice and snow. That task had been accomplished, and the crowds gathered to greet their Emperor's return waved swords and axes high in recognition of his victories.

Bells pealed from every tower that had one and the schoolhouses emptied as word spread throughout the city. First the arrival of the Grand Knight of the Empire, and now the return of the Emperor. Truly the city of Reikdorf was blessed. Thousands of men, women and children lined the streets, cheering and alternately shouting the names of Sigmar and Ulric.

Conn Carsten and a hundred Udose warriors marched with the Emperor, grim-faced men in long kilts and baked leather breastplates. Each carried a long, basket-hilted broadsword over their shoulders and a round leather-covered shield was slung over their backs. They carried themselves with a rowdy confidence, utterly sure of themselves and cheerfully scornful of the ordered ranks of the Unberogen.

Clad in his dwarf-forged plate and silver helm, Sigmar kept Ghal-maraz held high. The symbol of his rule, it served to remind his people of the bond of loyalty that existed between his people and those of the mountains. The Empire had come close to disaster at Middenheim, and in times of trouble it was good to remind people of all that stood in their favour. It had been many years since King Kurgan had visited Reikdorf, and Sigmar longed to visit the mountain hold of his fellow king and friend someday.

Wolfgart had not returned to Reikdorf. He had ridden south with Sigmar as far as the castle of Count Otwin of the Thuringians, before heading eastwards toward the lands of the Asoborns. Maedbh and Ulrike, his wife and daughter, now dwelled in the lands of Freya, Queen of the Asoborns. No one called Freya a count, no one dared. Like the Berserker King, she was one of Sigmar's allies that found it hard to shed her former title.

Behind the Emperor came an ornate bier, pulled by four white horses, the finest of Wolfgart's southern herd. Upon it lay an iron coffin, draped in the blue and cream of Middenheim. The body of Pendrag lay within, preserved with camphorated wine and powdered nitre. For his service and friendship, Pendrag would be rewarded with a place of honour within Warrior Hill. Sigmar rode through the streets of his city, basking in his subjects' adulation, the image of the heroic warrior-emperor his people needed and wanted.

THE FIRES OF the longhouse burned fiercely, filling the length of it with warmth and light. Three wild boars hunted that morning from the forests north of Reikdorf turned on spits and the smell of roasting pork was making every man in the great hall salivate. Blessings to Taal had been said in thanks, and serving maids bearing trays laden with platters of roasted meat and wooden mugs of beer circulated amongst the celebrating tribesmen.

The Udose drank heavily, singing achingly sad songs of lament to the wheezing, skirling music of the pipes. Unberogen warriors joined in, though the singsong language of the northern tribesmen was all but impenetrable to their southern ears. The mood in the hall was hearty, for both groups of warriors had fought side by side for the last year. Many oaths of brotherhood had been sworn between Udose and Unberogen, the kind that lay at the heart of what made the Empire strong.

Sigmar sat upon his throne, stripped of his armour save for the gleaming breastplate and a thick bearskin cloak. Two of his hounds, Lex and Kai lay curled at his feet, while Ortulf – ever the opportunist – circulated through the longhouse in search of scraps. Conn Carsten sat in the place of honour to Sigmar's right, while Alfgeir and Eoforth sat to his left. Though both these men had helped steer the Empire through some of its darkest hours, Sigmar found himself missing the earthy counsel of Wolfgart and Pendrag.

This hall had once echoed with Wolfgart's dreadful singing and off-colour jokes, but more and more, he was spending time in Three Hills with his family. Sigmar couldn't blame him, Maedbh was a hard woman to refuse. As was any Asoborn woman, thought Sigmar, remembering how he had secured Queen Freya's Sword Oath.

Conn Carsten had filled the void of leadership left by the death of Count Wolfila, binding the argumentative clans of the Udose into a fighting force in the face of the Norsii invasion. But for Carsten's merciless hit and run raids, the north would have fallen long before the armies of the Empire could have marched to save Middenheim.

This night was to honour his courage during the war against the Norsii and confirm his appointment as Count of the Udose. It should have been an occasion for great celebration, and certainly was amongst Carsten's warriors. But since this night had begun, Conn Carsten had said little and responded to any query with curt answers. He nursed his beer and seemed content to simply watch proceedings rather than participate.

Sigmar regarded his newest count's brooding countenance, his gloom-swept face having surely seen more than its fair share of hardship. His silver hair was cut tight to his skull and his beard was similarly trimmed. Where his warriors were bellicose and roaring, he was quiet and ill-suited to conversation.

None of the other counts were in attendance, nor had Sigmar expected them to be. After the mustering of their armies for the relief of Middenheim, the tribal leaders were attending to matters in their own lands. Since his return, Sigmar had read missives from Freya and Adelhard of increased greenskin activity in the Worlds Edge Mountains, of warbands of twisted forest beasts in the southern reaches and increased coordination between brigands and reavers in the north. Krugar and Aloysis both begged the Emperor's help in quelling numerous incidences of the dead rising from their tombs to attack the living, and Aldred of the Endals reported increased attacks from unknown seaborne corsairs.

Eoforth had once said that winning the Empire had been the easy part. Holding on to it would be the real challenge. Sigmar was now beginning to see what he meant. Something so precious would always attract enemies, and the true legacy of Sigmar's creation would be how long it endured against the encroaching darkness.

As much as he found it hard to enjoy Carsten's company, Sigmar knew this man was key to keeping his land safe. Better the northern marches were ruled by a competent, disagreeable man than a gregarious friend who didn't know one end of a sword from the other. Yet it sat ill with Sigmar that he could not reach the dour clansman, as though some unknown gulf existed between them that he could not cross. He did not expect to be as close to all his counts as he was to his friends, and as their ruler he knew he ought not to be. Yet to count a man as his ally and not to know him, that would not stand.

Sigmar turned to Conn Carsten and said, 'Can I ask you something, Conn?'

The newest count of the Empire nodded slowly, as though wary of Sigmar's purpose.

'This should be a grand day for you,' said Sigmar, knowing that flowery words or an indirect approach would only irritate the northerner. 'You are a count of the Empire now, a man of great respect and responsibility. Yet you seem distracted, like you stand at the grave of your sword brother. Why is that?'

Carsten put down his beer and wiped his lips with the back of his sleeve.

'I have lost too many men in the last year and a half to celebrate, my lord. The wolves of the north wreaked great harm on my tribe and devastated our lands. Every village among the Udose has widows to spare, and the black shawls of mourning are too common a sight among my people. We are always first to feel the bite of Norsii axes. That makes it hard to know joy.'

Sigmar shook his head, gesturing at the gathered warriors. 'Your warriors seem to have no difficulty in finding it.'

'Because they are young and foolish,' said Carsten. 'They think themselves immortal and beyond death's touch. If they live a little longer they will see the lie of that belief.'

'A grim view, my friend.'

'A realistic one. I have buried three wives and six children in my life. I once believed that I could have it all, the life of a warrior with its glory and battles, with a loving wife and family to come back to. But it is impossible. You of all people should know that.'

Sigmar felt the touch of Ravenna's memory, but instead of pain, it now brought him comfort, a reassurance that she was alive within his heart.

'You're right, I *do* know the pain of losing loved ones. I lost the love of my life many years ago and my best friend was killed by a man I once called a brother. Every death in Middenheim was a grievous loss, but I know that a life lived without hope or joy is a wasted one. I know the reality of life in the Empire, my friend. I know it is dangerous, often short and violent. That is precisely why we must take what joy we can from what the gods give us.'

'That may be the Unberogen way, but it is not my way,' said Carsten. 'Live in hope if you must, I will live in the knowledge that all things must die.'

Sigmar said, 'Look at Reikdorf, look at all we have achieved here and how the Empire's cities grow larger and stronger. One day we will have borders that no enemy, no matter how strong they are, can breach. We will have peace and our people will know contentment.'

Conn Carsten took a mouthful of beer and smiled. 'It would not do for me to call you foolish, my Emperor, but I think that is a naïve belief. We will always have to fight to hold on to what you have built. Already you have defeated two major invasions. Many more will come. It only takes one to succeed and the Empire will be forgotten in a generation.'

'I have heard that before, Conn,' said Sigmar with a grim smile. 'The necromancer Morath tried to break me with a similar argument. If we live fearing that all we have will be lost, then we would never build anything, never *achieve* anything. I cannot live that way; I will build and defend what I have built with my life. You are part of that, Conn, a vital part. I cannot do this without your support. You alone can keep the clans united and be my sword in the north.'

Carsten smiled and his face was transformed in an instant. Sigmar's words were flattery, but the northern clansman saw the sincerity in them and his dour expression lifted. He raised his mug of beer and Sigmar toasted with him.

'I'll drink to that,' said Carsten. 'But I know what I am, a cantankerous old man the clan chieftains tolerate as their count because they know that every other clan hates me too. I have no sons left to follow me, so the other chieftains look at me and know they will be rid of me in a few years. They can wait.'

Sigmar extended his hand and Conn Carsten took it.

'Make the bastards wait a long time,' said Sigmar.

Conn Carsten laughed and somewhere beyond the longhouse walls a bell tolled.

THE REVELRIES CONTINUED for another three hours, though Conn Carsten excused himself not long after their conversation. As the last of the tribesmen staggered or were carried from the longhouse, Sigmar stood from his throne and paced the length of the dwarf-built structure. Its walls were fashioned from black stone quarried from deep beneath the Worlds Edge Mountains, carried on wagons from the east and raised by surly craftsmen of the mountain folk under direction of Alaric.

Sigmar knew the dwarfs called him Alaric the Mad, a name that rankled, for a more level-headed, pragmatic individual would be hard to find. Alaric now laboured deep beneath the mountains to forge twelve mighty swords for the counts of the Empire. Before Black Fire, Pendrag had crafted wondrous shields for each of the tribal kings, and King Kurgan had decreed that he would present Sigmar with swords to match.

Alaric himself had delivered the first of those swords to Sigmar at the battle for the Fauschlag Rock, a blade without equal among the realm of man. It had been given to Sigmar, but he had presented it to Pendrag as the Count of Middenheim, and upon his death it had been taken up by Myrsa – once the Warrior Eternal, now the new count.

Sigmar sat on a bench, idly tracing the outline of a wolf in a spilled pool of beer. He missed his friends. Time and distance had seen them pulled to the corners of the Empire, and though each was in his rightful place, he still wished they could be near. He even found himself missing the reckless wildness of Redwane. The young warrior and his White Wolves were now quartered atop the Fauschlag Rock as honour guard to Myrsa, a position Sigmar saw no need to rescind.

The hall smelled of cold meat, sweat and stale beer. It was the smell of maleness, of warriors and companionship. Sigmar looked up as the moon emerged from behind a long cloud and its light flooded the hall. He remembered catching Cuthwin and Wenyld trying to sneak a glance at the warriors within on his Blood Night, smiling at the memory of those long ago days. Two and a half decades had passed since then, and Sigmar shook his head at the idea of such a span of time. Where had it all gone?

'Thinking of the past?' said Alfgeir, sitting opposite him and depositing a pair of wooden mugs of beer on the trestle table. 'Isn't that the job of old men?'

'We *are* old men, Alfgeir,' said Sigmar with a grin.

'Nonsense,' said the Grand Knight of the Empire. He was drunk, but pleasantly so. 'I'm as strong as I was when I first took up a sword.'

'I don't doubt it, but we're not the young bucks of the herd anymore.'

'Who needs to be? We have experience those with milk from their mother's teat on their thistledown beards can only dream about.'

'Those that are old enough to have beards.'

'Exactly,' agreed Alfgeir, taking a long swig of his beer.

Sigmar knew that Alfgeir would pay for this indulgence tomorrow. It wasn't as easy to shake the effects of Unberogen beer as it had been in their youth. Sigmar had ridden to Astofen after a heavy night of drinking and had felt no worse than any other morning, but he now had to nurse his beer or else he'd feel like the gods themselves were swinging hammers on the inside of his skull. His friend was still a powerful warrior, yet Sigmar knew he was slowing down. A young man when he served King Björn, Alfgeir was now approaching his sixtieth year.

'Do you remember when we climbed to the top of the Fauschlag Rock?'

'Remember it? I still have nightmares about it,' said Alfgeir. 'I still can't believe I went with you. I must have been mad.'

'I think we were both a bit mad back then,' agreed Sigmar. 'I think youth needs a bit of madness, or else what's the point?'

'The point of what, youth or madness?'

'Youth.'

Alfgeir shrugged. 'You're asking the wrong man, my friend. You want clever answers, you should ask Eoforth.'

'I would, but he went to his bed many hours ago.'

'Always was the clever one, eh?'

'The wisest among us,' said Sigmar, taking a long mouthful of beer.

They drank in silence for a while, listening to the good-natured arguments of drunken warriors outside as they wended their way to their bedrolls. Sigmar could well imagine the substance of their strident roughhousing, the same things he and his sword brothers had squabbled over when they were young; women, war and glory.

'I sometimes miss it though,' said Sigmar. 'When all you had to do was strap on your armour, carry a sharp sword and ride out with the blood thundering in your ears. You fought, you killed the enemy and you rode back with your cheeks blooded. Things were simpler back then. I miss that.'

'Everything seems simple to the young.'

'I know, but it would be pleasant to live like that again, just for a while. Not to have to worry about the fate of thousands, to try and protect all you've built and fear for what will happen to it when you're gone.'

Alfgeir gave him a sidelong look down the length of his nose. His eyes were unfocussed, but there was a clarity to his look that Sigmar knew all too well.

'The Empire will endure,' he said, taking his time not to slur. 'The youngsters behind us may be foolish just now, but they're good men and they'll grow wiser. You've built a grand thing in the Empire, Sigmar, grand enough that it'll endure without sons of your blood to keep it strong.'

Sigmar nodded and looked into the thinning froth on his beer. Alfgeir had hit a raw nerve, and he took a moment to consider his answer.

'Ravenna and I talked of a family,' he said.

'She would have borne you strong sons,' said Alfgeir. 'She was a bonny lass, but she had strength too. Every day I wish Gerreon a thousand painful deaths for what he took from you.'

'What he took from us all,' said Sigmar. 'But I don't want to talk about Ravenna. The world will have to make do without my sons.'

'And mine,' said Alfgeir. 'Never wanted to make a woman wait for me every time I rode to war. Didn't seem fair, but I wish I'd sired a son. Someone to carry on my name after I die. I wanted there to be someone who'd remember me after I was gone.'

'The saga poets will remember you, my friend,' said Sigmar. 'Your deeds will be immortalised in epic verse.'

'Aye, maybe so, but who'll read them?'

'They'll be sung from the longhouses of the Udose to the castles of the Merogens. I'm the Emperor, I can make it law if you like.'

Alfgeir laughed and the maudlin mood was banished. That was the Unberogen way, to laugh in the face of despair with a drink in one hand and a sword in the other. Alfgeir threw his empty mug over his shoulder into the gently glowing firepit and nodded.

'Aye, I'd like that,' he said. 'Make it happen.'

'First thing tomorrow,' promised Sigmar, draining the last of his beer and lobbing his mug over Alfgeir's shoulder. It broke apart on the coals, the last dregs of the beer hissing as the alcohol burned with sudden brightness.

'So how was Carsten?' asked Alfgeir, apropos of nothing. 'Looked like you cracked the granite of his face at the end.'

Sigmar took a moment to consider the question. He and Carsten had established a connection tonight, one he hadn't expected to make, but Sigmar still felt like he hardly knew the man.

'We're never going to be friends, but I think I understand him a bit better.'

'What's to understand? He's a dour-faced misery, though he's a devil of a fighter.'

'I knew that already, but I know why he's the way he is. He's known great pain and suffering and I think it got the better of him.'

'We've all known suffering and loss,' said Alfgeir, raising his mug. 'To the dead.'

'To the dead,' said Sigmar.

BENEATH THE LIGHT of Mannslieb a hundred warriors of the Menogoths marched from the hill fort of Hyrstdunn. They followed an oft-used road that led through the fields and villages clustered around the sprawling settlement like children afraid to venture too far from a parent's protection. Many warriors carried tall spears tied with green and yellow cords, flanked by groups of hard-eyed men in lacquered leather breastplates with unsheathed broadswords. Torchbearers accompanied the marching warriors; each robed in black and with their hoods pulled up over their heads. At the head of the column rode Count Markus of the Menogoths, draped in the black cloak of mourning and with his own swords sheathed across his back.

The fortress city at their back had stood for hundreds of years, a forest of wooden logs with sharpened tips and strong towers. The land hereabouts was rugged and undulant, rising in gentle sways towards the haunches of the Grey Mountains that bordered Menogoth lands to the south. The earth here was fertile and rich in resources, yet the price for that bounty was a life lived in the shadow of the monsters that made their lairs within the mountains: greenskins, cave beasts twisted by dark magic or strange monsters with no name and ever more fearsome reputations.

King Markus had carved a life for his tribe in this wild land, but not without great cost. His people were hardy, yet their souls were forever caught in the shadow of the mountains. Often gloomy and fatalistic, the Menogoths were viewed as a miserable tribe by their more northerly cousins, but had they spent a year in their lands, not one Unberogen, Cherusen or Thuringian would fail to see why.

Count Markus rode beneath a streaming banner of yellow and green silk carried by his sword champion, Wenian. The banner had been a gift from Marius of the Jutones in the wake of the great victory at the Fauschlag Rock, and its fabric was said to have come from lands far to the east beyond the Worlds Edge Mountains. Markus had cherished the gift ever since.

His wife and daughter rode in an ornate coach pulled by four black horses that had been harnessed in bronze and plumed with black feathers. The coach was of lacquered black wood, hung with ebony roses, spread-winged ravens and, at its front, the image of a great portal. The women had their heads bowed, and heavy veils hung with black pearls obscured their faces.

This was a grim night for the Menogoths, for the only son of Count Markus was dead.

Borne on a palanquin of spears, Vartan Gothii went to his rest among the tombs of his ancestors. An honour guard of the Bloodspears carried the body of Markus's son, granted this honour for their courage in standing firm at Black Fire while their brother warriors had run.

Markus led the procession through his lands towards

the flat-topped hill where the Menogoth heroes of old were buried. Called the Morrdunn, its height should have made it the natural place to build one of the forts that gave the Menogoths their name of hill people, but the first tribesmen to settle here had instinctively known that this was not a place for the living. A number of torches flickered at its summit as the grim procession wound its way up the hard-packed earth of its burial paths.

They passed the tomb of Devyn of the Axe, the heroic warrior who had saved the first king of the tribe from an ogre's cook pot. Further up, Markus nodded respectfully to the mausoleum carved into the hill where Bannan, the greatest Swordmaster of the Menogoths, lay at his final rest. Odel the Mad lay within a simple sepulchre of polished grey granite built into the upper slopes of the hill, and Markus touched the talisman of Ranald at his chest to ward off the malign influence of the berserk huscarl.

He rode onto the crest of the hill, its summit enclosed by a ring of rune-carved stones like spikes on an ancient ruler's crown. The priests of Morr were waiting, a dozen men in black robes tied with silver cords and each carrying a thin book bound in soft kidskin. The black coach rumbled onto the hilltop, and the Bloodspears moved to the centre of the hill, where the only priest of Morr with his hood drawn back stood ready to fulfil his duty to the dead.

'Who comes with a lost soul to be ushered into the realm of Morr?' intoned the priest.

Markus and his champion dismounted, walking alongside the Bloodspears towards the centre of the hilltop tomb. Wenian planted the banner before the priest as Markus answered.

'I do, Markus Gothii, King of the Menogoths.'

Markus used his old title, for this was an ancient rite of

his tribe, one in which his new title of count had no part.

'Morr would know this soul's name, King Markus of the Menogoths.'

'I bring my son, Vartan Gothii, slain by greenskin warriors while defending his people.'

'Slain in service of a higher calling,' said the priest. 'Then he will find rest in the realms beyond this world of flesh.'

Markus clenched his jaw. He was the master of the Menogoths, a warrior of superlative skill. He rubbed a hand across his shaven scalp, tensing his lean, wolfish physique as the grief threatened to unman him before the priests who would see his son to the realms of the dead.

The priest saw his battle and opened the book he carried as the Bloodspears gently lowered Vartan Gothii to the ground. The acolytes of the head priest came forward and knelt in a circle around the body. Markus looked at the unmoving features of his son, so pale and serene that they might have been carved from marble.

'Keep it simple, priest,' ordered Markus. 'Vartan hated ceremony.'

'As you wish, King Markus,' said the priest, flipping to a shorter passage.

Markus's wife and daughter came alongside him and he took their hands as the priest began his recitation of the benediction to the dead. The priest's voice was clear and strong as he read, and Markus took comfort in the words he heard.

'Great Morr, master of the dead and dreams, you have made death itself the gateway to eternal life. Look with love on our fallen brother, and make him one with your realm that he may come before you free from pain. Lord Morr, the death of Vartan Gothii recalls our human condition and the brevity of our lives in this world. For those who believe, death is not the end, nor does it destroy the bonds forged in our lives. We share the faith of all men and the hope of the life beyond this frail realm of all flesh. Bring the light of your wisdom to this time of testing and pain as we pray for Vartan Gothii and for those who loved him.'

The priest closed his book and bowed his head. The hillside was silent, even the black horses and the torches seeming to understand that it would be unseemly to intrude on a king's mourning.

A slow clapping came from the far side of the hill, and a figure armoured in gleaming silver and gold emerged from behind one of the great menhirs. A mantle of white silk spilled from his shoulders, contrasting sharply with the soft caramel colour of his skin and the oiled darkness of his lustrous hair.

'Very poetic,' said the warrior, his accent soft, rounded and obviously cultured, though it was of no tribe Markus had ever encountered. 'You mortals do so enjoy indulging in the luxury of woe.'

'Begone,' declared the priest of Morr, brandishing his prayer book like a weapon. 'This is a sacred moment you are defiling.'

The warrior snatched the book from the priest and hurled it into the darkness. 'This? Utter nonsense! Don't believe a word of it, but what can you expect from a man who has not passed over to see the other side for himself?'

THE BLOODSPEARS LIFTED their weapons and the swordsmen tensed as the warrior walked slowly towards the mourners at the centre of the Morrdunn. His movements were unhurried and casual, yet Markus's expert eye caught the telltale signs of a man perfectly in balance with his body. This man was a killer, no doubt about that. He seemed utterly unafraid, which marked him either as a madman or a man who knew something Markus did not.

'Who are you?' he said, struggling to keep his voice calm. 'I am burying my son, and you are being disrespectful. That can get a man killed in these lands.'

'So can being in the wrong place at the wrong time,' said the warrior. 'But in answer to your question, I am Khaled al-Muntasir, though I am sure that will mean nothing to you.'

'You're right, it doesn't,' said Markus. 'Now begone before I have you slain.'

Khaled al-Muntasir laughed, a rich sound full of dark amusement. He smiled and swept back his cloak to reveal a slender-bladed scabbard of pale wood inlaid with mother-of-pearl and jade. The warrior placed his hand on the sword and drummed his fingers on the pommel of jet.

'If you are looking for a fight, then you are a fool,' said Markus.

'I am many things, Count Markus: a man of culture, an artist, a writer of sorts and a dilettante in all things mystical. I have some knowledge of the celestial mechanics wheeling above us and am a passable tailor, weaponsmith and crafter of fine jewellery and ornaments. But one thing I am not, is a fool.'

'Let me gut him, my lord,' hissed Wenian, drawing his sword with a hiss of metal on leather.

Markus hesitated, knowing full well how skilful Wenian was, but fearing that any duel fought here would be an unequal match.

'Yes, let him,' said Khaled al-Muntasir, drawing his own weapon. The blade reflected Mannslieb's glow such that it shone like a sliver of moonlight itself. 'I have been cooped up too long in Athel Tamera, and it will be good to wet my blade in mortal flesh again.'

'You talk big, fancy man, but you'll bleed just the same,' said Wenian, spinning his sword to loosen his shoulders.

'Actually, I think you'll find that–'

Wenian didn't give him a chance to finish, launching himself at the finery-clad warrior. Khaled al-Muntasir's blade swept up in a blur of white gold, flickering like sunlight on ice. Wenian's charge carried him past the warrior, but before he turned, he sank to his knees and toppled to the side. His head fell from his shoulders, rolling to a halt before one of the great menhirs.

Markus was horrified. Wenian was one of the greatest swordsmen he knew, more skilful than any *droyaska* of the Ostagoths, and twice as fast as any Cherusen Wildman. Yet this effete warrior had beheaded him without so much as batting an eyelid.

Khaled al-Muntasir knelt beside Wenian's corpse and wiped his sword blade clean of blood. He looked up at Markus with a predatory gleam in his eyes. They were dark and liquid, like the oil that burned in sunken pools deep in the reeking canyons of the Grey Mountains, and he found it hard to look away. Markus had seen that kind of look before, in the eyes of a wolf with its prey firmly locked in its grip.

'What are you?' he said.

Khaled al-Muntasir stood and smiled. 'I am your worst nightmare. Or at least one of them.'

'Kill him,' ordered Markus, and the Bloodspears moved to surround this lone warrior. No one, no matter how skilful could survive against such numbers. Fifty spearmen advanced towards the warrior, the iron blades of their weapons aimed at the swordsman's heart.

'Really?' said Khaled al-Muntasir, as though disappointed. 'You are a king, are you not? This is the best you can do? I'm insulted you think I would fight like some common brawler. Luckily, Krell here excels at this sort of fight.'

A terrifying roar swept over the summit of Morrdunn, the echoes bouncing from the menhirs and filling every heart that heard it with the naked fear common to all prey creatures. Something moved in the shadows and a hulking red shape flew through the air to land with a crash of metal and stone in the centre of the ring of spearmen.

It was a warrior, but a warrior unlike any other.

A full head and shoulders above his tallest rival, Krell was clad in brazen plates of ancient iron so stained with blood that their original colour was impossible to gauge. A great skull rune was stamped or branded into his chest, and Markus's courage deserted him at the sight of it. Great horns of bone extended from the monstrous warrior's helm and Markus saw Krell's face was a skeletal horror of yellowed bone and leathery flesh. A hideous emerald glow burned in his empty eye sockets, and any warrior brave enough to meet his gaze saw the manner of his death there.

A vast axe with a blade of utter darkness swung out and a dozen men died, their bodies hurled through the air like corn stalks at threshing time. The red-armoured warrior bludgeoned its way through the Bloodspears, hacking them down with insane ferocity and without mercy. Khaled al-Muntasir watched the slaughter impassively, as though bored by such violence.

In seconds, every warrior of the Bloodspears was dead, chopped into ragged hunks of gory meat. It was impossible to tell one warrior's remains from another, such was the scale of butchery. Markus ran to his wife and daughter, gathering them to him and shielding them from the whirlwind of destruction that killed his warriors.

The sword bands fared no better; cut down in a frenzy

of bloodletting that left Markus horrified and disbelieving. The summit of the Morrdunn was soaked in blood, the ground sodden with the vital fluid of a hundred men, slain in less time that it would take to count them. The slaughterman returned to Khaled al-Muntasir's side, a constant stream of blood pouring from the black blade of his axe.

Only now did the swordsman look interested in the slaughter. A thin network of veins pulsed beneath the skin of his temples, his jaw clenched and his nostrils flared at the bitter reek of blood on the air.

'Ulric preserve us,' whispered Markus, backing away from the two warriors.

'The wolf god?' smiled Khaled al-Muntasir. 'He won't hear you. And if he does, he won't care. Isn't that what his priests teach, that his followers should be self-reliant?'

'You are daemons,' said Markus, drawing his sword and standing before his family. 'Fight me if you must, but let my wife and daughter live. They are innocents and do not deserve this.'

'Innocent?' hissed Khaled al-Muntasir, as though enjoying the taste of the word. 'There is no such thing in this world. Just by being born mankind corrupts this world. Every step a mortal takes, he destroys a little piece of it. No, do not think to appeal to me with thoughts of compassion. I forgot that emotion before your tribe even crossed the eastern mountains.'

'What are you?' demanded Markus.

Khaled al-Muntasir stepped closer, and Markus saw that the pale hue of his complexion had nothing to do with the moonlight. Khaled al-Muntasir smiled, revealing two elongated fangs descending from his upper jaw.

'You are a blood drinker!' hissed Markus. 'A creature of the dead.'

'I cannot deny the truth,' said Khaled al-Muntasir. 'And your daughter's terror is such a tantalising sweetmeat that I think I shall leave her until last. As much as it would give me great pleasure to make you watch them die, I will savour her terror all the more as she watches her parents bled dry before her young eyes.'

'Why are you doing this?' said Markus, fighting to control his terror of this beast of the night. His blood was sluggish in his veins, and it was all he could do to keep hold of his sword.

'It is not I,' said Khaled al-Muntasir. 'I am but a humble servant in this drama.'

A vast shadow moved in the darkness behind the warrior, a slice of the deepest, darkest night given form and motion. As Krell towered over Khaled al-Muntasir, so too did this giant figure loom over them all. It stepped into the flickering circle of light cast by the fallen torches, yet no hint of illumination touched its blackened form.

A mighty figure cloaked in night and armour from the darkest forges of the damned, its eyes burned with the same green light as shimmered in Krell's vacant skull. One arm clutched a forked staff in the form of an elongated snake while the other had a sickly metallic sheen to it, like iron with a rainbow scum of oil slithering across its surface.

Grotesque and twisted with vile animation, the grim visage was that of death itself, a horror cast from the nightmares of men and women since the dawn of time. Markus's wife fainted dead away with horror, and he felt his own fragile grip on sanity slipping in the face of such irrevocable knowledge of his own death. His sword fell to the ground and tears spilled from his eyes as he turned his daughter's face away from the monster.

She sobbed uncontrollably, and Markus knew it would be a mercy to cut her throat rather than have her face what was to come. Until this moment, Markus had not feared death, knowing his courage in battle would surely earn him a place in Ulric's Hall. One look into the lambent pits of this horror's eyes told him there would be no journey to the next life to hunt in the forests of eternal winter. Even the horror of the grave, with cold earth embracing his rotting flesh and the worms growing fat on his meat was to be denied him. Compared to the fate this creature was soon to visit upon them, such an end would be a mercy.

Markus dropped to his knees before this dreadful apparition as it closed on him.

'It is fitting that you give homage to the new lord of these lands,' said Khaled al-Muntasir.

Markus fumbled for his dagger, thinking to end his and his family's life, but before his hand even closed on the hilt, the blood drinker was at his side and holding him in an unbreakable grip, the cold flesh of his face inches from his own.

'No, not yet,' whispered Khaled al-Muntasir. 'Not when there are such sights left to see.'

Darkness boiled from the towering black warrior's form, filling the sky with unnatural gloom, blotting out the moon and filling the sky with evil clouds and the screeching of bats. Wolves howled in the darkness, blood-hungry beasts of the deep forest, not the noble creatures of the northern woods that carried the chill winds of Ulric in their veins. The darkness closed on Hyrstdunn, obscuring it from view, but Markus heard the screams and knew his city was doomed.

'I want you to say his name,' said Khaled al-Muntasir.

'I don't know it,' said Markus, wishing that were true.

'Come now,' chided Khaled al-Muntasir, digging a manicured nail into his throat. 'It lives in mortal minds as a nightmare of distant lands and forgotten days. It is a name of death that travels with fearful taletellers and poisons the lips of scared men huddled around fires in the foolish belief that they are safe from his reach. Say it, mortal. Say it now.'

'No,' wept Markus. 'I cannot.'

'Of course you can, it's just wind noises passing through your throat.'

'He is… he is…'

'That's it, go on,' urged the blood drinker.

'He is *Nagash*,' said Markus, spitting the name like a curse.

As though giving voice to the name of the dread necromancer from the ancient horror tales gave it power, the mighty form slammed its vile metal hand into the earth of the Morrdunn. A booming peal of thunder split the heavens and the green light in Nagash's eyes blazed with incredible power, flowing through his withered, monstrous body to pour into the earth of the Empire like a corruption.

Flickering green light danced over Markus's son's body, like wisps of corpse light in the swamps. Though he was cold and dead, Vartan sat up with stiff movements, as some dread force other than his own wasted muscles empowered him. Markus wept at this violation of his son's flesh, hating these beings of darkness more than he had hated anything in his life.

Vartan turned his dead gaze upon Markus, the cold empty green light flickering in his sunken, shrivelled eyes. Cold horror crept over Markus as his son stood on limbs he himself had washed and oiled the night before, the metal links of Vartan's armour clinking together as he took his place at the blood drinker's side.

The ground of the hill trembled and a deep groaning from its heart rumbled far beneath Markus's feet. The grass rippled, as though an army of snakes writhed beneath its surface, and a hand punched up through the earth. Dried flesh clung to the bones and fragments of rusted armour emerged as the dead warrior clawed its way from beneath the hill.

More and more followed it, hundreds of Menogoth dead torn from their eternal rest by the dark sorcery of the ancient necromancer. The hill shook as the honoured slain broke open their mausolea, tombs and barrows and marched to the summit of the Morrdunn.

Markus felt his anger crowd out his fear, but Khaled al-Muntasir's grip was unbreakable.

'Know that your Emperor's realm is doomed,' said the blood drinker. 'Know that all you love will die and rise again to serve this army of darkness. Know this and despair!'

Khaled al-Muntasir's fangs sank into his neck and Markus felt his life being sucked from his flesh. Yet as he slipped down into the black abyss of death, his thoughts were that once again the Menogoths had failed their Emperor.

━◄ FIVE ►━

Homecomings

ANOTHER ARROW THUDDED home in the straw man hung from the pole, spinning him around with a foot of Asoborn wood protruding from his chest. Wolfgart watched as the black and gold chariot rumbled a weaving course through a long line of stakes hammered in the dry ground. Maedbh guided the two horses pulling the chariot with an expert hand, while his daughter loosed carefully aimed arrows from the fighting platform behind her.

'Only a youngster and already she can handle a bow better than I,' he said.

The chariot turned at the end of the strip of land and came back towards him. Maedbh gave her daughter a hug and Ulrike waved her bow for him to see. He waved back, but inwardly he hated the sight of his little girl with a weapon. Too small to practise with spears, Maedbh had not wasted the year he had been in the north with Sigmar, and Ulrike had transformed from a small girl into a budding young woman.

Maedbh hauled back on the reins and the chariot came to a halt next to the piled logs on which he sat. Situated on the outskirts of Three Hills, this wide strip of land had been used by Asoborn youths to hone their skills with bow and spear and chariot for decades. A huge square of hard-packed earth and stone, the wheels of countless chariots and the hooves of unnumbered cavalry mounts had long since beaten any fertility from the soil.

At the field's northern end, a group of Asoborns marched back and forth, getting used to the notion of fighting and manoeuvring in ranked-up blocks of sword bands. It wasn't the usual way Asoborns fought, but after Black Fire had proved its worth, Sigmar had pressed every tribe to master such organised warfare.

Men and women marched together, and Wolfgart smiled. Some of the tribes of the Empire thought the Asoborn armies comprised of only women, but such an idea was ridiculous. Any tribe that sent only its women to war would soon be extinct without mothers to birth the next generation of warriors and farmers.

'Did you see, father?' cried Ulrike as Maedbh brought the chariot to a halt beside him. 'I didn't miss a single one! Even Daegal can't manage that!'

'Aye, dear heart, I saw,' he said, wondering who Daegal was. 'No greenskins will get by you with that bow of yours.'

'I know,' she said, miming the act of pulling the bowstring back. 'I'll kill them all. Swoosh, swoosh, swoosh!'

'Our daughter's a natural,' said Maedbh, stepping lightly from the chariot and lifting Ulrike down. The little girl ran over to Wolfgart and leapt into his arms, curling her own wiry limbs around his neck. She kissed his cheeks and he hugged her back, the most precious thing in the world to him.

'Easy there, Ulrike,' he said. 'You'll squeeze the life out of me like that.'

'Sorry,' she giggled. 'I don't think I could do that. You're too strong.'

'Aye, maybe you're right,' he said, squeezing her until she squealed at him to stop.

She rested her head on his shoulder, and Wolfgart hated that he had been away for so long. He had missed so much of her childhood with war calling him from one corner of the Empire to the other. Too often, Wolfgart felt like he was being pulled in different directions. Maedbh had eventually tired of living in Reikdorf and after months of sullen silences and furious rows, she had declared that she and Ulrike were moving back to the Asoborn settlement of Three Hills.

Wolfgart had remained in Reikdorf as one of Sigmar's Shieldbearers, but had travelled often between Unberogen and Asoborn lands. The times between each visit grew longer as he and Maedbh would often end up arguing, and if not for Ulrike, Wolfgart wondered whether he would come at all.

'When are you going back?' asked Ulrike, and Wolfgart hated that this was always one of the first questions she asked when she saw him.

'Ach, don't let's talk about that just yet, lass,' he said, prising her from his shoulder and setting her onto the ground. 'Gather your shafts and show me again how good you've gotten with that bow.'

Ulrike nodded enthusiastically and ran off towards the gently swaying straw men to pluck the arrows from their abused forms. Wolfgart straightened and sighed as he saw the fiery look in his wife's eyes.

'Well?' said Maedbh.

'Well what?' he said, though he knew fine well what she was asking.

'You didn't answer your daughter,' said Maedbh. 'When are you going back to Reikdorf?'

'Can't wait to get rid of me, is that it?'

Maedbh stared at him coldly, and even in such an ill-temper, she was still beautiful. Her fiery red hair was bound in two long scalp locks that fell to her waist and her figure was gloriously curved and full. Desire swelled in him, but one look at her icy eyes quelled it.

'You always have to start a fight, don't you?'

'That's rich coming from an Asoborn,' he said, though he knew it would only inflame the situation. 'As I recall, you're the ones who prefer to hit first.'

Maedbh sighed, and Wolfgart wanted to reach for her, to hold her close to him and tell her that he loved her, that he knew she still loved him and that this fighting was stupid. But his pride wouldn't let him. She was a hellion in war and in the bedchamber, but her viper's tongue drove him to words he knew were foolish.

'I do not want to fight, Wolfgart, but I need to know you will be here for Ulrike. She misses her father. She *needs* her father. *I* need him.'

'I'll stay as long as I can,' he said. 'There's trouble in the south, and we're hearing rumours that the forest brigands have banded together in the northern marches. They'll need rooting out before they become too strong. Not to mention the greenskins coming down from the mountains and the beast raids along the Taalbec.'

Maedbh moved away from him and rubbed the horses' necks, loosening the bits at their mouths now that they were at rest. He saw the disappointment in her posture and rose from his seat on the logs.

'Look, what do you want me to say? I'm oath-sworn to Sigmar, I can't just leave him.'

'He is an Emperor,' snapped Maedbh. 'You think you

are his only warrior, that the Empire will fall if you are not at his side?'

'It almost did once before,' he said. 'There was that business with the crown I told you about.'

'I know,' she said. 'I know you are his oldest and dearest friend, but you also swore an oath to me, remember?'

'I remember,' he said, taking her hand. 'It was one of the happiest days of my life.'

She pulled away, watching as Ulrike plucked the last of her arrows from the straw men.

'She will make a fine warrior,' said Maedbh. 'A proud Asoborn warrior woman.'

Anger touched Wolfgart and he said, 'Does she have to be?'

'What do you mean?'

'A warrior. She's my little girl; she shouldn't be using any weapons at all. It wasn't so long ago she chided me for wanting to go to war. She said it was stupid, and she wasn't wrong, but here you are pushing her into the battle lines.'

'As every Asoborn child is,' pointed out Maedbh. 'Or is there some reason you think she shouldn't learn to defend herself?'

'She's a girl,' protested Wolfgart. No sooner were the words out of his mouth than he knew he'd made a terrible mistake.

'She's a girl,' repeated Maedbh. 'Like me, you mean? Unberogen women may not fight, but you are in Asoborn lands now, Wolfgart. And if you don't like it go back to Reikdorf and stay in your draughty house without us.'

'Aye, well for all the warmth you bring to it, I might just do that.'

Maedbh's face turned to granite and she looked away as Ulrike returned with her quiver restocked. Wolfgart wanted to take his harsh, thoughtless words back, but it was too late.

'Come on,' said Maedbh, lifting Ulrike back onto the chariot. 'Let's try again, and this time I'll make it more difficult for you.'

As the chariot pulled away, Ulrike waved to him and shouted, 'Watch me! Watch me hit them all again!'

Wolfgart waved back, though a leaden weight settled in his belly.

ELSWYTH KNELT BY the dwarf's pallet bed, cleaning the wound at his shoulder, tutting at Cuthwin's crude application of herbal poultices. Inflamed joints had forced Cradoc to hang up his healer's satchel, but his apprentice had proved to be no less capable, though her manner was just as abrasive as the old man's.

'Did he tell you his name?' Sigmar asked Cuthwin, looking at the dwarf's pallid features.

Sigmar had seen his share of battlefield injuries and though he'd seen many a man and dwarf recover from such a wound, few of them had travelled for six days through the wilderness before being properly treated.

'Yes, my lord,' answered Cuthwin. 'Grindan Deeplock. Said he was from Zhufbar.'

'And an engineer by the looks of it,' added Elswyth, lifting the dwarf's hand. Scarred and callused, the tips were dark with powder burns and the nails were caked with the residue of oils and coal dust.

'He said he was an engineer, aye,' nodded Cuthwin. 'Said he worked for the Guildmasters of Varn Drazh. Didn't say what that was though.'

'It's a vast lake, high in the mountains,' said Sigmar. 'Alaric told me of it long ago. Supposedly a comet fell from the sky and blasted a huge crater in the mountains. Alaric said there's lots of dwarf settlements nearby, because the rock around the lake is rich with iron and precious metals.'

'Really, Cuthwin, were you *trying* to help this dwarf to die?' cut in Elswyth. 'This wound is so dirty and infected that I don't know if anything I can do will halt it. You might as well have packed the dressing with nightshade.'

Cuthwin shrank from the healer's sharp words, and Sigmar hid a smile. Though many considered Elswyth a fine looking woman, few dared attempt to court her, for her tongue was well known amongst Unberogen men, though for all the wrong reasons.

'We were on the run from greenskins,' protested Cuthwin.

'They were only goblins,' pointed out Elswyth.

Cuthwin's face darkened. 'I didn't have time to redress his wound. It looked fine.'

'Did you check? Or did you just drag him here through all the muddy, stagnant pools of water you could find?'

Cuthwin looked set to lose his temper. Sigmar smiled and put himself between the scout and the healer before violence ensued.

'He got him here alive is what matters,' said Sigmar. 'Now it's your job to keep him that way. Can you do that?'

'I won't promise anything, not even to you, Sigmar,' said Elsywth. 'I'll keep his wound clean and change the dressing hourly. If he recovers consciousness, I'll have him drink a berberry tisane with some sweet balm. That's all I can do, and it probably won't be enough, so you'd best get Alessa at the temple of Shallya to say some prayers for him.'

'You talk about me like I'm dead already,' croaked the dwarf and they all jumped.

Sigmar joined Elswyth at Grindan's bedside. He placed a hand lightly on the dwarf's chest. The effort of talking was taking its toll on the dwarf and runnels of sweat poured down the age lines carved in his face.

'Where am I?' asked Grindan.

'You're in Reikdorf,' said Elswyth. 'Under the protection of Sigmar Heldenhammer.'

'Ah,' said the dwarf. 'So the young lad got me here then…'

'Aye, that he did,' said Sigmar. 'He's a canny one is Cuthwin.'

'I'm in your debt, youngling,' wheezed the dwarf, his eyes screwed up in pain.

'Think nothing of it,' said Cuthwin.

'Don't be a damn fool, youngling,' snapped Grindan. 'You think the life debt of a dwarf is given lightly? Bear the tale of my doom to the Deeplock clan and you and all your line will become Umgilok to them.'

'I'll do that,' promised Cuthwin.

'It means a man worthy of praise,' said Sigmar, seeing the scout's look of confusion.

'You know your Khazalid, young Heldenhammer.'

'Master Alaric has taught me a tiny bit,' said Sigmar. The dwarf's chest rasped like a punctured forge-bellow with every word. He looked up at Elswyth, who shook her head.

'Ah, the Mad,' grunted Grindan. 'He toils night and day for you, manling. Another year and he'll have a second sword for your kings. Foolish to rush these things, I say, but it'll outlast any man it's given to so I suppose it doesn't matter.'

The dwarf's chest hiked and his eyes widened as a memory returned to him and he gripped Sigmar's shoulder urgently. He looked past the Emperor to Cuthwin and fixed him with a desperate gaze.

'Youngling! Did they get it? The grobi, did they find it?' demanded Grindan.

'Get what?' said Cuthwin. 'I don't know what you mean.'

'The Barag... the Thunder Bringer...' wheezed Grindan. 'We... we were bringing it home. Prince Uldrakk of Zhufbar... loaned it to the third son of... of Mordhaz, lord of the Grey Mountain clans, three hundred and seventy-five years ago. We'd gone there to get it back, but the grobi ambushed us... too much beer and not enough caution...'

Red flecks sprayed from the dwarf's mouth as he spoke and his words were forced out though the effort was killing him.

'Hush now,' said Elswyth. 'Don't talk any more. That's an order.'

But Grindan paid her no mind and squeezed Sigmar's shoulder even harder.

'Promise me!' he hissed. 'Go back... find it. We buried it deep, so the grobi wouldn't... wouldn't think to look... the Barag...'

'What's he talking about?' said Cuthwin.

'I don't know,' said Sigmar, taking the dwarf's hand and holding tightly.

'Promise me!' demanded Grindan. 'You must or the Deeplock clan will be disgraced! Heldenhammer, you are oath-bound to my kin... do this thing for a dying son of Grungni and I will meet my ancestors with pride.'

'Aye,' nodded Sigmar. 'I am a sworn brother to King Kurgan, and I give you my oath that I will find the... Barag.'

Grindan nodded and laid his head back on the bed, satisfied with Sigmar's words. His chest rose and fell in jerky spasms.

'The Halls of Grungni,' sighed Grindan, looking off into realms beyond the sight of mortals. 'How grand they are...'

Grindan Deeplock's last breath rattled from his throat, and his ore- and fire-blackened hand slid from Sigmar's grip.

'Go with honour to your rest, friend Grindan,' said Sigmar.

WOLFGART SADDLED HIS horse, a fine grain-fed stallion from his herds around the Barren Hills. The horse's coat was dappled dun and chestnut, with a long russet mane. The finest beast in his herds, he'd called him Dregor in honour of Sigmar's grandfather, a gesture his friend had appreciated immensely.

He adjusted the blanket beneath the saddle and tightened the girth under Dregor's belly, lowering the Taleuten-style stirrups to his preferred riding style. Wolfgart was a natural horseman and liked to ride low in the saddle, leaning over his horse's neck as he fought. He slung his panniers over its rump, the packs laden with enough food and spare clothing to see him to Reikdorf. He had a bowstave and string in case he needed to hunt, but hoped he wouldn't have to, as his eye wasn't as sure as it had been in his youth.

He patted Dregor's flank. 'At least you don't talk back to me, eh lad?'

The horse stared at him with a curious look in its eyes, unused to being taken from its stables at so early an hour. Wolfgart wanted to be gone before Maedbh roused Ulrike from sleep. He didn't think he'd be able to leave if she was awake. Wolfgart took a deep breath, resting his forehead on the warm, oiled leather of the saddle.

He didn't want to leave, but nor could he stay with such a poisonous atmosphere between him and his wife. Ulrike was already picking up on it, and the last thing he wanted was for her to see her parents at each other's throats. No child needed to see that.

Dregor was stabled with the royal horses of the Asoborns, and they were powerful beasts: strong and wide shouldered. Bred to pull war chariots, they had stamina and strength, but little in the way of real speed. Even the least of Wolfgart's herd could outpace an Asoborn mount in a straight sprint. But harness one of his mounts to a chariot and it would baulk at such harsh treatment.

Two hundred horses were stabled here: an underground collection of stalls, haylofts and exercise yards where Asoborn horse breakers trained the beasts for a life of war. He'd watched them at work, and while the effectiveness of their methods was without doubt, Wolfgart preferred to establish a bond with his beasts instead of bending them to his will.

The air was close and reeked of animals and dung, but it was an earthy fragrance that reminded Wolfgart of home. Even at this early hour, grooms and stable boys and girls were busy attending to the tribe's stock. Animals were being led over the cobbled floor toward the curved tunnels that led towards the surface and bales of hay were dropped down chutes cut through the earth of the hill.

Wolfgart checked Dregor's bit wasn't too tight and made a circuit of the animal, ensuring all was well before mounting. He gripped the saddle horn and hauled himself onto Dregor's back, relishing the sensation of owning so fine a beast.

He touched his spurs to the horse's sides and walked him slowly towards the sloping tunnel that led back to the surface. A group of men and women marched down the tunnel into the stables, hard Asoborn warriors armed with lances and swords. Clad in iron breastplates chased with silver and black, and golden-winged helms, these were the Queen's Eagles, the elite guardians of the Asoborn royalty.

Wolfgart's mood darkened further as he saw who they escorted – a pair of young men, both thirteen summers old and fair haired. One had pale blue eyes, while the other's were deep green. Wide shouldered and tall, they were already men, having ridden out on their first blooding three years ago.

Sigulf and Fridleifr, the sons of Queen Freya.

Wolfgart pulled Dregor to the side as they marched past, and he kept his head down, not wishing to look upon these boys a moment longer than necessary. Few outsiders had seen the queen's sons, for they rarely ventured beyond Asoborn lands, and were constantly attended by the Eagles. Wolfgart had first laid eyes upon them at a feast held beneath the Queen's Hill to honour their first kills after riding out to battle at the age of ten.

No sooner had he seen the two boys beside their flame-haired mother than he was catapulted back to the days of his youth and a shocked paralysis had seized his limbs. The breath froze in his lungs and he felt a gabble of words ready to spill from his throat.

Maedbh had clutched him and dug her nails into the muscle of his arm.

'Say nothing,' she warned him.

'But Ulric's balls, they're–'

'I know,' she hissed urgently. 'I warn you, say nothing. The queen has demanded it.'

Wolfgart had turned to her in surprise. 'You knew?'

'All the Asoborns know.'

Wolfgart looked back at the two lads, both laughing and drinking beer as their proud mother smeared Asoborn war-paint on their cheeks. Freya was a fearsome-looking woman, all curves and flame, a hellion in form-fitting armour and shimmering mail that left nothing to the imagination. The years since Wolfgart had first met her appeared to have left no mark upon her; the queen's flesh still war-sculpted and firm, her hair still long and fiery, her breasts still high and full.

Wolfgart tore his gaze from Freya's intoxicating beauty and looked back at her sons.

'By Ulric and Taal, they're his image…'

'That they are,' agreed Maedbh, 'but you're to say nothing. Do you understand me, Wolfgart?'

'By all the gods, he has sons!' said Wolfgart. 'The man has a right to know.'

'Maybe in Unberogen lands, but Asoborn queens take many lovers during their reign, and precedent comes from the maternal lineage, not the line of the father. Give me your word that you'll say nothing. Do it now or I'll send you from Three Hills right now.'

'What? That's no kind of bargain.'

'It's not a bargain,' Maedbh had warned him.

Left with no choice, Wolfgart had acceded to his wife's demand and sworn the oath she demanded. He'd spent the rest of the night trying not to stare at the two boys, struggling to contain a strange mixture of joy and sadness at the thought of all they could represent and what they would mean to their unaware father.

The Queen's Eagles and the royal twins passed him, heading towards where their own mounts were stabled. Wolfgart didn't watch them go, but rode up and out of the hill, emerging onto the hard-packed ground in the midst of Three Hills.

Torches were lit at the settlement's perimeter and a low morning mist still clung to the ground. The grass glittered with dew and the stars were visible in the purple sky. Where Reikdorf was a city that represented the Empire's progress, with its stone walls, ornate buildings, many schools, and great library, Three Hills was a pastoral settlement, without walls or defensible location. Its security came from its fusion with the landscape, such that any enemy would find it next to impossible to locate it, so cunningly were its dwellings crafted in the earth.

Archers watched the approaches from miles beyond its furthest extent and chariots roamed the wild lands to the east. Three Hills might look undefended, but the truth was altogether different. An enemy coming against the Asoborns would be harried by chariots and archers for many miles before they even came within sight of Three Hills.

It was a wild place, a savage realm of a people equally fierce and lusty. Wolfgart would be sorry to leave, but he hoped he would come back one day soon. Perhaps time and distance would allow old wounds to heal, harsh words to fade and absence to fill cold hearts with love once again.

Wolfgart turned Dregor towards the Reikdorf Road.

'Come on, lad,' he said. 'Let's go home.'

SIGMAR GATHERED HIS knights in the longhouse, twenty men of hardy Unberogen stock and proven courage. The fires burned brightly, filling the hall with warmth, for the night beyond its walls was chill, and oppressive clouds hid the moon. Eoforth studied an unrolled map with Cuthwin, listening attentively to the scout's tale of his rescue of Grindan Deeplock.

He sat on the edge of a long trestle table, judging how long it would take them to reach where the dwarf wagons had been ambushed.

'I reckon four days to get there and back,' said Alfgeir.

'Assuming no trouble,' replied Sigmar. 'That part of the forest's not travelled much. The beasts and greenskins have grown bold in the south.'

'They'd have to be bolder than I've known them to attack twenty knights, plus you and me.'

'They attacked a convoy of dwarfs,' pointed out Sigmar.

'I suppose,' said Alfgeir with a shrug. 'These are my best, and can handle any trouble that comes our way.'

Sigmar nodded, shivering despite the heat of the nearby fire. He pulled his bearskin cloak tighter about him. Eoforth stood straight, rubbing the small of his back with one hand and pinching the bridge of his nose with the other.

'Well, High Scholar?' asked Sigmar. 'What do you have for us?'

Eoforth scowled at Alfgeir and said, 'I think I have a good idea of where young Cuthwin came upon the goblin raiders, on the old mountain road about two miles north of the Thaalheim mines.'

A murmur passed through the armoured knights, and it was Orvin who spoke up. Sigmar had fought alongside Orvin many times, and knew him as a warrior of great personal courage, quick temper and unpredictable moods.

'Dangerous country,' remarked the knight. 'The greenskins we routed were from around there. I'll wager they came from under the mountains via the mineworks.'

'More than likely, Orvin,' said Eoforth, and Sigmar caught the tension between the two men. He knew Orvin's son to be a source of frustration to Eoforth, and wondered how much of the father had passed to the son.

His thoughts were interrupted as he heard a sudden commotion from the main doors to the longhouse. His hand flashed to Ghal-maraz at his belt in anticipation of danger. His crown grew warm at his brow, a runic warning of fell sorcery and unnatural powers at work.

'To arms!' he shouted as the doors to the longhouse burst open and a swirling gale of icy wind blew inside. The fire was snuffed out in an instant, its fitful embers glowing dully with all the heat that remained to them. Frozen gusts of dead air flew around the longhouse like poisonous zephyrs, carrying with them the scent of death and far off lands that baked beneath an oppressive sun.

A lone figure stood silhouetted in the doorway, a tall warrior in silver and gold mounted upon a hellish black steed with rippling flanks and eyes of smouldering red. Stinking steam like marsh gasses gusted from the beast's flared nostrils. The rider walked his nightmarish mount into the longhouse, its iron-shod hooves sparking from the flagstones like heavy hammer blows.

He dismounted with easy grace and folded his arms across a gleaming breastplate. His manner was confident to the point of arrogance and a white cloak flowed like snow from his shoulders. The knights drew their swords and roared in anger, moving to surround the elegant warrior, his long dark hair swept back over his ears and his swarthy complexion cut from a cruel mould. His eyes were black and without pupil, his mouth twisted in a malicious grin of spiteful mischief.

Alfgeir took a step towards the intruder, but Sigmar held him back.

'No,' said Sigmar. 'This man is death.'

'Your Emperor is a wise man,' said the warrior, his voice liquid and seductive. 'I have heard that about him. You should listen to him, for I would kill you before you could even swing that lump of pig iron in your hand.'

'You talk big for a man surrounded by twenty warriors,' said Alfgeir.

'Then that should tell you something about how good I am.'

Sigmar stepped towards the warrior, his hand tight on the grip of Ghal-maraz. Everything about this warrior sent pulses of anger and hate from the ancestral hammer of the dwarfs into his hand. The weapon longed to be unleashed, but Sigmar kept his urge to fight in check. He knew this man was no ordinary foe.

'I am Sigmar Heldenhammer, Emperor of these lands,' he said. 'By what right do you come before me into my longhouse?'

The warrior bowed elaborately. 'I am Khaled al-Muntasir, and I bring a message to you, Sigmar Heldenhammer.'

'A message from whom?'

'My master, the lord Nagash,' said Khaled al-Muntasir.

'You lie!' hissed Alfgeir, making the sign of the horns over his heart. 'There's no such being; he's just a story to frighten children. You can't scare us with old ghosts.'

'Can't I?' laughed Khaled al-Muntasir. 'I beg to differ.'

Sigmar had heard the tales of Nagash, there were few in the Empire who had not. No two stories were the same, lurid tales of walking corpses, fallen warriors stirring from their tombs and legions of the living dead marching to the howls of carrion wolves as darkness covered the land and the living cowered in terror.

But all the tales agreed on one thing. Nagash was the supreme lord of the undead, an evil king from an ancient land far to the south where a world-spanning empire had once risen from the desert sands. That empire had been destroyed in an age long forgotten, and only dusty tales and half-remembered legends survived from those times.

Sigmar knew from bitter experience that the dead could indeed rise from their graves. He and his warriors had destroyed a sorcerer of the undead many years ago, but if even half the tales of Nagash were true, then his power dwarfed that of the necromancer of Brass Keep.

'You are not welcome here, Khaled al-Muntasir,' said Sigmar. 'So deliver your message and begone.'

'No threats?' said Khaled al-Muntasir. 'No promises of a swift and brutal death?'

'I sense you are not a man cowed by threats.'

'True, but that doesn't stop the foolish from making them,' said Khaled al-Muntasir. He gave Sigmar an elaborate bow and threw his cloak back over his shoulder. The knights tensed, but made no move against the warrior, as a blade that shimmered with dark power was revealed at his side.

'You have something that does not belong to you,' said Khaled al-Muntasir. 'A crown forged by my master over a thousand years ago. You know this crown belongs to another, yet you keep it from its true lord. It will be returned to him.'

'I know this crown can never be allowed to fall into the hands of evil men.'

'I was not offering you a choice.'

'The crown remains where it is,' said Sigmar. 'If your master wishes to try and take it back, he will find all the armies of the Empire ranged against him.'

Khaled al-Muntasir smiled, a winning smile of pristine white teeth. Sigmar was not surprised to see two sharpened fangs at the corners of his mouth. His heart beat a little faster as he knew he faced a vampire, a creature of the night that fed on blood and murder.

Sigmar saw the monster's eyes widen a fraction and knew it could sense the increased flow of blood around his body. The hunger was upon this creature – he could no longer think of Khaled al-Muntasir as a man – and the danger of every one of them dying within the next few moments was very real indeed.

'You cannot stand against my master,' said Khaled al-Muntasir.

'Others have said similar things, yet the Empire endures.'

'Not against the legions of the dead it won't,' promised Khaled al-Muntasir. 'Your friend Markus, king of the Menogoths, is already dead. He and his family and his tribe have swollen the ranks of my master's army and more will follow.'

Sigmar sensed the furious shock of Khaled al-Muntasir's revelation sweep through his knights. They badly wanted this warrior dead.

'Hold!' cried Alfgeir, also seeing the angry urge to attack in the faces of his knights.

Sigmar's voice was colder than the Norscan ice as he met the blood drinker's gaze.

'Get out,' he said. 'And if you return you will be killed. This is the word of Sigmar.'

Khaled al-Muntasir turned and vaulted onto the back of his terrible steed. Its eyes flared brightly and it reared up onto its hind legs. He rode from the longhouse and Sigmar's knights ran after him with Alfgeir at their head.

No sooner was the vampire beyond the walls of the longhouse than a pair of wide black wings of impenetrable darkness unfolded from the steed's sides. The beast leapt into the air and its wings boomed with the sound of a mainsail catching a stormwind. It rose swiftly into the night sky, a bat-like slice of darkness against the black vault of the heavens.

Alfgeir watched it vanish over the hills and treetops, his face pale and fearful.

'Do you think he was lying?' he asked. 'About Markus, I mean.'

Sigmar shook his head. 'I fear not, my friend.'

'Damn,' whispered Alfgeir. 'The Menogoths gone...'

Sigmar turned and re-entered the longhouse, barking orders as he went.

'Bring every scribe and runner in Reikdorf here,' he said. 'I want word of this on its way to every one of the Empire's counts before sunrise. Eoforth, search every scroll in the library for tales of Nagash. Sift what facts you can from the legends. We're going to need to know what we're up against. Draft orders for sword musters to be gathered in every town and village from the Grey Mountains to the Sea of Claws. I want to be ready for these monsters when they come at us.'

Alfgeir nodded. 'I'll make it happen,' he said. 'I take it we'll not be heading south now?'

'I cannot, but you must lead these knights and Cuthwin to find what the dwarfs buried. Find it and bring it back here. I swore an oath and I mean to see it kept, even if I cannot do so myself.'

'I'll see it done, my Emperor,' promised Alfgeir.

'And Alfgeir?' said Sigmar. 'Be swift.'

'The crown is really that important to Nagash?' asked Alfgeir.

'You have no idea,' said Sigmar.

─◄ SIX ►─

Dead Flesh

THE MADMEN CHANTED and danced with wild abandon, like Cherusen Wildmen in the grip of a bane leaf frenzy. Redwane shifted uncomfortably in his saddle, trying to gauge the right moment to ride in and end this. He glanced at the rider next to him, a wide-chested warrior in red plate and thick mail with a sodden wolf pelt cloak draped over his shoulders.

Like every White Wolf, Leovulf didn't wear a helm, and his wild mane of black hair was plastered to his skull by the rain. Apparently to go bareheaded into battle was considered an act of bravery, openly displaying a warrior's contempt for the foe. Redwane wasn't so sure that going without a helm was a good idea, but since the White Wolves he'd recruited from Middenheim followed Leovulf's lead in all things, he couldn't very well go against it.

The man had carved himself a legend in the fighting that had raged through the streets of the northern city, and though he was lowborn, Count Myrsa had decreed that station was no barrier to entry into the ranks of the White Wolves. Courage was all that mattered.

'Madness,' said Leovulf, watching the madmen with bemused distaste. 'Why would anyone do such a thing?'

'I have no idea,' said Redwane, wincing as he watched a screaming man jam a long iron nail through the palm of his own hand. 'But Myrsa wants it stopped.'

'*Count* Myrsa,' said Leovulf.

'Of course,' replied Redwane. He'd known Myrsa for a long time, and still couldn't get used to the idea of calling him count, though he'd more than earned that title during the siege of Middenheim. 'Force of habit.'

He returned his gaze to the centre of the village, shaking his head at the sight before him.

Two hundred men dressed in rags filled the centre of Kruken, a gloomy, stockaded miners' settlement a day's ride to the west of Middenheim. Built upon ancient dwarf ruins, Kruken nestled in an undulant range of hills in the midst of the Drakwald Forest. It had found prosperity with the discovery of tin beneath the high ground, but that prosperity had quickly faded as it became clear the seams were nowhere near as deep and rich as had been thought.

Wailing and moaning, the madmen whipped their bare backs bloody with lengths of knotted rope bound with thorns and fishhooks. Some cut into their chests with gutting knives, while others jammed splinters of sharpened wood beneath their fingernails.

Each man chanted meaningless doggerel interspersed with monotone dirges in an unknown tongue that sounded part gibberish, part incantation. A wooden log had been hammered into the ground near the centre of the square and a pile of kindling set at its base, though Redwane wasn't sure what they were planning to burn.

A drizzle of rain drained the life from the day, and only

made the utilitarian nature of the soot-stained buildings, mine-workings and dormitories of Kruken all the more depressing. Perhaps a hundred people were gathered in the town square, watching the carnival of madness at its centre with varying degrees of dour amusement. Children threw stones at the chanting men, while yapping dogs snapped and bit at their bloody ankles.

In the days since the defeat of the Norsii horde, the people of the north had suffered great hardship; the forest beasts that had fled the destruction of Cormac Bloodaxe's horde had returned to hunting men as their prey, banditry had increased, harvests had gone uncollected and famine was widespread. In the aftermath of the fighting, outbreaks of pestilence in the settlements around the western foothills of the Middle Mountains stretched the resources of the land still further.

Life in the north was always hard, but this last year had been especially hard, so any diversion, no matter how absurd or bloody, was welcome.

No one had noticed these wandering bands of madmen at first, for the Empire was a land of strangeness, of the bizarre and dangerous. They had been tolerated as an aberration that would soon burn itself out, but as the year grew darker and life harder, it became obvious that, far from dying out, these roving bands of lunatics were growing in strength.

The largest of these bands was said to be led by a man named Torbrecan, a man who – depending on which fanciful tale you listened to – was either a warrior driven mad by a life of bloodshed or a priest of Ulric who'd spent too long alone in the winter woods. Torbrecan's host marched in bloody procession from the isolated towns and villages north of the mountains, curving in a southerly bow towards Middenheim. Pestilence marched alongside them, and thus Middenheim's warriors blocked the roads to the city. Something had to be done, and so Myrsa had despatched Redwane and the White Wolves to break up this band and take Torbrecan prisoner.

Redwane shook his head as he watched a man drag his dirt-encrusted fingernails down his face then drop to his knees and plunge his scarred features into the mud. Was he Torbrecan? Who could tell? Each man looked just as ferociously insane as the next.

Leovulf shook his head. 'We'll need to move if we want to stop this getting out of hand.'

'Aye,' said Redwane. 'But I want to make sure we don't start trouble going in too early.'

'Trouble's started already. We're just limiting it.'

Leovulf's gloomy assessment of the situation wasn't far off the mark. Like most northern tribesman, Leovulf had a grim worldview, one born out of years of harsh winters and the constant struggle for survival in the inhospitable wilds of the northern marches. The people of the north were tough and hard as oak, but weren't noted for their lightness of spirit.

A tall figure in a mud-spattered robe that might once have been white, but which was now a grimy brown danced towards the centre of the square. His shoulders were stained red, and he carried a metal-studded switch that dripped blood. Matted and unkempt hair hung lank and limp to his shoulders and his beard was tied in a number of braids like tangled tree-roots. Each burned with a small coal that sent acrid fumes into his nostrils.

'You think that's Torbrecan?' asked Leovulf.

'Must be,' agreed Redwane. 'He looks mad enough.'

The man walked a ragged circle around the square, his eyes wild and staring, his mouth open in a silent scream. He beat himself over the shoulders with his switch and laughed hysterically with each blow. His followers gouged and tore at themselves with each crack of his switch.

'People of Kruken!' howled Torbrecan. 'Listen well to me, for I speak of your doom! It is the doom of us all, for the gods have turned their faces from this world! Who among you has not seen the signs of the End Times? Who among you has not seen heralds that portend our extinction from this world? Plague destroys your towns, beasts hunt your children and ungodly men seek to take what is not theirs with blade and bow! We are doomed, and it is no one's fault but our own. We turned from our proper devotions and led the gods to abandon us. The terror that stalks the land is one of our own making, for we are a godless people, condemned to die unless we can wash away our sins in blood and pain.'

The crowd jeered him, but not as many as Redwane expected. Some looked like they were seriously enter-taining this insanity, and some were even nodding their heads like he was making some kind of sense.

'The gods are far from us,' went on Torbrecan, jabbing a scabbed fist at the sky, 'and they grow farther with every passing day. Only through the ecstasy of pain shall we draw their attention to us. Only by the exquisite wails of our suffering shall we turn their gaze back upon us.'

Redwane shook his head, unable to believe that folk weren't simply laughing this man out of their village. Surely life was hard enough without people like this wanting to make it worse?

'This has gone far enough,' said Redwane, jabbing his spurs into his mount's flanks.

'Aye,' agreed Leovulf. 'Bloody lunatic needs to be shut up for good.'

Redwane shook his head. 'No killing. Myrsa, *Count* Myrsa, was very specific about that.'

Leovulf nodded and passed the word through the

ranks. The White Wolves shucked their pelt cloaks from their right shoulders to clear their hammer arms. Ustern unfurled the banner, a glorious piece of red linen with a wolf picked out in silver thread, and Holstef blew two rising notes on his clarion.

Redwane led his riders into the village, the crowds parting as their heavy horses plodded through the mud towards the centre of the square. Torbrecan saw them coming and aimed his switch at them. For a second, Redwane wondered if he was going to charge him, but instead he threw his hands up as if in praise.

'The very warriors who serve the doombringers come to silence my words! They fear the truth and the knowledge that they are blind fools serving a master who cannot see the forces ranged against him. They have not the strength to suffer as we suffer, to bleed as we bleed. Brothers, show them the strength of true belief! Show everyone!'

A dozen men ran from the mob of ragged lunatics towards the stake hammered into the earth. They fought to climb the stacked kindling, biting and punching each other in their desperation to reach the upright log. Two fought harder than the others, and clutched the tall log as close as a lover. One carried a set of hooked chains and he wrapped these around their waists, binding them fast to the wood. Those denied the chance to reach the log took up lit torches and Redwane's jaw dropped open as he realised what they were going to do.

'Ulric's mercy, no!' he yelled, but it was too late. The torches were thrust into the kindling, which lit with a rushing *whoosh* of ignition. Redwane smelled the oil and not even the misting sheets of rain could dampen the flames as they leapt high. The two men clung to one another as the fire took hold of their robes and set them alight from head to foot. So swiftly did the flames leap to life that Redwane knew their bodies must have been doused in oil too.

The crowd pulled back in horror as the two men shrieked in agony. Their robes vanished and Redwane watched in revolted fascination as their flesh blackened and blistered in seconds. As though to aid this martyrdom, the rain ceased, and the air filled with the reek of burning meat and hair. The men screamed as they were consumed, fatty smoke pouring from their melting flesh.

Their fellows danced around the flames and the burning men sagged against the log, their lower limbs little more than blackened stumps of bone. The smoke would surely have killed them by now. At least Redwane hoped so.

He spurred his horse to greater speed and rode through the ragged mob of chanting madmen. They clawed at him with broken fingernails, screaming and howling without words or sense. They weren't attacking as such, more clamouring to be punished. Redwane obliged one man with a filth-encrusted face, slamming the haft of his hammer down and sending him sprawling to the mud. The man screamed as the horse rode over him, but Redwane didn't spare him a glance.

His horse barged through the crowd of raving lunatics, scattering them as he angled a course towards the ringleader. Keeping the reins loose in his hand, he steered his mount towards Torbrecan. The laughing madman's switch beat against his chest and a triumphant stare of vindication bored into Redwane's eyes.

'Deliver me unto the arms of the gods!' yelled Torbrecan, hurling himself to the ground in front of Redwane's mount. Redwane hauled back on the reins and his horse reared up, its front legs pawing the air. The gelding's hooves stamped down into the mud, inches from the madman's head. Redwane kicked his feet free of the stirrups and jumped down. He dragged the mud-covered man to his knees and slammed the butt of his hammer into his face.

Torbrecan's nose burst across his face, but he laughed as blood spilled into his mouth. Redwane hauled him to his feet as the screaming mob pressed in. Ustern's horse came alongside him and the weak sunlight caught the red of the banner like a flash of glorious crimson.

Redwane drew himself up to his full height and yelled, 'Enough! In Ulric's name, enough!'

His voice cut through the baying mob of lunatic screeching, and the blood-smeared men dropped to the ground, moaning and yelling in equal measure. Redwane realised they were waiting for the White Wolves to ride them down, to crush their skulls with hammers or trample them beneath the hooves of their mounts.

'Hold!' he yelled. 'White Wolves hold!'

His warriors pulled up, circling their horses around the madmen and corralling them away from the villagers. Realising they weren't to be killed, many of the madmen sprang to their feet and sprinted off into the forest. Redwane watched them go, knowing most of them probably wouldn't survive more than a day alone in the forest.

The people of Kruken cheered, amused by the spectacle as much as anything. The fire burned brightly at the centre of the village, but the black smoke from the damp kindling thankfully obscured the ravages of the fire on the dead men's flesh. Melting fat fizzed in the fire and sharp cracks sounded as bones split in the heat.

Redwane hauled Torbrecan to his feet and thrust him towards Leovulf.

'Get him out of my sight,' he said.

NIGHT HAD CLOSED in on Kruken, and Redwane sat with Ustern and Holstef in what passed for the village tavern.

To ride through the forest now would be too dangerous. The night belonged to the beasts, and even thirty armed warriors would likely never be seen again were they to travel its haunted paths in the dark.

The tavern was a high-ceilinged building built of heavy timbers atop square-cut blocks of stone that were clearly of dwarfcraft. A fire burned within an inglenook that had once been a doorway, with faded angular runes carved into its lintel. Redwane guessed the tavern was normally sparsely populated, but today's drama had brought the locals out in force. A number of hard-bitten men sat in huddled corners nursing their dark beer and casting furtive glances their way.

The beer was peaty and flavoursome, but it was too strong for Redwane's tastes. The other White Wolves seemed to like it though. Conversation had been muted, for Kruken wasn't a town that welcomed outsiders much, even ones in the service of Count Myrsa.

'I reckon we've seen the last of those idiots,' said Ustern between puffs on his pipe, a long-stemmed piece with a bowl in the shape of an upturned drinking horn. Ustern bore the White Wolves banner, and was always the first to venture a grim opinion. 'Aye, the beasts'll do for them and no mistake.'

'I'd not be too sure,' said Holstef. 'They survived this long, what makes you think that just because we got Torbrecan they'll end up beast food?'

One the youngest White Wolves, Holstef was an eternal optimist, which made him a perfect foil for the banner bearer. He and Ustern argued like an old married couple, though neither seemed to mind, as though it was all part of their friendship. Ustern leaned forward and jabbed his pipe at Holstef.

'How d'you even know it's Torbrecan who we got?'

'He was the leader, stands to reason doesn't it?'

'You think that lot care about "reason"?'

'Why was he the one doing all the talking then? Why would a leader let someone else talk?'

'So he wouldn't be caught by the likes of us,' suggested Ustern.

'Crap,' replied Holstef. 'Someone that mad wouldn't think like that.'

'How d'you know? Touched by a bit of moon-madness are ye?'

'Must be,' said Holstef. 'Why else would I fight along-side you?'

Redwane let them bicker and watched the tavern's patrons as they drank and argued. They were a motley bunch, miners and woodsmen mostly by the look of them. None looked like they'd worked in a while, though that hadn't stopped them coming in here to spend their coin. Redwane recognised an underlying connection between the snatches of conversation he heard, knowing a familiar thread ran through every one.

Fear.

Their expressions spoke of fear of one sort or another. Fear of poverty, fear of starvation, fear of being alone, fear of the dark and, worst of all, a fear that the madmen in the square today were right.

In the last year, Redwane had seen the same expression on many faces throughout the northern marches, a pinched desperation for things to be better. Sigmar's Empire had promised great things, but for many of its people it had yet to deliver.

He followed one of the tavern's serving girls, a good-looking woman with a body that time hadn't yet caused to sag and a face in which bitterness had its claws, but hadn't yet won the battle. She wore a black bow tied around her wrist that told him her man had been killed, most likely in the war against the Norsii, though in the north he could have met his end in any number of ways. She sensed his gaze and looked over, a thin smile creasing her full lips. She couldn't quite keep the grimace from her face, but she nodded and her eyes flickered towards the stairs.

Redwane sighed and nodded back to her. Was this what it had come to, a fumbled liaison in a cold tavern room, loveless and bought with copper coins? He remembered having the pick of the girls, a different one every night if he'd wanted. But that was before the battle at the centre of the Fauschlag Rock when he'd swung his hammer at the daemon lord. He could still feel the searing pain as it had exploded against its infernal armour and sent red hot shards of iron into his face.

Now no woman would look at him unless he paid them.

A cold wind gusted into the tavern and the locals grumbled as candles flickered and the fragile heat in the building slipped outside. Their mutterings ceased at the sight of Leovulf in his armour and heavy wolf pelt cloak. Redwane's second stamped the mud from his boots on a threadbare mat and pulled off his cloak. Still clad in his armour, he sat next to Redwane and shouted at the tavern keeper to bring him some beer.

'Everyone bedded down?' asked Redwane.

'Aye,' agreed Leovulf. 'I've told them to keep the gambling and drinking to a minimum and that I'll take my hammer to anyone who isn't ready to ride out at daybreak.'

'Good, I want to be back at the Fauschlag before nightfall,' he said. 'There's an evil feel to the forest just now.'

'Isn't there always?' put in Ustern.

'More than normal I mean,' said Redwane.

'It's the pox,' said Leovulf. 'Gets everyone on edge. It's an enemy you can't fight. Show me a beast or a greenskin and I'll break it in two with my hammer. But the pox… that's something a man *should* be afraid of.'

'You sound just like Ustern,' said Redwane.

'Ulric save me, but things must be bad,' said Leovulf with a shake of his head. He removed a thin pipe from his belt and lit it on the candle at the centre of their table. More beer arrived on a platter, and the White Wolves each took a tankard.

'To Ulric,' said Redwane, raising his beer.

'To Ulric,' echoed the White Wolves.

Their conversation turned to the logistics of their journey home, but Redwane's attention was fixed on the serving girl. She finished her rounds and spoke a few words to the tavern keeper, who glanced over at their table. He grunted something and waved her away. She looked over at him and headed upstairs.

Redwane drained the last of his beer and said, 'I think I'll leave the rest of the drinking to you northerners.'

'See,' said Ustern, nudging Holstef. 'Told you the southern tribes couldn't hold their beer.'

Redwane knocked over his empty mug. 'You call that beer. Harder stuff than this falls from the sky over Reikdorf. Our pigs drink better than this.'

'That's no way to talk of your women,' said Holstef, emboldened by several beers.

'Easy, soldier,' cautioned Leovulf. 'Watch that tongue of yours.'

Redwane left them to it and made his way towards the stairs, climbing to the upper level where the girl was waiting for him. She stood in a doorway of the corridor and threw him a smile. He knew it was false, but didn't care.

She looked at him, trying to conceal the horrid fascination she had of his scars. She reached up to touch them, but he grabbed her hand before her fingers touched his face.

'Don't,' he said, turning his head away. 'Please.'

She nodded and led him into the room.

WOLVES HOWLED AT the moon and feasted on the dead as carrion birds lined every rooftop or billowed in sweeping clouds of feathered bodies. Death had come to Hyrst-dunn and not a single soul had lived through the battle to break down its walls. With their dead king now fighting in the ranks of the enemy, the defence of the city had been without heart and the mortals had fought with desperation born of knowing they could not win.

Khaled al-Muntasir walked the darkened streets of the city, revelling in the sounds of its doom as a conductor might enjoy a musical recital. The sounds of death were familiar to him; as well they should be after centuries of inflicting them upon the living. He made out the sound of splintered wolf teeth tearing at human meat, the *peck, peck, peck* of beaks battering at skulls to get to the soft matter within. Beyond that, he could hear screams of the last survivors as they were dragged from hidden cellars or attics.

King Markus walked listlessly behind him, his flesh pale and dead, his eyes flickering with green embers as the vampire's will remade him. Dried blood caked his ravaged neck, and though he bore the semblance of the man he had once been, nothing now remained of that mortal vessel. Khaled al-Muntasir had delivered the blood-kiss to the Menogoth king, knowing the effect it would have on mortals to see their fallen leader fighting alongside the army of the dead. Markus would soon emerge from this catatonic state, and a new blood drinker would walk the land. It gave Khaled al-Muntasir perverse pleasure to see the panicked faces of mortal cattle as they realised that neither prince nor pauper was safe from death's touch.

The sound of crying children drifted on the midnight wind, and this was the most exquisite sound of all. Innocent blood was the sweetest elixir, and though his hunger was long sated on the blood of warriors, there was always desire for such epicurean delights.

The city itself was a poor specimen of architecture: a random collection of muddy timber structures built upon older ruins. No two were alike, a mishmash of prosaic, peasant architecture that offended his cultured eye. His lips curled in distaste as he looked up at the count's dwelling, a ridiculous hall of crudely hewn stone with a thatched roof and laughably childish daubings of antiquated gods on timber panels.

'To think that you, a king of men, lived in this hovel is absurd,' said Khaled al-Muntasir, shaking his head in disbelief. 'I was but a lesser prince and I grew to manhood in a sun-kissed palace of marble towers, glittering fountains and triumphal domes that enclosed vast spaces of such beauty that they could move a man to tears. You primitive savages could never achieve something so magnificent.'

Markus didn't answer of course, and Khaled al-Muntasir waved his thin hands at the hall's swaybacked roof. 'Such inelegant design is so utterly primitive for a land that claims to be the greatest empire of man. The notion that you people actually believe that to be true is so ludicrous that it makes me want to laugh. Or maybe weep, I haven't decided. Oh, how the race of man has fallen.'

He shook his head in sadness and moved on, keeping to the centre of the cobbled thoroughfares to avoid the sewage leaking down the edges of the road. He held his white cloak draped over his forearm to keep it clean. Filth encrusted every surface of the city, and thousands of dead bodies lay strewn around like burst sacks of grain.

A pack of wolves ran through its streets, fighting over scraps of flesh. Flocks of crows followed them, eager for their leavings.

Khaled al-Muntasir climbed the steps towards the king's longhouse, smelling the aroma of fresh-spilled blood from within. The doors were splintered and sagging, and skeletal warriors in rusting armour of bronze stood like silent guardians of a tomb. He turned to look back into the city, watching as the army of Nagash completed its destruction.

Beneath the light of the moon, armoured skeletons marched between the buildings, gathering the dead and dragging them into the open, where they were deposited on rotted carts pulled by shambling animated corpses. Ghoulish scavengers loped through the streets, fighting the rotten-furred wolves for warm flesh torn from the bone. Pale-fleshed and scabbed with open sores, these carrion feeders hissed and bit with grave-dirt claws, their bodies thin and wasted, yet ravenous and tenacious.

And holding court over this glorious tableau of death was its lord and master.

Nagash himself was surrounded by ghostly flocks of revenants, howling wisps of light and shadow that curled in supplication around his monstrous limbs. Krell, the hulking champion of the northern gods marched at Nagash's side, a physical manifestation of his master's rage and aggression. Darkness went with them, a shroud of bleak misery that invigorated Khaled al-Muntasir, but which sapped the living of their courage and filled their hearts with fear. More than just the fear of death, it spoke of an eternal life of servitude to a cruel master, of paradise denied and the promise of a life that would go unrewarded by the gods.

The vampire stood on the highest point of the city and watched with relish as his personal retinue of warriors climbed the steps towards him. Each skeletal champion dragged a screaming child behind it, none older than six or seven summers. They wept and fought, but the dead men who carried them to their doom were as inexorable as their fate was inescapable.

His fangs tingled with anticipation, his eyes filling with killing red as the first dead warrior pushed a struggling girl-child towards him. He lifted her head with a finely manicured nail, tracing its razor edge around her chin.

'Hush, child,' he said. 'Do not cry. There is no need for tears, they are a waste of something precious.'

The girl looked into his eyes, and she saw his hunger.

Before she could scream, he sank his fangs into her neck and began to feed.

KHALED AL-MUNTASIR DROPPED the shrivelled husk of the last child, glutted on innocent blood and his senses afire with the rush of undiluted life energy. His eyes beheld the world around him with greater clarity than before, every living thing glinting with its own internal fire. To his eyes, the world was ablaze in silver light.

He smiled, feeling the rush of another's blood filling his atrophied veins and unused organs with a semblance of life. Sensuous, erotic and deliciously painful, it was a fleeting sense of wonder, absolute knowledge of the thoughts and life of another living being as they were extinguished forever.

Yet as soon as it was drunk and revelled in, it was gone. The curse of the blood drinker was never to know satiety, to always crave the blood of the living. He wiped the droplets from his chin, licking his fingers clean and enjoying the last sensations of life as a starving peasant would relish the crumbs of a prince's discarded meal.

His vision was already returning to its more mundane outlook as he saw the great lord of the undead climb the steps towards him, his pall of shadow like a soothing balm of radiant energy. Nagash towered over Khaled al-Muntasir, his power straining at the boundaries of existence, almost too intense for his undying frame to contain. Even with sight far beyond that of mortals, Khaled al-Muntasir could see only a fraction of the great necromancer's power. It was immense and unstoppable, an energy that existed in worlds beyond understanding, crossing the gulfs of death and empowered by a dark wind whose source had been a mystery to even the greatest practitioners of the arts in his sand-swallowed city.

The necromancer's shimmering metallic hand glimmered with power, a reservoir of untapped energies drawn into its mysterious structure by the slaughter of this pitiful city and its inhabitants. Walking its streets, Khaled al-Muntasir had laughed to feel the stirring spirits below his feet, knowing that this land was already a tomb.

This region of the Empire was awash with forgotten sepulchres and barrows of long dead warriors. The people of this place lived atop a great mound of corpses, buried beneath the earth thousands of years ago, and didn't even know it.

Khaled al-Muntasir closed his eyes and let his senses flow out around the city, searching for any sign of life, any living thing that had somehow escaped the killing. There was nothing, and he looked up into the emerald fire of the necromancer's eyes.

He shook his head and the necromancer thrust his hand towards the sky.

A blazing pillar of green light filled the heavens with its necrotic glow, piercing the clouds and unnatural darkness with its brightness. The light built within Nagash's body, a lambent glow that slithered down through his invisible flesh. It filled the necromancer's skull, infused his dried bones, formed phantom organs and coursed through his debased body into the heavy plates of his armour. A black wind sighed, and the silver light that suffused the earth was snuffed out in an instant. The ground shook as the impossibly powerful will of Nagash spread through the land, reaching deeper than the roots of the mountains and out into the wilds far beyond.

The wolves of the city threw back their heads and howled. The darkness was suddenly lit by thousands of pinpricks of green light as the dead of Hyrstdunn were dragged from their rest to serve in the army that had slain them. Bloody men, half-eaten wives and murdered offspring screamed as their dead flesh was filled with horrid animation.

Dead Menogoths climbed to their feet, reaching for weapons that had lain beside their brutalised corpses. Those without weapons wrenched sharpened timbers from their former homes, gathered up meathooks, gutting knives or cleavers from butcher's blocks.

At some unseen command, they shuffled towards the northern gate of the city, moving with dreadful purpose and monotonous unison. The army of the dead, already thousands strong, swelled by thousands more. And all across this degenerate empire, the dead would be stirring in the damp earth that contained them, roused to wakefulness by the most powerful necromancer ever to rise from the lost kingdom of Nehekhara.

High above Nagash, a black miasma saturated the heavens, a roof of oppressive coal-dark cloud that roiled outwards from its boiling epicentre. The dark of night was nothing compared to this, for it was an umbra of complete emptiness, the *oblivion* of light not just its absence.

The dread blackness slipped over the sky like a slick of oil on a lake, creeping towards the horizon in mockery of the coming sunrise and life itself.

Death had come to the Empire.

BOOK TWO

Down Among the Bone Men

Some, though headless, stood erect,
From some the arms were hacked,
Some were pierced from front to back.
And some on horse in armour sat,
Some were choked while at their food.
Some were drowned in flood,
And some were withered up by fire,
Some raving mad and others dead.
Merciful Shallya of the Sorrow
pours bright tears from her eyes
Weeping and wailing the fate of Men
Alas my grief that ye did not heed her cries.

━◄ SEVEN ➤━

Portents of Death

A COLD, SALTY wind blew off the ocean and a bell chimed high on the Tower of Tides. Gulls wheeled over the docks of the lower town, and Count Marius of the Jutones took a moment to savour the smells of his city. Unlike many cities in the Empire, those smells were not shit and refuse and livestock. Jutonsryk smelled of wealth, prosperity and contentment.

The buildings of his city were a haphazard mix of stone and timber, the oldest jutting from the cliffs and spurs of the rock forming the natural bay that made it such a perfect location for a port. Dominating the city was the Namathir, the leaf-shaped promontory of dark rock upon which Marius's castle was built. Crafted of pale stone with many slender towers and shimmering roofs, the fortress of the Jutone count was a curious mix of power and grace. High walls of stone surrounded the city on its landward side, patched and rebuilt by dwarf masons hired at ruinous expense in the aftermath of Sigmar's siege.

Always a nautical city, most buildings of Jutonsryk sported some recognition of the sea that had made its fortune. Tall masts with billowing sails jutted from numerous rooftops, while figureheads from wrecked ships, cargo netting and entire forecastles made up frontages, roofs and gables. Effigies of Manann in his aspect of a bulky man with an iron crown were common, as were images of crashing waves and sea creatures. Warehouses and loading bays for the hundreds of ships that berthed here every week crowded the seafront, finely-built structures paid for by the wealthy merchants and traders who had grown fat on Jutonsryk's prosperity.

Hundreds of ships filled the harbour, a myriad of sails of many colours and different kings. Udose ships sat alongside those of the Endals and ones bearing flags of nations that most people in the Empire had no knowledge of. Ships of all size and shape jostled for space on the quayside and a forest of lifting hoists worked in a never-ending procession of unloading and loading.

Trade was Jutonsryk's lifeblood, and it had brought undreamed-of wealth to Marius's city.

Yet only a few years ago, it had come to the edge of destruction at the hands of the man to whom Marius now gave homage as Emperor. Smiling to himself, he knew he should have allied with Sigmar a long time ago, but not for the reasons the Emperor would have liked to hear.

Always independent, the Jutones had stood apart from Sigmar's burgeoning Empire, but as Marius looked at how his city and people had benefited from that alliance, he knew it had been a worthwhile investment. The streets were clean, part of an initiative proposed by his physicians as a means to alleviate sickness among the poor, as was the building of a new almshouse to care for the ailing and needy. Taxes on incoming trade ships had paid for these institutions, and such was the influx of new trade that followed his Sword Oath with Sigmar, that each year brought more gold than he could spend.

Marius rode past the Tower of Tides on a white stallion, a gift from Sigmar's warrior friend, and its caparison was of fine blue and green cloth woven by Thuringian women as a tribute from the Berserker King. He leaned back in the saddle as he negotiated the winding, cobbled streets that led down to the old town and the docks. Citizens of Jutonsryk bowed as he passed and he favoured them with his most magnanimous smile.

Yes, it was a good day to take the air, though a smear of darkness on the horizon portended storms to come. He shivered, pulling his exquisite cloak of bearskin tighter about his shoulders. His clothes were finely made, a tasteful mix of eastern silks and hard-wearing Ostogoth tanned leather that gave him the unmistakable appearance of wealth, yet retained the look of a man who knew how to wield the sword buckled at his waist.

A troop of lancers accompanied him, their pale blue cloaks falling tidily over the rumps of their mounts. Spoiling this image of perfection was the wobbling form of Vergoossen, his latest aide, who rode his chestnut gelding about as well as a bale of hay might.

Ever since Bastiaan had stabbed him at Middenheim in the height of the fighting, Marius had forbidden his aides to bear arms. Looking at Vergoossen, it didn't look like he knew one end of a dagger from another, yet he had a head for numbers and a total lack of ego to be bruised by Marius's frequent tirades and verbal abuse. All of which made him a perfect aide.

'My lord,' said. 'If you'll just look over these documents…'

Marius sighed, his good mood evaporating in the face of Vergoossen's pleadings.

'What is so important that you need to spoil a perfectly good day?' he demanded.

Vergoossen held out a sheaf of papers. 'My lord, I have petitions from a number of merchants, and–'

'Let me guess, Huyster and Merovec.'

'Amongst others, but yes, the majority of correspondence is from them.'

'So what do they want, as if I can't guess?'

'Master Huyster wishes to bring to your attention the latest increase in berthing fees and the imposition of the new import tariffs,' said Vergoossen. 'And Master Merovec asks if you have had time to consider his request for permission to extend his warehouses along the north shore.'

Marius felt his anger grow at these foolish, greedy merchants. Their coffers were already swollen with gold, yet still they wanted more. It seemed a lust for gold wasn't simply confined to the mountain folk. What angered Marius most was that he saw a reflection of his old self in their grasping, transparent greed. He took a calming breath.

'Tell Huyster that the berthing fees are paying for additional docks to be built along the shoreline, which will allow him to double his revenue within the year. And if he wants it known that he feels aggrieved with the berthing fees, then he is only too welcome to bring that to the attention of the stevedores' guild. I'm sure they would be happy to hear of his dissatisfaction.'

'Really?' said Vergoossen, missing his sarcastic tone. 'I would have thought it a recipe for disaster to say such a thing.'

'Of course it is,' snapped Marius. Vergoossen was efficient and thorough when it came to organising Marius's affairs, but he had no head for understanding people. 'The stevedores' wages are paid from berthing taxes, and any shipmaster who wants to pay less will find a greater than usual percentage of their cargoes inexplicably lost or accidentally dropped into the sea.'

'But that's blackmail, my lord,' exclaimed Vergoossen.

'All trade is blackmail of one sort or another,' said Marius. 'But that is a lesson for another day.'

'And what shall I tell Master Merovec?'

'Tell him that I know he already owns more quayside frontage than city regulations permit. He may fool others with his straw men, but I was finding new ways to earn gold while he was soiling his swaddling clothes. Tell him that if he *really* wants me to have you investigate his assets to adjudge his property holdings with a view to his future expansions, then I am more than happy to oblige him.'

'I understand, sir,' said Vergoossen. 'He wouldn't want that.'

'No,' agreed Marius. 'He wouldn't. Now is there anything else that needs my subtle hand of diplomacy, or do you think you can actually do your job and handle the minutiae of running a busy sea port?'

'There is one other matter, my lord,' said Vergoossen.

'Go on then, what is it?'

'Some sailors from Tilean lands are refusing to pay their berthing fees.'

'Typical bloody Tilean,' said Marius with a shake of his head. 'Their coin purses are sealed tighter than a Brigundian virgin's legs. Why are they refusing to pay?'

'They say they don't have any cargo to unload, so they don't see why they should pay a berthing fee.'

'No cargo? Then why are they here?'

'They claim they were attacked and had to ditch their cargo to escape.'

'Pirates?'

Vergoossen consulted his notes, as though reluctant to voice the reason the sailors had given.

'Well, in a manner of speaking, my lord,' stammered Vergoossen.

'Oh, just spit it out, man!' ordered Marius.

'Yes, my lord. Sorry. They claim they were attacked by ships crewed by dead men.'

'THIS IS THE place?' asked Alfgeir. 'You're sure of it?'

Cuthwin gave the Marshall of the Reik a look that said he was sure, and that he'd have liked to see the knights find this place again. Instead he simply nodded. A life lived in the wilderness was a solitary, silent one, and even when in company, Cuthwin found himself limiting his speech to short answers.

'Yes, this is the place,' he said.

'There's nothing here,' said Orvin, dismounting from his gelding and looking around. 'You said there was a fight here.'

'There was,' said Cuthwin. 'You'd see that if you looked.'

Orvin stepped towards him. 'Are you cheeking me, scout?'

'Leave it,' warned Alfgeir, and Orvin backed off, returning to his horse's side. Twenty of the Empire's finest knights stood at the edge of the road, where Cuthwin had forced them to dismount lest they spoil the tracks. It had taken them two days to reach the road, much less than it had taken Cuthwin to reach Reikdorf, but then he'd been on foot and had a wounded dwarf to carry.

He squatted at the edge of the road where he and the dwarfs had fought the goblins and wolves. He could picture the wagons, where he had come out of the forest and how he had moved through the fight. The road was empty now, no sign of any bodies or wagons to indicate that a life and death struggle had played out here.

At least to the untrained eye.

Alfgeir stepped onto the road, moving from smudged track, to discoloured patch of earth and broken branch. He moved well for an old man, kneeling to dust earth from a stone and follow the course of the fight through the telltale marks such a struggle inevitably left behind.

'You killed the first one here,' said Alfgeir, miming the act of drawing a bowstring.

Cuthwin nodded as Alfgeir wended his way through the fight, moving as though he fought it anew. At last he turned to face Cuthwin, his face betraying a grudging respect.

'You took a big risk in helping these dwarfs, scout,' said Alfgeir. 'That took courage.'

Cuthwin shrugged, uncomfortable with praise. 'It seemed like the right thing to do. It's what Sigmar did.'

'And we all want to be like Sigmar,' laughed Alfgeir. 'Good lad. Now the wagons were over here, yes?'

Cuthwin rose and smoothly made his way to join Alfgeir, carefully avoiding the earlier tracks and making sure to stick to the hardened ground to leave no trace of his own passing. The knights followed him, leading their horses and without the care he showed.

He pointed to a disturbed area of ground at a bend in the road.

'There,' said Cuthwin. 'That's where the wagons were.'

'So where are they now?' asked Orvin.

'Maybe the goblins took them,' he said. 'Maybe the forest beasts broke them up for firewood or weapons.'

'Can't you tell?'

Cuthwin shook his head. 'Maybe if your horses hadn't trampled the ground I could have.'

Alfgeir put a hand on his shoulder and said, 'You do enjoy provoking people, scout.'

'I reckon the goblins took the wagons,' said Cuthwin, pointing back down the road. 'There's a stone path leads up into the mountains about a mile back. Could be they took them that way.'

'Do you think they found what the dwarf buried?'

'Hard to say,' said Cuthwin. 'Let me look.'

He waved away the knights and dropped to his hands and knees, lowering his face to the earth, scanning left and right for any trace of something out of the ordinary. Moving like a bloodhound with the scent of its prey in its nose, Cuthwin ghosted over the ground as though listening to it. He ignored the chuckles of the knights. Let them laugh; they'd be choking on it when he found something.

He moved over where the wagons had been circled, touching the ground and feeling the tension in the soil, brushing it with his fingertips. The earth here was looser, less densely packed, as though disturbed. Where the wagons had been pulled around and turned into makeshift barricades, the earth was hard-packed, but this patch in the middle was loose.

Cuthwin rose to his feet, circling the area and searching for any other obvious signs of something buried. He brushed the ground with the sole of his boot, closing his eyes as he relied on senses honed in the wilderness over many years.

'It's here,' he said, dropping to his knees. He drew his dagger and sketched a rough rectangle in the dirt, encompassing where he knew the dwarf had buried what Grindan had called the Thunder Bringer.

Alfgeir knelt beside him. 'I don't see anything.'

'It's here, trust me,' said Cuthwin. 'The mountain folk are masters of digging. If anyone can bury something they don't want found, it's them.

'Aye, that's true enough I suppose,' agreed Alfgeir. He looked over to his knights. 'Orvin, you and the others break out the shovels and start earning your pay.'

'By digging?' said Orvin, as though the notion was beneath him.

'By digging,' confirmed Alfgeir. 'Get to it.'

Orvin shook his head and, together with five other knights, began shovelling earth from the spot Cuthwin had indicated. They dug relentlessly and swiftly moved a large amount of soil. Cuthwin watched with Alfgeir as they dug down around four feet into the ground without finding anything.

Just as he was beginning to entertain doubts that there was anything buried here, Orvin's shovel clanged on something metallic. Orvin used the end of his shovel to clear away the black earth, using his hands when the shovel proved insufficient for the task. At length, he leaned back to allow those above him to see what he had uncovered.

Cuthwin looked into the hole the knights had dug. He caught a gleam of tubular iron, like the funnels on Govannon's forge, spars of splintered timbers and what looked like an iron-rimmed wheel.

'What in Ulric's name *is* that?' said Alfgeir, tilting his head to the side.

'The Thunder Bringer,' said Cuthwin. 'And we have to get it back to Reikdorf.'

THE SHIP WAS a long merchantman, sleek-hulled and coloured a garish blue and green with wide, dark eyes painted beneath its prow. An elaborate figurehead jutted provocatively from her forecastle, representing Myrmidia and Manann entwined in an embrace that Marius was sure the temple priests of Jutonsryk wouldn't find in any of their holy books. Its flag was one Marius had seen before, but he couldn't remember to which distant princeling it belonged. He saw so many ships in any given week, it was hard to keep track of them all.

Hundreds of people bustled to and fro: sailors, tax collectors in blue robes, maritime enthusiasts, dwarf masons and shipwrights, rope-makers, labourers, hawkers, map-makers, whores and sell-swords. The taverns were doing a brisk trade, as a number of ships had just finished their unloading and their crews were eager to spend their wages.

The air tasted of saltwater and hard work, and Marius felt his brow turn thunderous as he saw the crew of the impounded vessel pressing against the ring of armed lancers preventing them from leaving the quay. Olive-skinned sailors from the south, they waved their arms and jabbered in their foreign tongue, apparently oblivious to the fact that they were on Empire soil and ought to be speaking Reikspiel if they wanted to be understood.

'To be fair, they do look rather unsettled,' said Vergoossen.

Marius waved away his aide's comment. 'Nonsense, these foreign types are always ludicrously animated when they converse. The way they talk to each other, they could be discussing the weather and you'd swear they were relating news of the End Times.'

'But still,' pressed Vergoossen, 'what if they aren't lying?'

'Of course they're lying,' snapped Marius, rounding on his aide. 'It's the oldest trick in the book for fly-by-nights and thieves. Listen, Vergoossen, one of two things has happened here. Either they've stolen their master's cargo and transferred it to another ship, which we'll see in a few days with false papers of lading, or they have come here claiming they had to ditch their cargo to outrun some pirates so they don't have to pay the berthing tax. Then they'll miraculously find a hugely lucrative trade deal when they get ashore. Either way, I won't stand for it. I'll have them locked in the tower for trying to cheat Marius of Jutonsryk.'

His lesson in tax evasion dispensed, Marius marched towards the merchantman, noting how high it was riding in the water. Its holds were empty, that was for sure, but he'd wager they'd been empty long before the sailors had come within spitting distance of the city.

The Sergeant of Lancers turned as he heard Marius approach. He gave a formal salute and placed his clenched fist against his chest before bowing curtly.

'My lord,' he said. 'Sergeant Alwin. We detained these men when the Master of Taxes informed us they refused to pay the berthing fee.'

Marius scanned the sailors, a grimy bunch of men with colourful complexions and dark hair to a man. He counted around a hundred men on the quayside or clustering the rails of the ship. They looked desperate to get onto dry land, and many threw furtive glances over their shoulders out to sea.

'Is this all of them?' asked Marius.

Alwin nodded. 'A couple of them may have gotten into the city before we arrived, but looks like there's more or less a full ship's complement here.'

That seemed about right, and Marius looked for the sailor in the least grubby clothes, the one that likely captained this vessel. His eyes immediately fixed on a man with skin like tanned leather and a mane of slick black hair. His manner was agitated, but from the looks the others were giving him, it was clear he was in command.

'You,' said Marius, beckoning the man through the line of lancers. 'You speak Reikspiel?'

The man nodded and gratefully pushed through the lancers towards Marius. Two of his personal bodyguard quickly searched the man for weapons, taking a pair of daggers and a gunwale spike from his belt.

'I am Count Marius of Jutonsryk, lord of this city. What is your name?' said Marius, careful to enunciate each word carefully.

'My name is Captain Leotas Raul, and I speak Reikspiel very well.'

'Good, then we won't have any misunderstandings,' said Marius. 'This is your ship, yes?'

'It is,' said Raul, his voice prideful and yet melancholy. '*Myrmidia's Spear*, sole surviving ship of Magister Fiorento's fleet.'

'Yes, well I'm sure he will be overjoyed to hear that his last ship is soon to be impounded,' said Marius.

Before Raul could react to Marius's dire pronouncement, the count of Jutonsryk said, 'Tell me, Captain Raul, what do you think of my harbour? Is it adequate for your magnificent ship?'

Raul looked confused, and Marius said, 'Would you like me to repeat the question?'

'No,' said Raul, a hard look entering his eyes. 'That will not be necessary.'

'Well? Are my docks fit to berth your ship?'

'These are very fine docks, Count Marius,' answered Raul coldly.

'Good, so why don't you tell me why you've taken the liberty of berthing in my perfectly good harbour and yet refuse to pay the berthing fee.'

'We have no cargo,' replied Raul. 'No cargo means nothing to tax.'

'Oh there is always something to tax, Captain Raul,' Marius assured him. 'But if you have no cargo, then you have come a long way for nothing. Magister Fiorento must be a wealthy man indeed to despatch ships with no cargo all this way.'

'We did not come here with empty holds, my lord,' said Raul. 'We were forced to abandon our cargo.'

'So tell me, what manner of cargo were you carrying before you abandoned it?'

'A thousand bales of embroidered cloth,' answered Raul. 'Dyes and oils from the warmer climates of the southern islands.'

'I see, and you threw these overboard because...'

'We were attacked by black ships with crimson sails of ragged cloth and crewed by dead men. Sailors from the depths of the ocean risen from the sea to hunt the living.'

'Very poetic,' commented Marius. 'Of course, you realise I don't believe a word of it?'

'I speak no lies,' hissed Raul, and Marius smiled at his conviction.

'Then, please, elaborate,' said Marius, knowing even a skilled liar would often trip themselves up in the details of an over-elaborate farrago.

'As we rounded the Reik headland from the south a noxious fog arose from the sea and a host of crimson-sailed vessels moved to intercept us. Not a breath of wind stirred their sails, yet they came on at speed, as though all the fiends of the deep pulled their rotted hulks through the waters. More appeared around the northern headland, trapping us between them, two hundred vessels at least.'

'Two hundred?' laughed Marius. 'Now I know you are lying. There are, I'll grant you, a few corsairs who raid the shorelines of the far Reik, but none with so large a fleet.'

'These were no corsairs,' insisted Raul. 'As their ships drew nearer we smelled the stench of rotten, waterlogged timbers and saw the decaying flesh of the skeletal crewmen aboard each vessel. We tried to outrun them, but they were too fast, and our sister ship, *Shield of Glory*, was overtaken. A hundred dead warriors swarmed her decks, and they tore the living apart to eat their flesh. Though our fellow brothers of the sea were being devoured, not a man aboard ship dared turn to help them. *Golden Goddess* tried to evade, but she was too heavy, and more of the ships of the damned cut her off. She too was lost with all souls.'

'But you escaped,' said Marius.

'No sooner had I seen how many ships opposed us than I knew we were too heavily laden to escape. I ordered our cargo ditched, but even then we only barely made it through the line of mouldering hulks.'

'These ships of the dead did not pursue you? How convenient.'

'They did not,' said Raul. 'But they are still out there, this I swear on the life of my mother. They are out there and no more ships will come to your city. And while they lurk in the fog, none shall leave.'

Marius had heard enough and shook his head. 'A fanciful tale, Captain Raul, but one I am disinclined to believe.'

He turned to Sergeant Alwin. 'Impound the ship and lock these men up in the Old Town gaol. Vergoossen, draft a letter to Magister Fiorento and tell him that if he wants his ship and crew released then he'll need to pay their fines and taxes. Be sure to inform him of the increasing levy of fines the longer he leaves them here.'

'As you wish, my lord,' said Vergoossen.

Marius turned and walked away as the lancers began rounding up the protesting sailors.

'Dead corsairs, indeed,' he said. 'Ridiculous.'

THE FIVE CHARIOTS thundered over the rugged flatlands to the south of Three Hills, the horses running at battle pace as Maedbh let them stretch their muscles. Asoborn beasts needed to have their head now and again. The training fields allowed the youngsters to get a feel for the beasts and how the chariot behaved, but there was nothing like riding tall at battle pace to get the heart pounding and the blood racing.

Two chariots sped along either side of her, each with an Asoborn youth at the reins. Not one was over thirteen years of age, but they worked the reins like veterans. The ground here was dotted with thin copses, unexpected slopes and random patches of rocks, but so far they had steered around them without losing valuable speed. Ahead, the Worlds Edge Mountains soared to the sky and a black line of thunderheads rolled like a giant wave crashing over the distant peaks to the far south.

Looking at those clouds gave Maedbh a shiver of dread, though they would be long back at Three Hills before any storm broke. She returned her attention to the ground before her chariot as they rolled over a rough patch of earth and the wheel spun in the air for a moment. The chariot wobbled, but Maedbh brought it back level without effort.

'Careful, mother!' squealed Ulrike with frightened delight.

'Are you still secure?' called Maedbh, sparing a quick glance over her shoulder.

'Yes, mother! Of course I am!'

Ulrike had her right ankle braced against the side armour, her left against an angled ridge of wood Wolfgart had crafted to compensate for her narrower stance. Her knees weren't locked, her legs flexible and her posture loose; the perfect position for a charioteer spear-bearer. Maedbh smiled, seeing the same fierce determination in her young features she saw in herself. And, if she was honest, she saw in Wolfgart.

Thinking of her estranged husband brought a lump to her throat. She missed him, and it rankled that she felt like that. An Asoborn woman needed no man to complete her, she was a fiery warrior princess with the winter fire of Ulric flowing in her veins. Maedbh knew all that was true, but she knew there was no shame in wanting to be part of a union that had created so beautiful a life as their daughter.

She and Wolfgart were too alike, that was what she loved about him, and, perversely, was also the problem. Like two bulls in a pen, they locked horns every day to establish dominance, though surely there was no need. She regretted her harsh words to him, but like arrows of fire, they could not be taken back and had struck where they would do the most damage. Maedbh knew herself well enough to know that pride was but a facet of stubbornness, a quality both she and Wolfgart possessed in abundance.

It wasn't in her nature to back down, and yet Ulrike needed a father. She had cried when Maedbh told her that Wolfgart had returned to Reikdorf. Part of her hated him for leaving without saying goodbye, but she recognised that any such farewell would have resulted in a bitter quarrel, and couldn't blame him for wanting to avoid such a confrontation.

'Mother!' cried Ulrike, and Maedbh cursed as she wheeled the chariot away from a scattered tumble of rocks in a dry riverbed. Her attention wasn't on what she was doing, and that was dangerous. Many a careless charioteer had run themselves into rocks or trees through their inattention, and such inglorious fates were amongst the most shameful among the Asoborns.

She pushed Wolfgart from her mind and fixed her attention on her wild ride, weaving a deft path through a sparsely wooded forest in the shadow of a long ridge that ran from east to west. The chariots formed a line in her wake, smoothly changing formation in response to her manoeuvres, and she smiled at the youths' deft touch on the reins.

The horses were breathing hard, their flanks lathered with sweat and Maedbh drew them in, gradually slowing them until they were gently trotting. The horses came to a standstill and Maedbh coiled the reins through the loop of iron fixed to the chariot's wooden frame. She was sweating, her limbs pleasurably sore from their ride.

'Why are we stopping?' asked Ulrike. 'I like going that fast!'

'The horses need to rest, my dear,' said Maedbh. 'They've had a hard morning. Think how tired you are after you've run around the training ground five times. These horses have done that and more.'

'They need to rest then.'

'Yes, my dear, they do,' said Maedbh. 'We all do. See to the horses, and I'll fix you some food once you're finished.'

'Can't I have food first?'

'No, always see to your horses as soon as you stop,' instructed Maedbh. 'You can go without food for a little while, but your horses may need to ride fast at a moment's notice, so be sure they're watered and rubbed down before you see to yourself.'

Ulrike nodded reluctantly, but began expertly brushing the sweat from the horses' heaving sides. The chariots had halted in such a way as to form a rough circle, a perfect defensive formation and one that allowed each rider to set off without fear of hitting another. Maedbh watched the others follow Ulrike's lead, rubbing their horses down with handfuls of straw before allowing them to drink from a trickling stream of clear water.

Satisfied the horses were being looked after, Maedbh stepped down from the chariot and sat on its base, untying a bundle of black bread and cheese from an internal pannier. She broke the bread and set out a portion for her and Ulrike, enjoying this chance to get out in the wilds. Any Asoborn warrior preferred the wind in their hair and the sight of open horizons to the feel of enclosing walls and buildings of stone. Though Three Hills was far from oppressive, Maedbh still relished the chance to explore the far reaches of Freya's lands, to ride the wild woods and race along the open flatlands beyond the hills.

'That was well done, my beauties,' said Maedbh, as the others led their horses back to the chariots. They didn't hobble the horses, but let them roam freely, knowing they would come with a whistle. They beamed at her pride, knowing that as charioteer to Queen Freya, her praise was not given lightly.

As they gathered around her, Maedbh offered instructional tips, helpful pointers and the occasional admonishment to her charioteers. Each had performed well, but there was always room for improvement, and nobody could afford to rest on their laurels.

'You're leaning left when you crack the reins, Osgud,' she said, angling her hand as she spoke. 'It makes the horse pull away from the line, and you need to keep your spacing close when you're riding in close to the enemy. And Daegal, follow through with your spear thrusts, but remember to twist the blade at the extent of your thrust, otherwise it will be torn from your grasp. Ulrike, you need to watch your balance, always keep your back foot braced or you'll be thrown out if the wheels strike a rock or hit a dip in the ground.'

They listened intently, and Maedbh was pleased with their progress. With their midday meal eaten, they broke into smaller groups, practising with their spears and posture. Ulrike ran to join them and Maedbh watched the young Asoborns with a fierce maternal affection. They were *all* her children, not just Ulrike.

She rested her head on the side of the chariot, letting

the sounds of the wilderness wash over her: the burble of the water, the sigh of the wind through the trees and the distant caw of a carrion bird over something dead. It had been a long day and she closed her eyes briefly, letting a warm lethargy sneak up on her.

Again the carrion bird cawed, and Maedbh opened her eyes.

The sound was closer than before, louder and more strident, which was strange, as food for crows didn't normally move. She didn't react, but let the sensations of the world come into sharper focus. The wind was coming from the north, the carrion bird was to the south and getting closer.

Maedbh rose to her feet as the wind changed and the horses' heads came up, their ears flat against their skulls and their eyes wide with fear. They snorted and tossed their manes, walking back towards the yokes of the chariots. A wolf howled to the south, and Maedbh tensed. Such a sound would normally be auspicious, but there was something wrong with this howl, it had a hollow, hungry edge to it that no animal servant of Ulric would possess. An answering howl answered the first, this time from the west. A wolf pack was circling them, and Maedbh fought down her rising fear.

'Get the horses yoked back to the chariots,' she shouted, authoritative, not frightened.

The young Asoborns moved to obey, too slowly.

'Get a move on!' she cried. 'If you were under attack, is this how fast you'd move?'

Maedbh gathered the two horses of her own chariot and swiftly harnessed them to the yoke with quick tugs of the bronze buckles. A shadow flitted across the chariot's frame and she looked up to see a flock of circling birds with black feathers. Eaters of the dead.

'Hurry it up, for Ulric's sake!' she said, scooping up

Ulrike and depositing her in the chariot. She unlimbered her bow from the side of the chariot and quickly bent it back to string it.

'String yours too,' she said to Ulrike. 'And keep a wary eye out.'

'What's going on, mother?' said Ulrike, sensing a measure of her mother's unease.

'Nothing, my dear,' she said. 'Just do it. Hurry.'

She climbed onto her chariot seeing that the rest of her group were almost ready. The birds cawed again and another wolf howl echoed over the desolate wilderness. That one was unmistakably from the north, and as the wind changed again, Maedbh caught the reek of dead flesh, of mangy, maggot-ridden fur and stagnant, bloody saliva.

Someone screamed and she looked up to see a line of huge timber wolves on the ridge above them. Their fur was rotted and patchy over yellowed bone and torn muscle. Vacant eye sockets glimmered with emerald light and drooling ropes of bloody saliva hung from their exposed fangs.

Some dead things *did* move, it seemed.

'Ride!' shouted Maedbh.

─◄ EIGHT ►─

The First to Die

THOUGH HE HAD faced the horror of the living dead before, Sigmar's soul rebelled at the sight before him. Once Ostengard had been a prosperous, well-populated logging village, home to two hundred Cherusen woodsmen and their families. Now it was a charnel house, a field of blood and death.

'Ulric's bones,' swore Count Aloysis, his face pale and the tattoos that curled across his face bleached of colour. His shaven head was criss-crossed with scars and his long scalp lock was more silver than black, bound with circlets of cold iron. 'Those were my people.'

Aloysis's scarlet cloak flapped in the cold wind and his hand twitched on the hook-bladed sword at his side. His eyes were wide with fear at what lay below them.

'Not any more, they're not,' grunted Count Krugar, trying to mask his own fear. 'Now they're dead meat for hewing.'

The Taleuten count was wide and powerful, clad in a shimmering hauberk of silver scale. He hefted Utensjarl from hand to hand. The ancient weapon of Talenbor was slender-bladed, but Sigmar had seen Krugar hew Norsii like saplings with its lethal edge. Despite Krugar's bluster, Sigmar knew both counts were afraid. He didn't blame them.

'Krugar speaks the truth, Aloysis,' said Sigmar. 'These are not your people. Remember that.'

'Aye, I know,' said Aloysis. 'That doesn't make it any easier to take a blade to them.'

Sigmar knew that only too well, having fought against dead things that had once been men of the Empire in the Middle Mountains. This would be hardest on Aloysis, but it would be a test every one of them would have to face soon, of that Sigmar was certain.

A thousand warriors lined the hillside above Ostengard, a mix of Cherusen axemen and foresters, the Red Scythes of the Taleutens and Unberogen swordsmen. Though the Cherusens and Taleutens had almost gone to war a few years ago, their leaders had since become staunch allies, their bond forged by the nearness of their death at Sigmar's hands when the dread crown of Morath had poisoned him with its evil.

In the wake of Khaled al-Muntasir's appearance in Reikdorf, Sigmar had gathered a sword host of five hundred warriors and ridden with all speed towards Taalahim, the great forest city of the Taleutens. If the dead were on the march, then it seemed their first move was in the north. Both counts had sent desperate missives asking for the Emperor's troops to quell the rising dead, and Sigmar had answered their calls.

The Unberogen had ridden hard, meeting the Cherusens and Taleutens in the rugged southern skirts of the Howling Hills. Too late to save the people of Ostengard, but not too late to avenge them.

Clustered around a central thoroughfare that led to the

river, Ostengard had been built in a horseshoe shape, with a grain store and carpentry building at its centre. Numerous dwellings were built around these structures, and an elaborate shrine to Taal stood at the riverside. Vast swathes of the forest had been cleared around the village, and much of that had been given over to cultivation, with fields of golden corn and barley waving in the gentle breeze.

The village seethed with activity, unnatural activity. Pallid-skinned creatures with thin, wiry limbs and enlarged skulls feasted on the dead, loping from corpse to corpse to fight for the choicest shanks of meat. Shambling corpses in muddy rags gathered together in moaning bands of rotting flesh, stumbling and dragging themselves towards the hillside where the warriors of the Empire watched.

The dead had risen from the mulchy earth and devoured Ostengard, and a gathering darkness held sway over the day, though the sun was only just past its zenith. The horde of dead things, sensing the warm meat of the living, came for them in an inexorable march of dread patience and insatiable hunger.

Sigmar guessed they faced at least five hundred living dead, a number that could normally be easily overcome, but this was a foe that fought with fear as their greatest weapon.

'Aloysis, you and your axemen are with me. Krugar, split your horsemen and ride around the enemy to hit them from behind,' said Sigmar. 'Ride down to the village and come up through its main street.'

'They won't break and run,' pointed out Krugar, mounting his horse, a powerful, grain-fed stallion of midnight black. 'The dead don't fear anything.'

'They fear this,' said Sigmar, lifting Ghal-maraz from his belt. The dwarf runes etched into its surface shimmered with silver light, and he could feel the weapon's ancestral hatred of the living dead. 'Somewhere down there is a will that is controlling this horde. Ghal-maraz will find it and I will destroy it. With its destruction this horde cannot exist.'

'Then let me be the one to fell it,' begged Aloysis. 'My people demand their count's vengeance.'

Sigmar nodded. 'So be it, but enough talk, it's time to fight.'

Krugar dug his heels into his mount's flanks and said, 'May Ulric give your arm strength, brothers.'

The Taleuten count wheeled his horse and joined the Red Scythes. At a curt command, the horsemen split into two groups with the smooth ease of practiced warriors. They rode with incredible skill, crouched low over their mounts' heads as they moved to encircle the host of the dead.

Aloysis offered Sigmar his hand, and he shook it, feeling the clammy sweat coating the Cherusen count's palm. The man was terrified, but he was facing that terror with iron courage. Sigmar had always respected Aloysis, but this was a level of courage beyond simple bravery.

'Ready?' he asked.

'No,' answered Aloysis honestly. 'But let us fight together, my Emperor.'

Sigmar took Ghal-maraz in a two-handed grip and raised his voice so that every warrior on the hillside could hear him.

'Men of the Empire, you fight a terrible enemy today, but know this. The dead can die. Lay them low as you would slay any foe. Sword and axe will fell them as surely as any living man. Fight in Ulric's name and we will prevail! For Ulric!'

A ragged cheer erupted along the hillside and Sigmar

led the warriors forward in two solid blocks, Sigmar in command of the left, Aloysis the right. They marched towards the enemy, and Sigmar felt the fear of the dead spread through the ranks.

He raised Ghal-maraz and the man next to him hoisted the Imperial standard high, a magnificent banner of red, blue and white. A glorious beast of legend was picked out in gold, with a silver crown encircling its breast, and the sight of Sigmar's new heraldry filled the hearts of all who saw it with fresh courage.

Closer now, the dead were a truly horrific sight, a collection of all degradations time could wreak upon the frailty of human form. Decomposing flesh hung from the bones of those who had clawed their way from earthen graves, loose jawbones hanging like grotesque ornaments from splintered skulls. Those more recently dead were bloody and raw where grasping hands, grave-dirt claws and broken teeth had torn the meat from their bones.

Worse than that, the dreadful aspect of their very existence sent cold spikes of unreasoning fear through every man who stood against them. A man could face another man with courage and know that he could prevail by the strength of his sword arm alone. To face the dead was another matter entirely, for to look into their eyes was to see your own death, to know that your existence in this world was fleeting. To face the dead was to face mortality itself.

Sigmar increased his pace to a loping run, lifting Ghal-maraz over his shoulder and letting loose a fearsome Unberogen war-shout. His warriors echoed him, bellowing the name of Ulric and matching his pace. The Cherusens whooped and hollered, their painted faces recalling the days they had fought near-naked and chewing on wildroot and bane leaves.

Where the Unberogen marched in close-packed ranks, the Cherusen fought as individuals, their mighty felling axes requiring space to swing without hitting a fellow warrior. Aloysis had his sword drawn, a long cavalry sabre more useful on the back of a horse, but a fine enough weapon to strike down the dead on foot.

Less than twenty yards separated the living from the dead.

Sigmar shouted, 'For Ulric!' and broke into a furious charge.

The Unberogen and Cherusen came with him and they struck the dead with all the force and vitality the living could muster.

MAEDBH HAULED THE reins left as a savage beast with blood-red eyes leapt towards her, its taloned paws slashing. The feral wolf slammed into the side of the chariot with a heavy thump, its claws tearing down through the wooden sides. Ulrike screamed in terror and Maedbh risked a glance back to check her daughter was safe.

Ulrike loosed a poorly aimed shaft. The arrowhead scored through the wolf's fur and bounced from its skull. It howled and fell away from the chariot.

'Keep them back!' shouted Maedbh.

Only three of the chariots had escaped the riverbed, breaking through the encircling packs of wolves. The horses yoked to Yustin and Kreo's chariot were torn apart before they could get moving, and the youngsters were brought down moments later. A huge, black-furred wolf snapped its jaws on Yustin's head, killing the youth instantly, while two wolves with bare skulls and exposed musculature tore Kreo's arm off with brutal sweeps of their claws.

Henia and Torqa got their chariot moving, but a pair of wolves leapt from the ridge straight onto them. Torqa skewered the first with her spear, but the second wolf bit her in two and smashed Henia's spine with one slash of its claws.

The rest of them had broken free and rode with all speed to the north.

Maedbh looked around. The wolves were loping alongside them, their decayed bodies ravaged and wasted, yet powerful and untiring. Six followed them and another four ran on each flank, content to drive them into the path of wolves Maedbh knew were lying in wait somewhere up ahead. These were dead creatures, but they hunted like living ones.

A steady stream of arrows flew from the backs of the chariots. Of all the youngsters, Ulrike had the best eye, and her arrows struck home more than anyone else's. Already she had brought down two wolves. Even amid this desperate chase, Maedbh was proud of her.

The wolves howled and closed in. A slavering beast loped in from the right, its eyes fixed on Maedbh's throat. She pulled the reins in hard, almost tipping the chariot, and its right wheel came off the ground. The wolf hit the spinning wheel and its momentum carried it under the chariot. It gave a mournful howl before its bones were crushed and whatever animation empowered it was extinguished.

Ulrike loosed an arrow at the creature behind it, the shaft punching through the beast's eye socket, and its body writhed as the unnatural energies that bound it together faded and it dropped without a sound. The other creatures cared nothing for the deaths of their pack brothers, and drove the chariots onwards. Maedbh saw three wolves closing on Osgud's chariot and steered around a patch of rocks to sweep in behind him.

'Bloody fool never could keep his spacing,' she hissed. The wolves saw her coming, but too late, and she drove over the rearmost creature, flattening it beneath her wheels. The second loped away, but the third was too fixated on its prey to pay her any mind.

'Osgud! Hard right!'

The terrified youth obeyed instantly, his training making the movement automatic. The two chariots slammed together, crushing the wolf between them. Ulrike screamed as she was jolted from her perch. Maedbh reached back and grabbed her daughter's arm as she slid off the chariot.

Ulrike flailed with her free arm, desperately clawing her way back on board. Spying a target of opportunity, a ravaged wolf with a spectral gleam in its eyes and a hollowed skull bounded towards her, stinking grave dirt spilling from its fang-filled jaws. It leapt towards Ulrike, claws outstretched.

A heavy spear slammed into its side, punching through its ribs and skewering it in mid-air. The blade twisted and the wolf fell away, its bones dissolving and its fur rotting to ash in the wind. Daegal drew back his spear as another wolf leapt for the back of his chariot. The blade stabbed into its skull, and the wolf howled as it died anew.

Maedbh hauled Ulrike back into the chariot, pleased at least one of her students had listened to her. She lashed her horses to greater speed, pulling in close to Osgud's chariot and making sure Daegal's was close by too.

Eight wolves remained, but one of those was slain by a pair of arrows that pierced its chest and skull. Another died when it dared to come too close to Daegal's chariot, and ended up beneath its wheels. Six left, and the ground was rising towards the hills where they would find sanctuary. She heard the howls of wolves from ahead, and knew that was just where the wolves were driving them.

'Circle up!' she cried, and the chariots rolled around,

each moving in a smooth arc until they had formed an ad-hoc fortress with one another. The wolves surrounded them, wary at this change of strategy on the part of their prey. Ulrike dropped one wolf with an arrow to the head, and Daegal hurled his spear into the flank of another. Both yelped as their bodies crumbled away to stinking ash.

Realising they could not afford to wait, the remaining wolves hurled themselves at the Asoborns. Freed from the need to control the chariot, Maedbh loosed a quick arrow that tore the throat from a leaping wolf. She threw her bow aside and drew her sword as the rest of the wolves attacked.

Osgud killed a wolf with a spear thrust, and was borne to the ground by a second. Ulrike stabbed a throwing spear into the side of a snapping beast as it climbed over the sides of the chariot. The shaft snapped off in the creature's ribcage, but Maedbh stepped in and hacked the wolf's head from its shoulders with one blow.

The last wolf backed away from the Asoborns, its fangs bared and its eyes alight with killing fire. A living wolf would have slunk away in defeat, but this dead creature circled the chariots at speed before finally leaping onto Osgud's chariot and plucking the fallen youngster from his position there. Its jaws closed with the sound of two spars of wood slamming together and Osgud's body came apart in a spray of crimson.

Four arrows sliced into its body and a heavy throwing spear all but severed its spine. Its rotten bones fell apart and Osgud's remains flopped into his chariot, little more than torn limbs and ruptured meat.

Maedbh cast a wary look north. She saw no signs of wolves and let out a pent up breath.

'Gather up your arrows!' she ordered. 'Quickly, there's likely more of these things out there.'

Ulrike and the others ran to obey and she was proud of them all. Maedbh retrieved her own bow, constantly scanning the horizon for fresh threats. The darkened skies to the south worried her, more than they had before. Something evil was coming to the lands of the Asoborns, and this was just a foretaste.

The youngsters ran back to the chariots, and they mounted up.

'We ride west!' shouted Maedbh.

'No!' protested Ulrike. 'We can't go west. Three Hills is north.'

'And so are the wolves,' answered Maedbh, coming down to Ulrike's level. 'If we go west through the hills, no wolves will be able to find us. When it's safe, we'll cut back north.'

'I was scared,' said Ulrike, holding onto Maedbh's arm.

She saw the fear behind her daughter's eyes, a fear for her own life, but also that of her mother. Only now, with the immediate danger averted, did Maedbh realise how close she had come to losing Ulrike. The thought terrified her, and a sickening feeling in the pit of her stomach sent a dreadful nausea through her entire body.

'I know you were, my dear,' said Maedbh, fighting to keep her voice even. 'So was I, but you were very, very brave, my girl. You were scared, but you didn't run, you fought like a true Asoborn. I'm so proud of you.'

Ulrike smiled, but Maedbh saw the fear hadn't left her entirely. She stood on trembling legs, and took hold of the chariot's reins. Her hands shook and she gripped the leather tightly to keep her terror from showing.

'Perhaps Wolfgart was right,' she whispered, fighting back tears.

SIGMAR SLAMMED HIS hammer into the face of a long dead man in mouldering rags. The skull caved with a wet, tearing sound and his hammer broke through the corpse's collarbone and burst from the ruined chest cavity. He jabbed the butt of the hammer through the throat of a nearby corpse and kicked out at a fallen dead thing that grasped his legs with broken fingers. All around him, the battle raged with one-sided fierceness. The dead clawed and bit at the living, but there was no passion or courage to their violence. An animating will filled them, but did so without the spark that drove living warriors to risk their lives for something greater than themselves.

Yet for all their monotonous rigour, the blows of the dead were no less fatal. The flesh of the living was a choice sweetmeat to them, the craving for the warmth and softness of their flesh a hunger that could never be satisfied.

Sigmar's armour bore numerous dents and scars from viciously wielded clubs and cleavers, and blood flowed from a deep cut on his shoulder where a dead logger's axe had smashed the pauldron from his armour and bitten through the links of his mail shirt. He fought alongside Unberogen veterans of the battle of Middenheim, each hacking a path through the dead while watching for threats Sigmar could not see.

He ducked a slashing axe and drove Ghal-maraz up into the pelvic cavity of a skeletal warrior clad in ancient armour of corroded bronze. The head of the hammer shattered the dead warrior's spine and broke the body in two. It collapsed in a rain of dusty bone and Sigmar swung his hammer around, knocking three more revenants to the ground. Hoarse cries of Ulric's name echoed from the hillside as the Cherusens hewed a path into the dead, felling them like dead wood with every crushing blow of their axes.

Sigmar's warriors fought as one, each pushing forward

with the support of the man next to him. Only Unberogen discipline allowed such close-quarter fighting, and it was paying dividends, as few were falling to the blades of the enemy. Lone Cherusen axemen fought until their arms grew weary and they were overwhelmed by the dead, dragged down and torn apart by the voracious enemy.

The pallid cannibal creatures darted through the trees in cowardly packs, skulking at the edges of the fighting and darting in for opportunistic slashes and bites. Sigmar paid them no mind, forging a path onwards towards Ostengard as he saw the Red Scythes ride along the arms of the horseshoe shaped settlement and form a deadly wedge of cavalry in a magnificent display of horsemanship.

'Hold them!' shouted Sigmar, spotting a black-cloaked warrior in the heart of the enemy host, a warrior with the bleached bone of a skull beneath a full-faced helm of bronze. Jade light burned in the sockets of his eyes, and Sigmar felt monstrous will gathered there, a black sorcery of abominable darkness that was holding this dead host together.

He smashed a pair of skeletal things aside with one blow of his hammer, angling his course towards the Cherusens.

'Aloysis!' he yelled, spotting the slender count of the Cherusens as he beheaded a rotten-fleshed cadaver with expert skill. 'Fight with me!'

The count of the Cherusens heard him and gathered his closest warriors, cutting a path through the dead warriors towards Sigmar. They met in a ring of dead things, both blooded and both breathing hard. Yet for all the carnage around them, they both grinned with fierce battle fury.

'You're hurt,' said Aloysis.

'Not badly,' answered Sigmar, pointing Ghal-maraz towards the black-cloaked warrior with the bronze helm. 'There yonder, that's the source of their power. Destroy it and the host will crumble like morning ashes.'

Aloysis nodded and with a wild, ululating yell, set off downhill towards the nightmarish master of the dead. Sigmar followed him, breaking through the lumpen ranks of the dead to aid his count. Once more they were surrounded by the dead, but with numbers on their side, the strength of the mortal warriors was telling.

The thundering wedge of Krugar's Red Scythes smashed into the rear ranks of the dead, trampling corpses and splintering bone beneath their hooves. Long lances punched into rotten bodies and the host of living dead were split apart. Krugar wielded Utensjarl as though it weighed nothing at all, its blade cleaving dead things in two with every stroke. Most mortal foes would have broken and run at this sudden attack, but the dead cared nothing for this new enemy, fighting with the same horrid determination as ever.

Sigmar and Aloysis fought their way towards the black-cloaked warrior, but with every step more of the dead seemed to rise and block their path. Bones once broken fused together and skulls split open reformed in a dreadful parody of healing. All around Sigmar, the dead pressed in, grasping with decayed hands.

'Sigmar!' shouted Krugar. 'Duck!'

Knowing never to question a shouted battlefield command, Sigmar threw himself flat as something whirling and silver flashed over his head. He rolled swiftly to his feet and bludgeoned two dead warriors with quick jabs of his hammer. He looked left and right for fresh opponents. None of the dead came near him, and as he sought out the black-cloaked master of this dead host, he saw why.

The creature whose will drove the horde was dying.

Utensjarl had been bathed in the fire of Ulric in Middenheim after the great victory, and was now buried deep in the monster's chest. Baleful energies flared from the dead thing, green fire streaming from its eyes as it sought to hold its unmaking at bay. An armoured warrior leapt towards it, a slender-bladed cavalry sabre arcing towards its bony neck. Aloysis's blade found the gap between the dead warrior's breastplate and helmet, his power and rage driving it through unnaturally formed sinews, bone and sorcery.

The bronze helm and skull parted from the body, falling to the ground and rolling downhill. A torrent of icy energy swept out from its disintegrating form as the bones collapsed and a spectral scream of hideous rage split the forest.

No sooner had its vile echoes faded than the dead host fell apart. The recently dead slumped over like drunks and the skeletal warriors risen from their graves fell to pieces like poorly made puppets. Sigmar blinked as the loathsome twilight they had fought this battle beneath was dispelled and sunlight returned to the forest.

Sigmar took a deep breath, feeling the air as a clean draught in his lungs, not the stale, stagnant miasma he had endured in the fighting. His warriors and those of Krugar and Aloysis stood amazed as life and vitality returned to the land. There was no cheering, no victory cries, for this was simply survival.

Krugar rode up to Sigmar and vaulted from his horse. He lifted Utensjarl from the rusted pile of armour and mouldering cloak. Its blade shone like new, and he turned it over to ensure no lingering trace of the dead warrior remained to taint its edge.

Sigmar stood next to Krugar as Aloysis joined them.

'My warriors gave me a stern lecture the last time I

hurled my weapon in the middle of a fight,' said Sigmar.

Krugar shrugged. 'And they were right to do so, but I never miss.'

'You've done that before?' asked Aloysis.

'Once or twice,' grinned Krugar. 'After all, it never hurts for a leader of warriors to have the odd trick or two up his sleeve.'

Aloysis nodded and looked around the grim spectacle of the destroyed village. Sigmar felt his count's pain, for it was his pain too. These people were Cherusens, but they were also Sigmar's people, men and women of the Empire. This attack had brought them together as warriors and it united them as men.

'People will return,' said Sigmar. 'That is what those who make pacts with the dead will never understand. Life will always return stronger than ever.'

'I hope you are right, my lord,' said Aloysis. 'I fear that belief will soon be put to the test.'

— ❮ NINE ❯ —

Darkness Closes In

GOVANNON RAN HIS hands along the cold metal cylinder, feeling the smooth, almost perfect finish the craftsman had applied to its surface. Even the most highly polished metal forged by man had imperfections, a roughness to the surface that no amount of sanding and finishing could erase. This had none of that, and if what he believed was true, then this was no decorative piece to be found in a king's palace, but something far more interesting.

'What is it, da?' asked Bysen. 'Is it a bellows, is that what it is, da?'

'No,' said Govannon. 'It's not a bellows, son.'

'So what in Ulric's name is it?' asked Master Holtwine, staring at the device. 'And why did you need me here?'

No sooner had Govannon given what Alfgeir's knights had recovered from the earth a cursory examination, than he knew he'd need Holtwine's help. He'd sent Cuthwin to fetch the master craftsman, knowing the man would not be able to resist this challenge. Holtwine was a stout man of average height with a scowling face and thinning blond hair. He had been a superlative bowyer and archer in his youth, but his time as a warrior was cut short when a greenskin spear had pierced his chest and nicked his left lung.

Turning his dextrous hands to woodwork, he quickly discovered a natural talent that carpenters who had worked the wood for decades couldn't match. The man was a master of his art, a craftsman who could shape timber in ways that were simply incredible. Govannon had seen his most fabulous pieces, exquisite tables and chairs, decorative cupboards and beds. Even kitchen furniture was given his special attention, resulting in pieces almost too good to be placed in such a harsh environment.

'The dwarf called it a Thunder Bringer,' said Govannon.

'His name was Grindan Deeplock,' Cuthwin reminded him.

Govannon heard the grief in the boy's voice. Since losing his sight, Govannon had become adept at picking the truth from people's voices. He'd heard from Elswyth that this young scout had rescued the dwarf clansman from the forest, though his wounds had been too severe and he'd later died.

'Aye, that it was, Master Cuthwin,' said Govannon. 'My apologies. You saved his life, and it's thanks to you that he'll keep his honour in death. It's all too easy to feel responsible for that life when it ends, trust me I know.'

'No, it's me that needs to apologise,' said Cuthwin. 'I know you meant no disrespect. It's just that I promised that I'd get this machine back to his clan.'

'And so you shall, my boy,' Govannon assured him.

Govannon circled the machine, once again letting his hands inform him of its dimensions and construction.

Five long cylinders of cold iron were fixed in a wooden brace harness, which in turn was mounted on a broken carriage with two iron-rimmed wheels supporting the machine. Govannon could tell that each was precisely the same size, which was no mean feat.

Four of the five cylinders were perfectly cast, no blemishes, miscasts or air pockets that he could hear when he tapped the iron with his finishing hammer. The fifth was badly dented at its furthest extremity, as though pinched between enormous tongs, though Govannon shuddered to think of the strength that would be required to compress so strong a casting.

'You still haven't answered my question,' said Master Holtwine.

'Don't you know?' asked Govannon. 'Even Bysen here could guess.'

Holtwine took an irritated breath. 'I am a master craftsman, Govannon, not a player of games, so why don't you just tell me? I have a weapons cabinet to finish for Count Aldred, and the individual walnut panels require chamfering before they can be fitted.'

'I am sure Count Aldred would understand were he here right now,' said Govannon, letting the moment hang. 'This, my good friend, is, in the dwarf tongue, a barag.'

'What does that mean?' asked Cuthwin, leaning down to inspect the machine.

'What indeed?' asked Holtwine, his patience wearing thin.

'Is it Thunder Bringer?' suggested Cuthwin. 'Grindan called it that before he died.'

Govannon smiled. 'I am no expert in the dwarf tongue, but Wolfgart told me that the dwarfs who fought in the tunnels beneath Middenheim used a weapon known as a baragdrakk, which was a bellows-like machine that hurled gouts of sticky fire at the enemy. I'm guessing barag is a term for war machine, a dwarf version of the great catapults we use.'

Holtwine leaned over the device, his eyes roaming the expert shaping of the wood, the fabulous joint-work, the inlaid carvings and elegant cuts that ran with the grain. 'Really? It's a bit small. What manner of wall could you bring down with this?'

'I don't think this is meant to bring down walls,' said Govannon. 'I think this is designed to kill living things, a great many at once if I'm not mistaken.'

'How's it do that, da?' asked Bysen, peering down the length of one of the iron cylinders.

Govannon ran his hands towards the back of the war machine, to where a complex series of flint and powder trap mechanisms in the shape of iron hammers and brass cauldrons were fitted to the back of each cylinder. He pulled each of the hammers back then hauled on the length of leather cord hanging from the base of the mechanism. The first hammer slammed down in the empty cauldron with a hard clang of iron. One by one, the other triggers battered down in their cauldrons, and sparks flew from the impact of flint and iron.

Everyone jumped, but it was Cuthwin who spoke first. He tapped the iron hammer. 'It's a kind of trigger mechanism, isn't it? Like the firing lever on a crossbow.'

Holtwine leaned in, and Govannon could smell the beeswax, woodsap and polish on his skin. He smiled, knowing this device intrigued the man.

'A trigger mechanism, eh?' mused Holtwine. 'Then this small cauldron would be filled with their fire powder? Ulric's breath, is this some manner of enormous thunder bow?'

'That is exactly what I think it is,' said Govannon.

'So what do you plan to do with it?'

'I plan to return it to the dwarfs,' said Govannon. 'But first, I intend to fix it. And I need you to help me.'

REDWANE DREW ON his pipe, letting the fragrant smoke swirl around his mouth before blowing a series of perfect rings. Though the sun was shining, the day still seemed gloomy and cold. The clouds over the Middle Mountains were black and threatening, the skies to the south not much better. His relaxed posture and long wolfskin cloak hid his readiness for trouble, and his free hand never strayed too far from his hammer.

He and the other war leaders of the north made their way through the narrow, greystone streets of Midden-heim, talking in the open air, as was Myrsa's custom. The man hated being indoors, and insisted on conducting all planning with the northern wind in his hair and the open sky above him. The wardens of his northern marches, Orsa, Bordan, Wulf and Renweard, walked with him and the mood was grim.

Redwane had thought the dark clouds gathering over the Middle Mountains were a bad omen when he'd first seen them on waking. Now he knew that to be true.

Sigmar's herald had arrived from Reikdorf at first light, bearing evil tidings of a coming war with the living dead. Count Myrsa had listened in stoic silence to the herald's words of the Lord of Undeath's return, and immediately summoned his northern wardens to a war counsel.

They strode down Grafzen Street, on the eastern side of the city, with the Middle Mountains soaring to their left and the rising walls and towers of the great temple to Ulric rearing up to their right. Redwane averted his eyes from the mighty structure, his dreadful scarring and the fight with the daemon lord too fresh and raw for comfort. He still dreamed of that terrible battle, wondering if he could have aimed his blow differently, if there was any outcome that would not have left him so disfigured. A dolorous bell pealed from the temple of Morr, its echoing toll unmistakable. Somewhere, someone was dead, and Redwane whispered a prayer for their journey into the next world.

Redwane glanced at the magnificent sword sheathed at Myrsa's side, the runefang crafted by Alaric the Mad of the dwarfs. That blade had unmade the daemon lord's malefic protection, allowing Sigmar to destroy it with the power bound to his enchanted warhammer.

In the wake of the battle, Sigmar had named the blade Blodambana, which meant *Bloodbane* in the ancient tongue of the Unberogen, and not a day passed when Redwane didn't wish that Myrsa had reached the battle sooner.

He shook off his gloomy thoughts, concentrating on what was being said around him. He was the senior bodyguard of the count of Middenheim, and his attention was wandering far too much these days. Not that he had any real reason to fear for Myrsa's safety. A ring of White Wolves surrounded the council of war, twelve fur-cloaked warriors with hammers resting on their shoulders. The citizens of Middenheim gave them a wide berth, sensing the bellicose mood of the count's guards.

'There are people streaming south from the villages in the foothills of the Middle Mountains,' said Wulf, the lean and wiry Mountain Lord whose hardy warriors watched the high valleys and deep canyons of the Middle Mountains for trouble. 'Many claim that the living dead are rising up in their hundreds, and I'm inclined to believe them. I've heard their stories and looked in their eyes as they spoke. They're not lying.'

'The dead, are they coming from Brass Keep?' asked Myrsa, unable to contain his revulsion. 'I prayed that we had broken Morath's power.'

'We did, my lord,' said Wulf with gruff confidence. 'Brass Keep is nothing more than a refuge for the few Norsii bastards who escaped the slaughter last year. If there's dead rising in the mountains, then they're not coming out of the peaks. It's mainly the villages' own dead that are rising, and it's happening all over. Some of the local sword bands have contained the smaller attacks, but that won't last long. The dead are rising in greater numbers, and they're gathering together, like some damned pack instinct is at work.'

'Nonsense,' put in Bordan. 'You put too much faith in peasants' scare stories. And you're giving the dead too much credit. It's simple hunger that brings them together, nothing more.'

Bordan's title was Forest Master, and the safety of the numerous villages and trails through the western woodlands were entrusted to his foresters and huntsmen. It was a thankless task, and had ground Bordan down into a cynical man with little patience for others. In return, few had time for him, Redwane included.

'You were not at Brass Keep, Bordan,' said Myrsa. 'Wulf and Redwane and I were, and I am in no hurry to dismiss the Mountain Lord's reports. I understand only too well the malign cunning that animates the living dead, and we should not dismiss any tales of malevolent intelligence.'

'As you say, my lord,' said Bordan, suitably chastened.

'Tell me, Bordan, how fare the forests?' said Myrsa, knowing when to scold and when to embolden. 'I know there are many barrows and forsaken places within the Forest of Shadows. Have any of them been disturbed?'

'The western settlements have faced increased raids, my lord,' replied Bordan. 'The beasts and brigands grow bolder and more desperate with the early onset of winter. There have been a several instances of pestilence, but I have heard of no attacks by the walking dead.'

'There's a surprise,' grunted Redwane, unable to contain himself any longer.

'What did you say?' snapped Bordan.

'You heard me,' said Redwane. 'Your own grandfather could climb from his grave and bite you on the arse and you wouldn't notice.'

Bordan's hand flashed to his hunting knife, but one look into Redwane's horrifically scarred features convinced him that to draw it would be folly of the worst kind.

'You insult me, White Wolf,' hissed Bordan. 'Men have died for less.'

Redwane laughed at Bordan's threat, tapping the warhammer at his belt. 'Come at me with that toothpick of yours and I'll knock that damn fool head off your shoulders. You stood by and allowed Torbrecan's band of lunatics to march through the forest unimpeded. Now you've got hundreds of them in the city shouting for his release and Ulric knows how many of them camped outside the city.'

Bordan shrank before Redwane's words. Ever since the White Wolves had brought Torbrecan back to a Middenheim gaol, the mood in the city had been ugly. Contrary to Ustern's gloomy prediction, the madman's followers hadn't died in the forest, they had followed their captive leader back to the Fauschlag Rock, their numbers growing in strength with every village they passed through.

Hundreds had entered the city before Renweard had closed the gates to their kind. Now the growing flock of screaming, dancing and chanting madmen made camp at the base of the rock, whipping themselves into deliriums of agony-fuelled rage. A group of the ragged lunatics had set themselves ablaze and hurled themselves from the top of the rock, tumbling like falling stars to their doom below. Such heinous acts and their doom-laden presence set the entire populace of Middenheim on edge, and tension spread like a plague to every nook and cranny of the cloud-wreathed city.

'If they are camped around the rock, then surely it is the Way Keeper's duty to break up these fanatics' camp and disperse them,' said Bordan.

'Oh, it is, is it?' said Orsa, the barrel-chested and big-hearted man who sought only to see the good in men. Redwane liked him a great deal, though he knew there was no love lost between Orsa and Bordan. 'Telling me how to do my job are you? Fancy becoming the Way Keeper, do you?'

'No,' said Bordan. 'It was just a suggestion.'

Orsa grunted and shook his head.

'Duly noted, Forest Lord, duly noted,' said Orsa, turning his attention to Myrsa and giving his report. 'We've suffered increased attacks on the workers building the great road, and I've authorised new watch-houses to be built along the route it needs to take through the forest, but even they're proving vulnerable to sustained attack. One was burned to the ground by the forest beasts last week, and another would have fallen but for timely aid from the Berserker King's warriors.'

Throughout these reports of hard times, Myrsa had largely kept his own counsel, but now he turned to the last of his warriors, a youthful man encased in burnished white plate armour named Renweard. The demands of ruling a city in Sigmar's name had become too much for Myrsa to bear alongside his duties as Warrior Eternal, and though it had broken his heart to set aside the role that had defined him for two decades and more, he had bestowed his armour and title to a successor.

Young and courageous, Renweard was a perfect choice for the role. He had no vices as far as Redwane could tell, who *knew* how to spot a man's vices, and was as a devout an Ulrican as it was possible to find. Even Ar-Ulric himself, were he ever to return from the frozen wilderness, would surely approve.

'Well, Warrior Eternal,' asked Myrsa. 'What is happening beyond our walls?'

'It is true that more and more people are coming to Middenheim, my lord,' said Renweard with arch formality. 'And the Mountain Lord is correct that a great many are fleeing packs of the dead. As to this Torbrecan's followers, I think we shall be rid of them soon enough.'

'How so?' asked Myrsa.

'It seems they plan to march on Reikdorf soon.'

'Reikdorf?' said Redwane. 'Why?'

Renweard shrugged with a clatter of cream plate. 'It is hard to be certain, White Wolf, but it seems they believe that the great battle between life and death is to be settled there. When Torbrecan is eventually released, they plan to march on Sigmar's city in a great host.'

'Perhaps we should let them,' said Redwane, surprised to find he was only half joking.

THE DREAM WAS always the same, rank and malignant tree roots growing up from beneath the earth and spreading their poisonous taint to the far corners of the world. She knew, of course, what it signified and what was causing it, but no amount of prayers to Shallya could keep it at bay. High Priestess Alessa rose from her bed and poured some water into a mug from a copper ewer.

She drained the entire mug and rubbed her eyes, looking towards the curtained window at the far end of her room. It was still dark outside and the fire in the hearth had burned to low embers. Alessa rose and threw another log onto the fire, knowing there would be no more sleep tonight.

She wanted to wake someone, anyone, just to have another living person to talk to, but that was selfish, and she did not want fear of what was buried beneath their temple to spread among the novices. Ever since it had been brought here, she had feared to face it.

She remembered Sigmar and Wolfgart bringing her the damned crown of Morath, locked within an iron casket and sealed with holy words recited by every priest in Reikdorf. The shaft they had sunk beneath the temple to bury the crown was a hundred feet deep, lined with iron rods and filled with blessed earth. That artefact of evil had been removed from the world of men as far as any object could be.

Then why did she feel that the precautions they had taken were nowhere near enough?

'It feels the nearness of its maker,' she whispered, seeing her breath mist before her, despite the warmth growing in the hearth. She shivered and returned to the bed, gathering up her woollen blanket and wrapping it around her shoulders. Alessa clutched the dove pendant around her neck and whispered a prayer to Shallya.

She smiled at her own weakness. Shallya answered prayers of the needy, of those who could not help themselves. Alessa was no helpless victim, no unfortunate at the end of her tether. She was a high priestess, a servant of the goddess of healing and mercy, her instrument for good in this world. There were others more deserving than she, and Alessa gave thanks for what she had and all she had been allowed to do in her life.

She had served the people of Reikdorf for over twenty years, first as a novitiate tending to the small riverside shrine dedicated to the goddess, then later as a temple maiden, before finally becoming high priestess of the temple built by Sigmar ten years ago. It had been a fulfilling life, a worthy one, and she had blessed many children as they came screaming into the world, and eased the passage of those whose time in it was done. Alessa had healed the sick, tended the wounded and comforted the dying.

Alessa left the room and made her way through the cold corridors of the temple. Faint starlight gleamed through the windows as she made her way past the infirmary, where many of the sick of Reikdorf were treated, heading towards the chapel. She felt at peace there and, with the last traces of the nightmare lingering in her mind, she needed the solace just kneeling before the shrine to Shallya brought before facing her greatest fear.

Inside it was quiet, as she had expected it would be. A few low-burning candles guttered behind glass panels and white banners stitched with gold thread hung from the walls, each depicting Shallya in her many aspects; the maiden before the bubbling spring, the soaring dove, the bleeding heart and the benevolent mother of all.

She made her way between the long rows of benches toward the small shrine at the end of the nave. Set within a curved chancel, a marble statue of a beatific figure of a woman shawled in white knelt beside an injured warrior and healed his wounds. Though most warriors offered praise to Ulric, they all prayed to Shallya eventually.

Alessa knelt before the image of her deity, closing her eyes and placing her hands over her heart. She recited the healing litanies, listing the ten sacred virtues of selflessness, and felt her serenity return and the vision of the black tree roots burrowing into the world lose its potency.

'I will not fear you, for even death is part of the cycle of life,' she whispered. 'I will face you and I will be restored by resisting you.'

Alessa rose and moved around the statue, where a wooden table laid with a muslin cloth was set. Upon it was a softly glowing lantern, a washbowl and a collection of cleansing oils. She pulled the table to one side, revealing a heavy iron trapdoor set in the flagstones. She lifted a silver key from around her neck, and slipped it into a keyhole worked from the same blessed metal.

The lock clicked and she pulled the heavy trapdoor open, its bulk offset by a system of counterweights and pulleys designed by Govannon the smith. A cold gust blew up from the depths, but she paid it no mind as she took up the lantern and descended the spiral staircase that disappeared into the earth.

She followed the stairs until they opened out into a long corridor of black stone. Verses to ward off evil influences were inscribed on the walls, and just looking at them gave her the strength to follow the corridor to its end. A door fashioned from yew and rowan barred the way forward, but once again the silver key unlocked it.

Beyond the door was a diamond-shaped chamber, its wood-panelled walls aligned east to west to attract the influences of the sun and rubbed in essence of valerian and jasmine. Incense vials placed around the chamber filled it with the ripe scent of crops, verdant growth and burgeoning life. The floor was hard-packed earth from the fertile Reik estuary, and though nothing would grow down here away from the light, corn seeds were sown in its loamy richness as the fields above were planted.

It was cold, and Alessa shivered, knowing the chill had nothing to do with being below ground. She moved to the centre of the chamber and dropped to her knees, once again clasping her hands over her heart. With her eyes closed, she let her awareness of her physical surroundings fall away, allowing her spirit to fill the void in her senses.

Immediately, she could feel the crown's evil pulsing below her. Even contained within its iron casket and bound with wards and charms passed down through unremembered generations, its power was strong enough to bleed out. Alessa could feel its influence reaching out to her, promising eternal life, the return of her youth, and an existence free from fear of disease, disfigurement or infirmity.

'You cannot tempt me,' she said through gritted teeth. 'Everything you promise is a lie.'

Her mind filled with its blandishments, each more fanciful than the last. She saw herself renewed, her skin unblemished like the cool marble statue of Shallya. She could not deny the attraction of what the crown offered; yet one look into the eyes of this immortal vision of her eternal features betrayed the truth of it. Immortality was an affront to nature, an abominable state of existence where growth was impossible and stagnation the only outcome.

She banished the crown's promises, feeling its hold on her thoughts grow weaker as her will to resist it grew stronger. *This* was why she had come here, knowing that only by facing her fear of its temptations could she overcome them.

'Only those who feel fear can know true courage,' she whispered. 'And my faith was meaningless unless put to the test. I know now it is stronger than anything you can offer.'

Alessa felt the crown's fury, its icy touch retreating into the depths of its prison. She let out a shuddering breath, feeling as weak as a newborn, but renewed in her heart. She rose to her feet and left the chamber, locking the door behind her and mounting the steps to the temple with a lightness of spirit she had not felt in months.

As she locked the trapdoor once again, she felt a last spiteful stab of venom from the buried crown. A searing image burned itself into her mind, and she dropped the lantern as her limbs spasmed in fear.

She blinked, but there was no erasing the horror of the vision.

Sigmar Heldenhammer, riding through the gates of Reikdorf with the crown of the damned once again upon his brow.

THE GREAT LIBRARY was quiet, as it always was, but this quiet was more than just the absence of hushed voices and the rustle of parchment. It was a silence that told Eoforth he was alone in the building and always would be. That was ridiculous of course, but such was the emptiness he felt here that it was easy to believe no one would ever come here again.

He loved his Great Library, feeling more at home amongst its wealth of knowledge and the accomplishments of Man than he did anywhere else. It was a place of solace, where he could retreat from the world of violence and lose himself in a Brigundian treatise on mathematics, a colourful Ostogoth tale of family histories or the incredibly complex blood-feuds between the Udose clans. This was his refuge, yet tonight it felt like a tomb, a cold and empty place where no one ever came and no one ever would.

He blamed it on the stacks of books and piles of rolled up scrolls scattered around him, for who would choose to remain in a building with such evil reading material out in the open? For weeks, Eoforth had pored over every manuscript he could find that had some mention of Nagash, however tangential. Most of it was surely nonsense, but Sigmar had tasked him with unearthing everything that could be found on the Lord of Undeath, and Eoforth was not about to let him down.

A great many of the most useful tomes had come from

the dusty library of Morath, the necromancer of Brass Keep, though copies of translated manuscripts from the far south had come to Reikdorf's Great Library via the Empire's southern kings. Oral tales told by traders returning from the southern lands of searing deserts or from across the Worlds Edge Mountains had been painstakingly compiled by the library's scribes.

Lack of material was not the problem; sorting the embellishments and exaggerations from the truth was proving to be the hardest part of this task.

Trying to cross-reference and corroborate details was proving to be next to impossible, for no two manuscripts or tales agreed on any details of worth. Eoforth sat up straight as the small of his back flared in pain. His joints were aching and it felt like he had a desert's worth of sand trapped beneath his eyelids. He yawned and put his head in his hands.

People called him wise, as though that were enough to reach back across the gulfs of time to pluck the truth from the mass of conflicting information. He knew a great deal, it was true, more than most men, but in the face of all he needed to discover, his knowledge was a paltry thing indeed. Eoforth rubbed his eyes with the heels of his palms and stared at the manuscript before him once again.

Its edges were curled and blackened, as though it had been plucked from a fire, and the writing was an old form of Reikspiel, one that only a handful of the oldest men and women in the Empire could decipher. It was a depressing thought that he was one of those oldest men.

Endal mariners returning to Marburg from a mapping expedition to the far north over a century ago had discovered the manuscript aboard a smouldering galley drifting at the mouth of the Reik. No trace had been found of any ship that might have attacked the galley, nor were any of its crew found aboard.

It was a mystery that had never been solved, but the sailors had found a treasure trove of trinkets and tomes of unknown provenance aboard the galley, all of which they took back to their city and presented to King Alderbad, the great-grandfather of Count Aldred. Eoforth had travelled to Marburg many years ago to study these artefacts – golden effigies of jackal-headed monsters, strange, beetle-like creatures and elaborate death masks of gold and jade.

Many of the manuscripts Eoforth had studied made reference to ancient gods of similar aspect, naming them as forgotten kings of a lost land named Nehekhara. It was said that these kings had been laid to rest in fabulous tombs and mausoleum cities now lost to the desert sands. In many of the manuscripts, Nagash was blamed for the final doom of these kings in a single night, though how anyone, even Nagash, could have laid an entire civilisation low so swiftly was beyond Eoforth.

If such tales were to be believed, then Nagash had walked the earth for over two thousand years, a fantastical span of time that Eoforth had trouble in grasping. It seemed absurd, but then the ultimate goal of the necromancer was to cheat death and live forever, so perhaps it was not so unbelievable after all.

Some of what Eoforth read was plainly nonsense, tales of a beautiful queen of the dead who had become his consort and sired the race of blood drinkers, an alliance with a burrowing race of vermin creatures who infested the hidden corners of the world and, most incredible of all, the building of a vast obsidian pyramid somewhere in the southern mountains that prevented the necromancer from ever truly dying.

All the accounts agreed on one thing: Nagash was the

bane of life, a twisted and corrupt sorcerer whose existence had transcended his human origins to become something more monstrous and more evil than anything that had ever walked the face of the world. His powers were beyond imagining, his reach limitless and his armies legion.

Inextricably linked with the tale of Nagash was the tale of the crown he had forged and into which he had bound the essence of his damned soul. This, the ancient taletellers agreed, was the source of Nagash's greatest power and his greatest weakness. The manuscript from the burning galley spoke of an ancient warrior named Al-Khadizaar who slew the Lord of Undeath with a dreadful sword of fell power and cast his bones and crown into a great river.

Frustratingly, the manuscript said no more of the crown, but in a long-dead trader's recounting of his travels in the blasted lands south of the Black Mountains, Eoforth unearthed mention of a ruined ancient city that bore all the hallmarks of having been destroyed by a greenskin invasion. When Sigmar had told him of the battle against the necromancer of Brass Keep, he had spoken of a phantom city beneath the ice; a vision conjured by Morath to recreate the fallen glory of his lost city of Mourkain. Like the cities of Nehekhara, it too had been made great and then brought low by Nagash's crown.

A greenskin invasion had destroyed the city, but had they been drawn to destroy Mourkain by the crown's influence? Everywhere the crown appeared in history, great devastation quickly followed: terrible invasions, cataclysms of dreadful power or corruptions of once noble civilisations into barbarism. The crown was a talisman of woe, a bringer of destruction that brought only misery and death whenever it came to light.

And it was buried in the heart of Reikdorf.

A soft gust sighed past Eoforth, and he heard a dry, dusty chuckle that echoed from the blackness between the stone pillars. It drifted on the still air, and Eoforth knew in that moment he was not alone. Deathly eyes were turned upon him, mocking his feeble attempts to unlock the nature of a creature that had walked the haunted paths of the world from the earliest ages of Man. Cold chills travelled the length of his spine and Eoforth slammed the book shut, his breath misting before him as the light from the flickering candles dimmed and the shadows crept closer.

Gathering up his notes, Eoforth fled the library.

~< TEN >~

Creeping Death

A DOZEN RIDERS fled north, whipping their mounts in a frenzy of terror and desperation. Khaled al-Muntasir watched them go with a wry grin of amusement on his lips. A city of nearly eight thousand people, and twelve men were all that now lived. He watched from a high balcony of the Count's Palace, a grand tower decorated with finery from all across the Empire and a number of artefacts he recognised as belonging to civilisations from the other side of the world.

'You were a man of culture,' said Khaled al-Muntasir, lifting a delicately-wrought vase of pale white ceramic decorated with exquisite images picked out in blue ink. The artist had skilfully rendered a man and women drinking tea at a low table in a bamboo-framed home. The brushwork was flawless and the detailing incredible. In any land this piece would fetch a small fortune.

Khaled al-Muntasir tossed the vase from the balcony, watching as it tumbled down the cliff to smash to fragments on the way down. The vase's owner didn't bat an eyelid at his prized possession's destruction.

'Yes,' said Khaled al-Muntasir, moving back into the Great Hall, its walls painted with colourful frescoes depicting scenes of hunting and battle. 'You have some wonderful pieces here. This rug, for example, bears the handiwork of the dreamweavers of Ind, while this wall hanging is from the silk-worms of the Dragon Emperor is it not?'

The vampire stopped beneath a podium of oak, upon which was mounted a pair of giant ivory tusks. He stroked the monstrous fangs, marvelling at their size and contemplating the scale of the beast from which they had been torn. The vampire looked towards the warrior standing motionless in the centre of the audience chamber, a tall man in golden armour and a crown of the same metal upon his brow. His hair was white and flowed across his shoulders like a frozen waterfall.

'Ordinarily, I would say these belonged to a dragon, but I know of no such beasts in these lands any more. So tell me, Siggurd, what manner of creature once owned these?'

The warrior turned to face Khaled al-Muntasir, his face drained of life and his throat a ruined mess of torn sinews and muscle. Blood coated his chest and his eyes were now sunken, filled with a hideous red light. His mouth opened and closed, but no words came out, just a hiss of dead air from his opened throat.

'Ah, yes, of course...' said Khaled al-Muntasir. The vampire muttered a petty incantation of dark magic and the torn meat of Siggurd's throat began to close up, the necrotic flesh weaving the ghastly wound closed. 'Now, you were saying...?'

The count of the Brigundian tribe's mouth opened and a rasping death rattle emerged, a sound dragged from the abyss that carried such pleasing anguish that Khaled al-Muntasir couldn't resist a wide grin.

'Skaranorak...' hissed Siggurd. 'A dragon ogre...'

Khaled al-Muntasir's eyes widened, and he stroked the heavy tusks with his carefully clipped nails, a new-found respect in his deathly eyes.

'You killed this beast yourself?' he asked.

'No,' said Siggurd, his voice returning. 'Sigmar killed it.'

'Ah, yes, Sigmar,' said the vampire. 'I should have guessed.'

Siggurd walked out onto the balcony, a perch from where he had once surveyed the lands belonging to his tribe, lands that had once brought trade and wealth to his city, but were now overtaken by darkness and fear. Swollen by the Menogoth dead, the army of Nagash had taken Siggurdheim in a matter of days, its rugged peak climbed by hundreds of ghoulish infiltrators as thousands of dead warriors marched along its steep winding roads to batter their way in through the heavy gateway. The city had fallen in a night that still held sway, the Great Hall's many windows admitting no light, only the darkness of eternal night.

'Are you not going to stop them?' asked Siggurd, his flesh finally losing its vigour and warmth as the Blood Kiss destroyed the last of his humanity and completed his journey to become an immortal killer of the living.

'Why would I care to do that?' said a voice laden with thousands of years of blood and slaughter. Like tombstones crumbling, it was the sound of toppled civilisations, cultures destroyed and entire realms drained of life.

Siggurd and Khaled al-Muntasir bowed as Nagash entered the Great Hall. The darkness beyond the windows was eclipsed by the bleak presence of the arch necromancer, a thick miasma of dark energy that filled his servants with macabre vigour. The coiled snake staff crackled with simmering power, and his metallic fingers dripped beads of dark magic to the stone floor of the hall.

The hulking violence that was Krell marched at Nagash's right hand, his black axe strapped across his armoured back. The fallen warrior of the Dark Gods had run rampant through the city, killing with a frenzy that would no doubt have pleased his former master. To Nagash's left was the wolfish figure of Count Markus, his lean frame now invigorated with slaughter. His blade and chin were covered in blood; his eyes alight with the thrill of feeding on so many fearful hearts.

'They will carry word of what has happened here,' said Siggurd, staring hungrily at the blood on Markus's blade. 'It will give them time to prepare for your attack.'

'It matters not,' said Nagash. 'Already my vassal forces spread fear to the furthest reaches of this land. Man is a beast and it is good that fear fills him.'

'And that fear will drain men's hearts of courage,' said Khaled al-Muntasir, returning to the balcony. 'But more than that, it tastes so sweet…'

Khaled al-Muntasir watched as the riders fleeing Siggurdheim's destruction disappeared over the horizon, their life lights as bright as stars. 'Where will they go?' he asked.

'North to Asoborn lands,' answered Siggurd, licking his lips and pacing the hall like a restless stallion. 'They will flee to Queen Freya in Three Hills. She lives for war and will muster her warriors as soon as she learns what has happened here.'

'Then that is where you will go, Khaled al-Muntasir,' said Nagash. 'Hunt down this queen and destroy her.'

Khaled al-Muntasir bowed and dropped into the throne that had once belonged to the Brigundian count.

'I will leave her lands as desolate as Bel Aliad itself.'

'What of the Merogens?' asked Siggurd, his hands clawed into fists. 'Is Henroth dead?'

'Henroth's people huddle around flickering candles within their castles of stone, surrounded by the dead. They will be no threat,' said Nagash as Markus walked over to Siggurd and took hold of his chin.

The former count of the Menogoths turned to Khaled al-Muntasir. 'The birth-hunger is upon him,' he said.

'It is,' agreed the vampire.

'He will need to feed soon or else go mad.'

'There are living yet within this city's walls,' said Khaled al-Muntasir, languidly twirling a finger through the air, as though stirring its flavours. 'Young Siggurd must learn to hunt on his own, just as you did.'

Siggurd took Markus's hand from his chin, his eyes hostile, and they circled like two virile males in a wolf pack. Khaled al-Muntasir smirked at such posturing in newly-ascended blood drinkers.

'Give a mortal a taste of true power and it all but overwhelms them,' said Nagash.

'If either survive to learn how to use that power they will be formidable killers,' said Khaled al-Muntasir.

'The fate of blood drinkers interests me not at all,' hissed Nagash ducking below the balcony's archway and casting his immortal gaze over the landscape. The darkness of his armour and tattered cloak swirled around him like sable light, the faint glow from within his bones like the last sunset of the world. 'Only the crown matters.'

'Then why am I to ride north?' asked Khaled al-Muntasir. 'Surely we should march straight to Reikdorf.'

Krell took a thunderous step towards him, his axe unsheathed in a heartbeat and the light in his skull shining with the threat of furious violence.

'You question my purpose?' said Nagash.

'No, my master,' said Khaled al-Muntasir, smoothly swinging his legs from the arms of the throne and giving an elaborate bow. 'I am your humble servant in all things.'

Nagash's eyes bored into him, and Khaled al-Muntasir instantly regretted his flippant tone. He felt himself touched by a fraction of the necromancer's power, a dreadful extinction that held everything that lived or once drew air into its lungs with contempt. Even the living dead were not immune to the necromancer's touch. His enormous reservoirs of power could snuff out unlife as easily as a mortal blew out a candle.

Khaled al-Muntasir had passed the point where he feared much of anything, but the one fate that still struck horror through his undying flesh was oblivion. To live forever, to hunt the living and to indulge his every sense and vice was the sum total of his desire, and the thought of that ended filled him with dread.

Nagash saw his acquiescence and the lambent glow in his eye sockets shimmered at his vassal's fear. The Lord of Undeath turned to the darkened landscape beyond Siggurdheim.

'Spread the terror of death before you and drive those you do not kill toward my crown,' hissed Nagash. 'Lay waste these petty kingdoms and scour the seed of mortals from this land.'

'It shall be my pleasure,' Khaled al-Muntasir assured Nagash.

A LOW BELL tolled, echoing across the Old Town harbour, and Sergeant Alwin of the Jutonsryk Lancers paused to watch the beacon fire atop the Tower of Tides light up, signalling the end of another day.

'Regular as always,' he said to himself. 'Good to know that some things never change.'

He moved on, walking with an unhurried gait, his sword sheathed at his side and his blue cloak flitting behind him in the choppy evening wind blowing off the seafront. It was a quiet night, which made a nice change, the drunks keeping a low profile instead of roistering in the streets or brawling in the taprooms.

The docks were quiet, just the slap of water against the quay, the creak of ships' timbers and the sigh of wind through the rigging and flags. His lancers followed behind him, four men of proven character, all of whom he could rely on in a tight spot. Not that he expected any tight spots tonight; the day had been without incident, as though the thousands of sailors, tradesmen and inhabitants of the city had been reluctant to remain outdoors for any length of time. He'd thought it odd, but anything that helped keep the peace in Jutonsryk was a boon as far as Alwin was concerned.

He paused by the westernmost spur of the docks, putting his foot up on one of the iron mooring rungs set in the quay. The *Ormen Lange*, an Udose vessel familiar to the docks of Jutonsryk, was moored here, and he waved up to the bearded clansman at ship's watch in the forecastle.

'All's bonny,' called the man. 'None reddin the fire the night, eh?'

'Indeed,' agreed Alwin, though he had no idea what the clansman had just said.

He moved on, looking up at the Namathir to Count Marius's castle, its many windows glowing with colour and light. The lord of Jutonsryk was a hard man to like, but Marius knew how to run a busy port, understanding that commerce and trade would only flow into a city if its streets could be made safe. Merchants would not come to a city where they feared for their life and cargo. Which wasn't to say the city was a utopian society where crime didn't happen, far from it, but those who flouted the law were punished by Marius's only penalty – death. Justice in Jutonsryk was harsh, uncompromising and final. Which made for a city where all but the most foolish drunks or desperate footpads observed the law.

Alwin followed the line of the docks as he and his lancers made his way towards Taal's Fire, the most southerly beacon brazier of the docks. It burned with blue fire, a shimmering lodestone for incoming ships. Further north, around the curve of the bay, Ulric's Fire wavered with a green light. Differing herbs altered the colour of the flames, and it was thanks to these beacons, together with the one atop the Tower of Tides, that not a single vessel had been lost while navigating the treacherous channels around the Reik estuary.

As Alwin looked north, the light from Ulric's Fire was momentarily obscured, as though a shimmering curtain had been drawn in front of it. He frowned and squinted through the darkness as it flickered and disappeared.

'Did you see that?' he said, turning towards his warriors.

They nodded and Alwin looked south towards Taal's Fire. It too was gone.

'Damn me,' hissed Alwin. 'I don't like that, no I do not.'

He looked back at the Tower of Tides, reassured to see that its beacon light was still lit. Low clouds clung to the distant tower, tendrils of mist that seemed not to move with the wind. Alwin looked out to sea, and his mouth fell open at the sight of a rolling grey fog coming in from the darkness. Living by the ocean, with a coastline of marshland to the south, a man got used to mists, but this was something more. It hugged the water, undulating over its black surface like a scum of sea filth as it crept towards the city.

The fog was thick and reeked worse than a bloated

corpse dragged from the water. It drifted over the hundreds of berthed ships, slinking and creeping over their timbers with an unclean touch. It slithered up the quayside, oozing onto the docks with dreadful purpose, and Alwin knew he'd never seen anything quite so unpleasant.

'It's only mist, damn it,' he chided himself, irritated that something so banal had him spooked. Even as he told himself it was only weather, he couldn't shake the feeling that it portended something far worse. No sooner had he formed the thought than he heard the dolorous peal of a brass ship's bell, a talisman to guide a vessel through just such a fog, yet this familiar sound gave him no comfort.

The sound was dead, without the natural echo or earthly touch of an instrument forged by man. Another bell answered it, then another. Soon the quayside was echoing to the ringing of dead bells, hundreds of flat peals that slid through the darkened streets like midnight assassins. Sailors and traders were emerging from the taverns, drawn by the deathly echoes and an instinctual understanding that these sounds were just *wrong* in every way it was possible to be.

Alwin wanted to tell these people to run, to flee whatever doom was soon to overtake the city, but he couldn't think of what to tell them that wouldn't sound ridiculous. He looked back out to sea, searching for the source of the hollow bells, now hearing the sluggish passage of water over rotten timbers. Lights began to appear in the fog, drifting corpse lights that rose and fell with the tide, a hundred or more of them.

They shone like a host of candles for the departed, poisonously evil flares that bridged the gap between the living and the dead. Or guided the dead *to* the living...

'Reinen, get back to the barrack house,' ordered Alwin.

'Gather everyone you can find and have them arm themselves before getting down to the quayside.'

'Sir? What's going on?'

'Don't argue with me, just do it!'

Reinen nodded and sped off, grateful to be freed from remaining at the water's edge. Moments later, Alwin heard a clatter of armour behind him as his lancers fled the quay, leaving him alone on the dockside. Though he knew hundreds of people were nearby, he could see none of them as the fog thickened around him.

Isolated in his mist-wreathed world, he saw nothing but the approaching lights and heard nothing beyond the sullen bells, his thudding heartbeat, the slurp of water and the rattle of dusty bones, chains and rusted iron.

A shape emerged from the fog; a black-hulled vessel wreathed in a spectral light and which could surely never have remained above the waves such was the rotten, holed nature of its hull. Its timbers were swollen and decayed, and whole swathes of its side were missing. Stagnant water poured *from* it as though recently raised from the deeps. The fog lifted momentarily, and Alwin saw hundreds of these ships of the damned surging into Jutonsryk harbour, each with tattered crimson sails that hung lank and limp, stirred by no wind and made fast without ropes or crew.

Captain Raul claimed he had seen two hundred vessels of the dead, and Alwin now knew the southern captain's estimate of numbers had been conservative. The black ships moved against the wind, relentless and inexorable as they drifted over the sea to the quay. Black things moved through the sky, horrors thankfully concealed in the thick fog, swooping over the city with murder in mind. Chittering flocks of bats billowed in their wake and a distant screech of something monstrous echoed through the fog-bound city.

Muffled by the fog, Alwin heard cries of alarm from the moored ships. Alarm bells began ringing, on the ships and throughout the city, but Alwin knew it was too late for any warning to save Jutonsryk. He heard a sickening crash of timbers and looked back over his shoulder to see the *Ormen Lange* cloven in two by an eastern war galley built in the style of a hundred years ago. The galley slammed into the quayside with a thunderous crash of splitting timbers, and Alwin had his first look at the damned crew aboard this abominable vessel.

All along the gunwale, dreadful figures with piercing green lights for eyes stared at him with hungry fervour. Pale corpses, rotted skeletons in corroded armour and hunched figures with water streaming from their wounds clutched spears, axes and short blades in their dead hands.

They streamed onto the land, a host of dead sailors come for revenge on the world of the living. Alwin heard the first screams from further along the quay. The sound broke through the paralysing terror that held his limbs fast, and he drew his sword, determined to fight these seaborne invaders with whatever courage he could muster.

He ran back to the *Ormen Lange*, seeing the clansman he had spoken to earlier crawling from the wreckage of his ship. Bloated, grey-skinned dead men hacked at him with sharp cutlasses. As soon as they saw Alwin, they abandoned their victim and lurched towards him with a dreadful hunger in their sunken, dead eyes.

Alwin wanted to run, to live, but he was a Jutone warrior, and he brought his sword up.

'Come on then, you dead bastards!' he shouted, hurling himself at the damned.

His first blow clove a rotten corpse in two. Its flesh was soft and yielding, and his blade easily cut through its

sodden meat. Alwin slashed the neck of another
drowned man, and a froth of stagnant water bubbled
from the wound. A grinning skeleton came at him and
he slammed his blade through its skull, dropping it in a
clatter of bone. The dead pressed in, dying by the dozen,
but they poured in unending numbers from the hundreds of ships.

He buried his sword in the guts of another waterlogged
corpse, twisting the handle to relieve the suction of wet
flesh on the blade. A corpse fastened its teeth on his arm
and bit through the meat there. Alwin cried out and
punched the dead thing in the face. Its jellied eye
squirted ooze, momentarily blinding him, but momentarily was all the opening the undead needed.

Clawed hands fastened on his throat and tearing limbs
pinned his arms to his side, as they bore him to the
ground. Sharpened teeth gnawed at his flesh and Alwin's
sword was torn from his grip. He struggled furiously, but
there were too many and the pain was too great. He
screamed as they devoured him, biting chunks from his
legs and stomach like warriors with hunks of roast boar
at a victory feast. Blood burst from his mouth, and the
stink of it drove his killers to fresh heights of hunger.

Alwin's last sight was the beacon fire atop the Tower of
Tides as it died, plunging the world into a darkness
which it could never survive.

THE MUSTER FIELDS of Three Hills were thick with horses
and the clamour of warriors. Maedbh wound a careful
path through the thousands of people gathered here,
nodding to those she knew and picking out the differing
tattoos of various tribal sword bands. Even within the
Asoborns there were fiercely clannish groupings, and
though they were united by Queen Freya's call to arms,
each swaggered with something to prove.

At the centre of the maelstrom, Freya directed her warriors with fiery sweeps of her spear and shouted pronouncements. Her twin boys were at her side, their faces downcast and sullen. Maedbh could guess the reason why, now understanding a measure of Wolfgart's reluctance to see Ulrike trained in the arts of war.

Five hundred chariots were lined up along the edge of the field or rolled in to take up position by the rutted track that led towards the river. Two acres of forest had been felled to corral the horses and a neverending train of wagons was assembling on the far side of the hills to carry their fodder. Sword bands in their hundreds milled around the field, warriors from all across Asoborn lands greeting one another like long lost friends. Many of these warriors would not have seen each other for years, and Maedbh lamented that it took times of such darkness to bring them together.

Ulrike walked beside her, holding tightly to her hand. Every night since the attack of the wolves, she had woken in the darkness, screaming and weeping uncontrollably. Maedbh had held her tight, hating that her little girl was suffering like this. She remembered her own first blood, a desperate chariot ride before a mob of greenskins raiding the eastern lands of the Asoborns. Freya's mother, Queen Sigrid, had broken the enemy horde, but Maedbh never forgot the exhilarating terror of riding close enough to the enemy that she could smell their rank, rotten-meat breath and feel the bite of their axes on her chariot.

'Is the queen going to fight the wolves?' asked Ulrike.

'Yes, my dear,' said Maedbh. 'That's exactly what she's going to do. All these men and women are going to ride south and hunt them down. They're going to kill every one of them so they never hurt anyone ever again. Do you understand me? The queen doesn't tolerate bad wolves in her lands.'

'Good,' said Ulrike. 'I hope they kill them all. I hate wolves.'

'Those weren't real wolves,' said Maedbh, stopping and coming down to Ulrike's level. She looked her daughter in the eye and said, 'Real wolves are servants of Ulric, the god you were named for, so don't hate them. Those things that attacked us were once noble wolves, but an evil man made them into monsters with his dark magic.'

Ulrike nodded, though Maedbh saw she was yet to be convinced. Maedbh led her through the sword muster, passing mail-clad fighters of the east, bare-chested horse archers of the hill folk, colourfully tattooed women of the Myrmidian sects and burly horsemen from the northern woodlands with their long iron-tipped lances. Everywhere she heard proud boasts of the monsters the warriors would kill, tall tales of martial prowess and bravado, but it rang hollow to Maedbh's ears.

Mixed in with the Asoborns were perhaps two hundred Brigundians and a hundred Menogoth warriors; all that had survived the invasion of the dead. Hundreds of refugees from both tribes were sheltered in Three Hills, but these men, with their grief-etched faces and hollow eyes, sought only vengeance. Maedbh didn't blame them; their lands had been ravaged, their homes destroyed and their families murdered. With nothing left to lose, they were only too glad to join the Asoborn war muster.

Maedbh knew how she would feel if Three Hills suffered as their lands had suffered, and that thought gave her stride fresh purpose as she marched through the uprooted warriors towards the Asoborn queen.

Freya stood beside her chariot, a gold and bronze creation of deadly power. Its sides were reinforced with iron cords and layered wood against the grain. Golden fire was inlaid in finely crafted carvings of flaming wheels and blazing comets. A dozen of the Queen's Eagles surrounded her, mounted on tall, wide-chested geldings, their golden-winged helms shining like sunlight on silver. Sigulf and Fridleifr harnessed two beasts Maedbh recognised as having once belonged to Wolfgart's herds to the chariot, though it was clear the boys were less than happy with their mother.

Freya herself was clad in her finest armour of bronze and iron, and, as always, the queen was attired to impress as much as protect. Bronze mail hung in a weave from her shoulders, and the plates protecting her chest and belly were moulded to the form of the muscles beneath. Iron greaves and vambrace were strapped to her shins and forearms, leaving the curved sway of her hips and thighs bare. A scarlet cloak was pinned to her shoulders with silver brooches in the form of snarling wolves.

'Maedbh!' cried the queen as she saw her approach. 'A fine gathering is it not?'

'Yes, my queen, very fine,' said Maedbh, looking around the muster field. 'How many answered the call to arms?'

'All of them it seems,' laughed Freya. 'Near five hundred chariots, two thousand warriors on foot and a half century of horsemen. A host to chase the dead back to their tombs, eh?'

'A mighty army indeed,' answered Maedbh. 'Our lands must be empty of warriors.'

The queen nodded, her face darkening at Maedbh's insinuation. 'I know you think me rash to ride off like this, and, yes, this muster will leave us vulnerable for a while. But brother Siggurd's lands are aflame and what manner of queen would I be if I left his murder unavenged? You heard what Sigmar's herald said, the dead are rising everywhere and the Menogoths are already gone. Now Siggurd's city is taken and our southernmost scouts say there's an army moving on Three Hills. No one invades my lands, Maedbh, no one.'

'I understand, my queen,' said Maedbh. 'But I have faced this enemy, and it is not cowed by threats, boasts or reputations. It is a foe that lives to kill and create more of its kind.'

'You can still come, Maedbh. I need you with me,' said Freya, indicating her chariot. 'I can find another rider when battle is joined, but no one has your skill with a chariot. No one has your fire and daring.'

Maedbh glanced down at Ulrike, pulled by the desire to ride with her queen and the need to protect her daughter. She had crewed Freya's chariot ever since the queen had taken the throne, and the idea that she would go into battle without Maedbh rankled. Yet one look at her daughter's need told her she could not ride with this army. In that moment she understood the demands on Wolfgart, but to Maedbh, the choice was clear. She could not leave Ulrike.

'Thank you, my queen,' said Maedbh, 'but I cannot. I have Ulrike to think of.'

The queen shrugged and said, 'Your child is blooded now, she should ride with us too.'

Anger touched Maedbh. 'As Sigulf and Fridleifr do?'

The queen's face darkened and she climbed aboard her chariot.

'You know why they do not march with me,' hissed Freya, mercurial as ever. 'If you will not ride with me, then I charge you to protect them. Keep my boys safe, Maedbh, promise me this and I might forget your insolence.'

'I will watch over them as though they were my own,' promised Maedbh.

Freya smiled, her earlier anger forgotten.

'I know you will,' said the queen. 'I will leave a sword

band of my Eagles too, but it is a great honour I do you, Maedbh.'

'I understand, my queen,' said Maedbh, bowing as Freya took her sons in a crushing embrace. The queen hugged them to her breast, whispering something to each of them in turn and pushing them towards Maedbh. They stood with Ulrike, hurt that they were not riding to war with their mother and resentful that they were under the protection of another.

Freya took up a spear from her chariot and raised its bronze blade high. At her signal, the Asoborns let loose a whooping war shout, which was taken up by every warrior gathered in the muster field. The queen of the Asoborns cracked the reins and her chariot rumbled away, leading her army towards the route south.

Maedbh watched her go, her heart heavy at the sight of so many warriors going into battle without her, yet secretly relieved she wouldn't have to leave her daughter. She looked at the three children she was now beholden to protect, and the maternal urge flowed through her entire body.

She would die before she allowed any harm to come to these youngsters.

'Are you our guardian now?' asked Sigulf.

'Yes,' said Maedbh. 'I am.'

⫷ ELEVEN ⫸

Unwelcome Guests

THE VIEW FROM the top of the Raven Hall was spectacular, and Princess Marika never tired of looking out over Endal lands. A relentless grey twilight gripped the day, as it had done for the last few weeks, but on a clear day it was possible to see all the way to the Great Road and the marshes beyond. She suppressed an involuntary shiver at the thought of the marshes, recalling an unhappier time when Aldred had almost sacrificed her to the mist daemons to save their ailing kingdom.

Marika and her brother had publicly made their peace, though she could never quite forget the nearness of her death. As count of Marburg, Aldred had done what he thought best to lift the curse from his people, his good intentions twisted by Idris Gwylt, a manipulative priest of an ancient faith now outlawed in the Empire. That didn't make it any easier for her to forgive.

Gwylt was dead now, executed in the manner of the Thrice Death, but Marika still woke with the stink of the daemon queen in her nostrils more nights than not.

The reek of the swamp took her back to that dark time, but she was a princess of the Endals and destined for great things. As a child, a soothsayer had told her that she would one day bear the first king of a great city of union, a place of wealth and prosperity that would one day stand taller than all others. It was a child's fantasy, yet one that made her smile on a day like this, when even a child's dream was a welcome relief from grim reality.

'So many of them,' said Eloise, her lady in waiting, her hands clasped before her heart in an unconscious supplication to Shallya. 'Those poor people.'

Marika shook her head, thinking there were no more than two thousand people trudging along the coast road towards Marburg.

'So many? No, it should be a lot more,' she said. 'Jutonsryk was a mighty city. This is less than a third of its population.'

'Where are the rest of them?' asked Eloise, and Marika rolled her eyes. Servants could be wilfully dense sometimes.

'They're dead,' said Marika, turning and making her way towards her brother's chambers.

SHE FOUND ALDRED with Laredus in the throne room of the Raven Hall, donning his armour in preparation for meeting his fellow count. Laredus helped buckle Aldred's bronze breastplate, its front moulded to replicate abdominal muscles Marika knew were nowhere near as sculpted as the armour would suggest. Aldred pulled his sword belt around his waist, shifting Ulfshard's hilt to be within easy reach.

Twin shafts of weak sunlight shone through the eyes of the carved raven's head that surmounted the top of the tower, and a warm fire burned in the hearth, filling the glossy-walled chamber with glistening reflections. It was a cold room, one that had seen its share of bad decisions in its time. She had long since vowed to see that no more were made here.

Her brother wore a long dark cloak of feathers, and as she watched Laredus buckle on the last portions of Aldred's armour, Marika saw an all too familiar melancholy settle upon Aldred. Laredus lifted a tall, black-winged helm from the armour stand behind the count's ebony throne, where the majestic Raven Banner was seated in a socket cut into the backrest.

Marika took her brother's hands and looked into his sad features. The years had been difficult for him. The death of their father at Black Fire cast a long shadow, and when their brother Egil died of the mist daemons' plague, a black outlook had settled upon Aldred like an indelible stain on his soul.

'You should hurry,' said Marika, adjusting his cloak. 'He'll be at the gates soon.'

'They're here?' asked Aldred without looking up at her. 'They've moved fast.'

'So would you with the dead nipping at your heels,' she said.

'I suppose,' he answered as Laredus handed him his helmet. Aldred tucked it in the crook of his arm and said, 'How do I look?'

'Grand,' replied Laredus. The captain of the Raven Helms was a warrior born, a man who had fought all manner of enemies in his service to the royal bloodline of the Endals. 'You do your fellow count honour to meet him warrior to warrior.'

'He's damned lucky I'm meeting him at all,' said Aldred. 'The man's insufferable. First he refuses to stand with us at Black Fire, and then we have to lay siege to his city to earn his Sword Oath. Now he's a hero of the

Empire? I've a damn good mind to shut the gates on him and his bloody people.'

'Don't be foolish,' said Marika, moving in close and adjusting his sword belt. 'What kind of message does that send? You will be gracious and welcoming.'

'His people drove us from our homes,' said Aldred.

'Thirty years ago, after the Teutogens drove them from theirs,' pointed out Marika.

'Semantics.'

'History.'

'History,' he grunted, 'Is written by those who now live in lands they took by force.'

'No, it's written by scribes cleverer than you and I,' she said. 'Now come on, you don't want to keep Marius waiting.'

Aldred eyed her suspiciously. 'If I didn't know better I'd swear you were in a hurry to meet this mercenary.'

Marika smiled. 'Marius may be a mercenary, but he is a count of the Empire. You should remember that.'

'Like you'll let me forget,' he muttered.

THE GATES OF Marburg swung open and a group of blue-cloaked horsemen rode through on tired mounts. Most were warriors, their armour torn and mud-stained, though one was a young man who was clearly no horseman. A scribe perhaps? Their mounts were lathered and winded, and Marika saw they were near the end of their endurance. Only a fool would ride their mount to such extremes, but what other choice was there when death was the only other fate?

The cobbled courtyard was lined with spearmen in the blacks and browns of the Endals, and a lone piper filled the air with a skirling lament. The lancers looked uneasy, as well they might, for the Endals and Jutones had long been enemies. The coming of the Empire had made them allies, but no amount of Sword Oaths could erase the memory of centuries of bitter fighting.

Count Marius rode at the head of his lancers, incongruous amongst their raggedness by looking as though he had just stepped from his dressing room in search of a grand feast. His long blond hair was kept from his classically handsome features by a silver band, and his blue eyes regarded the warriors lining the courtyard with amused disdain. Where his warriors were dirty and weary, his clothes were immaculate and tailored to make the most of his lean physique. Marika had met Marius briefly atop the Fauschlag Rock the previous year, and had been dazzled by his quick wit, easy smile and roguish charm. Though she bore as much ancestral antipathy towards the Jutones as any Endal, she had found herself warming to him and the cosmopolitan description of his coastal city.

That city was now gone, scoured of all life by an invading fleet of the dead, and all that remained was a decaying charnel house. Or so the fastest refugees had told it. Looking at the bedraggled column of frightened people travelling in the wake of Marius, she was inclined to believe that description.

Marius rode toward Aldred and dismounted. The Raven Helms tensed, though there was surely no threat here. In a gesture of uncharacteristic humility, the dispossessed count of the Jutones dropped to one knee and bowed his head.

'Count Aldred of Marburg,' said Marius. 'I am here to ask for your help, though Ulric knows, you've reason enough to turn me away.'

'Aye, that I do, Jutone,' said Aldred, his tone icy as he drew Ulfshard. The fey-forged blade shone with a sapphire light in the wan afternoon sun, and Marika gasped as her brother stepped towards Marius. 'It's thanks to your tribe that we live on the edge of a marsh, afflicted by disease and cut off from our ancient lands. The spirits of my ancestors cry out for vengeance, so give me one good reason I shouldn't kill you right now.'

Marika was horrified at her brother's reaction, but to his credit, Marius took Aldred's anger in his stride. He nodded, as though he'd been expecting such an outburst.

'Our tribes have never been friends, it's true,' said Marius, 'but I ask you to look past our shared enmity and give my people shelter. They have lost everything and have walked many miles to escape death. There is nothing left of Jutonsryk, the corpse army destroyed it all. Thousands of the living dead came in from the sea and killed most of my subjects. Fires burned out of control through the city and I had no choice but to lead the survivors from its burning gates. My castle is ruined and my walls toppled. Only the Namathir remains, and the dead now haunt its tunnels and catacombs. Deny *me* a place within your walls if you must, but do not punish those who have not earned your ire.'

The count of the Jutones rose to his feet and Marika saw the anguish in his eyes, a genuine sorrow that she had never expected to see in him. Aldred still held the softly glowing blade of Ulfshard out before him, unwavering in his hatred. His anger had blinded him to what he was doing, and Marika decided to take matters into her own hands.

'Marika! What are you doing?' hissed Aldred as she walked towards Marius

'What *you* should be doing, brother,' she said, keeping her gaze fixed on the Jutone count.

She extended her hands, and Marius took them, bending to kiss her palms. His lips were soft and he smiled at her as he stood straight.

'You are a magnificent woman, my lady,' he said. 'As radiant as the sun.'

'I know,' she replied.

Aldred stormed over to her side, but before he could speak she rounded upon him.

'Do not say a word, Aldred,' she warned him. 'I am the daughter of Marbad, and this is my city as much as yours. And you owe me, remember?'

'You're never going to let me forget that, are you?'

'Is there any reason I should?' she hissed.

'But he's Jutone!' protested Aldred.

'No, he is a man of the Empire,' said Marika. 'As are you. Would you be known as a murderer or a man of mercy? A man of compassion and forgiveness or one who left thousands of innocents to die?'

'Damn you, Marika,' said Aldred, though there was relief in his tone. 'You are the better angel of my nature. I sometimes think it would be better if you ruled Marburg.'

Aldred took a deep breath and sheathed his sword. He removed his helmet and met Marius's gaze, his murderous anger dissipated, yet his hostility intact. It would take more than her simple, if heartfelt, words to quench his long-burning hatred of the Jutones.

He extended his hand to Marius and said, 'You and your people are welcome in Marburg, Count Marius. In the face of our enemies, we are one nation. Your enemies are my enemies.'

Marika saw Marius was genuinely surprised and he nodded, accepting the truth of Aldred's words in his heart.

'Thank you, brother,' he said. 'A small beginning, but a beginning nonetheless.'

Aldred said, 'Laredus will see that your people are given shelter and food.'

'You have my thanks, and the thanks of my people,' said Marius.

Aldred nodded stiffly and turned away, marching towards the gatehouse that led into the city of Marburg. A detachment of Raven Helms went with him, leaving Laredus and Marika with Count Marius.

The Jutone count favoured her with a grateful smile.

'You are an exceptional woman, Princess Marika,' he said.

'In all kinds of ways,' she replied with a smile.

SIGMAR STARED INTO the fire, more weary than he could ever remember. His horse was hobbled with the rest of the mounts, and three hundred Unberogen swordsmen huddled around their fires with their weapons within easy reach. They kept tired eyes averted from the flames, looking out into the darkness for their foes, but hoping not to see them. The night offered no respite from the armies of the dead, for they marched with hellish vigour and had no need to sleep, eat or rest.

Count Krugar sat across the fire, drinking from a battered leather canteen. The Taleuten count had always been a powerful figure of a man, broad of shoulder and square of jaw, but these last weeks had strained even his formidable constitution. His left arm was in a sling, and his chest was bandaged from where a rusted spear had punctured his silver hauberk. Utensjarl was laid across his thighs, its scabbard torn and dented, yet the blade within as sharp and lethal as ever.

Since the battle at Ostengard, the combined force of Taleutens, Cherusens and Unberogen had destroyed five more such hordes, yet it was an unending war. Each battle cost lives, but no matter how many of the dead they felled, more could always be brought back to hunt the living.

This camp was within a cratered basin on the edge of the Howling Hills, which was Cherusen land, though the Unberogens were camped with two hundred riders of Krugar's Red Scythes. Count Aloysis had led his warriors north to the Old Forest Road, where barrows clustered like blisters on the eastern foothills of the Middle Mountains had disgorged thousands of skeletal warriors to ravage the countryside. Dozens of villages had been destroyed, their victims dragged from death to serve in Nagash's army.

'You're sure you won't come with me to Taalahim?' asked Krugar.

'I cannot,' said Sigmar. 'But I appreciate the offer.'

'My city is closer than Reikdorf,' persisted Krugar. 'It will be safer.'

'If the situation were reversed, would you ride to somewhere safer instead of your own homeland?' said Sigmar.

'No,' admitted Krugar, 'but I'm not the Emperor.'

'Which makes it even more pressing that I return to Reikdorf.'

'Well, don't say I didn't try to save your life,' said Krugar, passing the canteen over to Sigmar.

'I'll be sure it's remembered,' said Sigmar, taking a drink, and not surprised to taste the fiery bite of harsh Taleuten corn spirit.

'Ulric's beard,' said Sigmar, wiping his mouth with the back of his hand. 'It's a wonder you Taleutens are able to stay on the back of your horses drinking this stuff.'

'Makes it easier to stay on if you're a little looser in the saddle,' said Krugar, taking the canteen back with a smile. 'Why do you think our horsemen invented stirrups?'

They lapsed into a companionable silence, neither man wishing to break this moment of peace amid so dark a time. Count Krugar was preparing to ride to Taalahim and rally his people to defend their tribal heartland. Over the weeks of fighting, the army of the dead's grand stratagem was becoming clear: isolate smaller villages in a black noose of corpses and choke them. No village could hold on its own, but gathered together in greater numbers the people of the Empire might be able to resist this terrible threat.

'Any word from across the land?' asked Krugar.

Sigmar shook his head. 'Little, my friend. I have to assume the southern kings are under attack too. With Markus gone, Henroth and Siggurd are sure to be next to face Nagash's wrath.'

'If they haven't already,' pointed out Krugar. 'What about the west? Marius and Aldred?'

'No,' said Sigmar. 'And nothing from the north either. The dead are cutting us off from one another and denying us our greatest strength.'

'And what's that?'

'Our unity,' said Sigmar. 'The strength that comes from knowing we are one people who can count on our fellow men to honour their oaths of brotherhood. Nagash knows this; it's why he's forcing us to fight like this, as divided as we were before I founded the Empire. He's drawing our forces into battle all across the Empire, trying to pick us off one by one and keeping us from gathering our strength.'

'Then you definitely need to get back to Reikdorf,' said Krugar, setting down the canteen and drawing Utensjarl from its sheath. The blade shone like a sliver of gold in the firelight. 'I swore on this blade that I would fight and die for the Empire, and I stand by that.'

'Which is another reason for me to go home, for I'll have no one dying needlessly. I'm the Emperor and I don't know what's happening in my own lands. If Nagash is half as cunning as the old legends make out, he won't be attacking from just one direction, he'll be pressing hard on all sides. We've done good work here, but it's time for me to go.'

'It'll be a dangerous journey,' said Krugar. 'Take a hundred of my Red Scythes with you.'

'Thank you, my friend, but that's not necessary,' said Sigmar.

'Nonsense, they know this terrain better than anyone, better than the Cherusens even. They've raided these lands more than once over the years.'

'I thought I told you that it was bandits, remember?'

'Ah, yes,' said Krugar. 'I forgot. So it was. Look, I'm not offering, they're coming with you and that's that.'

'Very well,' smiled Sigmar, knowing it was pointless to argue. 'I will be glad to have their blades.'

'Damn right,' said Krugar, handing over the canteen once more. 'It may be some time before I see you again.'

'It may indeed,' agreed Sigmar.

'Then drink with me as friends do around a fire. Let's talk of happier times when the sun was golden, women were maidens, and old age something that happened to other men.'

'I'll drink to that,' said Sigmar, taking another swig.

THE GATES OF Reikdorf swung open as Wolfgart led two hundred of his finest warriors across the Sudenreik Bridge. He glanced at the panels carved into the inner faces of the bridge, heroic endeavours from the history of the Unberogen and its greatest heroes rendered by the woodcarver's art. Master Holtwine had crafted the latest panels, depicting the heroic defence of Middenheim's viaduct and the rout of the Norsii army from the base of the Fauschlag Rock. No panel depicted the desperate fighting in the tunnels beneath the rock, and Wolfgart was glad, only too happy to have that terror forgotten.

To see the high walls of his home lifted his spirit in

ways he could never describe. The blue and red flags fluttering from the towers and high buildings within were a shining light of hope in the long night. To see Reikdorf, it seemed impossible that darkness could ever truly hold sway.

Though Reikdorf was a welcoming sight, his pleasure at seeing it again evaporated at the thought of returning to his empty home. Without Maedbh and Ulrike it was just a hollow structure of stone and timber, without life and warmth. He missed them terribly, but covered that loneliness by riding to war at every opportunity. And with the dead rising all across the Empire, there was no shortage of opportunities.

This latest ride had seen them fighting on the edge of the Skaag Hills, where the dead had pressed north along the River Bogen. A number of mining settlements in the hills had sent word of the dead emerging from cairns in the high slopes, and Wolfgart led yet another band of warriors to fight them.

They had destroyed the host, but with every ride, it seemed the dead were arising closer and closer to Reikdorf. How much longer would it be before they were clawing at the walls of Sigmar's city? The Emperor was in the north, and though Alfgeir was more than up to the task of defending Unberogen lands, Sigmar's presence was greatly missed.

Not least by Wolfgart, for he had left Three Hills in order to fight alongside his friend.

He and his warriors rode through the gate and into the streets, following a curving route that led towards the open square of the Oathstone. It never failed to amaze Wolfgart how the city had grown over the years. He remembered when it had been little more than a small settlement of timber structures, none taller than two storeys, huts of wattle and daub, and riverside lean-tos.

Now most of the city was built of limestone and granite, the city's masons learning how to shape stone with ever-greater skill from travelling craftsmen who came down from the fortified mountain holds of the dwarfs.

Wenyld, one of Wolfgart's battle captains, rode alongside him and said, 'This isn't the route to the stables.'

'I know,' said Wolfgart. 'I want to stop at the Oathstone.'

'Any particular reason?' said Wenyld. 'The horses are tired, and the men need rest.'

Wolfgart wondered if he should even try to explain. Wenyld was only seven years younger than Wolfgart, but carried a weight of war upon his face. A wide scar split the left side of his jaw where a greenskin axe had smashed through his shield, and one eye was covered with a rough cloth patch. The claw of a ravening ghoul-creature had taken the eye on their last ride, and the wound had festered. Elswyth had done what she could, but Wenyld had lost the eye.

'I want to touch the past,' said Wolfgart at last.

'What?'

Wolfgart sighed, knowing any explanation would sound foolish to the younger man. In truth, he didn't understand his reasoning himself, he just knew he had to go there.

'Take the men back to the stables then, I'll meet you there when I'm done.'

Wenyld nodded and issued the orders to the armoured horsemen, who gratefully turned their mounts and rode towards the stables. Wolfgart saw they were exhausted after the long ride to the west and two major battles. It had been inconsiderate of him to put his own desires ahead of his warriors' needs.

He turned his horse and rode away, twisting in the saddle as he heard iron-shod hoof beats coming after him.

'You should go with them,' he told Wenyld, as the man rode next to him.

'A good battle captain never leaves his commander until the ride is over.'

Wolfgart did not want company, but had not the energy to argue with the younger man.

'Fair enough, though it'll be longer until you get to your bed,' he said.

Wenyld shrugged, a few torn links in his mail slipping from his corslet and falling to the ground. 'It's as far now, whichever way I go. I'll ride with you.'

'Suit yourself,' said Wolfgart, riding onwards in silence.

The streets were quiet, the unnatural greyness of the world keeping people indoors, as though to see so grim a day would remind them of the gathering threat. Word of what was facing them had spread throughout the city, and though the temples were busy, little else had the power to tempt people from their homes. Every doorway was hung with talismans of Morr and every keyhole was plugged with dried fennel. Those men and women on the streets avoided eye contact and hurried into side streets and doorways as the armoured horsemen passed.

'Some welcome home, eh?' said Wenyld. 'Don't they know we're out there risking our lives to keep them safe?'

'They know,' said Wolfgart, 'but no one likes to be reminded of what we're fighting. It's bad luck to dwell on the dead, and only a fool wishes for more ill-fortune at times like this.'

'I suppose,' replied Wenyld.

Wolfgart turned his horse into the square of the Oath-stone, the hard-packed earth almost as solid as stone. There had been talk of paving the square, but Sigmar had refused to allow this ground to be covered.

'If we sever our links to the earth beneath us completely, then we are doomed. The Oathstone shares its bed with no other slab,' the Emperor had said, and the matter was closed.

The square was empty save for a few wild dogs fighting over scraps stolen from a nearby butcher's slops, and the sound of hoarse bellows roared from within Beorthyn's forge. Wolfgart smiled. The old smith had been dead for twenty years or more, yet still the name stuck. It belonged now to his apprentice, Master Govannon, a worker of metal considered by many to be a greater craftsman than Beorthyn had ever been.

'What do you suppose they're doing in there?' asked Wenyld, as a sooty black cloud billowed from the iron chimney stack and a thunderous bang echoed from the walls of nearby buildings. Even over that noise, Wolfgart could hear Govannon cursing.

'Who knows? Something with that giant thunder bow Alfgeir and Cuthwin brought in I expect.'

'Is Cuthwin still in the city?'

'I don't know, maybe,' said Wolfgart. 'Why?'

'We were friends as youngsters,' answered Wenyld. 'The years have taken us down different paths, but it would be pleasant to see him again.'

'I vaguely remember the pair of you trying to get a look at my Blood Night, the evening before Sigmar rode to Astofen for the first time.'

'You remember that night? I thought you were too drunk.'

'Not so drunk I don't remember you falling on your arse and running like the Ölfhednar themselves were after your manhood.'

'Aye, well it's not every day you're caught by the king's son on his Blood Night.'

'Sigmar and I tried it once, and we got the thrashing of our lives.'

'Maybe you should have run as fast as I did.'

Wolfgart smiled. 'Maybe, lad, maybe.'

He reined in his horse and dismounted before the Oathstone, the earth around it trod by a thousand people every day. He knelt beside the red stone, its rough surface warm and threaded with golden veins. Those veins were thinner than they had been when Sigmar had made them swear their oath to help him build the Empire, and he hoped that wasn't an omen.

'I miss you,' he whispered, thinking of Maedbh and Ulrike.

No sooner were the words out of his mouth than he felt the Oathstone grow hot to the touch. He tried to pull his hand back, but it was stuck fast to the stone. Wolfgart gasped as he felt the heat travel up the length of his arm, his vision swimming as unknown power held him in its grasp.

'What…?' he managed as his vision greyed and he saw a host of chariots riding through hills of rolling greensward in his mind's eye. Armoured in black and gold, they were escorted by hundreds of horsemen and painted warriors in mail shirts who marched beneath banners of gold and red.

He recognised the landscape around Three Hills, and the chariot at the front of the army as that of Queen Freya. The woman at the reins was not Maedbh, and a gathering evil loomed over the Asoborns, a doom that none could see, but which was slowly enveloping them in its encroaching shadow.

The vision of Freya's army was overlaid with the sight of Maedbh and Ulrike standing side by side on a wooded hillside. Both loosed arrows into an oncoming horde of the dead, but he could tell from their expressions that it wouldn't be nearly enough to stop them. His heart broke to see the fear on their faces.

Death stalked these lands, and he wanted to scream,

but he had no voice, no way to warn the Asoborns that their enemies were almost upon them or that he was aware of their plight. He heard wolves, noble, white-furred heralds of Ulric, and knew they were calling to him, demanding he take action.

A sudden, twisting sense of vertigo seized him, and he felt himself falling, his arms windmilling for balance. The visions faded from sight, and the harsh angles and stone walls of Reikdorf snapped back into focus. Wolfgart's stomach lurched and he put a hand out to steady himself, his gut churning in fear.

'What in Ulric's name just happened there?' demanded Wenyld, and Wolfgart looked up to see the warrior holding onto his shoulders. The golden lines on the Oathstone pulsed with life, now even thinner, as though the stone had all but exhausted its power to grant him this vision.

'I have to go,' said Wolfgart, pushing himself unsteadily to his feet. He ran to his horse and vaulted into the saddle.

'What are you talking about?' demanded Wenyld. 'We've only just got back.'

'My family is in danger,' said Wolfgart. 'And I have to go to them.'

── ◄ TWELVE ► ──

Three Thrusts to the Heart

FREYA'S ARMY LEFT Three Hills in triumph, cheered by those whose age or wounds prevented them from joining their queen. Three thousand warriors marched or rode south-east through the rolling landscape, moving quickly towards the River Aver, the watercourse that effectively divided Asoborn lands from those of the Brigundians.

Within three days, the army came within sight of the mighty river that ran from the Worlds Edge Mountains through the Empire before emptying into the sea at Marburg.

Here, the coming winter had made the landscape flat and hard, ideal for chariots and cavalry, and the army moved into marching column as it followed the river east towards the river crossing at Averstrun.

Despite the grim skies that wreathed the world in bleak twilight, the army's spirits were high. Freya was an inspirational presence, taking many lovers en route and ensuring that overblown erotic tales spread through the camp quicker than a dose of the pox. As always, Freya led from the front, her black and gold chariot unmistakable among the less ornate chariots of the Asoborn warriors.

With the river on the army's right flank, Asoborn horse archers galloped wide, while the heavier lancers rode closer to the main body of the infantry and chariots. By noon of the fourth day of march, Freya sent word back down the line that she had spied the river crossing and their enemy.

Blocking the crossing were a thousand dead warriors in ancient armour, arranged like a row of obsidian statues in a mausoleum. All were clad in rusted bronze, the weak light glinting from the corrosion on the rings of their mail. An eldritch green light glimmered in the empty eye sockets of each warrior and a hundred knights sat on skeletal horses on either flank. Flocks of carrion birds gathered for the feast and the few trees in the scattered patches of woodland were thick with screeching bats.

A warrior in gleaming silver armour sat upon a hellish steed at the centre of the host, black wings like smoke billowing from its flanks. Khaled al-Muntasir was an incongruous sight amid this army of darkness, and his wondrous form drew all the light to him, such that he shone like a legendary hero of old.

Freya wasted no time in arraying her army for battle, issuing orders with customary fire and fury. The Asoborn infantry moved into four blocks of five hundred, spears and swords held in fists that demanded vengeance for the loss of the Brigundians and Menogoths. With the chariots thrown out before her main battle line, the heavy horse rode out to the flanks, ready to roll up the line of the dead warriors.

Bare chested horse archers whooped and yelled as they rode around the army of the dead, loosing flurries of arrows into the massed ranks of skeletal warriors.

Though the dead had no flesh to damage or organs to pierce, the barbed shafts felled them just as surely as they would a mortal man. Intended to provoke a reckless charge rather than inflict mass casualties, the arrows of the horse archers did little but fell a few score of the dead warriors.

Ululating Asoborn war horns signalled the advance, and the infantry moved forward, moving at a brisk trot to cover the ground between the two armies. Freya led the advance, her chariot thundering towards the serried ranks of the dead with hundreds more behind her. The hard ground threw up no dust with their passage, and the entire army witnessed the horror of what happened next.

Before Freya's horn blew to signal the turn, Khaled al-Muntasir aimed his sword at the earth before the charging chariots. The hard ground cracked and split as hundreds upon hundreds of dry, fleshless corpses clawed their way to the world above, dust and earth spilling from their empty skulls and opened jaws. Unable to stop or turn, the chariots slammed into them with a tremendous crash of dried bone and wood.

Asoborn chariots were never meant to be run straight into the enemy, but raced along the front of a foe's formation. Archers would loose arrows into the faces of the enemy at point-blank range, and spear bearers would hurl heavy, iron-tipped shafts into the warriors pressing in from behind. To run a chariot straight into the foe would certainly kill a great many of the enemy, but would, more often than not, destroy the chariot and kill the riders and horses.

The chariots came apart in a screaming bray of pain, both animal and human. Most simply shattered in the impact, but some overturned, crushing their crews and breaking the horses' legs. The queen's chariot vanished in a crash of shattered timber, broken apart by the violence of the impact. Hundreds more were destroyed in explosions of splintering timber, hurling their crews to the ground or breaking them beneath the wheels of those behind them. Only the quickest crews were able to avoid the catastrophic collision of dead bodies and screaming horses, but in doing so they bled off the speed that kept them safe.

Grasping skeletons clawed their way onto the chariots, attacking with broken swords or cudgels salvaged from the vast swathe of wreckage left by the destruction of the chariots. Khaled al-Muntasir swept his sword up and hundreds of rotten-fleshed wolves burst from the ranks of the dead warriors at the river. They fell upon the struggling Asoborns with dreadful hunger, jaws tearing open throats and claws raking warm flesh from the bone.

The warriors blocking the river crossing marched forward in dreadful unison, each bony footfall crashing down at the same time as they fell upon those the wolves hadn't yet killed. Swords and spears stabbed and slashed with mechanical precision, and the entangled Asoborns were cut down without mercy.

Freya's shield maidens dragged her bloodied body from the wreckage, fighting with all the fury of berserkers as the rest of the army raced forward to rescue their fallen queen. The black skeletons chopped through the ruin of the chariots, killing anything living they could find.

Asoborn cavalry charged towards the flanks of the dead army, but the corpse knights wheeled their skeletal mounts and raced towards them as hundreds of leathery-winged bats launched themselves from the trees. Green fire flickered around the undead knights, their blades shimmering with ghostly light, and the two forces met in a thunderous clash of iron. Asoborn lances smashed through ancient armour, splintering as the weight of the dead broke them apart. Screeching bats tore at the Asoborn riders, clawing their faces and entangling their blades with their wings and stinking bodies. Both forces of horsemen swirled together, hacking at one another with swords and axes, but within seconds it was clear the Asoborn charge was doomed.

In the centre of the battle, Khaled al-Muntasir danced through the fighting, his gleaming sword slaying all it cut. No weapon could touch him, no warrior lay him low, and he slid through the scattered Asoborns like a ghost, leaving a trail of bodies in his wake. Tattooed warrior women of the Myrmidian sects formed a ring of screaming fury around him, but within moments, all were dead, gutted, beheaded or fatally pierced by his quicksilver blade. Malign clouds of sable light billowed around the blood drinker, a miasma of dark sorcery that drained the life from any who came near him and animated the corpses of those he had killed.

The ranks of the dead swelled with every passing moment, for the newly slain rose up to attack their former comrades, bloodied and mangled charioteers clawing at men and women they had broken bread with only that same morning. The encircling horns of the dead army began to envelop the Asoborns, but even at this desperate moment, the battle could have been saved.

At that critical moment, when one spark of heroism or fear could have turned the tide of the fighting, a warrior named Daegal, a lad no older than twelve summers who had trained and fought with Maedbh, turned and fled from the horror of the bloodletting. His sword and shield forgotten, Daegal ran in blind terror, and his panic spread to those around him.

Within moments, hundreds of Asoborns were fleeing the battle, desperate to escape the slaughter and frantic to live. The battle line collapsed as the fragile courage of the mortal army broke in the face of this nightmare horde.

But there was to be no such easy escape.

The dread knights rode down the fleeing Asoborns, trampling them beneath the pellucid fire of their mounts' hooves or chopping them down with pounding blows of their swords. The encircling army of the dead surrounded the dying Asoborn host, drawing it into a black embrace of massacre.

Only a handful of mortals escaped the slaughter, the queen's shield maidens and a hundred or so warriors who had been first to flee. Their shame burned almost as hot as the relief that they still lived, and as darkness fell, barely a tenth of the queen's army escaped into the hills.

Khaled al-Muntasir stood triumphant, his army arranged across the battlefield in silence as the crows and ravens pecked the choicest morsels from the defeated army. The blood drinker let them have their feast, for what could be more terrifying to a mortal warrior than to later face one of his own kind with eyes pecked out, flesh partially eaten and tongue hanging loose on rotten sinews?

As Morrslieb slipped from behind the clouds to bathe the blood-soaked field in its rich, emerald moonlight, he uttered the words given to him by Nagash and laughed long into the night as the vanquished Asoborns rose to their feet once more.

Without any orders needing to be issued, the army of the dead arrayed itself for march, moving in deathly silence and utter precision as they followed the route Queen Freya's doomed army had taken.

Back towards Three Hills.

VOLLEYS OF ARROWS flew overhead, slashing down the causeway and slicing into grey, lifeless flesh. Bordan's foresters loosed more arrows, and another clutch of the dead were felled. The viaduct from the ground was thick with dead warriors, partially decayed men and women lurching and swaying towards Middenheim with horrid purpose and grotesque hunger moaning from their slack jaws.

'Got to hand it to Bordan's men,' said Holstef, the beast-horn clarion clutched tightly in his gauntleted fist. 'They're killing everything they hit.'

Ustern grunted. 'They can't miss. Even I could loose an arrow that would slay something.'

'Probably one of us,' added Leovulf, undoing the leather thong that held his black hair.

'You cut me deep,' said Ustern, tapping smouldering ash from the end of his pipe.

Redwane let them talk, it was their way of easing the tension before a charge. Though the White Wolves feared no living foe, the horde arrayed before them today was something much worse. Redwane had fought the living dead before, but the same fear was still there, still poisoning his gut with a sour-bile taste. The thoughts that had haunted him on the march towards Brass Keep returned to him anew; the dread of dying alone, the fear that his best years were already behind him and that he was on a grim descent into dotage and infirmity.

Redwane took a deep breath, looking to the sky in a bid to cast off such gloomy thoughts, but he found no refuge there. The sky above the Fauschlag Rock was as black as his mood.

It had been that way ever since the dead had isolated Middenheim from the Empire.

The noose had closed slowly, with villages blotted out one by one and the steady stream of traders, mercenary companies and pilgrims diminishing until it was impossible not to see that something terrible was developing in the haunted forests surrounding the city.

Despite his dislike of the man, Bordan's foresters had quickly discovered the roads cut by lurking bands of the dead and packs of fiery-eyed wolves. The villages and camps around the city were hastily evacuated, their people brought within Middenheim's walls. Even Torbrecan's band of lunatics had come into the city, which had surprised Redwane until he remembered that they had foreseen their deaths before the walls of Reikdorf. Despite his insistence that no one be left beyond the city, Redwane suspected that Myrsa was already regretting his decision to allow the self-mutilating madmen into Middenheim. They marched through the streets, preaching their prophecies of destruction and pain, while whipping themselves into maniacal frenzies. No warriors could be spared from the fighting to stop them, and the mood in the city soured as more and more of Middenheim's citizens joined in their cavalcade of blood.

'If they're so eager for death, I say we help them on their way. Give them a sword and stick them on the walls,' Redwane had muttered at one of Myrsa's war councils, and few disagreed with him. Yet for all their apparent lust to die, the madmen refused to take arms to defend Middenheim. Clearly they weren't insane enough to want to die just *yet*.

Within a day of the gates closing, the living dead host swallowed the lands around Middenheim, throwing themselves at the fortresses clustered around the city and the chain lifts. Those bastions still held, but the horde had soon discovered another way up. Led by shadowy, dark-cloaked figures on black steeds, skeletal warriors armed with spears, axes and swords climbed the great viaduct towards the city. Frothing, blood-hungry corpses scrambled up the rocky sides of the Fauschlag Rock, and Orsa's city defenders had their hands full hacking them down as they reached the summit.

Trapped beyond the walls, Wulf's mountain pathfinders had tried to cut through the dead towards the viaduct, but they had been overrun before making it halfway. Redwane had watched as the Mountain Lord was dragged down and eaten by wiry, hairless things with tearing claws and distended jaws. Orsa led a party of axemen to retrieve the bodies of their fallen comrades, but had been beaten back without success.

Now Wulf marched with the dead, his ravaged flesh hanging from his bones in rotten strips. His warriors fought beside him, as loyal in death as they had been in life. It had been a blow losing Wulf, for he had been well-liked and the tale of his ending had circulated to become a macabre scare story, growing in horror with every retelling.

'They'll be calling for us soon,' said Leovulf.

'Expect you're right,' said Ustern.

Redwane looked towards the fighting raging at the head of the viaduct. Since the war against the Norsii, a more permanent defensive barrier had been built across the head of the viaduct, a curved wall flanked by two drum towers and with a heavy gate of Drakwald oak and good northern iron at its centre. Atop the walls, Count Myrsa led the defenders in battle, the runefang cleaving glowing arcs through the ranks of the dead. None of them could resist it, the dwarf-forged blade slicing through mouldering bones, rotted armour and decayed flesh with its runic edge. To see so magnificent a weapon borne by such a hero lifted the hearts of all who fought beside him. Myrsa's banner bearer battled alongside him, the blue and ivory standard soaked and limp. No wind stirred the fabric and instead of lifting the spirits of those who saw its colours, it only served to remind the warriors of Middenheim of how grim their situation truly was.

The dead swarmed the defensive wall, scaling its rugged surfaces with bony claws digging into the stonework in a way no living warrior could manage. They fought with a speed and ferocity Redwane remembered all too well, dragging men from the battlements and pushing through any gaps in the line.

Myrsa and Renweard commanded the defenders on the viaduct, while Bordan and his men occupied the high ground behind the walls. Perched on rooftops, clock towers and watch posts, the foresters thinned the dead host as best they could. Orsa's men patrolled the city, hunting down any dead warriors that found their way through the caves that honeycombed the rock or successfully scaled its sides.

Redwane had defended this city once before from an attacking army, but this felt very different. Then he had been one of Sigmar's warrior companions, but now he was part of Middenheim's defence, a city that was not his by birth. As much as Sigmar might declare that all men of the Empire were as one, he couldn't shake the feeling that he ought to be in the south, fighting to protect Unberogen lands. This city wasn't his, no matter what oaths he had sworn to Myrsa and the White Wolves.

'Redwane,' hissed Leovulf, leaning in close.

'What?' he muttered absently.

'You're our leader, so damn well lead,' said Leovulf.

Redwane snapped out of his gloomy reverie, and nodded, ashamed he had allowed his mind to wander when he needed to focus now more than ever.

'Aye, sorry,' he said, looking towards the walls for Myrsa's signal.

'Whatever is on your mind, deal with it later,' said Leovulf. 'They'll be looking for us soon. And we need you with us.'

'You're right,' he said, holding himself tall in the saddle. He unhooked his warhammer and slipped the leather thong at its base around his wrist. The White Wolves saw him and repeated the gesture, and every man's shoulders squared. Leovulf had spotted what he should have seen. The defenders on the wall were at the limit of their endurance, the dead finding more breaches and pulling men to their doom in ever greater numbers. Myrsa raised the runefang high and his banner bearer swept the flag from side to side. Now the wind caught it, and the billowing standard flew with glorious brightness against the sepulchral sky.

'That's it,' said Leovulf, turning to Holstef.

Holstef raised the war horn to his lips and blew a three note blast.

Redwane raked back his spurs and shouted, 'White Wolves, ride in the name of Ulric!'

His horse leapt forward, and two hundred heavy horsemen followed him, galloping across the cobbled esplanade towards the city gate in a column ten riders wide, twenty deep. Ustern raised their banner high, and each man loosed a feral wolf howl to banish the fear they all felt as they charged towards the gate. A team of stout men hauled the gates open, but before the dead could take advantage of this new opening, Redwane's White Wolves thundered through and struck the enemy host like a hammerblow.

MARIUS LET OUT a groan of pleasure as Marika rolled off him and lay back on the bed with a contented sigh. Her eyes were closed, and she purred like a satisfied cat, blonde hair tousled with errant strands across her face. He stared at her for a moment, relishing this rare moment of escape from the world of plans, defences and warriors. Marburg was a city readying for invasion, and it felt good to take a moment for himself amid the frenetic battle preparations.

'You're staring again,' she said.

'How do you know?' he asked.

'I'm a princess,' she said, as though that answered his question. 'If we can sense a pea in our beds, we can surely sense when a self-satisfied man is staring at us.'

'Self-satisfied?' he said with mock hurt. 'You have a viper's tongue, Marika.'

'You weren't complaining about my tongue last night,' she said, finally opening her eyes and pushing herself up onto her elbows. Marius smiled and traced his fingertips down her slender neck, over her small breasts and down her flat stomach.

'Indeed I wasn't,' he agreed. 'Though I can't help but feel your brother wouldn't approve of the use you put it to or your choice of lover.'

She laughed and rose from the bed, fetching a silver ewer filled with water. Marius stared at her naked body, the sway of her hips and the beads of sweat running down her spine sending a tingling warmth through his entire body. She half-turned and nodded.

'Aldred never does,' she said. 'He'd have me live out my life as a virgin spinster.'

She laughed. 'Ranald's balls, if he knew half the men I'd bedded, he'd have me locked in the Raven Tower, never to see the light of day again.'

'And that would be a crime against the pleasures of the flesh.'

She padded back to bed with the ewer and a pair of goblets, pouring one for each of them. Marius took the proffered drink and drained it in one gulping swallow. The march along the coast through the swamps had given him a terrible thirst that never seemed to be quenched.

He dropped the goblet to the floor and leaned up to kiss Marika.

'Why me?' he asked suddenly.

'Why you, what?'

'You know fine well what I mean,' he said. 'Why take me as your lover, a man your brother would cheerfully gut? Is it because I am an energetic and thoughtful bedmate with the body of an athletic god or is it simply because I am a count of the Empire?'

'A little of both,' she admitted. 'You are an enjoyable bed partner, but I need more than that. I need a man who can achieve things. A man who can match my dreams with an ability to shape this world to the way it ought to be.'

In any other woman, such candour would have surprised him, but Princess Marika had proven to be a far more interesting woman than any he had met before. She had an open honesty to her ambition that he liked, a mind free of the subterfuges and coquettish games played by most women of his acquaintance. Amid such grim times, the company of a beautiful woman free from the normal petty games of her sex was refreshing.

And these times were indeed grim.

In the week since the Jutones had arrived at the gates of Marburg, Marius and Aldred had clashed many times in deciding how to defend the city. He had come to believe the Endal count *wanted* his city to fall, such was his obstinate rejection of any stratagem or defensive measure Marius suggested.

These interludes with Marika had provided a welcome diversion from talk of war and the dead. Marius liked to think of it as affirming the joys of life. After all, weren't sex and death but two sides of the same coin? Wasn't the moment of climax known by some poetic souls as the Little Morr?

Marika rolled onto her side, interrupting his train of thought. Her face was inches from his, and he felt the directness of her gaze.

'I know what you did with Jutonsryk,' she said. 'You turned a small fishing village into the most prosperous city in the Empire. Ships came from all across the world to your city.'

'That they did,' said Marius, knowing her flattery was intended to stroke his ego, but enjoying it nonetheless. 'If there's one thing I understand it's how to take what the gods have given me and use that to turn a coin.'

'I want you to do the same with Marburg,' she said. 'Aldred is a good man in his own, limited way, but all he wants is to maintain what our father built. Marburg is ideally placed to become as great as Jutonsryk ever was, if not greater, but only if rulers of vision are prepared to make it so. Aldred has no vision to make Marburg great, but you do.'

'You might be right, but Aldred is count of the Endals, not me.'

'That can change,' said Marika.

'How?'

'If you and I were to be married,' she said, leaning forward to kiss him.

Now it was Marius's turn to laugh. He rolled onto his back, pillowing his head on his hands. 'That's your plan? Your brother would never allow it. Manann's thunder, he'd have my manhood on a spike if he thought I'd even kissed you let alone bedded you.'

'Aldred won't be count forever,' she said. 'After all, if what you've been saying in the war councils is true, then this city is likely to be attacked soon by these undead corsairs. Aldred's a decent enough warrior, but anything can happen in a battle, can't it?'

Marius turned to look at Marika, his eyes narrowing as he saw the extent of her ambition.

It matched his own and he felt the stirrings of opportunity.

'What are you suggesting?' he asked.

'Suggesting?' she said, pulling the sheet down and rolling on top of him. She sat up, allowing his eyes to feast on the seductive curves of her body. 'I'm not suggesting anything, I'm just saying that if something were to happen to Aldred, then there would be nothing to stop you marrying me and becoming lord of all the lands from here to Manann's Teeth.'

Marius slid his hands up her sides and cupped her breasts with a smile.

'You are a cunning fox, aren't you?' said Marius.

'Takes one to know one,' she said.

REDWANE CRUSHED SKELETAL warriors in crumbling iron armour beneath his horse, swinging his hammer in a mighty underhand arc that smashed collarbones, broke shoulders apart and sent skulls flying. His horse trampled the dead beneath its hooves. To either side of him, Leovulf, Ustern and Holstef fought with brute ferocity as they battered a path down the viaduct, winning Myrsa and Renweard time to move up fresh warriors and relieve those who had fought to exhaustion.

'Holstef, spearhead!' bellowed Redwane, and the clarion blew a long, rising blast.

The White Wolves smoothly formed a wedge on Redwane, pushing hard into the choking, massed ranks of the dead. Redwane lost himself in the simple purity of this fight, bludgeoning the dead with his hammer and letting his horse kick and crush its enemies with wild abandon. He heard screams around him as grasping, skeletal hands dragged warriors from their saddles or screeching things with elongated jaws and red eyes tore the throats from horses to spill their riders to the ground.

Their charge was slowing, the press of dead warriors too great for even the mighty White Wolves to smash through. And as they slowed, more of Redwane's warriors were falling to the blades of the dead. A fiery-eyed wolf leapt towards him and Redwane swayed in the saddle, intercepting the beast's opened jaws with his hammer. Its head split apart and its corpse slammed into him. Its dissolving body unravelled, looping, rotted guts spilling into his lap and stagnant fluids hissing as they burned his armour.

'Time to go!' shouted Leovulf.

Redwane nodded and turned to shout at Holstef to sound the retreat, but the saddle next to him was empty. He circled his horse, finally seeing Holstef pinned to the ground by a scabrous ghoul with foam-flecked jaws and needle-sharp talons. Holstef screamed as it tore his guts out, its arms bloody to the elbows as it disembowelled the White Wolf. Redwane hauled back on his reins and his horse reared up onto its hind legs. Its hooves flailed as it came down, crushing the creature beneath its weight, though it was too late to save Holstef.

The White Wolves fought on, the dead pressing in from all around as the sheer number of skeletal warriors finally arrested their charge. The viaduct was choked with the debris of the fighting, a welter of bones, rusted armour and leering skulls.

Though it was probably suicide, Redwane leapt from the saddle and dropped to the ground beside Holstef. The man was already dead, his ruptured stomach steaming in the cold air. Redwane reached for the war horn. Unless he blew the retreat, the White Wolves were as good as dead.

An armoured foot slammed down on the horn,

shattering it into fragments, and Redwane leapt aside as a black sword slashed towards him. He rolled to his feet, swinging his hammer up to block a descending blow. The force of the blow rang up his arms and emerald sparks flew from the impact. He backed away, taking in the measure of his opponent as he fought the rising tide of fearful bile in his throat.

Redwane's heart chilled as he saw he faced a dead knight in black armour who was shawled in a cloak woven from nightmares and woe. Its sword and armour were archaic, coated in grave dirt and rust, though the lambent glow that surrounded the ancient warlord told Redwane that this was a champion of the dead, a supreme killer of the living. It wore an open helm, and the green fire in its eyes promised a death as quick as it would be meaningless.

Its sword swung for his neck and Redwane threw himself back as it attacked with a speed and skill no living swordsman could match. Without a shield, Redwane could only block and parry with his hammer, but no matter how skilful, a fight between sword and hammer could only end badly for him.

The champion's blade slipped past his guard and Redwane screamed as its icy tip punched through his armour and slid between his ribs. Numbing waves of cold spread from the wound, and Redwane's heart stilled as the blade twisted in the wound. He staggered away from the champion, and no sooner had its sword scraped free of his armour than his heart thumped painfully in his chest.

The dread champion came at him again, but before it could strike him down, a black horse slammed into it, sending it crashing back against the viaduct's parapet. Leovulf reached down and extended his hand towards Redwane as the champion climbed to its feet, broken bones knitting together once more and its grinning skull welcoming fresh meat to slay.

'We can't fight it…' gasped Redwane.

'I know!' shouted Leovulf. 'Get on!'

Redwane grasped Leovulf's hand, hauling himself painfully onto the horse's rump. The dead were closing in, and Redwane feared that Leovulf's horse would never make it with two heavily armed warriors on its back.

The dead champion strode towards them, but it had taken only a handful of steps before it halted, as though sensing a greater threat than the two warriors before it. Redwane's entire body was cold, his flesh icy and grey from the wound dealt to him, but a deeper cold swept over him as the sound of winter gales howled from the forests. Swirling snowflakes and fragments of ice slashed from the sky, and the dead paused in their relentless attack, as a surging wind roared up the viaduct, echoing with the howls of wolves.

The chorus of lupine fury was utterly without mercy, and Redwane watched in amazement as a blizzard of winter wind blew over the dead warlord who had so nearly slain him. Ice formed on its ancient armour and decaying flesh as the chill wind froze the champion in place. A bitter squall of hail tore at it like a storm of razored glass, and a deafening howl of winter's fury broke its bones apart in an explosion of long dead remains.

The dead parted as something pushed its way up from the ground, a hulking figure in thick wolf pelts and cloaked in a blizzard of freezing ice. He carried a long staff that shimmered with hoar frost and was topped with a glittering blade of ice. A wolf-skull mask obscured his face, and his heavily muscled limbs were bare to the elements, though he seemed to feel no ill-effects from the deathly cold. Two wolves loped through the motionless dead as he stalked towards them, one pale as moonlight, the other black as jet. The fighting on the viaduct ceased, and the White Wolves drew together as the wolf-clad warrior stopped before them.

'The fire of Ulric calls me,' he said, his voice echoing as though coming from the furthest reaches of the frozen north. Redwane had seen this warrior once before, at the coronation of Sigmar in Reikdorf, and a wave of frozen pain washed through him.

'Ar-Ulric!' cried Leovulf. 'Ar-Ulric has come!'

─≺ THIRTEEN ≻─

The Next to Die

MAEDBH RAN TOWARDS the centre of Three Hills, hearing the shouts of the sentries and their cries of alarm. Fear clamped her heart and she looked back over her shoulder to make sure Ulrike and the boys were with Garr's Eagles. Asoborns armed with bows and spears were pouring from their homes, dwellings cunningly secluded within hidden arbours and sunken hollows. Any enemy would have a difficult time in locating their homes, but it sounded like someone had done just that.

Her own bow was slung over her shoulder, but she carried a long, leaf-bladed spear that normally sat in the queen's chariot. A priest of Taal had blessed its blade, and its keen edge never failed to find its prey. A thousand possibilities flew through her mind, the living dead had found a way to locate Three Hills, the greenskins were invading from the mountains, the forest beasts had followed a scent trail to the Asoborn homeland…

None of those made sense. Queen Freya's army was between Three Hills and the living dead, and though the greenskins had been more active of late, the mountain scouts had reported no signs of a gathering horde. That just left beasts...

Freya had entrusted the care and safety of her sons to Maedbh. Bad enough that she couldn't have marched with the queen, but to allow enemies within Three Hills would be unforgivable. Maedbh rounded a grassy hillock, overgrown with trees and nettles, finding a line of Asoborn women with bows lined up with their backs to her. Their bowstrings were taut, yet their arrows remained unloosed. Children scampered around their mothers' legs, but there was no sense of fear, no sense that something dangerous had come amongst them.

'What in Taal's name is going on?' said Garr, coming alongside her with the children in tow. Ulrike held his hand, while Sigulf and Fridleifr had their hunting knives bared. Clad in baked leather armour and a bronze-reinforced kilt, Garr was handsome and strong, with a cropped scalp of fine black hair. One of the youngest Queen's Eagles, Maedbh had heard enough stories of Garr's stamina and prowess to know that he was a true Asoborn in all areas the queen required. He had taken to the children well, and they to him, which made their confinement to Three Hills marginally less troublesome.

'I don't know,' replied Maedbh, resting the spear over her shoulder and walking towards the line of Asoborns. She heard gruff voices and the clank of metal beyond, and her trepidation turned to curiosity with every step. The Asoborns parted before her and she found herself looking at a hundred armoured dwarfs, clad from head to foot in armour of silver, gold and bronze. Stained with the dust of many days travel, the dwarfs seemed unconcerned by the bent bows aimed at them or the assembling chariots rumbling around their flanks.

Leading the dwarfs was a broad figure in a suit of

glittering gold and silver. The visor of his helmet was shaped in the form of a stern, bearded god and he rested his mailed fists on the haft of an axe almost as tall as he was. The warrior flipped his visor up to reveal a craggy face like the flanks of a cliff and eyes that twinkled like shards of obsidian. The dwarf's beard was plaited with iron cords and he spat a mouthful of dust.

'Which of you manlings is in charge here?' said the dwarf.

Maedbh stepped forward, planting her spear before her in the earth.

'I am,' she said. 'Maedbh of Three Hills. Who are you and how did you get past our sentries? No one enters Queen Freya's lands without permission.'

'I am Master Alaric, Runesmith to King Kurgan Iron-beard of Karaz-a-Karak, and your queen is likely dead,' said the dwarf, and a horrified ripple of disbelief swept through the assembled Asoborns. Maedbh felt a cold hand take hold of her heart. She struggled to maintain her composure in the face of such terrible news.

'As to how we got here,' continued the dwarf, oblivious to the effect his words were having, 'Do you think the paths *over* the land are the only ones? The roots of your manling town reach so rudely into the earth that even a skrati couldn't miss them. There are routes to the surface all over this place. I'm surprised you haven't found them and taken steps to secure them, but then you are only manlings…'

Maedbh struggled to hold her annoyance at the dwarf's insult, instead focusing on the news he had brought.

'What are you talking about?' she said at last. 'Queen Freya's army set out from here only a week ago.'

'Freya?' said the dwarf. 'Tall woman with red hair, doesn't wear enough armour to cover a small child? Rides a chariot of black and gold?'

'Yes,' said Maedbh.

'Aye, that's her,' said Alaric. 'It's hard to tell you man-lings apart sometimes. Anyway, the dead destroyed her army at the river crossing. It was messy, not many escaped. A blood drinker swordsman commands the dead, and those he slew now march north with him.'

Maedbh swallowed, grief twisting her gut into a painful knot. She knew little of the dwarfs and their ways, but knew the Emperor counted them as his sworn allies and that they did not lie or embellish.

To the mountain folk, truth was like the hardest stone, unyielding and enduring.

'How many?' she said. 'And how long do we have?'

'His army is near four thousand now,' said Alaric. 'I reckon they'll be here within the day and don't even think about hiding. They'll sniff this place out as sure as gold glitters.'

'Then we need to leave here,' said Maedbh. 'We need to head west to Reikdorf.'

'Aye,' agreed Alaric. 'That you do, manling. And right quick too.'

THE ATTACK ON Marburg came in the dead of night. Spec-tral fog gathered over the marshland around the mouth of the Reik where it spilled over the treacherous sandbars and narrow channels of the harbour. Marburg wasn't as naturally blessed as Jutonsryk in its geography, but it had the advantage of being on the Reik, which meant it could control the traffic of ships to Reikdorf.

That thought alone made Marius's mouth water.

'A city of gold,' he whispered. 'That's what this place could be.'

His lancers looked over at his words, but none spoke. Unlike some counts, he didn't encourage fraternisation between commoners and their betters.

Marius and a hundred of his warriors stood on the southern shore of the main channel that led to the curving ring of the docks where Aldred and the Raven Helms awaited. The quayside was deserted, all those ships that could flee the city having sailed around the coast to safer ports in the south. It made for a strange sight to see a port bereft of ships.

Despite her brother's urgings to remain in the city, Marika commanded a host of archers on the rooftops and forecastle-shaped towers set in the curve of the citadel's lower walls. From there her archers could rain down arrows upon the dead without fear of retaliation.

Rearing up behind her archers was the Raven Hall, the monstrous tower dominating the skyline with its beaked upper chambers and swept-back wings. Impressive enough in its own way, Marius found it rather vulgar, like something the ancient tribal kings might have raised to some long forgotten animal god. Hundreds of crows and ravens alighted on its ledges and carvings, such that it shivered with feathers as though coming alive.

Endal warriors occupied positions all along the docks and shoreline, their spears and shields wavering like tiny specks of starlight in the darkness. Aldred had been a hard man to convince of his own danger, but with Marika's help, Marius had been able to persuade him to evacuate many of the oldest and youngest along the river towards Reikdorf. Marburg was a city of warriors now, but as night after night passed without an attack, fear gnawed at the courage of every man.

Truth be told, it was almost a relief when the dead finally came.

Huntsmen watched the coastal approaches to Marburg, and Marius had persuaded Aldred to send out sentry ships to watch for the undead corsairs. One of those ships now bobbed in the dark swells of the harbour, its sails torn and holed, listing to the side where planks had been torn from its ribs by bony fingers. Its crew still stood on its decks; the helmsman at the tiller and its captain behind the wheel, but it was clear to all who saw them that these men were dead.

The ship had drifted into Marburg an hour before the watch fires were lit, and as darkness closed in, the city's defenders rushed to their posts. Yellowed fog rolled in from the sea, and Marius heard the flat, toneless sound of ships' bells, the same bells that had rung the death knell of his city. He smiled weakly as he realised he was afraid. That was a new sensation. Even when Bastiaan had stabbed him in Middenheim he had been more angry than afraid.

The monotonous sound conjured images of skeletal ferrymen and a black river crossing from which no living soul could return. Bobbing corpse lights followed the echoes of the bells, and Marius saw a host of ships drift into the harbour, over two hundred of them, each with torn sails, splintered oars and swollen, barnacle-encrusted hulls. They came on without need for wind or sail, dread ships of the forsaken and the damned.

'Now,' hissed Marius, willing the defenders ranked up along the line of docks to hear his whispered imprecation. 'Come on, Aldred, don't be a fool all your life.'

The ships came on until a single fiery arrow arced up into the night sky.

Flames rippled around the curve of the docks as oil-soaked braziers were sparked to life and the city's entire complement of war machines were unmasked from behind wicker mantlets. Marius heard the creak of wind-lasses as heavy ballistae cranked, followed by a *whoosh* of the barbed tips of great javelins being set alight. Ten of these machines had been dismantled from their positions on the city's eastern walls and carried down to the

docks, where they had been rebuilt in makeshift earth-
works of good Reikland mud.

The heavy iron bolts leapt towards the enemy ships
and six were struck, the flaming missiles punching
through their rotten timbers and setting them ablaze.
Holed beyond the ability of their masters' dark magic to
sustain, they slid beneath the water and distant cheering
drifted up to the Jutones' position.

'Don't get carried away,' said Marius. 'The dead don't
fear a bit of water.'

More missiles leapt from the war machines, smashing
masts and breaking open hulls with every bolt as the war
machines' crews found their range. The ships of the dead
scattered, moving with greater urgency towards the
shoreline. A flurry of arrows rained down from the high
town, thudding home on the decks of the hulks or piercing the dead meat of their crew.

Marius saw Marika among the archers, loosing white-
fletched shafts from a bow he was sure was of fey origin.
He had sent a similar bow to Sigmar before Black Fire,
which he'd heard the Emperor had broken over his knee.
Such a shame, the bow had been worth more gold than
Sigmar would have seen in his life.

Nothing more had been said of his and Marika's conversation the other night, but Marius was savvy enough
to know that it still hung in the air between them. He
could do nothing to act on her unsaid plan just yet, but
perhaps his doing nothing was just what she wanted.

'My lord,' said Vergoossen, appearing from the darkness and shivering in a thick woollen cloak. 'Should we
not be on the move? Much as I am loath to approach
anything resembling a battle, was our plan not to move
to occupy the southern tip of the docks upon the appearance of the dead?'

'Indeed, it was,' said Marius, watching the battle unfold

as the ships of the dead reached the docks. The first of the drowned sailors leapt from their ships and no sooner had they done so than Marika loosed a flaming arrow that lit the oil spread around the quayside in wide troughs hacked into the stone. A wall of searing flame leapt up and ran around the docks like a fiery snake, setting hundreds of corpses alight and spreading swiftly to their ships.

'Is that not our plan now?' asked Vergoossen. 'I do not recall any tactical amendments from Count Aldred.'

'No, you wouldn't have, Vergoossen,' said Marius. 'This one came from Princess Marika. She and her brother clearly share an… interesting relationship.'

'I see, my lord.'

'No you don't,' said Marius. 'But it doesn't matter. Watch and learn, Vergoossen. Watch and learn. This is how things change in this world, not with diplomacy and words, but with swords and gold and ambition.'

The wind carried the stink of rotten, burning meat, and Marius covered his mouth with a pomander scented with exotic fruits and rose petals. The fire on the docks was dying now, and yet more of the dead were pouring from their ships or climbing from the muddy waters of the shores. The Raven Helms charged, smashing into the dead with heavy broadswords, cutting them down with brutal strokes. They pushed the dead back, driving them into the water as Endal tribesmen fought to keep the flanks of the elite warriors safe.

'Ah, now things get interesting,' said Marius, as hundreds of the living dead waded ashore below them. Water spilled from opened bellies and vacant ribcages. Green fire guttered in rotted eye sockets. The dead lurched in the direction of the Raven Helms, ignoring the Jutones on the higher ground.

'Won't the Raven Helms be flanked if we do not move?' asked Vergoossen.

'Of course,' said Marius, drawing his sword. 'And the bloodshed will be terrible, but at the last moment, the heroic Marius will save the day. Saga poets will sing songs of my bravery for years to come.'

'I hope you are right, my lord,' replied Vergoossen.

'Of course I am,' said Marius.

MARIKA LOOSED ANOTHER arrow into the flaming horde below, struggling to contain her horror at these decaying revenants as they shambled ashore from their doomed boats. Dozens were ablaze in the harbour, banishing the crepuscular gloom with the fury of their demise. To see so many of the dead clawing at the living brought back all the memories she'd buried of her time in the marshes. The lingering doubts she'd had regarding her unspoken pact with Marius were forgotten as the suffocating terror of that night returned to her.

'Another quiver!' she shouted, and Eloise passed her a fresh batch of arrows. Her maidservant had refused to leave with the rest of those who fled for Reikdorf, but Marika saw she was now regretting that decision.

She nocked another arrow and sighted on a skeletal warrior with a rusty cutlass and a hole in its breast where a heart once beat. She let out a breath and loosed before drawing another. Her arrow flew straight and true, slashing into the dead warrior's chest and dropping him to the ground in a pile of disconnected bones. It was a fine shot, but ultimately a waste of a shaft. Marius had told them to look for the host's sorcerers, evil beings who gave life to the army of the dead.

Without these fell magickers, the dead could not sustain their existence and would return to the grave. She didn't know how Marius had learned of such things, but supposed that with enough gold, you could learn anything in the world.

Marika scanned the docks, finally spying a hunched figure lurking by the gunwale of a wrecked ship listing against the quayside. She pulled another arrow and took her time with her aim, allowing for the gentle sway of her target's ship and the slight wind. The figure turned towards her, and she saw its face was that of a man, though one ravaged by some hideous wasting sickness or starvation.

Her arrow punched through his right eye, the barbed tip bursting from the back of his skull and pinning him to the gunwale. The dead things clambering from his ship lurched drunkenly as their dissolution overcame them. Armoured warriors of bone and rotted meat collapsed where they stood and the bloated corpses of drowning victims sagged and fell back into the sea. Perhaps fifty of the dead cracked and crumbled to ash with the death of the black sorcerer, and Marika's heart surged with sudden hope.

To face the dead was to know fear like never before, but to fight them... that was the sweetest elixir. She whooped with newfound fearlessness. She shouted to the rest of the archers, reminding them of what to look for, feeling her heart race with surging life.

'My lady?' whimpered Eloise. 'What's that?'

The light of the moon was obscured as the carrion birds took off from the eaves and garrets of the Raven Hall. Marika had seen birds behaving like that before. The birds were flocking not to feed, but to flee. She looked to where Eloise was pointing, seeing hundreds of screeching bats swarming in from the sea. Their leathery wings sounded like a fleet of ships at sail, but behind them came something far larger, far worse and far more terrible than she could have dreamed in her worst nightmares.

* * *

ALDRED WATCHED THE sky darken as hundreds of bats swarmed the night with their hideous furred bodies. Ever creatures of ill-omen, bats were vermin with a thirst for blood, and claws that carried all manner of foulness. Arrows flashed toward them from the citadel walls, and though he hated to admit it, Marius was right to deploy the archers further back.

The fighting around the docks raged in the leaping shadows of dying fires, a frantic fight for survival against a foe that cared nothing for pain. His warriors had beaten back one attack and he had driven Ulfshard into the chest of one of the robed sorcerers Marius had told them to look for. That death had unmade two ships' worth of the dead and Aldred felt unbridled joy as their spirits were released from bondage.

Endal tribesmen fought to prevent the dead from getting a foothold on the docks, but their enemy's numbers were telling in every backwards step they were forced to take. The wail and skirl of pipe music echoed over the water and filled the hearts of every warrior with courage. While the ancient tunes of glory played, no man could fail to fight without feeling the judgemental eyes of his ancestors upon him.

A dreadful shriek echoed over the water, and Aldred flinched as something monstrous flew overhead. He heard screams, and saw a winged shadow swoop down on the city, a terrible monster of darkness with a black armoured figure astride its bony, elongated neck.

His terror nearly overwhelmed him as a stray shaft of moonlight reflected from its exposed bone and dead scale hide. Ragged wings of death-stiffened hide flapped with ponderous slowness and its rotted jaws opened wide exposing broken, jutting fangs of yellow.

'It's a dragon... a dead one...' he said, unable to believe his eyes, feeling his fragile courage melting away at the sight of so terrifying a monster in the flesh. Its body shimmered as though not truly corporeal, and Aldred's soul wept to see a creature from the elder days of the world violated in such a hideous manner.

Necrotic flesh withered on its millennia old bones, and flaps of skin trailed from ancient lance wounds in its flank. Its elongated head was horned and hooked, barbs of bone and tooth making its jaw a serrated blade as long as a warship's keel. Sat astride its bony neck was a hooded figure robed in black, its body wreathed in baleful energies of undeath. Pale wisps of bleak twilight billowed around the rider and wherever its gaze turned, men fell dead in terror, the flesh withering to ash on their bones.

The mighty dragon swooped down over the citadel walls, and a billowing cloud of noxious breath streamed from its jaws to engulf the ramparts. The stench was overpowering, even from so far away, and Marius coughed at the grave reek. He could hear men dying, choking and coughing as their internal organs liquefied and the flesh melted from their bones.

Wails of terror spread along the docks as warriors threw down their weapons and fled in terror from the corpse dragon. Alone among the Endals, the Raven Helms held firm, but one look at their faces told Aldred they were close to breaking. He held Ulfshard aloft, and the pale blue glow of the fey enchantments woven into its arcane metal poured iron into their veins.

The living quailed before the sight of the dragon, but the dead cared nothing for its dreadful magnificence, and threw themselves upon the Raven Helms once more. Notched blades clove armour, claws and teeth ripped flesh. Aldred blocked a slashing cleaver and beheaded its wielder as he saw that he and the Raven Helms fought on alone. Endals were dying all around him, borne to the ground by the dead or skewered on rusted spears.

The defence of the docks had become a rout, hundreds of warriors fleeing towards the lower walls of the citadel. The gates were open and men fought to reach the safety of the walls. Laredus fought through a press of the dead warriors towards Aldred, the top portion of his sword snapped off and his black armour torn by bloodied claws.

'We need to go, my lord!' he shouted. 'We can hold them at the walls.'

Aldred nodded, too weary to even reply. His sword arm felt like his veins had been filled with lead and the exhaustion of the fighting settled upon him like a cloak of iron. He knew he was no longer as fit as he needed to be. This one fight had almost drained him.

'Sound the retreat,' he gasped.

'There's no need,' said Laredus. 'We're all that's left. Raven Helms! With the count!'

Aldred and Laredus turned and ran towards the gates of the citadel, but they had covered barely half the distance when the ground trembled. Glittering particles swirled in hundreds of miniature whirlwinds, dust devils that spun and twisted like living things of spectral light. They gathered form and solidity until hundreds of translucent figures stood between them and the citadel, a lambent host of ancient men and women with eyes of pale white and mouths stretched open in soundless screams.

The blood froze in Aldred's veins.

An army of the dead behind them and a host of hungry ghosts ahead of them.

They were trapped.

MARIKA SAW THE host of shimmering spirits arise from the dust and her humanity rebelled at the sight of these wretched souls denied their final rest. She could feel their pain and the horror of their blasted existence, and tears welled at the thought of such a fate. What manner of man could tear these souls from Morr's realm and force them into slavery, denying them their rightful place in the next world?

These dreadful wraiths flickered in the air like wavering candle flames, drifting against the wind towards Aldred and the Raven Helms. A ring of dead warriors and glowing spirits surrounded them, and there was nothing anyone could do. No warrior dared leave the citadel while the looming dragon and fear of the restless spirits held their courage in check.

Screams and groans of pain surrounded her. The dragon's breath had swept the ramparts and its pestilential exhalation choked the life and vitality from all those who breathed its foulness. Young men in the full fire of youth had fallen to the ground, transformed into ancients with withered skin, brittle bones and sunken flesh. Some coughed up bloody froth as their lungs dissolved, while others had the flesh scoured from their bones by the noxious corruption.

A handful of arrows slashed up at the beast, but every single one bounced from its dead hide. The war machine crews attempted to bring down the beast, but some hideous force protected it from their missiles. Unable to harm the dragon, the survivors of its attack turned their bows upon the dead spirits, loosing volley after volley at the glowing figures. Their arrows passed through the spirits' forms, clattering on the cobbled streets and shattering as though they had been frozen in flight.

They might as well have been loosing arrows at clouds for all the effect they were having.

Undeterred, Marika pulled back her bowstring and loosed a shaft from the bow her father had given her on her fifteenth birthday. The bowstave was fashioned from a wood no Endal craftsman could name or work, its length inlaid with silver threads woven through the grain of the wood in swirling patterns that changed with the seasons.

Her arrow leapt from the bow, arcing up and slashing down through the spirits, and where its point struck, one of the forlorn revenants vanished in a flare of light.

'They *can* be slain,' she said, looking in amazement at her bow. The metallic threads shimmered with life and the wood grew warm to the touch. Her father had told her the bow had been crafted by the fey folk from across the ocean, but she hadn't really believed him until now. She bent her bow and released over and over, freeing more of the damned spirits from their hellish servitude in shimmering twists of light.

But as many as she banished, there was no way she was going to destroy enough to save Aldred and the Raven Helms.

ALDRED AND LAREDUS stood back to back as the dead drew near. Ulfshard shimmered with a blue light, the blade brighter than Aldred had ever known it. The moans of the dead cut through the din of battle and the dry roar of the dragon and its screeching bats. The Raven Helms fought the dead coming in from the sea with desperate strokes, blocking ship's axes and cutting down dead men who came at them with nothing but their clawed hands reaching to pluck the eyes from their heads.

The spirits of the dead enveloped them, swirling in a cloying mist of screams and tormented wailing. They tore at the Endals with insubstantial claws that passed through the thickest armour yet drew no blood. The merest touch of these damned spirits sucked the vitality from a warrior like a leech drawing blood from a wound. None came near Aldred, flinching from him as soon as he brought Ulfshard to bear. He swept his sword through the misty substance of the spirits, feeling their joy as the connection to the evil sorcery binding them to the world of the living was severed.

Yet it was not enough. The spirits shrieked and wailed as they were dissipated by Aldred's blade, but there were too many of the fleshy undead to defeat. The ring of Raven Helms shrank as the ranks of the dead swelled still further. More ships were crashing into the shoreline to disgorge yet more of the doomed warriors of the dead.

Aldred heard a furious clamour from the citadel and saw a banner of bright colours borne through the mêlée, a flag no Endal would dream of bearing. It was a Jutone flag, ostentatiously colourful and garish, and beneath it rode a host of armoured lancers in pale blue cloaks fighting with curved sabres. Marius fought at their centre, cutting a dashing path through the dead with the elegant sweeps of a duellist. His blade was a golden streak of sunlight, and like Ulfshard, the dead feared it.

The Jutone cavalry smashed through the encircling dead, and Marius backhanded a reverse cut into the skull of a dead warrior, neatly removing the top of his head. Marius fought with fluid grace, as much a showman as a killer. His skill was undeniable, though Aldred saw he favoured his right side.

The charge of the Jutone horsemen was devastating, smashing the dead apart with ferocity Aldred had hitherto not suspected. The Endals had long believed the Jutones had gone soft in their city of merchants, preferring the luxuries gold could buy instead of living as warriors. Clearly he had underestimated Marius, and the thought disturbed rather than reassured him.

While the Raven Helms and Jutone lancers held the

dead at bay, Marius reined in his horse beside Aldred, his face flushed with excitement and the thrill of battle.

'I think you should be getting out of here, yes?' said Marius.

'Where in Manann's name did you come from?' demanded Aldred. 'Weren't you supposed to be holding the southern shore?'

'We were, but rather more monsters than we could handle came ashore and I had to fall back to the citadel to save my men,' said Marius. 'We mounted up as soon as we saw your danger, and here we are.'

'You allowed us to be flanked!'

'Yes, my deepest apologies about that, but I did send a runner informing you of our withdrawal,' said Marius smoothly. 'I suppose he must have been killed en route. That is a pity.'

'A pity!' stormed Aldred. 'We were almost overrun.'

'And you still will be if you insist on having this ridiculous discussion now,' pointed out Marius. 'Get up behind me if you want to live through this night.'

Marius held out his hand to Aldred, who bit back an angry retort as he hauled himself onto the back of the Jutone count's horse. Though it went against everything he knew to be right, he held his sword out to Marius.

'The spirit creatures fear the magic of Ulfshard,' he said. 'Use it to cut us a path.'

'No need, they fear mine also,' said Marius with a manic grin. 'Now let's be off.'

Marius kicked back his spurs with a wild yell, and his horse took off towards the citadel. The Jutone lancers fought alongside the Raven Helms as Marius forced the howling wraiths back with his enchanted blade. They rode back towards the citadel gates through the path the lancers had cut. Aldred heard cheers from the ramparts as they came within sight of the gates and laughed with joy. He saw his sister loosing arrows into the dead, and his relief fled as he saw the expression on her face.

It was disappointment.

━◄ FOURTEEN ►━

North, East and West

REDWANE PACED THE firelit interior of the temple of Ulric, a pulsing vein throbbing at his temple as he listened to Myrsa's pronouncement. Renweard stood at the count's side, the sword of the Warrior Eternal held loosely over his shoulder, while Bordan sat on a block of dark stone yet to be hoisted to the temple walls. The flame of Ulric burned cold in the centre of the stone-flagged plaza, white and stark against walls that rose daily to enclose it as the temple neared completion.

Ar-Ulric and his wolves circled the flame, their black eyes reflecting its glow and regarding Redwane as a fox eyes a wounded hen. The temple had changed a great deal since Sigmar's defeat of the daemon lord, all traces of the battle cleaned from the stonework and paved over with polished granite hewn from the quarries of the Middle Mountains. It had been a magnificent battle, yet no one wanted a reminder of that dread avatar of the northern gods to befoul a holy place of Ulric.

'I can't believe I'm hearing this,' said Redwane. 'You're really not going to march out?'

'I have made my judgement, Redwane,' said Myrsa. 'And my decision is final.'

'But Sigmar needs us. You heard what Ar-Ulric said – the armies of Nagash are closing on Reikdorf. We have to ride south.'

'We need to keep Middenheim safe,' said Myrsa, clutching the hilt of the runefang tightly. The count of the northern marches walked towards Redwane and laid a hand upon his shoulder. 'I know you and Sigmar are close, but the Emperor has entrusted me with the safety of Middenheim and I cannot let him down. If I ride south with my army then this city is doomed. Surely you must see that?'

'All I see is that we're abandoning the Emperor when he needs us most.'

'You are not thinking straight, my friend,' said Myrsa, concern written across his features. 'The deathly champion on the causeway wounded you deeper than you know.'

Redwane shrugged off Myrsa's hand, angry at the other man's pity. Two days had passed since Ar-Ulric's arrival, and his strength was only now beginning to return. The icy numbness and frozen chill that had stilled his heart still clung to his grey flesh. No heat warmed Redwane now, yet neither cold nor fear touched him any more. His body was alive, yet he felt no sensations of life. Food was tasteless, beauty meaningless, and all that remained to him was the pain of his many scars.

He turned to Ar-Ulric, his tone accusing. 'You agree with this? You crowned Sigmar, remember? You would cower in this mountain city and leave him to his fate? That is not Ulric's way, or if it is, I'll have no part of it.'

The wolves at Ar-Ulric's side growled, baring fangs of

ice and obsidian, their yellowed eyes boring into him with cunning beyond that of beasts. Redwane met their stare unflinchingly, daring them to gainsay him. Ar-Ulric crossed the temple towards him, his aura of frozen winters leaving Redwane untouched. Behind the great wolf-skull helm, Redwane saw piercing eyes like those of the wolves, one pale as a winter sky, the other blacker than a moonless night.

'You are soul-sick, Redwane of the Unberogen,' said Ar-Ulric, placing his glittering axe between them. Chill wisps of icy air wafted from the blade and haft, but Redwane felt nothing of the cold. 'You do not see the passage of time as I do. I roam the wild places of this world, following the breath of Ulric to the forgotten sites of primal power. I seek to follow the wolf god's path and instruct men in his ways of honour and courage.'

'Really?' said Redwane. 'Then why do we never see you? It's been over a decade since you've shown your damn face amongst the tribes. That doesn't sound like you're doing much in the way of instruction. That sounds a lot like hiding to me.'

'Redwane!' barked Myrsa. 'Hold your tongue!'

Ar-Ulric held up his hand to silence Myrsa. 'My days of wandering are over. From this day until the coming of the Red Eye, he who brings the End Times, Middenheim shall be my abode. But the Heldenhammer must face the dread Necromancer without the warriors of the north or he is not fit to be Emperor.'

'Why?' demanded Redwane. 'Tell me why.'

'Because if the Flame of Ulric is ever extinguished, then the Empire dies with it. Do *you* understand that, Redwane of the Unberogen?'

'I understand it, but I do not accept it,' said Redwane. 'And if that is the word of Ulric, then I spit on him and curse his name with my last breath!'

Gasps of horror spread through the temple at Redwane's blasphemy, and more than one hand found its way to a weapon. Renweard swung the sword of the Warrior Eternal down, and Myrsa's face flushed in anger.

'You dare speak such words in this place?' cried Myrsa.

'You're damn right I do,' Redwane shouted back at him. 'You're deserting your Emperor and your friend because this madman who roams the wilderness on his own tells you to. For all you know he's as mad as Torbrecan's lunatics. Well I won't abandon Sigmar, and if you won't march to Reikdorf, I'll go alone.'

'Then you'll die,' said Myrsa.

'So be it,' said Redwane. 'The gods don't seem to care one way or another.'

He spun on his heel and marched towards an archway to the city beyond, feeling dead inside yet filled with fresh purpose and determination.

'Damn you, Redwane, I forbid you to go,' said Myrsa. 'You are a warrior of the White Wolves! Sworn to the defence of Middenheim.'

Redwane turned and tore the wolf pelt from his shoulders. He dropped the cloak at his feet and unhooked the heavy warhammer from his belt. He let it slide from his grip, and it fell with a clatter of finality to the flagstones.

'Not any more I'm not,' he said.

THE STREETS OF Middenheim were cold, colder than he remembered them, but it didn't touch him. Redwane saw men and women huddled in doorways, pulling threadbare blankets around them as the breath misted before their mouths. Sunlight couldn't penetrate the oppressive gloom that pressed down, and it seemed as though the warmth was being leeched from the world day by day. Once again, the city was filled with refugees, and Redwane wondered what manner of gods could leave their people to suffer such an endless parade of misery as the people of the Empire were forced to endure.

Redwane walked the streets at random, keeping to the shadows and losing himself in the maze of stone structures. Faces passed him, men in armour and men in rags. He no longer knew where he was going, and he no longer cared. Men he had trusted and called friend were turning their backs on Sigmar, the hero who had given them everything. Now Sigmar was in mortal danger and they did nothing to help him. The certainties of loyalty and honour upon which Redwane had built his life were crumbling, and all that was left was the coldness in his heart that knew there was only one path open to him.

He passed through the streets as a ghost, numb to the world around him and feeling the pain of his scars as if they reached down through his skin and into his bones. The wound in his chest throbbed like a second heartbeat, one that pumped ice around his body instead of blood. People were looking at him strangely, but he paid them no mind, walking ever onwards as he unbuckled plates of his armour, shedding iron as a serpent sheds its skin to be reborn.

His path became clearer with every plate that hit the ground, his steps surer and more certain. His head came up and he saw the world around him, bleached of colour and life, and knew that this was its true face. Love was a lie and struggling against the pain and misery that life threw up was pointless.

He felt a hand on his shoulder and turned to see a face he knew, but couldn't place.

'What in Ulric's name are you doing, you fool?' said the black-haired man clad in red armour and wrapped in a wolfskin cloak. Another man stood behind him, one with a sour face that made him look like he'd swallowed a mouthful of vinegar.

'I know you,' said Redwane.

'Of course you damn well do,' snapped the man. 'It's me, Leovulf.'

'Leovulf, yes,' nodded Redwane.

'We heard what happened at the temple of Ulric,' said Leovulf. 'But what they're saying's wrong isn't it? You're still a White Wolf aren't you?'

'Doesn't look like it,' said the other man, lifting a discarded vambrace from the street.

'Shut up, Ustern,' said Leovulf.

Ustern, yes, that was it. Redwane turned away from them, making his way deeper into the city.

'Hey,' said Leovulf, taking hold of him once again. 'Were they right about you saying you're leaving for Reikdorf? To fight alongside the Emperor?'

'Yes, I'm going to Reikdorf,' said Redwane. 'That's what I told Myrsa, and that's what I'm doing. The Emperor needs us and I'll be damned if I don't go to him.'

'And I'll be damned if I let you go get yourself killed.'

'Don't try and stop me,' said Redwane, clenching his fists.

'I'm not going to, but I meant what I said. I'm not going to let you get yourself killed, so if you're set on marching to Reikdorf, then I suppose I'm going with you.'

'I'll come too,' said Ustern. Redwane and Leovulf looked at him in surprise. Ustern shrugged. 'A captain needs his banner bearer, else he's not a captain is he?'

'Good point, lad,' said Leovulf. 'Well?'

'Well what?' said Redwane.

'How are you planning to get to Reikdorf?' demanded Leovulf. 'In case you hadn't noticed, there's a host of the living dead surrounding this city. You'll need a damned army to break through, and I don't see Count Myrsa giving you his.'

'I know,' said Redwane, 'but I know how we can get another one.'

DAWN WAS LESS than an hour away, but Maedbh knew the rising sun wouldn't save them. She knelt beside a boulder at the edge of the river and dipped her cupped palms below its rippling surface. Splashing the cold water on her face sharpened her focus, but she knew it wouldn't last. Her entire body ached and she rubbed the heels of her palms against her eyes.

Even on campaign, when sleep was an elusive bedfellow, she hadn't been this tired. In times of war she fought alongside warriors, men and women who could look after themselves. This was very different.

Now she had people to protect who couldn't defend themselves.

The entire population of Three Hills and its surrounding villages had agglomerated into one long column of frightened people, making their way west with whatever possessions they could load onto wagons or carry on their backs. Perhaps six hundred people rested in the shade of a low ridge of hills, old men and women, children and those too sick or injured to march with the queen. Garr's sword band of Queen's Eagles stood watch and she gave thanks that Freya had thought to leave these fearsome warriors at Three Hills. Only thirty of them marched with them, but their presence alone was helping to keep spirits high.

Maedbh turned away from thoughts of the queen, the guilt that she should have gone with her assuaged by the fact that she could still protect her own daughter and Freya's sons. She clung to the hope that Freya might still live; after all, Master Alaric had said that some had escaped the massacre. If anyone could survive a battle with the living dead, it was Queen Freya.

This was their fifth day of march, and they had covered barely half the distance to the confluence of the great rivers. The oldest and youngest rode in the few wagons that hadn't been taken by the queen's army, but the rest walked. They were moving too slowly, and their pursuers did not need to stop to eat and rest as they must. Despite their stature, the dwarfs easily matched the pace of the Asoborns, moving ahead of the column and keeping watch on its vulnerable sides and rear. They took no rest, didn't seem to eat or sleep, and were as indefatigable as the foe that pursued them.

Packs of dead wolves dogged their every step, darting in from the flanks to savage a straggling family or to pick off a child that wandered too far from the column. The dwarfs had saved as many as they could, but Maedbh sensed their frustration at the slow speed the Asoborns were making. The dead were right behind them, and every time her people rested, they got a little closer.

Ulrike, Sigulf and Fridleifr lay asleep on the grass beside her, and Maedbh stroked her daughter's hair. She was loath to wake the children, but dwarf scouts had reported seeing sunlight on spear points no more than a few miles behind them. They would need to be on the move soon.

She wished Wolfgart were here, imagining him riding over the hills on his finest stallion to her rescue with his mighty sword hewing the dead like corn at harvest time.

'What I wouldn't give to see that,' she whispered. 'I miss you, my gorgeous man.'

Maedbh looked up from the river as she saw a stout warrior in heavy plates of gleaming metal and fine mail reflected in the water. She hadn't heard him approach.

'Master Alaric,' she said.

'The man you are bonded to is called Wolfgart?' asked Alaric.

Maedbh nodded, more surprised at the question than by the fact that the dwarf knew to whom she was bonded. 'That's right. Do you know him?'

'I do,' said the dwarf. 'I fought beside him at Black Fire, and we saved each other's life many times in the tunnels beneath Ulric's city.'

'Middenheim? Wolfgart would never speak of that battle.'

'That does not surprise me, for it was bloody and desperate,' said Alaric. 'I do not like to remember it, but if you are his bonded woman, then I must.'

'I don't understand.'

'A dwarf never forgives an insult, and never forgets a debt.'

Maedbh laughed mirthlessly. 'Wolfgart owes you money? He always was lousy at dice.'

'No,' said Alaric. 'Not money. Wolfgart and I fought the vermin beasts in the tunnels beneath Middenheim. The rats were all over us, and we fought in the cramped darkness by the light of dying torches. We fought with axes, picks and daggers or whatever came to hand. I hauled his arse from the jaws of a giant ogre beast with metal for arms and he slew an armoured rat-champion with a short-handled pick to its brain. We fought in those tunnels for days, but at the end of it all we were victorious. I remember every moment of that fight, and Wolfgart saved my life on seven separate occasions. I saved him six times.'

'I'm sure Wolfgart isn't counting,' said Maedbh.

'That matters not,' said Alaric. 'I am counting, and I owe him a blood debt.'

'What does that mean?'

'It means that I am indebted to him and his kin.'

'Is that why you came to Three Hills, to pay your debt to Wolfgart?'

'Not entirely,' said Alaric. 'We were coming to the Empire to take back a war machine your Emperor's warriors retrieved from a representative of the Deeplock Clan. That, and we heard that the great necromancer had returned. But mainly to retrieve the war machine. Your settlement was on the way and was the quickest way for us to get ahead of the blood drinker's army.'

'Then I'm indebted to you for warning us,' said Maedbh.

Alaric shook his head. 'There is no debt between you and I, Maedbh of Three Hills, but when I see you to Reikdorf, the debt I have with Wolfgart is settled.'

'That seems fair enough,' agreed Maedbh.

'To allow me to honour that debt, I need you to do something.'

'Yes, I know,' said Maedbh, pushing herself wearily to her feet. 'I will get my people moving, but they needed to rest.'

Alaric looked back to the east, as though he could see through the earth to spy upon the army of the dead. For all Maedbh knew of the mountain folk's skill, perhaps he could. Alaric sniffed the air and stamped a foot on the hard packed earth of the riverbank, as though listening to its echo through the ground.

'That is not what I mean,' said Alaric.

'Then what *do* you mean?'

'You know what I mean. My debt is to you, not these other manlings. You have to leave those who cannot keep up. Your kind lives and dies so quickly it will make no difference to your race. The old will be dead soon anyway, and you can breed more young in your belly. These ones aren't old enough to work or fight yet. What use are they to you?'

Maedbh struggled to hold her temper in the face of Alaric's request.

'You want us to leave our people behind?' she said, as evenly as she could.

'It is the only way some of you will live,' said the dwarf. 'Save those who can outpace the dead, leave the rest behind. Better to save some than none.'

'No, Master Alaric,' said Maedbh. 'That won't be happening. No one gets left behind.'

'Then you will all die.'

'Then we will all die,' hissed Maedbh. 'I'd sooner we all died right here than live with knowing I left my own people here to be killed.'

Alaric's face was unreadable in the dim light, but Maedbh thought he was more surprised at her decision than angry or disappointed. At length, he sighed.

'Very well, if you will not leave them behind, then my warriors and I cannot leave.'

'What? No! I don't want your deaths on my head.'

'That is not our custom, Maedbh of Three Hills,' said Alaric. 'The debt demands it.'

Further words were forestalled as Garr came running over, his sword drawn and the visor of his eagle-winged helmet pulled down over his handsome face.

'My lady,' he said, 'the mountain folk say the vanguard of the dead are upon us. You need to go right now. We will hold them off as long as we can, but you must get the queen's boys out of here.'

Maedbh took a deep breath, weighing the impossible choices before her.

'No,' she said. 'We're not leaving.'

'My lady?' said Garr. 'You have to move. Queen Freya–'

'Queen Freya is not here,' snapped Maedbh. 'And you will obey me, Garr. Do you understand?'

'Yes, my lady,' said the warrior. 'What is it you require of us?'

Maedbh looked around her for somewhere they could

make their stand, finally settling upon a wooded hill to the north. The river curled lazily around its eastern flank, and the thick trees would make any advance from the west next to impossible. The dead would have to come straight at them up the steep southern slope.

'Form up with Alaric's dwarfs on yonder hill,' she said, pointing to the ridge of trees above them. 'We can't out-run the dead, so we'll fight them. We'll fight them and make them wish they'd never invaded Asoborn lands.'

Garr quickly studied the lie of the land, and she saw his understanding that this could be nothing more than a last stand. Maedbh gripped his shoulder and jabbed a fist at the column of Asoborns.

'Get everyone who can hold a weapon in the battle line, no matter how old or young or wounded,' ordered Maedbh. 'Everyone fights, no one runs.'

He nodded and said, 'It will be done, my lady.'

The Queen's Eagle ran off to get the Asoborns moving and Maedbh turned to Master Alaric. She drew her sword and said, 'After today your debt is settled, whether we live or die. Will that satisfy your customs?'

'It will indeed, my lady,' nodded Master Alaric with a deep bow. 'It will be my honour to die alongside you, Maedbh of Three Hills.'

'Don't put me in the ground just yet,' said Maedbh as the sun rose over the eastern mountains, spreading its promise across the land. She smiled as fresh hope filled her heart and closed her eyes, tilting her face towards the sun. 'This is the Empire, and stranger things have happened than us living to see another dawn.'

Alaric heard the change in her voice and shook his head.

'Give me a hundred lifetimes and I'll never understand you manlings,' he grumbled.

* * *

THE THIRD NIGHT of attacks on Marburg's citadel walls
ended with the dawn, the dead melting away to the shadowed eaves of the lower town and docks. The base of the
walls were thick with bones and decaying corpses, the
detritus of the night's battle which would, come sun-
down, rise once more to claw their way up the pitted
stone.

Though the loss of the lower town was a blow, Marius's
rescue of Aldred had given the defenders fresh hope, and
the tale of his magnificent ride circulated throughout the
city, becoming ever grander and more adventurous as it
went. Each day saw the warriors defending Marburg
working in shifts to rebuild broken defences, shore up
gates that withered and rotted under the effects of wasting sorcery, stitch wounds and pray to the gods for
salvation.

Marius shook his sword free of ash from the grinning,
skull-faced dead man he'd just killed, and sheathed his
blade. The warriors around him cheered, and he smiled
modestly as he accepted a towel from a nearby lancer to
mop his brow.

'We may fight at night, but it's still damned hot work,'
he said, loud enough for the warriors along this stretch
of wall to hear. A few dutiful chuckles greeted his remark,
but most of the men were too exhausted and drained by
fear to acknowledge his words. Few had slept since the
battle had begun. Terrible visions plagued every man's
dreams and phantoms haunted the streets in ghostly
processions of long dead comrades.

Looping the towel around his neck, Marius rested his
elbows on a projecting merlon of the walls, scanning the
lower town for any sign of a fresh attack. A dank fug of
lingering smoke and mist hung over the abandoned dis-
trict, rendering its buildings blurred and its inhabitants
ghostly. At a distance, the docks of Marburg could almost

be normal; hundreds of indistinct figures filled its streets, shuffling from one shadow to the next, milling with apparent purpose, but really just meandering like ants from an overturned nest. Most of the corsair ships that had brought the dead to Marburg were wrecked now, their hulls holed by long shafts of iron hurled from the citadel's war machines or burned with flaming arrows.

Marius glanced skyward, looking for the dragon that had attacked the walls on the first night. It swooped over the fighting, filling the air with a drifting miasma that reeked of putrefaction and caused many of the wounded to sicken.

He turned as he smelled a scent of wildflowers, recognising the fragrant oil Marika liked to rub on her skin. She hadn't spoken to him after his rescue of Aldred, and Marius was intrigued to hear what she would make of that act. Marika wore leather buckskin, elegantly cut yet practical, and a quilted leather jerkin. Her bow was slung over one shoulder and a slender rapier was sheathed at her side. Marika's blonde hair was tied back in a severe ponytail, yet she was still devastatingly feminine.

Which was a welcome sight in a citadel defended by burly, seafaring men.

'Princess,' he said with a languid bow. 'It gladdens my heart to see you well.'

'Count Marius,' she said. 'Would you walk with me awhile?'

'It would be my honour,' replied Marius, hiding his amusement at the simmering anger he saw lurking behind her façade of courtesy. He proffered his arm and she hooked her own around it as they walked the length of the ramparts, looking like a courting couple out for a promenade along the seafront. A pair of Jutone lancers and four Raven Helms followed them, chaperones and bodyguards all in one.

When they had put enough distance between themselves and their warriors, Marika tilted her face towards him and said, 'What in Manann's name did you think you were doing?'

'I assume you're referring to my rescue of Aldred?'

'What else would I be referring to?' she snapped. 'It was perfect. He'd got himself cut off and all you had to do was watch him die. Why did you ride out?'

Marius smiled as they passed a band of Endal warriors gathered around a glowing brazier. He nodded to them as they tapped their fists against their mail shirts. Marika was cunning in a vicious, feral way, but he had been manipulating others for years and knew the way people's minds worked.

'What's so damn funny?' she said, seeing his smile.

'You, my dear,' he said. 'You think you're a wily schemer, but you're not looking at the big picture.'

He saw her anger threaten to spill out and raised a placatory hand. 'Let us assume for the moment that Aldred had died on the first night. You think that would be the outcome you desire, but you would be mistaken.'

'How so?' said Marika.

'If Aldred had died then, nothing would have changed in your tribe's perception of me. They would still hate me, and would never consent to our marriage. But look at how they see me now. Jutones are fighting and dying alongside Endals, and I have saved the life of their beloved count. Now I am not hated, now I am seen as a sword brother to Aldred. This battle isn't over, and a lot can happen between now and its end, including your brother's untimely end. If we play this game well, you and I will be heroes by its conclusion. *Then* we can marry and make this city the greatest seaport in the Empire. Now doesn't that sound like it's a plan that'll catch a fair wind?'

Marika listened to his words with a growing admiration, and Marius wanted to laugh at how simply she was impressed. He patted her hand and she turned to face him, giving her most winning smile. He saw through it, but it was a pleasant view nonetheless.

'I'm beginning to think I underestimated you, Marius,' she said.

'Most people do,' he replied with a self-satisfied smirk. 'It must be the cultured, debonair appearance of wealth I project. Though anyone with half a grain of sense would realise that you don't get to be this rich and powerful without having a head for intrigue and a heart for murder.'

'So what happens next?' asked Marika, pulling him on towards one of the towers flanking the citadel gates. Endal archers were stationed here and two of the bolt throwing war machines stood on elevated wooden platforms that could be turned in any direction.

Marius shrugged and leaned on the timber steps that led up to the war machine. 'We fight the dead and, like I said, this battle is far from over. Anything can happen, or anything can be *allowed* to happen.'

'Enemy!' shouted a voice from further along the ramparts, and Marius looked over the lower town, searching for what had triggered the warning. Archers loosed shafts into the grey skies as a vast shape moved through the mist, like a great undersea creature viewed from the deck of a ship. Marius prided himself on being afraid of nothing, but as the great dragon flew from the haze, he found himself rooted to the spot in terror.

A juggernaut of decaying meat and loose flaps of draconic hide, the colossal monster flew over the ramparts of the city with crackling sweeps of its ragged wings. Chains rattled and gears rasped as the war machines were hauled around and eight-foot barbs were loaded into bronze-sheathed firing grooves.

The dragon circled the Raven Hall, its wings beating the air in a parody of flight, for its mass was surely kept aloft by foul sorcery. Astride its neck, the black-robed sorcerer hurled a stream of baleful energies at the Raven Hall, wreathing it in crackling arcs of scarlet light from top to bottom.

Marius grabbed Marika and dragged her behind the war machine as the Raven Hall cracked and groaned, its structure aged a thousand years in the space of a breath. Crumbling stone poured like sand from its joints and a rain of powdered obsidian wept from the raven's eyes as the mighty structure sagged to the side. Booming cracks echoed over the city as the tower's stone split as cleanly as though struck with a giant mason's hammer.

The circling dragon roared with the rasp of a million plague victims' death cries, and beat its wings as it hurled itself at the tower. Its hind claws slammed into the Raven Hall and its enormous weight completed what the sorcerer's spell had begun. The top of the great tower of Marburg exploded in a rain of blackened stone, and its lower reaches keeled over like a felled oak. Vast blocks, each the size of a hay wagon, rained down upon Marburg, smashing buildings flat and wreaking untold damage throughout the city.

Thunderous booms shook the citadel as the rain of blocks hit in a series of percussive hammer blows, and billowing dust storms surged from the impacts. Marius pulled his cloak up over his face as the debris cloud rolled over him. He edged his way along the platform and threw off his cloak. Choking dust made him cough, and gritty fragments scratched his eyes. Marika huddled behind the war machine, her knees drawn up to her chest and her hands covering her face and mouth.

'Marika!' he yelled. 'Are you hurt?'

She looked up, numbed by the sight of the ancestral

seat of the Endal kings so comprehensively destroyed. She shook her head and rubbed her eyes free of dust. Marius pulled her to her feet. She was in shock, but he didn't have time to play nice.

He slapped her across the face, and said, 'Snap out of it, princess! The dead will be attacking any moment. If you want to rule this city, then you have to get your people ready to fight! Do you understand me?'

'I understand,' she said, her eyes filled with anger. 'And if you hit me again I'll kill you.'

Marius smiled and said, 'That's my girl. Aren't we a pair of lovebirds?'

The sound of clashing swords and clattering bone sounded from the lower town as the army of the dead marched towards the citadel once more. Endal sergeants and battle captains shouted at their warriors to stand to as the flapping of leathery wings filled the air. The howls of cursed wolves echoed over the black sea, and over everything came the bellowing, deathly roar of the skeletal dragon.

'Shall we?' said Marika, notching an arrow to her bowstring.

'We shall,' agreed Marius, drawing his blade.

BOOK THREE

Dust to Dust

Hollow footsteps, cloaked by night
of sadness known through tortured sight;
The willow weeps its tears of woe
as Owl moans the twin moons' glow.
Wind whispers through the willow's leaves,
and Owl, perched high, eternal grieves.
Raven drinks the blood of Sigmar's dead,
But soon flies off to hidden bed.
Weary 'neath death's black spell,
The dead know pain that none can quell.
Cursed to fight those they loved,
Forever lost, each journey taken,
plagues the mind; the nights awaken.
Troubled visions, thoughts of yesterdays,
that seem like beacons; lives away.
Random comforts cannot ease their soul,
For knowledge takes its weary toll
'Pon one who suffers with each breath,
Who slept once in peace, then awoke in death.

─◀ FIFTEEN ▶─

Reunions

THOUGH THE SUN was newly risen, light was already bleeding from the sky. The Asoborn battle line was silhouetted on the brow of the hill, three hundred men and almost a hundred women and children. Boys as young as six held long daggers, and men in their seventies gripped felling axes as they awaited the coming of the dead.

Maedbh kept Ulrike and Freya's boys close, trying to hide her fear from them. The desire to flee smouldered in the hearts of everyone, and all it would take to ignite would be one spark of fear. The Queen's Eagles held the centre of the line, thirty warriors in leather armour and golden winged helms. Each bore a long spear and carried a short, stabbing sword. Their presence was all that gave Maedbh hope they might withstand one attack at least.

Alaric had split his warriors into two groups of fifty, placing one on either flank. These redoubtable warriors bore wide-bladed axes slung across their backs, though each was presently armed with a heavy crossbow and bolts as thick as Maedbh's thumb.

Five hundred against four thousand; it was the odds of which sagas were made.

After five days of forced marching, it felt strange to be simply waiting for the enemy to reveal itself. The Asoborn way of war was to strike hard and fast, wreaking as much damage as possible before withdrawing and dragging the enemy onto the blades of the spearmen. To wait for the enemy to attack felt wrong, but what else could they do?

Maedbh felt a small hand tugging at her sleeve and saw her daughter looking up at her with wide, determined eyes. Maedbh's heart ached to see Ulrike afraid, but this was what it meant to be an Asoborn. Battle had to be given and courage earned in the face of fear. As much as Maedbh hated the idea of Ulrike fighting this foe, it would be the making of her.

'Are the bad wolves coming for us?' said Ulrike.

'Yes, dear heart, they are,' said Maedbh.

'But we'll see them off won't we? Just like we did before?'

'Yes, just like then, but this time we'll make sure they don't come back.'

Ulrike nodded and gripped her bow tightly. 'Good,' she said, nocking an arrow to her bowstring. 'I wish my father was here. He'd ride over them on his horse and that'd be the end of them, wouldn't it?'

'I wish that too,' said Maedbh, 'but the gods have already blessed us today, so we must be grateful for what they have given us.'

'How do you come to that conclusion?' said Sigulf, his features pale with worry. 'The gods haven't blessed us, they've forsaken us.'

Maedbh knelt beside the boy, his fair hair plastered to his scalp with sweat. His green eyes were wide and fearful. Sigulf had the soul of a poet, and though he had proved himself a capable fighter, Maedbh knew his heart was only truly free when he was writing music and composing verse.

His twin brother answered him. 'Because they have sent us an enemy to test our courage and the strength of our sword arms.' Where Sigulf was a gentle soul, his twin was a warrior born and bred. Fridleifr loved to fight, and had made a name for himself among the Asoborn as a fist-fighter of some repute. Skilled with sword and axe, he was happiest when the blood flowed and death hung upon every heartbeat.

Just like his father, thought Maedbh.

'They've blessed us because they gave us a beautiful morning, and sent strong friends to stand beside us,' said Maedbh. 'Ulric knows that no warrior should fight alone, and has sent us the warriors of the mountain holds to fight at our sides.'

'But we're going to die,' said Sigulf, his voice quavering. 'The dead are coming to kill us.'

'They'll try to kill us, but I won't be dying today, and neither will you, little brother,' stated Fridleifr. 'These are Asoborn lands and we are the sons of a warrior queen.'

'But the iron men said mother was dead,' said Sigulf.

'Aye, but I'll not believe it until I see her on a pyre,' replied Fridleifr, and Maedbh heard the strength and determination of the boy's father in his words. Both boys possessed qualities of their sire, but only one man of this age embodied such greatness combined. 'I'll wager a fist of gold she'll ride over the hill and send these bastards over the Worlds Edge!'

The boy's voice lifted with every word and Maedbh saw his conviction that they would live through this fight spread to everyone in the battle line. Even the Queen's Eagles took heart, and Maedbh was surprised to find that even she dared to hope he might be right.

A dwarf horn sounded a warning from the end of their formation and Maedbh saw the blood drinker's army for the first time. The sky above the enemy army blackened like dead flesh around an infected wound as a morass of carrion birds, bats and blood-sucking insects took to the air.

A single vast block of skeletons, two hundred wide and twenty deep, marched towards the Asoborns in perfect formation, their bodies armoured in scraps of iron and rusted bronze. Their spears rippled in unison as they brought them down, serrated tips aimed at the hearts of the mortal warriors opposing them. The blood drinker rode in the midst of a hundred black-armoured horsemen, his brilliant white cloak streaming behind him in the cold winds that blew around the deathly army.

Wolves howled and loped around the dread host, filthy, diseased mockeries of the noble heralds of Ulric. Exposed muscles and withered meat hung from their bones and their jaws slavered with rotten saliva. Worse than all of that, was the fact that many of the dead warriors had clearly once been Asoborns. Everyone gathered on the hillside had family who had marched to war beside the queen, and the thought that they might come face to face with a loved one was almost too much to bear.

Maedbh felt the hope drain away from her people at the appearance of the foe. The sight of so unnatural a horde, an enemy of life itself, struck at the very core of what made mortals great. To fight this enemy would test the courage of even the mightiest warrior, and the Asoborns gathered on this lonely hilltop were old men and children.

Yet though these people had either hung their swords up years ago or had yet to be formally blooded, not one moved and not one gave voice to the terrible fear stabbing up from their soul that told them to run, to flee this battle and perhaps earn a few precious hours of life. Maedbh had never been prouder to be a warrior of the Asoborns.

There was no attempt at parley – what would be the point? – and no theatrical displays of martial prowess. The dead marched to the bottom of the hill and began climbing towards the Asoborns.

'Do you WANT me to kill him?' asked Laredus, working the whetstone across the blade of his sword. 'Because I will if you need me to.'

Count Aldred shook his head. 'No, though don't think the thought doesn't appeal.'

'It could be made to look like the dead did it,' pressed Laredus. 'Or that he sickened.'

'Enough,' said Aldred, fetching himself a drink of water from an earthenware jug on the table of what had once been the seaward officers' barracks of the citadel. The Raven Hall was no more and his servants had been sent to Reikdorf, so this was what he was reduced to. Pouring his own drinks and sitting in a draughty room with no more appointments than a junior officer. Still, it was better than a great many of the Endals were forced to endure. The barracks were cold and damp, the sea air having long since warped the wood around the windows and letting in the clammy dampness of ocean mist.

'I know they're up to something,' said Aldred, 'but I don't want you to kill him. Think how it would look if Marius were to die while under my protection.'

'I told you, my lord,' said Laredus. 'It could be made to look like the enemy killed him.'

'No one would believe that, least of all Marika.'

'Does that even matter? You are the count of Marburg.

In any case, it's war, who's to say what happens in the midst of a battle?'

'And what of the other Jutones? Do you plan to kill them too?'

Laredus looked uncomfortable with the idea of such mass murder, but he straightened his back. 'If that's what it takes to keep you and this city safe, then that can be arranged too.'

'There are three hundred Jutone warriors here, not including Marius's lancers,' pointed out Aldred. 'Even the Raven Helms would have their work cut out in killing those men. And I rather think we need those lancers to help defend our city.'

Laredus nodded, though he clearly was deeply unhappy at the idea of relying on Jutones for anything. Laredus had fought the Jutones on many occasions, and there was no love lost between the two tribes. Though that was changing. Ever since Marius had ridden out to rescue him, Aldred had seen the beginnings of camaraderie between the two tribes. That should have been a good thing, but he couldn't help but feel it was the death knell for his city and his people's way of life.

Aldred stared into the fire. It crackled with the little wood remaining to them that hadn't been commandeered to craft fresh arrows and stakes for the defences behind the walls. It felt like evening, but the sun had risen only a few hours ago. The attack of the dead had shifted the diurnal cycle of Marburg, turning it into a ghost city in the daylight, a furious battlefield by night. He pulled his cloak tighter about himself, feeling a chill deep in his bones that had nothing to do with the temperature of the room.

'You should open your cloak, my lord,' said Laredus. 'Let the fire's warmth get to you.'

'I know. It's tiredness playing its part, but I feel the

touch of the grave deep in my heart, you understand?'

'I do, my lord,' said Laredus. 'It's settled in every man's bones since the army of the dead sailed into Marburg. And I expect it'll only lift once we defeat them.'

Aldred smiled mirthlessly with a shake of his head. 'Forced from our homeland to a scrap of land in the midst of a marsh, our king slain, the pestilence of the mist daemons ravages our city, and now this. We are not a blessed people are we?'

'We are the Endals,' said Laredus. 'Hardship makes us stronger.'

'Then we will be the strongest tribe of the Empire by the end of this war,' said Aldred.

Laredus tapped his fist against his breastplate in response and they lapsed into a comfortable silence, content to simply drink and enjoy this rare moment of quiet. Aldred wanted to close his eyes, but sleep brought nightmares and festering thoughts of being devoured by the wriggling creatures beneath the earth. When sleep did come upon him, he woke scrabbling at his eyes, fearing writhing masses of worms were feasting upon them.

'You still haven't said what you want to do about Marius,' said Laredus.

'There's nothing we *can* do,' said Aldred. 'To kill him, you'd need to slay all his men too, and that will simply hasten our ending. And I still have a hard time believing Marika would conspire with Marius. She's my sister.'

'I'm just telling you what I heard,' replied Laredus.

'That's just it though, you didn't hear it.'

'One of my men did, and that's good enough for me.'

'Who was it?'

'Daerian, one of my scouts. I had him assigned to the princess as a bodyguard, and he has the keenest eyes and ears I've known. He can see a hawk a mile distant and hear a whisper on the other side of seafront tavern. If he says they were talking about your death, then I'd wager a ship's worth of gold it's true. She still blames you for what happened with the mist daemons,' said Laredus. 'Even though you weren't at fault. It was Idris Gwylt skewed your judgement. She must understand that.'

'I had hoped she would by now,' agreed Aldred. 'But that woman can hold a grudge like no other. She reminds me of it at every turn, like I *wanted* to sacrifice her.'

'You had no choice,' said Laredus.

'No, I didn't,' said Aldred. 'I did what I thought was best for my people.'

'And the people know that, even if she doesn't,' ventured Laredus.

Aldred caught the hint of something unsaid, something too terrible to be given voice without tacit permission.

'What are you saying?' said Aldred. 'You can speak freely.'

'I'm saying that perhaps we're looking at the wrong person to kill.'

Aldred looked into Laredus's eyes, seeing no give there, only a fierce determination to protect his count. 'Marika?'

Laredus nodded. 'It's terrible and unthinkable, but I'm trying to save your life.'

'By killing my sister?'

'She's trying to kill you.'

'You don't know that for sure,' pointed out Aldred.

'Do you want to die to prove me right?'

Aldred said nothing, but the idea had already taken root.

THE BLOOD DRINKER unsheathed his sword and it glittered in the encroaching darkness with spectral light. Thunder split the sky above the Asoborns, and a crackling bolt of lightning zigzagged in a bright tracery, arcing downwards to be captured by the vampire's sword. The blade swept down and the wolves sprinted towards the mortal prey at the hilltop. In their wake, the skeletal warriors began marching uphill.

Maedbh watched them come, her mouth dry and her bladder tight. Sweat moistened the grip on her bow, and she flexed her fingers. She put an arrow to the string and pulled back, sighting downhill at the loping wolves. Those Asoborns with bows followed her lead, bending their bows towards the howling beasts.

'Remember to aim high,' she shouted, knowing that many archers would send their shafts into the earth when aiming at targets downhill.

Maedbh sighted on a wolf with a ragged pelt of decaying fur and one side of its skull exposed. The green corpse light shimmered in its eyes, and she let fly between breaths, sending her shaft slicing though its jaw. It ran on for a moment before collapsing in a dissolving mass of bone and rotten meat.

Two hundred arrows slashed downhill, but despite her advice most thudded into the earth in front of the charging wolves. At least fifty of the creatures were undone before they could reach the Asoborn lines. A flurry of crossbow bolts hammered the dead warriors behind the wolves, each one punching through rotten flesh and bone to slay the warped power at its heart. Every single bolt loosed by a dwarf crossbow found its mark, yet the dead marched on.

Ulrike's first arrow struck home as did her second, though her third went wide of the mark. Maedbh was able to loose three more times before the unnatural beasts reached them. She swapped to her sword as the wolves crested the summit of the hill. Snarling and clawing, they leapt with jaws stretched wide. Maedbh plunged her sword into a wolf's belly, spilling its decaying entrails to the earth. It screamed as its body was destroyed.

A wolf snapped at Ulrike, but the young girl ducked and rammed her knife into the creature's neck, tearing out the remains of its throat in a welter of grey meat and bone. Another snapped at her, but Maedbh's sword swept down and ended it. Swords and spears flashed in the dim twilight, and wolves died, but a score of Asoborns were pulled to the ground. Fangs snapped shut on skulls and throats were torn out with single bites. Rotten claws opened bellies and thrashing wolves howled as they ate the flesh of those they had killed. Maedbh fought side by side with her daughter, each protecting the other as though they had trained as sword maidens for years.

Sigulf and Fridleifr did not fight with bows, but with exquisitely crafted swords given as gifts to the queen by the dwarfs of the Worlds Edge Mountains. Long before Sigmar had sworn his oaths of brotherhood with King Kurgan, the eastern queens had counted the dwarfs of the mountains as their allies. As different in character as they were, they were alike in skill with a blade, Sigulf fighting with clinical precision, Fridleifr with furious passion.

The Queen's Eagles protected the heirs to the Asoborn crown, sweeping forward and fighting with all the skill that had seen them elevated from the ranks to become the guardians of Asoborn royalty. Garr fought at their forefront, his twin-bladed spear cleaving left and right as he hacked wolves down with every stroke.

The wolves attacked all along the Asoborn line, bounding around the flanks and punching through to attack the weakest members of the Asoborns. Alaric's dwarfs swung around like an opening gate, protecting the flanks and preventing the wolves from getting behind the battle line. They fought with mechanical strokes, relentless and merciless, hewing diseased flesh as easily as a butcher would prepare a bull's carcass. No claw or fang could penetrate their armour, and no wolf could pass them. Immovable and impenetrable, the dwarfs anchored the Asoborn defence.

In moments it was over, the wolves destroyed and the battle line restored. The moans of the wounded were somehow dulled by the oppressive gloom, and the youngest children dragged those hurt too badly to fight further back onto the hillside. There was little that could be done for them, but they could do no more good in the fighting ranks.

Maedbh wiped her sword blade on the grass at her feet and gave her daughter a weak smile. Ulrike's face was flushed with a mixture of fear and excitement, the adrenaline of battle outweighing the thought of facing an army of the dead.

There was no time for words, for the ranks of skeleton warriors in ancient armour were almost upon them. The wolves had been nothing more than a skirmish screen to protect the warriors following behind. The dead were less than fifty paces from the Asoborns, marching in perfect lockstep. Behind them, the vampire and his horsemen walked their skeletal steeds up the hill, ready to ride down any mortals who fled the field of battle.

Cold dread settled in Maedbh's bones, a terrible, suffocating fear of losing everything that she loved in one fell swoop. She looked into the eyes of the vampire lord, seeing a lifetime of cruelty and evil. She saw his blood hunger, and as his army marched onwards, she heard a thunderous rumble, a drumming on the earth like a distant thunderstorm drawing closer with every passing moment.

A wild series of horn blasts swept the hillside as a dozen ululating brays came from the trees behind the Asoborn battle line. What new horror had appeared behind them without warning? She had been so sure the dead would come at them head on that she hadn't even considered the possibility that their flank could be turned.

The horns blew again and Maedbh's heart leapt as she recognised the sound of Unberogen war horns. Shapes moved through the trees, galloping horsemen in their hundreds, but far from being riders of the dead, these were living, breathing warriors atop wide shoul-dered, powerful steeds clad in heavy hauberks of iron scale.

The riders thundered over the brow of the hill and Maedbh let loose a wild Asoborn war shout as she recog-nised the warriors at the head of the Unberogen horsemen. One she called Emperor and the other she called husband.

Sigmar and Wolfgart rode over the brow of the hill, weapons unsheathed and ready to fight to save those they held dear. Hundreds of Unberogen riders streamed past Maedbh, along with scores of horsemen armoured in mail shirts and bronze breastplates with blood-red cloaks. Maedbh recognised them as Taleuten Red Scythes and their crimson-pennoned lances lowered in glittering unison.

Ghal-maraz swept up, a shaft of brilliant sunlight breaking through the unnatural gloom to strike the Emperor's mighty warhammer and banish the darkness. Sigmar rode through the trees with his long hair unbound and his armour glowing with impossible radi-ance. Such was the skill of his riders that they rode through the Asoborn battle lines without trampling those they had come to rescue.

The charge of the Unberogen and Taleuten cavalry was ferocious and it struck the line of the dead with unstoppable force. The Red Scythes leaned into their stirrups and their lances punched into the ranks of the dead, skewering skeletal champions and hoisting them from the ground. Lances splintered with the impact and the riders drew heavy maces and morning stars as they plunged into the undead host.

Wolfgart's vast sword, forged by Govannon less than a year ago, swept from its shoulder scabbard and no sooner was its blade bared than it clove through the chest of an undead warrior clad in a rusted shirt of mail. Swords and axes smashed through bone and patchwork plates of bronze and iron. The dead reeled from the sudden attack, but did not break. Though hundreds were destroyed in the opening moments of the Unberogen charge, hundreds more remained to fight. Sigmar's cavalry plunged into the heart of the dead, breaking them apart as they split the host in two.

The dead cared nothing for the suddenness of the attack and merely turned to face the horsemen whose charge began to slow with the press of skeletal bodies. Sigmar fought at the centre of the dead army, the skull-splitter living up to its name as it shattered bone and pulverised armour with every blow. The dead tried to pull away from Sigmar, but he rode into them with ever greater force, destroying half a dozen with every blow.

Maedbh lifted her sword and charged after the horsemen, and the Asoborns followed her.

Alaric's dwarfs marched towards the dead, cutting through their mouldering ranks like loggers in a forest of saplings. The fear that touched mortal hearts seemed not to have so strong a hold on the dwarfs, and they broke through with sweeping strokes of their axes. Though the dead outnumbered the living by nearly two to one, the dead could not match the skill of those ranged against them.

Sigmar aimed his horse toward the white-cloaked vampire, but if he sought a duel with the blood drinker he was to be denied satisfaction. Sensing defeat for his host, the blood drinker turned and rode away, his black horsemen galloping south as the allies turned to fight the remaining undead warriors.

Attacked from the front and rear, and abandoned by their maker, the host of the dead began to waver, their physical forms unravelling in the face of mortal courage and vitality. The battle was far from over, but without the power of the vampire to bind the dark energies that held them together the dead were falling apart with every passing moment, like ice before the summer sun.

Horsemen rode through the dead, hacking them down with brutal sweeps of their swords, while the Asoborns hemmed them in and the dwarfs trampled them with the pounding force of their relentless advance. Sigmar and Wolfgart rode pell-mell through the diminishing host, their weapons reaping a magnificent tally of the dead.

Though it took another hour, the dead could not long linger, and as the last of the sepulchral twilight faded from the sky, the field belonged to the living. Sigmar turned his horse and it reared up, pawing the air in triumph, but Maedbh cared nothing for the sight.

She threw her weapon aside and ran towards her husband with her daughter in tow.

Wolfgart saw them coming and leapt from his horse, sweeping his wife and daughter into his arms and holding them so tightly she thought he might break them. He kissed Maedbh over and over and the intensity of the kiss was magnified tenfold by the nearness of death. Weeping with relief and the fear of what might have been lost, Wolfgart, Maedbh and Ulrike laughed and cried to be reunited, the bitterness and rancour of what had driven them apart forgotten in the rush of joy sweeping through them.

'You came for us,' said Maedbh, between breaths. 'I wished for it and you came.'

'Of course I came for you,' said Wolfgart, unashamed tears spilling down his face. 'You're my woman and I love you. And you're my little girl,' he added, dropping to his knees to hug Ulrike.

'I thought we'd never see you again,' cried Ulrike.

'Never think that, my beautiful girl,' said Wolfgart. 'No matter what happens, I'll always be there for you. Not even death can stop me from coming to you.'

They stayed locked together for many minutes, savouring this moment of reunion until a horseman rode up to them and Maedbh knew who it would be before she even opened her eyes.

'Sigmar,' she said, only reluctantly releasing her grip on Wolfgart and giving a short bow to the Emperor. 'Your timing couldn't be better. You saved us and you have my undying gratitude.'

Sigmar smiled and said, 'It's your husband you should thank. I was riding for Reikdorf when my outriders saw them heading east. I wanted to know where he was going with six hundred of my best horsemen and he told me you were in danger.'

'The Oathstone showed me this battle,' said Wolfgart. 'I don't know how, Maedbh, but it did. We hand-fastened over it, so maybe there's some lingering magic from that moment, something that brought me to you when you needed me most. I gathered up everyone I could to ride east. Turns out a lot of people wanted to help me.'

'I know,' said Sigmar, seeing her look of confusion. 'I

didn't believe him either, but he swore he'd ride east alone if need be, so I thought I'd best keep him safe for you.'

'I'm grateful,' said Maedbh.

Sigmar was about to reply when she saw a shocked expression freeze upon his face. He was looking past her, and Maedbh knew what it would be before she turned around. At the top of the hill, Sigulf and Fridleifr laughed and cheered as Garr and the Queen's Eagles blooded their cheeks.

'Who are those boys?' demanded Sigmar.

WOLFGART CAUGHT UP to Sigmar by the river. The Emperor's head was bowed and his arms were folded across his chest as he stared off into the distance. This was going to be difficult, and Wolfgart took a deep breath as he approached. Right here, right now, Sigmar was not the Emperor, not the ruler of the lands from the Grey Mountains to the Sea of Claws, he was simply his friend.

Sigmar turned his head as he approached, but said nothing.

They stood by the fast-flowing river, enjoying the sights and sounds and smells of a land resurgent after the touch of undeath. Water splashed over rocks and gurgled in pools by the riverbank. Birdsong had returned to the world, not the raucous cawing of ravens and crows, but the wondrously refreshing and hopeful warbling of songbirds. Wolfgart hadn't realised how much he'd missed the birds until now. The sky was a shimmering canopy of blue, the clouds scattered and white.

It was the perfect day but for the tension in Sigmar's body.

'They are Freya's sons, aren't they?'

'Yes.'

'And I am their father,' stated Sigmar.

Wolfgart nodded, though there was no need. It hadn't been a question.

'You knew about them, didn't you?' said Sigmar.

Wolfgart knew there was no need or good to be served by lying. 'I did, but Maedbh swore me to silence.'

'And you don't break an oath to an Asoborn woman,' said Sigmar.

'Not if you want to keep your manhood intact,' agreed Wolfgart, knowing he had let Maedbh down once already with his oaths.

'I understand why she wouldn't want me to know,' said Sigmar. 'Freya's not the family type. Not for her a husband and a doting father.'

'No,' agreed Wolfgart. 'She's not really cut out to be the faithful wife either.'

'But they are my sons,' said Sigmar, finally turning to face Wolfgart. 'I had a right to know them, to watch them grow up and become men! They are the sons I never had with Ravenna. Who will carry on my name when I'm dead, Wolfgart? Who?'

'There's still time, my friend,' said Wolfgart. 'You're not too old to sire sons, and there's plenty of strong women who'd be proud to bear them.'

Sigmar shook his head and knelt beside the riverbank, plucking a flat stone with a smooth face from the earth. He skimmed it across the water, watching as it skipped over the surface a number of times before sinking.

'I remember doing this as a child, and it still makes me smile.'

Wolfgart picked up a similar stone and skipped it across the water. His throw was better and made it farther across the river before sinking.

'You always were lousy at this,' said Wolfgart, stooping to pick up another stone. 'It's all in the wrist you see. Here, like this.'

Once again the stone skipped across the river, but Sigmar shook his head.

'I am who I am, Wolfgart, and it's too late for me to change. Ravenna was my love, and I swore that there would be no other.'

'You can change that, Sigmar,' said Wolfgart. 'You can get to know those boys. They're good lads, strong and brave, reckless and full of the same fire that drove you to build the Empire. Who knows what they might do with you as their father to guide them?'

'I wish it could be that easy, my friend,' replied Sigmar, 'but I am on a path that does not allow change. Others have that luxury, but I do not. The Empire needs me as I am, a warrior Emperor.'

'And what about what *you* need? Love, companionship, family?'

'I cannot be the man this land needs if I am drawn to hearth and home,' said Sigmar, looking over his shoulder to the Asoborns as they prepared to march west to Reikdorf. Freya's boys and Ulrike gathered around Maedbh, like chicks around a mother hen.

'Those boys don't need me, they're Asoborns,' said Sigmar. 'Their mother would never allow me to take them from her. That's what she fears, that I'll take them to Reikdorf and make them my heirs.'

'You should,' said Wolfgart. 'They *are* your sons after all. Doesn't the Empire need heirs, strong rulers to carry your name into the future? You said so yourself.'

Sigmar turned to look out over the landscape, and Wolfgart saw the beginnings of a smile crack his features.

'Aye, the Empire needs heirs,' said Sigmar, slapping a hand on Wolfgart's shoulder and walking him back to the column of people. 'And you are all my heirs. Everyone who lives in this land is my heir. Everyone who fights and bleeds to protect the Empire…'

The Emperor smiled. 'They will all be Sigmar's heirs.'

⊰ SIXTEEN ⊱

Murder Most Foul

THE DEAD ATTACKED Marburg again and again, clawing at
the walls with thin fingers of bone digging into the
stonework to pull themselves up. The entire lower town
thronged with rotten corpses, shambling cadavers and
skeletal warriors, and all of them threw themselves at the
walls of the citadel every night. Marius and his lancers
held the shorter stretch of wall between the main gate
and the eastern shore, while Aldred held the western
stretch of the walls and the barbican towers.

Marius swept his sword through the neck of a moaning
corpse with green fire in its eyes, kicking the rotting body
back down the walls. His sword was proving to be anath-
ema to the dead, and he silently thanked the eastern king
who had gifted it to him so long ago. It had saved his life
in Middenheim, and was saving him again now. His
lancers fought at his side, pushing the dead from the
walls, stabbing them with spears, hacking at them with
axes and bludgeoning them with heavy maces.

A skeleton came at him with a notched sword, and he

stabbed it through the jaw, wrenching its head from its shoulders. The animation went out of the long dead warrior and it collapsed over the stone parapet. Another clambered over its remains and a rusted axe swung down at him. Marius brought his sword up, but the force of the blow turned it aside and the dead warrior's axe slammed into his shoulder.

He grunted in pain and sent a reverse stroke into the creature's neck. The blade parted the bone easily and the warrior dropped to the ground. Marius stepped away from the wall and shouted, 'Take my place!'

Another warrior filled the gap Marius had left and he stabbed his sword into the earth at his feet, rotating his shoulder and prodding the flesh to feel how badly he'd been hurt. The skin was bruised and swollen, but he couldn't feel any blood pouring inside his armour, and he took a moment to survey the fighting.

The entire length of the walls pulsed with desperate combats, Endal and Jutone warriors struggling to keep the dead from getting in. A mobile reserve of Raven Helms stood behind the fighting at the ramparts, ready to bolster the defences whenever the dead punched a hole, but Marius saw they were stretched thinly. All it would take would be one too many breaches and there would be no one to stop the dead from overrunning them.

Marika's archers had taken up positions further back, loosing volleys of arrows over the heads of the warriors at the ramparts. The bat swarms flew overhead, circling the ruins of the Raven Hall or roosting in its tumbled structure. The mist that wreathed the lower town and docks seeped up into the citadel, a choking fog that settled in the lungs and gave every man a hacking cough.

Just thinking about it made Marius cough, though thankfully he'd managed to avoid the worst of it by virtue of having well heated quarters that were free from damp. There was more than one benefit from a close, physical relationship with Princess Marika, he thought with a smile.

A group of lancers formed up around him, and Marius nodded in weary appreciation of their efforts. He didn't waste words on them, for these men were just doing their job, and if a man needed thanks or encouragement just to do his job, then he wasn't worth employing.

Marius heard a shout of terror and the dreadful form of the dragon reared up over the walls, its patchwork wings spread wide as it hovered over the twin towers of the barbican protecting the citadel's gate. Arrows slashed out towards it, but only Marika's white-fletched ones seemed to cause it harm. Two of the war machines hurled iron barbs towards the vast creature, but both splintered against its necrotic hide.

A heaving breath of toxic vapours gusted from the dragon's mouth and enveloped the barbican. Men staggered from the ramparts, choking and vomiting as the hellish miasma did its evil work. The road to the lower town sloped down to the gates, and from his position behind the walls, Marius saw them wither as the timbers shoring up the already weakened structure rotted away to brittle deadwood. The mass of dead warriors on the other side buckled the decayed woodwork and the gates split apart in a flurry of rotten timbers.

A mob of groaning warriors poured through the gateway, but any thought that the dead fought without stratagems was banished the moment Marius saw what manner of undead forced their way inside. The chaff of the dead assaulted the walls, shambling corpses with no more will than to devour the flesh of the living. These new attackers were the champions of this host, warriors with black hearts whose dreadful malice transcended their own deaths to sustain them with pure hate.

Armoured in ancient hauberks of corroded bronze and bearing long-bladed halberds and great axes, they surged into the citadel and split left and right to sweep the walls clear of defenders. Marius looked around for the Raven Helms, but Laredus had already led them to plug a breach further along the western walls.

'Damn you, Aldred, you're practically giving me your city,' said Marius, dragging his sword from the earth. He led his lancers towards the dead champions pouring through the gate as a flurry of arrows sliced into them. A dozen fell, but most simply picked themselves up again, unfazed by the two-foot shafts jutting from their bodies.

The lancers slammed into the dead, cutting the head from the eastern push onto the ramparts. The warriors on the walls saw their danger and captains of battle sent men to stem the tide of flanking enemy. Marius ducked a ponderously swung axe, plunging his sword through a gap in a dead warrior's armour. His sword passed into his foe's body without resistance, its enchanted edge glowing as though heated in a forge. The champion convulsed and the magic sustaining it was broken. Marius spun away from the creature, wincing as the old wound in his side pulled painfully.

He pushed into the mass of dead warriors, fighting with his usual finesse and élan as he beheaded enemy champions with an ease that was as much to do with his blade as his own skill. His lancers fought in a wedge with him at its point, forcing the dead back and stemming the rush of their breach through the gateway.

A heavy halberd blade slammed into his stomach, but its edge was dulled and all it did was drive the wind from him. He doubled up, but before the halberd could be reversed, Marius thrust his sword into the groin of its wielder. The dead champion clattered to the ground as it was destroyed, and Marius surged to his feet, invigorated at yet another brush with death.

'It'll take more than that to kill me!' he yelled, plunging headlong into the mass of dead warriors. The fear was gone, and he felt utterly disconnected from even the idea of it. He heard the booming wing beats of the dragon beyond the walls, but even that held no fear for him. For one wild moment, Marius thought of charging through the gateway to face the dragon like the heroes of legend who were said to fight such monsters on a daily basis. Common sense reasserted itself as he saw Aldred and a detachment of Raven Helms fighting the dead forcing their way down the western stretch of the walls.

The Endals fared rather less well than the Jutones, and Aldred's warriors were falling to the black blades of the dead like cabin boys before a bosun's whip.

'Ten of you with me, the rest of you secure this gate!' he shouted. 'Nothing gets in or out!'

Without waiting to see if his order was obeyed, Marius ran towards the Endals. Pipe music drifted across the ramparts and Marius wanted to laugh with derision. Who in their right mind played music when there was a battle to be fought? His sword shimmered with light as he sliced it across the small of a dead warrior's back, almost cutting him in two. His lancers swung their swords and maces to break a path through towards the Endals.

Marius blocked a slashing blow to the head and hacked the legs from another dead man, spinning around to parry two quick thrusts and destroy another pair of dead champions. These warriors might be the best of the dead, but Marius was a count of the Empire and bore a blade that hated the undead with a vengeance. Its power flowed through his veins like an elixir, and though Marius was a fine swordsman, even he wasn't arrogant enough to believe he was *this* good.

Another blade of power flickered near him and he saw Aldred fighting against a towering monster of bone and iron. Like a vast statue of basalt, iron and discarded butcher meat, the monster slashed ponderously with an axe formed from some enormous creature's jagged-toothed jawbone.

Aldred darted in to slash his sword at the creature, and it turned its great axe upon him. The Endal count jumped back, giving Marius the chance to attack the creature, plunging his blade into its back. His blade flashed with angry light, as though encountering some force inimical to the enchantments worked into its metal.

Marius flinched as the blade stung him like a treacherous serpent, feeling his sudden euphoria and confidence evaporate in the face of this new beast. It turned to face him, its monstrous, bovine skull jammed with the fangs of a dozen different deadly creatures. It snapped at him, a jagged tooth catching the links of his mail shirt and tugging him off balance. The jawbone axe swung for him, but the blue fire of Aldred's blade caught the dreadful weapon in its downswing and deflected it into the earth.

As the beast struggled to free its blade, Endal warriors and Jutone lancers surrounded it, stabbing with spears and halberds. Marius righted himself and ducked beneath its slashing axe, slicing his own weapon towards the creature's belly. The sword scraped along the monstrously elongated thighbone, trailing sparks of orange fire until it bounced clear on the vast pelvis. Aldred attacked from the beast's other side, hammering Ulfshard against the beast's flank.

As mighty as the beast was, it could not resist the pressure of so many blades and portions of its form began to come apart under the relentless assault. Shards of bone and armour peeled loose from its body as Aldred and Marius clove their blades through its unnatural bulk. Fighting side by side, the counts of the Empire hacked the slow-moving creature down piece by piece.

Aldred was the one to deliver the deathblow, though Marius had seen the opening. Even in the midst of this desperate fight, he knew to leave the glory to the man whose city this was. As the creature tumbled back in a collapsing pile of rotted armour and mismatched bone, Marius heard a sudden clamour from the gateway as the defenders finally resealed the shattered portal. Wagons, debris, broken crates and rocks were rolled down the slope to block the entrance. It wasn't pretty and likely wouldn't hold out against another attack, but it would do for now.

Marius rotated his neck to work loose the stiff muscles and walked towards Aldred.

'Quite some fight,' he said with a laconic smile. 'Damn thing almost had me there.'

Aldred nodded, too weary to answer, and Marius swept his sword out in an elaborate bow before the Endal count. He heard shouts of alarm, but before he could pinpoint the reason for them, he was barrelled to the ground as someone in heavy armour slammed into him.

Marius rolled, but a mailed fist cracked against his jaw and he saw stars. Shouts of alarm became shouts of anger, but Marius was too dazed to understand what was going on. He felt himself being dragged away from where he'd fallen and struggled to get his feet underneath him. He heard Jutone and Endal voices shouting at one another, but couldn't make sense out of what they were saying.

Eventually his vision cleared enough to see that he was being dragged away by one of the Raven Helms, Aldred's chief lieutenant if he remembered correctly, though the man's name was a mystery. He rolled and swung his sword up. The man jumped back and Marius scrambled to his feet as Aldred ran over towards the confrontation.

'Laredus, what in Manann's name are you doing?' shouted Aldred.

'Getting this conniving, murderous bastard away from you!' shouted the Raven Helm.

'Are you mad?' demanded Marius. 'I was fighting alongside your precious count, you damned fool! I'll have you flogged for this, a hundred lashes from my strongest lancer!'

'Enough, both of you!' cried Aldred. 'Put up your weapons, there will be no flogging here. Laredus, I mean it, put up your sword.'

The Raven Helm stared at Marius with unbridled hatred, and Marius knew he saw through his deceptive façade of bonhomie and brotherhood. This man knew he intended to win the hearts and minds of the Endal warriors before engineering Aldred's death. Laredus was a dangerous man, and Marius knew he would have to find a way to be rid of him before continuing with his and Marika's plan to make Marburg their own.

Before any more could be said, a freezing shadow enveloped the ramparts as the mighty dragon and its sorcerous rider dropped from the sky to land upon the barbican towers with a thunderous boom of wings. Its hideous bulk shook the very foundations of the citadel as it reared over them with its jaws spread wide.

Despite his terror of this monster, Marius smiled as he realised the perfect means to be rid of Laredus had just presented itself to him in all its monstrous, draconic glory.

Assuming it didn't kill him too...

* * *

'CAN YOU HIT it from here?' asked Govannon, squinting towards the blurred outline of the empty barrel resting against the walls of Reikdorf. He'd placed the canvas bag on the barrelhead, but couldn't see it from here. Nor could he tell how far away it was, but Cuthwin assured him they were at least a hundred paces away. Bysen held onto his shoulder, eager to see if this composition would produce a more stable reaction.

Though Govannon's sight was virtually gone, he still felt Cuthwin's withering gaze.

'You could put it another fifty paces back and I'd still hit it,' the scout assured him.

'Sorry,' said Govannon.

'Is this one going to work, da?' said Bysen. 'Is it going to be big bang?'

'Hopefully, son, but not too big.'

Govannon had spent weeks working on the dwarf war machine, melting down almost every spare piece of armour and weaponry to forge a strong enough tube to replace the broken barrel. In every case the required centre of mass was off, the metal perforated with air bubbles or the weight not a precise match. These had proven to be costly mistakes, for each imperfection caused Master Holtwine's wooden carriage to fall out of balance. Dwarf engineering was unforgiving of errors.

But now they had it, a perfect twin of the other barrels; one that was completely in balance with the others and which was free from air bubbles and matched the precise density of the dwarf work. Though he never said so out loud, Govannon wished he could travel to the mountain holds of the dwarfs to hear their cries of astonishment at his accomplishment.

Holtwine's timber carriage was a work of beauty, an elegant recreation of the broken one that had been dug from the ground. Its flanks were embellished with carvings depicting Cuthwin's rescue of Grindan Deeplock, and his battle with the wolves. The machine was locked in Govannon's forge, but as magnificent as it was there was one problem.

Without fire powder, it was simply an expensive sculpture.

Govannon had forged plenty of shot for the machine, but he had no idea how to craft the dwarf folk's fire powder, which the device needed to function. In desperation, he'd made Cuthwin read him passages from accounts stored in the Great Library of Empire tribesmen who'd seen these weapons at war in action. From these accounts, Govannon had worked out how the devices functioned, which was more than any man had done before, but knowing how a device worked and recreating it were two different things.

With Eoforth's help, they had found a Jutone text purporting to be the writings of a trader named Erlich Voyst's journey to the lands of a far-flung eastern empire beyond the Worlds Edge Mountains where the death of a great king was marked by great explosions fired into the sky by a fine black powder. Voyst had tried to discover the secret of this powder, but had been stymied by his host's reluctance to divulge its composition. In the end, he had stolen a batch and tried to recreate it on the voyage home, though all he had managed to do was destroy three of his ships and lose a leg in the process.

It had been a painful process of illumination, for Cuthwin read slowly and Eoforth was too engrossed in his own researches to be much help. Throughout their researches, Govannon noticed that the venerable Grand Scholar took care to remain within sight of them at all times, as though afraid of being alone in his own library.

Armed with the many variations of Voyst's recipe for eastern fire powder, they had tried numerous experimental proportions of charcoal, saltpetre and sulphur, sometimes adding mercury and arsenic compounds for added effect. Most of their concoctions had burned too slowly, while others had blown smoking holes in the forge wall and begun fires that threatened to burn Reikdorf down. In the wake of such incidents, Alfgeir had threatened to shut down their work, but Govannon had, thus far, managed to persuade him of the validity of their researches.

'So are we far enough back, smith?' asked Cuthwin, breaking into Govannon's thoughts.

'Yes,' he said. 'We should be.'

'*Should* be?'

Govannon nodded. 'Yes, I'm almost sure of it. This new concoction has an added resin extract to slow the explosive reaction. It should react with just the right amount of violence, but enough control to allow us to fire the war machine without blowing it to pieces.'

'Or us,' added Bysen. 'We don't want to be blown to pieces neither, do we, da?'

'No, son, we don't,' Govannon assured him.

'Well, if you're absolutely sure,' said Cuthwin.

'I'm sure. Light the arrow.'

Cuthwin lowered the oil soaked arrowhead into the flame and Govannon heard his bowstring pull taut.

'Best cover your ears after you loose,' said Govannon as the arrow flashed from Cuthwin's bow. The burning shaft flew through the air and punched into the canvas bag. Almost instantaneously, a thunderous bang echoed from the walls and a fiery plume of orange light erupted from the bag. Acrid smoke coiled upwards, and a cloud of black streamed up from where the barrel had stood.

Cuthwin and Bysen led Govannon forward, his ears still ringing from the deafening blast. The barrel had vanished, leaving nothing but splinters the size of a child's little finger. A portion of the city wall was blackened in a teardrop shaped pattern and a number of angry warriors shouted down at them from above.

'Sorry!' shouted Cuthwin, waving at them.

'Did it work, da?' asked Bysen, sifting through the remains of the barrel and turning the smouldering fragments over in his hands.

'In a manner of speaking,' said Govannon, able to make out the extent of the black scorch marks on the wall despite his blurred vision. 'Even with the addition of the resin, the explosion was still too powerful. It would destroy the war machine.'

Though this concoction had failed to produce a workable compound, Govannon took out his measuring sticks and began to plot the dimensions of the blast. He shouted numbers for Cuthwin to note down, running through fresh ideas on how to retard the speed and violence of the reaction.

As Govannon measured the extent of the blast, a troop of horsemen rounded the curve of the wall. Even before he heard the lead rider's booming voice, Govannon knew who it would be. He braced himself for the Marshal of the Reik's ire.

'Damn you, smith! What in the name of Ulric's blood are you doing? I warned you about testing that fire powder!' shouted Alfgeir, dismounting from his horse and marching over to Govannon. He could smell the sweat and anger of the man coming off him in waves.

'Ah, Alfgeir,' said Govannon. 'Yes, you did warn me, I remember it vividly.'

'Then why are you trying to destroy the city walls with your damn foolishness?'

'You said you didn't want me to burn down the city,' pointed out Govannon. 'So here we are outside it. The wall may have suffered some slight damage, it's true, but nothing that should affect its structural integrity.'

'Some slight damage?' snapped Alfgeir, kicking over a pile of blackened timber. 'You damn near put a hole in it.'

'Scientific discovery requires some… experimentation and trial and error methodology.'

Alfgeir paced along the length of the wall, staring at them all one by one, struggling to hold his anger in check. Govannon wanted to remind him of what they might learn from this experiment, but knew the man needed to vent before he would listen to reason.

'Damn me, but if our advancement requires the work of a blind man, a simpleton and a huntsman, then we're doomed for sure,' said Alfgeir. 'And aren't you supposed to be making me a sword? Didn't I commission the finest blade in the land, and didn't you promise that it would be ready by the first snows?'

'It's not snowing yet,' said Govannon, looking towards the sky. 'It's not is it?'

'Not yet, but it will be a week at most, and I still haven't seen any hint of a blade.'

'You'll have your sword, Marshal of the Empire,' promised Govannon. 'And, if I'm any judge, something far more impressive.'

'What are you talking about?' said Alfgeir, kneeling beside the shattered pieces of timber, and Govannon heard the warrior's sudden pique of interest at the idea the weapon might actually function. 'Did it work?'

'No,' said Govannon wearily. 'It didn't, but we're close.'

'Close isn't good enough, Govannon,' said Alfgeir. 'Either get it working in the next few days or I'm loading it on a wagon and sending it east to the dwarfs. Do I make myself clear?'

'Perfectly,' said Govannon.

* * *

THE DRAGON ROARED, sweeping the ramparts with its deathly dry bellow. Marius tasted ash and caustic fumes, throwing himself flat as the hot breath billowed. As the heat washed over him, Marius realised these were not the corrosive fumes that stripped flesh from men's bones, but simply a terrible exhalation of long dead lungs.

Cries of terror spread away from the dragon as warriors fled from the nightmarish creature. He rolled onto his side, gripping his sword tightly as though his terror could be kept at bay simply by holding a weapon touched by protective sorceries. Incredibly, it seemed as though that were the case, as his terror diminished in the face of what was surely the most horrifying thing he had ever seen.

Its eyes were sunken, rotted orbs that burned with emerald fire. The rider astride its clattering bone neck loomed over them all, its mailed gauntlets crackling with dark energies that flowed into the dread mount and filled its dead limbs and corpse-flesh with animation. Reeking clouds of bloated, blood-fat insects swarmed around the monster, a haze of flesh-eating creatures ready to feast on the dragon's leavings.

Beneath the rider's hood, twin orbs of smouldering fire swept its gaze across the collection of mortals arranged before it, as though understanding that the masters of this city were within its grasp.

'Aldred!' shouted Laredus, running towards the count of the Endals. 'Get back!'

Marius felt the eyes of the black-robed sorcerer boring into him, a hollow gaze of utter evil, but his sword hilt grew hot in his hands and he felt the power of the creature swirl around him without effect.

He smiled, flexing his fingers on the copper-wound handle of his sword as the feeling of invulnerability surged through him once again. The dragon lurched forward, not sinuously, but with an awkward gait that was at odds with the grace it showed in the air. Marius was reminded of a fish scooped from the water onto a riverbank, or the wide-winged birds that lived on the cliffs above Jutonsryk – poised in the air, but waddling and graceless on the ground.

Its claws slashed out at waist height and half a dozen of the Raven Helms were smashed to bloody ruin. Its skeletal head snapped down and plucked another from the ground. The man screamed, but his cries were cut off as the dragon bit down and snapped him in two. Laredus fought to get Aldred back, but to his credit, the count of Marburg stood his ground. Ulfshard blazed with fey light that reflected from the tarnished scales that still hung from the dragon's bones.

Lancers and Raven Helms stabbed long pikes at the dragon, but the blades scraped down the beast's hide or bounced from iron-hard bone. Dozens surrounded it, hurling spears and jabbing its body with halberds. Marius worked his way around the edge of the fight, staying close enough to play a part, but keeping clear of the vast monster's slashing claws and snapping teeth.

The fire-eyed rider reared back and a gust of parched wind, like a sirocco blown of the southern deserts, swept down to engulf the ramparts. Endal warriors screamed and fell to their knees as their bodies were wracked by dark magic. Their flesh withered and rotted, their bones becoming brittle and dusty. Marius felt the seething energies around him, but he remained untouched. Likewise Aldred seemed impervious to the malefic sorcery, so clearly there was an advantage to bearing a sword enchanted by the fey or foreign kings.

Laredus staggered under the effects of the powerful magic, his skin pallid and the veins on his neck straining like hawser ropes. The dragon's neck came down and its jaws opened, still drooling a wash of blood and entrails from its last kill. The Raven Helm hammered his sword into the dragon's mouth and broke several fangs. Arrows bounced from its bony skull, and a huge javelin hurled by a war machine plunged between its ribs. Aldred ran to join his champion, but Laredus pushed him away.

'Stay back!' he yelled.

His distraction cost him dear, as the dragon's jaws snapped shut on his shoulders and head. Laredus came apart like a wineskin filled with blood, his upper body carved open with a gory 'V' shape in his torso. Aldred screamed his champion's name as Marius leapt forward to bring his sword down on the dragon's head.

His fiery blade clove through the bone of its skull, hacking a fist-sized chunk of bone from its body. The beast roared and snapped at him, but Marius was already moving. He dived beneath the dragon's jaw, rolling to his feet on its left-hand side. His sword plunged into its eye and a blaze of green fire spurted from the wound.

Aldred hurled himself at the beast, Ulfshard slashing a burning tracery across the dragon's snout. It reared back and its claws slammed down. A cracked talon slashed Aldred's chest open and the Endal count fell back. Blood streamed from the deep wound and Aldred toppled to the ground.

Marius ran to the injured Aldred, but the hooded rider hurled a forking blast of black lightning from his iron-sheathed fingers towards him. He staggered under the force of the dread sorcerer's power as ice poured through his veins, his sword's magic unable to prevent the darkness from overcoming him.

'Damn you!' he yelled, more angry than afraid. 'Not like this!'

His sword flared brightly, and the enchantments beaten into its folded metal by the wizards of the Celestial Tower of the Divine Dragon a thousand years ago unravelled before such dread energy. Its blade shone like the sun, cracks of light spurting all along its length as the magic dissolved. The sword exploded in radiant beams of light that spiralled heavenward with the sound of bells and shattering glass in a far away tower.

The full force of the black sorcerer's magic surged in Marius's body, but moments later it was gone. Marius blinked away dark spots from his eyes and saw Aldred on his feet before the rearing dragon, the sorcerer's arcing forks of black lightning being drawn into the pellucid blue form of Ulfshard.

It seemed impossible that any blade, enchanted or not, could survive such an assault, but Ulfshard was an ancient weapon of the immortal fey folk from across the oceans. Their smiths had mastery of magic and all its secrets since before mankind had crawled from muddy caves in the mountains. Those who had bound their arcane knowledge into its starmetal had done so with complete understanding of the winds of magic and how to defeat those who sought to pervert that power to evil purposes.

As powerful as this sorcerer's magic was, it was nothing compared to the power bound to Ulfshard's elder design. Marius watched in amazement as Aldred, blood pouring from the mortal wound in his chest, swept his blade down, casting the corrupt energies of undeath into the earth. The ground at his feet blackened and withered, its life drained in an instant as the dark magic was dissipated through the enduring rock of the citadel.

A white-fletched arrow flew through the air and buried itself in the chest of the sorcerer, who it let out an almighty howl of rage. Its magic was cut off abruptly as another arrow sliced through its black robe and flared brightly with a wash of pure light. As his strength began to return, Marius twisted to see Marika calmly walking towards the dragon and its rider, loosing arrow after arrow at the dread creature. Her bow shimmered with light, silver blue threads worked into the bowstave gleaming with the same pale light as suffused Ulfshard.

More arrows slashed into the dark sorcerer and Marius felt the creature's desperation as the magic of the fey folk severed the connection to its dread master. Marius surged to his feet as Aldred collapsed to his knees and slumped onto his side. Ulfshard dropped from his hands as Marika sent another arrow through the hood of the sorcerer.

It screeched with agony and scales fell from the dragon's body, its limbs spilling powdered bone from between its joints. The green fire in its remaining eye dimmed and Marius saw he had a chance to end this. He swept up Aldred's fallen sword and charged the reeling dragon. Ulfshard blazed with all the power the ancient smith and his archmage brother had bound to its edge.

Marius brought Ulfshard down on the dragon's neck, the blade shattering mighty bones as thick as a man's waist as easily as if they were fashioned from brittle clay. The sword cut through the dragon's neck and its head fell to the ramparts with a bellowing roar, like a whirlwind through a bone-filled desert. The sorcerous will animating the long-dead beast could not hold its form together in the face of Ulfshard's magic, and it began falling apart, bones and withered flesh falling like ashen flakes from its mighty form.

Its wings folded and rotted away, blown like cinders from a cold firepit. Its hollow bones disintegrated, and the black sorcerer upon the dragon's back fell to the ramparts. Its robes billowed around it like hellish wings and its hood fell back to reveal a loathsome face with gaunt cheeks, pallid skin and a narrow tapered jaw filled with needle-like fangs. Its eyes were sunken and violet, but

Marius saw they were all too human. This evil that had bound itself to Nagash was no unholy creature of darkness, but had once been a man.

A man steeped in evil and filled with unnatural power, but a man nonetheless.

Glowing arrows protruded from his body, shafts of white and gold that trembled as though working deeper into his magically sustained existence. The creature hissed and bared its fangs, but Marius saw it was wounded nigh unto death and stripped of its powers by Marika's arrows.

Marius stepped in and hammered Ulfshard across the creature's neck, the blade slicing as cleanly through the monster's flesh as it had the unholy dragon's. It died with a curse on its lips, but as its head flew through the air the body ignited with an internal fire that consumed it within the time it took Marius to bring Ulfshard around.

A cold wind blew over the ramparts and a foetid exhalation gusted along the length of the walls as skeletal warriors hacking their way over the walls collapsed into piles of decaying bone. Undead corsairs slumped on the docks and bloodied corpses that had, moments before, been clawing at the desperate defenders of Marburg now fell to the ground as the dark will empowering them was undone.

Thousands more remained beyond the walls, but this attack was over.

And that was good enough for Marius.

He sheathed Ulfshard, not surprised in the least to find it fitted within his scabbard, despite being almost a handspan longer than his previous blade.

Marika ran up to him and threw her arms around his neck. She held him tightly, and he responded in kind, though the gesture was automatic rather than heartfelt.

'We did it!' she cried. 'They're dead!'

Marius looked at the decaying remains of the sorcerer and his dragon, lying next to the corpses of Aldred and Laredus.

He wondered which deaths she meant, but realised it didn't matter.

'That we did, my dear,' he said with a satisfied grin. 'That we did.'

—◀ SEVENTEEN ▶—

The Price of Knowledge

EOFORTH HURRIED THROUGH the darkened streets of Reik-dorf, fear lending his exhausted limbs strength. The streets of the city, once so familiar and reassuring, were now threatening and unknown. Every turn was laden with uncertainty, each step echoing strangely as though this was a city that existed beyond the realms of men, a place forsaken by the natural laws of the world.

A gibbous moon hung low in the sky, casting stark shadows through the empty street. Eoforth knew that thousands of people, refugees from all across the Empire, packed Reikdorf, so the idea that the city could be so empty was surely ridiculous. Thousands of people filled every nook and cranny: refugees from Marburg and Jutonsryk, southern tribesmen and villagers coming up from the Grey Mountains and villagers fleeing the clos-ing net of the dead from the east and north.

Nor were refugees the only people to come to Reikdorf. The city had the feel of an armed camp, with warriors billeted throughout its many buildings. The majority were Unberogen, for they made up the bulk of the population around these parts, but many more were Asoborns and Brigundians fleeing the destruction of their lands.

Eoforth had heard snippets only of the news from across the Empire, for his researches into Nagash's history had driven him to the point of obsession. His head ached constantly and the aches and pains that plagued him on a daily basis seemed stronger and more insidious than ever before – as though the dread necromancer's reach was clawing him down into the ancient pages and scrolls gathered on the library's shelves. His breathing rasped in his lungs and every step sent a spike of pain shooting through his chest. Eoforth knew the eyes of the necromancer were upon him, mocking his attempts to uncover some secret that might give Sigmar and his warriors a means of defeating him. No such secret existed, and it amused Nagash to allow Eoforth to fritter away his time on such fruitless research.

Yet Eoforth *had* found something...

Not a hidden nemesis by which the necromancer could be defeated, but a character trait that might yet be exploited. He had to take what he had found to Sigmar's longhouse, yet the street before him seemed to stretch away into infinity. Scrolls fell from the bundle haphazardly stacked in his arms and he blinked stars from his eyes as his heart lurched painfully.

Sigmar had returned to Reikdorf two days ago, and the mood of despair that had settled upon the city had lifted as he rode through the Ostgate with Wolfgart and the Asoborns. News of what had befallen Freya's army had not dampened the spirits of Reikdorf's people, but Sigmar had not wasted any time and instructed every smith in the city to sharpen blades, repair armour and bolster the defences of the Unberogen capital.

Every man, woman and child within the city bent their efforts to ensuring the survival of the Empire, carrying armloads of arrows to the walls, establishing makeshift infirmaries for the wounded and doing all they could to help. Not one person or family stinted on their duties, and the sense of brotherhood that stretched from one side of Reikdorf to the other was palpable.

All that would be for nothing if Eoforth could not reach Sigmar's longhouse.

His moment of epiphany had come as the last glimmers of light faded from the library's high, lancet windows. Only when the dozen candles with which he surrounded his desk had blown out in the one instant had he realised he was alone.

Eoforth felt the gloom and the unseen whisperers in the darkness close in on him. Glimmers of light drifted from the farthest halls of the library, a host of sibilant voices sighing like distant choirs as they spiralled towards him, laughing in derision at his puny efforts to undo the schemes of their master.

He'd cursed himself for allowing himself to become so engrossed in his work that he'd forgotten the passage of time. He'd allowed the dead to get in and now he was going to pay for it. His heart beat an irregular rhythm on his thin chest, and a painful numbness flowed down his left arm. He flexed the fingers, trying to force the blood to flow. His heart was weak and to put it under such strain was too much for him to bear.

Eoforth rested against a stone building, trying to gather his strength. He heard whispers behind him and spun, clutching the scrolls he'd gathered in the dark before fleeing for the streets. Moonlight bathed the world in cold, heartless light and he saw shadows where no shadows should be. They slid across the cobbles and over the walls of nearby dwellings, stretching and swelling to resemble elongated figures with black, featureless faces, thin, wasted arms and curling claws.

They chattered with the rattle of unseen teeth, clicking their insubstantial claws on the stonework as they closed in on him. Eoforth pushed himself from the wall as they drew near, limping down the road with desperate heaves of tortured lungs rattling in his chest. Though it was cold and his breath misted the air before him, his skin was slick with sweat.

Despite the reek of boiling hops that turned his stomach, Eoforth set off down Brewer Street, weaving like the drunks who clustered around the beer makers' back doors, hoping for the slops.

The shadows on the walls followed him and he heard screeching laughter from the streets running alongside him, half-glimpsed phantoms flickering at the corners of his eyes. It seemed impossible that no one else could be aware of these spectres, or that he hadn't yet encountered another person.

Perhaps he walked in the world of the dead now, a living soul that moved unseen by those untouched by mortality. The enemy stalked him, perhaps fearing what he knew and might pass to Sigmar. The dead believed he had found something that could hurt them and that made him pick up his pace, forcing his wretched body onwards.

Eoforth clutched the silver dove pendant around his neck, mouthing a prayer to Shallya that he hadn't said aloud since he was a youngster.

'Merciful Shallya, meek and mild, watch me now, your helpless child,' he said, feeling the chill of the grave lessen with every word. He fought to remember his other prayers, especially ones to Morr and Taal. Morr for his hatred of the undead, Taal for his joy in life.

'Now I lay me down to sleep, I pray to Morr my soul to keep–'

His words were cut off by a feral snarl and Eoforth looked up to see a pack of wolves blocking the road ahead. Filthy, rotted creatures with bone and muscle exposed beneath mangy, dirt-encrusted fur, these were abominable creatures of darkness. They did not howl, but their broken teeth were bared and they stalked forward, limping and ungainly on broken bones and twisted spines. As malformed and broken in death though they were, Eoforth had no illusions as to his ability to outrun them or survive their attack.

He couldn't make it past them, and looking over his shoulder he saw the chattering shadows easing down the street with their stretched arms reaching out to him. There was no way he could reach the longhouse, and the Gardens of Morr were on the other side of the city walls, so he set off down the Street of Temples, to the only place that might yet grant him sanctuary.

They came after him, but slowly, as though they were afraid to follow him into this place of gods. These divine beings watched over mankind, and the minions of necromancers were their most hated foes, for the dead worshipped nothing.

Still clutching his dove pendant, Eoforth hurried down the street with the wolves padding behind him and the shadow hunters laughing at his feeble attempt to escape. He saw the building he sought, just as a sharp pain stabbed into his chest. Eoforth gasped with the shock of it. He stumbled, losing more of his scrolls, and ground his teeth against the pain spreading down his left side. Eoforth was no physician, but he knew his heart was giving out under the strain.

He cried out as he slammed into the temple door, the

pain of the impact spreading through his body as he slid down the stonework.

'Help… me…' he gasped, though he knew no one could possibly hear so weak a cry.

The shadows closed in and the wolves bared their fangs.

'In the name of Shallya, have mercy!' he cried with the last of his strength.

And then, a miracle. A sliver of light filled the street and the shadow hunters fled its touch, retreating to the forsaken corners of the darkness. The wolves backed away from the light, wary of its touch. They waited, uncertain and afraid, the torchlight reflecting in the empty sockets of their eyes.

Eoforth reached out to the light, as greyness smothered his vision.

His chest burned with pain and he fell into the arms of the woman who appeared in the doorway like the beauteous goddess of mercy and healing herself. His heartbeat became an arrhythmic crescendo as the light haloed her head and softened her angular features.

Eoforth had never seen anything so beautiful in all his life.

'My lady…' he said. 'You came for me…'

High Priestess Alessa of the temple of Shallya knelt beside Eoforth and cradled his head. Her eyes swept the street beyond her temple, and the wolves fled from her stern, unflinching gaze. No creature of darkness could face so holy and pure a vision without fear.

He felt himself sliding down into darkness, and tried to speak, but the words wouldn't come.

'Be at peace, Eoforth,' said Alessa, seeing immediately that he was dying. 'Whatever they were are gone now.'

'I must… speak,' he said, as a single tear slid down his cheek. 'Sigmar needs to know…'

Alessa brushed it away and said, 'Speak to me. Whatever you have to say, I will tell him. I promise. What would you have as your last words in this world?'

Eoforth gripped her shoulder and pulled his lips to her ear. With his final breath he whispered one last thing to the high priestess. As his eyes closed, he saw her face turn cold, and went into Morr's embrace terrified that she hadn't understood.

He heard wolves in the distance.

And then nothing.

SIGMAR KNELT BESIDE the body of his counsellor and kept his eyes closed. He gripped Eoforth's hand and wished he could have been there for his friend's final moments. This war against the enclosing forces of Nagash had already cost the Empire dear, but that cost had never been harder to bear than now. Friends and allies had fallen to the advance of the undead, but no one who had been as dear to him as Eoforth.

The venerable counsellor lay on Sigmar's bed at the rear of the longhouse, as though he were asleep and would shortly awaken and demand the honey-sweetened oats he liked so much. Lex, Kai and Ortulf lay curled at the foot of the bed, sensing their master's sorrow and knowing not to intrude on his grief. Kai yawned and stretched his back paws, looking up to make sure he wasn't needed.

Eoforth had steered Sigmar through the darkest moments of his rule. He had offered sage counsel and age-tempered wisdom to cool the Unberogen fire in Sigmar's heart that would otherwise have seen him become no better than a Norsii warlord. Over the years, Sigmar had lost his father, the love of his life, and some of his best friends. It had been a hard road to walk, but he had walked it knowing he could rely on Eoforth's steady, even-handed advice.

The dead man's face was at peace, the dimmed lanterns seeming to ease the furrows of care and smooth the lines of pain he had borne with quiet dignity. His pain was now gone, and Sigmar tried to find comfort in that, but all he could think of was that his friend was gone. Elswyth sat on the end of the bed, one hand resting on Eoforth's shoulder as she awaited Sigmar's leave to withdraw.

'Well?' said Sigmar.

Elswyth sighed. 'His heart gave out, nothing more sinister than that. I know you want another reason to hate Nagash, but I can't give it to you.'

'You think that's what I want?' he snapped. 'You are the Hag Woman's successor now?'

The healer scowled at him and leaned forward. 'You've lost a good friend, so I'll let that go, but speak to me like that again and it'll be the last time you see me in Reikdorf.'

'I'm sorry,' said Sigmar, instantly contrite. 'I just thought he'd be around...'

'Forever?' said Elswyth.

'Stupid, I know, but yes,' shrugged Sigmar.

'With his heart condition, it's a wonder he lived as long as he did. He wasn't a well man.'

'I didn't know that.'

'He didn't want you to. Thought you'd make him retire for good if you did.'

'Maybe I should have. It might have given him more life.'

Elswyth shook her head. 'Not Eoforth, you'd have killed him years ago if you'd made him step away from the sides of kings.'

'What are you talking about?'

'Men like Eoforth, men like you, they don't just fade into the background. What they are defines them and if you take that away, what's left to them? Like old Beor-thyn. When Govannon took over his forge after the old man's joints inflamed, he was lost and didn't know what to do with himself. Without purpose, Beorthyn felt like he didn't have anything left to live for and died a year later. Why do you think Govannon's not retired, even though he's mostly blind? He knows he'll be the same. What would you do if you weren't Emperor?'

'I don't know,' admitted Sigmar.

'You'd be a waster, a brigand or a sell-sword,' said Elswyth. 'You live for blood and battle, and even though you're the Emperor and say you want peace, you're secretly glad you'll never find it in your lifetime.'

'You have a healer's heart, but a viper's tongue,' said Sigmar.

'I say things as I see them,' said Elswyth. 'I've seen too many Unberogen boys brought to my home with the most horrific battle injuries to believe any warrior who says he wants peace while carrying a sword or axe. Or a hammer. And you know I'm right; else you'd have gotten angry.'

'Maybe you are right,' said Sigmar, 'but I can still mourn my friend, can't I?'

'Of course you can, you fool,' said Elswyth with a smile that made her beautiful. 'I never said you couldn't. You'd be made of stone if you didn't grieve for this old man. His counsel probably saved more lives than that hammer of yours.'

Sigmar shook his head. Elswyth's harsh tongue could deliver rebuke and praise in the same breath without a man even noticing.

'Eoforth advised my father and grandfather,' said Sigmar. 'I remember him back when I was a young boy. He seemed like he'd always advised the Unberogen kings, and always would. Now that he's gone, I feel... adrift...

like a guiding star that shone above me without me even knowing it was there has been taken away.'

'Eoforth was a good counsellor,' said Elswyth, 'but you were always the Emperor. You ruled with him to aid you, and now you'll rule without him. You have good friends around you, and they will help. Anyway, you know this already, so why I'm wasting time telling you is beyond me.'

'Because that's what you do, healer,' smiled Sigmar. 'You help people.'

Elswyth snorted as she gathered up her belongings.

'Only those that need it,' she said, patting his shoulder as she passed.

'It wasn't some magic of Nagash?' asked Alfgeir. 'She's sure? How can she be sure?'

'She's sure,' said Sigmar, pacing the length of the longhouse. 'I wanted it to be Nagash, but Eoforth was just old. I think we forgot how old sometimes.'

Alfgeir sighed and raised his mug of beer. 'He was a good man, and a good friend. I'll miss him.'

'Aye, we all will,' agreed Wolfgart, also raising his mug.

Everyone in the longhouse raised their drink, toasting the soul of the departed scholar and wishing him a speedy journey through Morr's gateway to the Wolf God's halls. Though Eoforth had not been a warrior, he had the soul of a fighter and Sigmar knew the old man would be welcomed as a true son of Ulric.

'To Eoforth,' said Maedbh, keeping one torq-wrapped arm around Wolfgart and the other around Ulrike. 'May the foolish fire of youth fill him again as he runs with the wolves.'

Since returning from the east, Wolfgart's family had been inseparable, as though the terror of potential grief had forged their bond stronger than ever before.

Sometimes it took nearly losing what you had to remind you of how precious it was.

Or sometimes you had to lose it forever, thought Sigmar, touching the golden cloak pin that secured the bearskin at his shoulders.

Worked in the form of a snake curling around to eat its own tail, it had been fashioned by Master Alaric in happier times, and the workmanship was exquisite, with small bands along the length of the snake's body engraved with twin-tailed comets. Sigmar had given the brooch to Ravenna as a symbol of his love, but it had returned to him all too soon thanks to Gerreon's betrayal.

Alfgeir offered him a mug of beer. The smell was inviting, but Sigmar shook his head.

'There's nothing I'd like more than to lose myself in a beer haze,' he said, 'but I want a clear head tonight.'

The Marshal of the Reik shrugged and took the mug for himself.

'Probably wise,' said Alfgeir, draining the mug. 'But Eoforth was the wise one.'

Like Eoforth, Alfgeir had served Sigmar's father, and the old man's death had hit him hard. Losing men in battle was hard, but every man who commanded warriors made their own peace with that fact. To lose friends to something as cruelly banal as a weak heart was, in its own way, harder to deal with. Though they had been opposites in almost all regards, Alfgeir and Eoforth had been true friends and comrades in arms.

Sigmar laid a hand on Alfgeir's shoulder and continued his circuit of the firepit.

The warrior Maedbh had introduced as Garr stood against the far wall, his arms folded across his chest and his expression hard to read. Sigmar knew the man was wary in this company, and given the identity of the boys he had been entrusted to guard, that was understandable. He had a fierce look to him that Sigmar liked, and his Queen's Eagles would be a formidable presence when battle was joined.

He had spoken briefly to Garr, assuring him that no one in Reikdorf had any intention of removing the boys he guarded from his custody. The man had nodded, but said nothing, as a perfect understanding flowed between them. Since then, Freya's boys had not been seen outside beyond their first arrival at Reikdorf.

Master Alaric sat on a stubby barrel of dwarf ale, his armour gleaming in the low firelight, and his axe propped next to him against a bucket of coal. Sigmar had been overjoyed to see his old friend, but thanks to his behaviour on the hillside where they had rescued Maedbh and the Asoborns, he had been forced to endure a stern lecture on the proper protocols on greeting friends. Alaric's dwarfs lounged around the edges of the longhouse, casting critical eyes around its structure, as though lamenting what men had done to the fine work they had crafted for them.

The Taleuten Red Scythes were represented by their captain, a warrior named Leodan, a man Sigmar had seen ride into the heart of the dead without fear. His skills were prodigious, but there was something missing to him, some part of him that wasn't entirely normal. At the moment, Sigmar didn't care whether the warriors he could count on to fight alongside him were normal. That they would fight was enough.

'Elswyth says it wasn't magic?' said Wolfgart. 'So why was the old man running for the temple of Shallya? They were using sorcery on him and he ran for help from the goddess of mercy. Makes perfect sense to me.'

'You might be right,' said Sigmar. 'You might very well be right, but I don't see that it makes any difference right now. Eoforth is dead, and when the priests of Morr have completed their rites, I will take him to a place of honour on Warriors Hill. But right now we have other matters to consider.'

'How close are the dead to Reikdorf?' asked Garr. 'You have word from your scouts?'

'I do,' nodded Sigmar. 'Cuthwin has seen the wolf packs and the eaters of the dead on the Reik, near the Wörlitz mines.'

'Two days' march,' said Wolfgart.

'About time Cuthwin tore himself from Govannon's side,' said Alfgeir, helping himself to another beer. 'They've wasted weeks on that machine, and it still doesn't bloody work.'

Sigmar nearly said something to Alfgeir, but a slight shake of the head from Maedbh convinced him not to. He glanced over at Master Alaric, but if the dwarf runesmith knew to what Alfgeir was referring, he said nothing.

'Did the scout say anything about their numbers?' asked Leodan.

'No, none of his men could get close enough,' said Sigmar. 'Many tried, but none returned. Nagash will be served by many thousands of revenants, and every day his army will swell with those who have died fighting him.'

'If you had to guess?'

'At least thirty thousand, maybe more.'

Leodan nodded, understanding the sacrifices Cuthwin's foresters and huntsmen had made in trying to gather information on the enemy. The number was staggering, and Sigmar could see that many of those gathered in the longhouse had trouble even picturing so vast a horde. Such a force had only ever been seen at Black Fire or around the foot of the Fauschlag Rock, and even then, no one really knew how many warriors had been present.

Sigmar saw the controlled anger in the captain of the Red Scythes. He wanted this battle finished so he and his warriors could return to defend their own homeland, for the Taleuten people were undoubtedly besieged within Taalahim.

'Can this city hold against an army of that size?' asked Garr, looking towards Alaric. 'The walls look strong and high, but I'm no expert on that sort of fighting.'

'The walls are serviceable,' said Alaric. 'Designed by a dwarf, but built by manlings, so who knows if they're strong enough? I'd need to test them to be sure, but I reckon they'll hold against what these grave-hoppers can throw at them.'

Alfgeir laughed, a drunken, nasal bray. 'Walls? It won't matter about the walls. We've a city filled to bursting point with refugees and warriors, and not enough food to last out the week, let alone a siege.'

'We have grain reserves,' said Sigmar. 'We can last a season.'

'And how long can the dead last?' snapped Alfgeir. 'They don't need to eat or drink, they don't need to sleep, and they don't need to worry about disease or fear or losing their friends. They don't even need to fight us. They can just trap us in here and wait for us to die!'

'They won't do that,' said a soft female voice from the doorway to the longhouse. 'And you're too old to be drinking that much beer, Alfgeir Gunnarson. The enemy is two days away and you'll still be puking your guts out if you have one more mouthful.'

'What are you, my mother?' said Alfgeir, though he didn't take another drink as he saw High Priestess Alessa standing in the longhouse door.

'Hardly, but the people of this city need you to fight,'

said Alessa, sweeping inside and making her way towards Alfgeir. 'Are you going to let them down?'

Alfgeir licked his lips and shook his head, putting the beer down on the table next to him. It was easy enough to shout at fellow warriors, but to snap at a priestess of Shallya would be boorish beyond even what his drunkenness would allow.

Maedbh rose from her seat and knelt before Alessa. The priestess touched the top of her head and smiled warmly, all hint of her irritation vanished. Alessa had blessed Ulrike when she had come into this world, and Maedbh would always be in her debt, for that protection had served her well over the years.

'High Priestess,' said Sigmar. 'I hadn't thought to see you at a gathering of warriors.'

Alessa turned to Sigmar and he was struck by the hostility he saw in her face.

'Nor would you under normal circumstances, but these are not normal times.'

'Then join us,' he said, gesturing towards an empty space on a long trestle bench.

'I'll stand,' she said. 'I do not relish being here, so I will say what I have come to say and then I will go.'

Sigmar nodded. 'You said that the dead won't simply trap us within the city and allow us to starve to death. Why do you think that?'

'It is the crown,' said Alessa. 'Nagash is desperate to retrieve it, and he will not wait for you to die from lack of food and water. He will want to break the walls of this place down as soon as he can and kill everyone inside. Eoforth knew as much, they were his last words to me before he died.'

'He spoke to you?' demanded Sigmar. 'Why did you not tell of this before now?'

Alessa's hostile confidence diminished and Sigmar saw

the agony of indecision within her. Whatever she had to say to him, it had taken a great deal of soul searching for her to come forward.

'He spoke about the crown I foolishly allowed to be buried beneath my temple.'

'What about it?' said Sigmar, seeing a number of confused expressions around the longhouse. The secret of what he had buried beneath the temple of Shallya was not widely known, and Sigmar would prefer it to stay that way. One look into Alessa's eyes told Sigmar that wasn't going to happen.

'Nagash is obsessed with it. It's the only thing he desires.'

'We already know that,' said Alfgeir. 'The blood drinker told us that.'

'But he would not have communicated how the great necromancer is consumed utterly by his desire, how his entire existence is bound to it in ways no mortal can understand. It is part of him, and without it he is less than nothing. To be close to the crown will drive all thoughts of restraint and reason from Nagash. It is his greatest strength and his most terrible weakness.'

'Eoforth told you all that?' said Wolfgart. 'He always did use ten words when one would do. Not bad for a dying man.'

'Of course he didn't,' said Alessa. 'He simply said, "The crown, tell Sigmar it's his Ravenna".'

'And you got all this talk of obsession and desire from that?' said Alfgeir.

'That and an understanding of what it means to be near the wretched thing,' whispered Alessa. 'You understand what I mean, don't you, Emperor?'

Sigmar nodded, only now seeing how pale Alessa was, how thin and undernourished. Her hollow cheeks and haunted eyes were a true testament to the insidious nature of Nagash's crown, a pervasive evil that sapped the vitality of the living by degrees.

'I do,' said Sigmar. 'And if we survive this coming battle, I swear I will hide this crown far from the lands of men, somewhere its evil will no longer wreak harm.'

Wolfgart turned to him. 'Do you know what Eoforth meant? Does it help us?'

'He does,' said Alessa, bowing her head and clasping her hands as tears flowed down her cheeks. 'Shallya forgive me, but I should never have told you.'

'What is she talking about, Sigmar?' said Alfgeir, rising to his feet.

Fear touched Sigmar as he understood the source of Alessa's reluctance to speak of what Eoforth had told her. They had shut the crown away from the world for good reason. Mortals were not meant to wield such magic, for their hearts were too malleable and too easily seduced to be allowed near such temptations as eternal life and ultimate power.

Sigmar had broken free from the malign effect of Nagash's crown once before, but could he do it again?

'There is only one way we can fight Nagash,' said Sigmar. 'Only one way I can face him with any hope of victory.'

He stood at the end of the firepit and took a deep breath, loath to even say the words, let alone contemplate the reality of what it would mean for the Empire if he failed.

'I have to wear Nagash's crown again,' said Sigmar.

◄ EIGHTEEN ►

The Dead of Reikdorf

THE HOST OF Nagash arrived before the walls of Reikdorf
on the leading edge of dark storm clouds. Winter cut the
air and the cold winds that blew from the vast horde of
the undead carried the stench of mankind's corpse.
Chain lightning flashed in the clouds and rumbles of
thunder that seemed to roll out from distant lands
echoed strangely from the walls of the city's temples, taverns and dwellings.

No sun rose on this day, the unnatural darkness covering the land in a bleak shadow from which it could
nevermore be lifted, a gloom that entered every mortal
heart and filled it with the sure and certain knowledge of
the fate of all living things. Skeletons marched at the fore
of the army, ancient warriors in serried ranks that
stretched from one line of the horizon to the other.
Cursed to serve Nagash for all eternity, they wore armour
of long lost kingdoms, clutched weapons of strange
design, and the grave dirt of far off lands clung to their
bones. Heavily armoured champions in heavy hauberks

of scale and corslets of iron marched at their head, exalted warriors of the dead whose skill with the executioners' blades they carried was more terrifying than when they had been mortal.

Where the warriors of bone resembled the army they had been in life, the thousands of bloody corpses dragged from shallow peasant graves or raised back from the dead in the wake of battle were a shambling mockery of life. Limping on twisted limbs and groaning with the torment of their existence, they were a stark reminder that even death in battle against this foe would be no escape from the horror. Hunched things in black robes moved through the shuffling horde of corpses, their fell sorcery directing its mindless hunger.

The sky above Reikdorf blackened with the fluttering wings of bats and every rooftop was lined with black-winged carrion birds. Ravens cawed in anticipation of a feast of flesh, hopping agitatedly from clawed foot to clawed foot, impatient for the slaughter to begin.

Hundreds of dark riders on skeletal steeds caparisoned in black and red and riding beneath banners of skulls and fanged maws took position at the centre and flanks of the army, the stillness of their mounts hideous and unnatural. These dread riders carried long black lances, their tips glittering with a loathsome green shimmer.

Scraps of lambent light billowed like pyre smoke around the horde, wailing with the torments of the damned. Spectres and howling revenants dragged from death, but whose remains were no more, spun and twisted in ghostly wisps, their eyes bright with aching need for the warmth of mortal flesh. Their howling struck terror into all who heard them, and scores of terrified people took blades to their own necks rather than face such an enemy.

Loping ahead of the host, a ragged line of corpse eaters

moved on all fours, wretched and debased, with only their monstrous appetites to sustain them. These degenerate monstrosities had once been men, but they had fallen far from the nobility of their former race. Some clutched sharpened bone, others fragments of swords, but most only needed their long, gnarled claws to tear out an enemy's throat. They gurgled and croaked as they skulked in the shadows, eager for the bloodletting to begin, but fearful to be the first into the fray.

No trace of the land could be seen as the black host spread out before the city, a tide of rotten meat, bleached bone and unquiet spirits. This was an army to end the reign of mortals, to plunge the world into eternal night.

Yet it was the figures at the head of this mighty army that drew the eye, a vanguard of three riders, one in silver plate, and the others in armour of black. Khaled al-Muntasir was easy to identify, but the two warriors alongside him were unknown to the defenders. Each clutched a flag so soaked in blood it was impossible to tell what heraldic devices it had once displayed.

Yet even among such dreadful abominations, the master of this army was clear, a towering column of fuliginous chill that seemed to draw in what little light remained to the world only to snuff it out within his immortal form.

This was Nagash, the Great Necromancer, the bane of life and undying corpse lord who had toppled empires and unleashed the curse of undeath upon the world. His dread form floated above the earth, and where he passed, the ground split apart, withered and destroyed as sable light was drawn upwards and coiled about his armoured and ragged-cloaked form. The creatures of the earth crept from the soil, crawling, buzzing and slithering away from the necromancer as his monstrous power sucked the vitality from everything around him.

Through the roiling miasma of deathly energies that surrounded him, black segments of iron and bronze could be glimpsed, shimmering coils of green light suffusing each plate, rivet and fluted line of beaten metal. A grinning skull of ancient bone loomed from the darkness, massive and long since bereft of flesh, muscle and life.

At Nagash's side, a towering warrior of brazen iron and ferocity. Broader and taller than even the mightiest tribesmen, Krell bellowed a martial challenge that not even death could contain. The bloody champion of undeath and slaughter brandished his axe, raising it to point at the city before him, as though claiming it as his own.

A wind from the depths of the earth sprang up around these fell lords of sorcery and battle, a chill breath of lifelessness and the withering passage of time. It roiled towards the city, billowing like a desert sandstorm. Where it struck the walls, the stonework cracked and spalled, aged a thousand years in a heartbeat. Wooden gates rotted and crumbled as though split apart by centuries of hoar frost. The cold wind blew through the city with a ghastly whisper heard by every man, woman and child.

It was the Necromancer's promise and threat all in one.

Man is cattle…

YET NAGASH WAS not the first to reach Reikdorf this day. As the fleeting light of dawn crested the eastern mountains before being smothered by the black canopy of the undead twilight, a ragged band of a hundred warriors limped towards the city's southern gateway. Led by her sword maidens, Queen Freya returned to the lands of Men, having fought her way through the infested wilds of the southern Empire.

These wounded, exhausted men and women were all that remained of the proud host she had led from Three Hills, warriors whose honour sought redemption by bringing the queen they had failed to safety. Death would be a release for them, should the enemy facing them grant such mercy. Maedbh was overjoyed to see Freya, as were the people of Reikdorf, for her survival was a lone beacon of hope in these grim times. That Freya could survive meant others could too. No sooner had she ridden through the gates than the Queen's Eagles surrounded her, bringing her sons to her side for a tearful reunion.

The joy that greeted Freya's arrival was soon tempered by word that the dead were no more than an hour behind them. The gates were sealed and barred, and the warriors preparing to defend the city with their lives manned the walls, clutching swords and axes in hands slick with fear. Though still gravely wounded, Freya took her place with the Queen's Eagles, and no words of admonition could shift Sigulf and Fridleifr from her side.

There could be no bystanders in this battle for survival.

All would fight, or all would die.

The bell on the temple of Ulric chimed, and the dead came to Reikdorf.

'I CAN'T BELIEVE we're doing this,' said Alfgeir, holding tightly to the reins of his horse as it tossed its head and snorted in fear. 'This is madness and you know it.'

'Maybe so,' said Sigmar, 'but it needs to be done.'

'I am never one to back down from a foe, but I agree with your Reik Marshal,' said Freya, riding alongside Garr and three of his Queen's Eagles. As the only one of Sigmar's counts present in Reikdorf, she had the right to ride out with him, but he found it hard to look at her without picturing the boys that carried his blood.

They rode through the rotted remains of the Ostgate towards the enemy army. Since arriving at the walls of Reikdorf, the undead host had stood in silence, content to let fear worm its way into the hearts of those mortals who would soon be joining their ranks. The only movement had been when the three armoured warriors in the army's vanguard had ridden forward beneath a lowered banner, the universal symbol of parley.

'Why should we respect this parley?' said Garr, one hand on his sword hilt. 'We outnumber them and should cut them down while we have the chance.'

Sigmar looked over at the man, irritated at his foolishness.

'You could try, but these are blood drinkers, and they would kill you before you even drew that blade,' said Sigmar.

Garr swallowed hard and released his hold on his sword.

'Damn, but what I wouldn't give to be riding out to these bastards with Redwane and a century of his White Wolves about now,' said Wolfgart.

Sigmar smiled. 'Aye, that would be most welcome, but Middenheim will have its own problems if I'm any judge.'

Further conversation was halted as the air grew dense and cold. The blood drinkers were ahead of them, blocking the road and silhouetted on the crest of the slope ahead of them. Sigmar felt his skin crawl at their nearness, the very core of what made him a man rebelling at being so close to creatures that so obviously violated the natural order of the world. An aura of freezing air surrounded them, as though warmth was repelled by their very presence.

Khaled al-Muntasir gave an elaborate bow from the back of his dark steed, smiling in welcome as though they were old friends and not mortal enemies. Sigmar's horse balked at the proximity of the undead, its ears pressed flat against its skull and eyes wide with fear. He heard a jingle of trace and harness as the horses of his companions whinnied and sought to gallop back the way they had come.

'Emperor,' said the vampire, and Sigmar saw the gleam of razor-sharp fangs in the corner of the monster's mouth. 'It is a great pleasure to see you again.'

'I cannot say the same,' he replied.

'No, I expect not,' agreed the vampire, turning his attention to the Asoborn queen with a mocking glint in his eyes. 'And Queen Freya, I am gratified to see you survived our previous encounter. I cannot promise you the same mercy I showed you at the river, but as you can see, many of your tribesmen now fight with me. Were you to join them, it would have a pleasing symmetry.'

Freya seethed with fury and hurt, and Sigmar saw it was taking every scrap of her restraint not to hurl herself at the vampire. She took a deep, shuddering breath.

'You defeat my army, but you run from a host of old men and children,' she said, each word a venomous barb. 'You are nothing to be feared. You and your kind are leeches, not warriors. A true leader would have died with his army, not run like a gelded catamite.'

Khaled al-Muntasir glared at her, but his angry expression turned to one of polite indifference, as if she had not spoken.

'Death is meaningless to me,' said Khaled al-Muntasir with a dismissive wave of a thin-boned hand. 'None of your inferior race can strike down one of my kind. The blood of ancient queens runs in my veins, and I will simply rise from any wound a mortal can deal me.'

Sigmar was studying Khaled al-Muntasir's eyes as he spoke, and almost missed the lie, so glibly did it trip from the vampire's mouth.

'I don't believe you,' said Sigmar, suddenly seeing a crack in the vampire's self-perpetuated aura of invincibility. 'You fear extinction like any mortal. More so. You've become so attached to the idea of immortality that just the thought of oblivion terrifies you.'

The vampire turned his gaze on Sigmar, and he felt the full might of his will, a potent force that had sustained his existence for centuries and which had seduced hundreds with its promises of a life undying. Its promises were empty to Sigmar, for he had faced the temptations of a being far older and far more dangerous than a mere vampire.

'I told you that you were not welcome in Reikdorf,' said Sigmar, without breaking the vampire's gaze and letting him know that the attempt to dominate him had failed. 'I said that if you returned that you would be killed.'

The vampire looked hurt at Sigmar's harsh words and said, 'You would not respect the sanctity of the parley? I had thought you a civilised man.'

'What do you want, fiend?' demanded Wolfgart.

The vampire's tongue flicked out, as though tasting the air like a serpent. He smiled and nodded toward Wolfgart. 'You should keep yapping dogs on a leash, Sigmar. They might have their throats torn out to teach them a lesson.'

'Now who's not respecting the parley?' said Alfgeir. 'What is it you want? Speak your offer so we can spit on it and get back to our drinks.'

'Very well,' said Khaled al-Muntasir, more offended at Alfgeir's disrespect than any notion of the parley being broken. 'I came here to offer you one last chance to hand over my master's crown. Ride out with it within a day and you will be…'

'Spared?' laughed Sigmar.

'No,' replied Khaled al-Muntasir. 'Not spared, but you

would become exalted champions of the dead, great kings among the host of the unliving. It is a great honour my master does you by even offering you this chance.'

'So why doesn't he come here himself to offer me this boon, ruler to ruler?' said Sigmar.

The vampire cocked his head to one side, as though trying to discern whether Sigmar was joking. Deciding he wasn't, Khaled al-Muntasir shrugged.

'My master does not lower himself to treat with lesser races,' said the vampire. 'Bring him his crown and your deaths will be swift, your rebirths glorious. Deny him and he will kill everyone in your ridiculous city, and bring your people back from the dead only after their corpses have been violated by the flesheaters. There will be no glorious resurrection for any of you, just mindless hunger and a craving for living meat that can never be sated.'

'Tough choice,' said Wolfgart. 'Can we think about it?'

Missing the sarcasm, the vampire said, 'You have one day. When the twin moons rise, the end begins.'

'Then we will fight you beneath their light,' said Sigmar, turning his horse back towards Reikdorf. Before he could rake his spurs back, Khaled al-Muntasir had one last parting shot.

'Where are my manners?' said the vampire with mock embarrassment. 'How rude of me not to introduce you to my new companions. My brothers, come greet our honourable foes.'

The two warriors accompanying Khaled al-Muntasir rode level with the vampire and raised their visors. Sigmar's heart lurched with a spasm of grief as he beheld the once-noble features of Counts Siggurd and Markus. Their faces were pale and bloodless, lined with spider-web patterns of empty veins, and their eyes gleamed red with hunger. Sigmar counted these men as his dearest brothers, warrior kings who had marched into the jaws of death with him and emerged victorious.

He had called them to his side time after time, and they had honoured their oaths to him without question. Now, when they had needed him, he had failed them. Their people were enslaved and their heroic lineage had been ended, each man cursed to an eternity of suffering and torment as a soulless blood drinker. They stared at Sigmar with undisguised thirst, fangs exposed and their bodies leaning forward, as though about to leap from their horses and bear him to the ground.

'You must forgive them their ill-manners,' said Khaled al-Muntasir with relish. 'They are little more than children, still driven by their own selfish desires and hunger. They have yet to master their appetites when in civilised company.'

'What have you done?' said Sigmar, overcome with anguish at the sight of counts.

'He has given us a great gift,' said Markus. 'One that can be yours if you so choose.'

'Gift?' spat Sigmar. 'You are both damned and you do not see it.'

He turned away from the vampires, disgusted and ashamed at what had become of them.

These abominations looked and sounded like his counts, but they were not Siggurd and Markus, and he wouldn't waste any words on the monsters that wore their faces. The brave men who had fought beside him at Black Fire and who had come to his aid at Middenheim were no more, and all that remained of them were memories.

Sigmar and his companions rode away from the vampire counts, each struggling with their emotions at the sight of the newest blood drinkers. Khaled al-Muntasir's laughter rang in their ears and Markus spurred his black horse forward to shout after them.

'We have been lifted from the mud of mortality,' the former count of the Menogoth tribe cried. 'Born anew to higher forms, and if you could feel what I feel, you would beg for my fangs to fasten on your neck!'

No one answered him. No one could.

THE SOUND OF hammers woke Govannon from a deep sleep, a percussive beat that set his whole room vibrating. It was dark, but that didn't mean anything. Since the dead had arrived it was always dark. He had thought that the loss of sunlight would not make much of a difference to him; his world was grey and lightless anyway. But even locked in his blind world he felt the crushing bleakness of a world without sunlight.

Though everyone in the city was afraid, including Govannon, he had no trouble in sleeping, for his work on the dwarf war machine had driven him past the point of exhaustion. He had yet to discover a workable fire powder compound, and his body was unforgiving in its protests at his treatment of it.

Rolling onto his side, Govannon yawned and stretched his tired muscles. He groped for his bearskin pelt, hanging on a hook beside the bed, and pulled it around his shoulders. The hammering was coming from below, but who would dare break into his forge to use his tools and materials without asking? They'd be in for a hiding, that was for sure. Bysen might have the mind of a child, but he had the right hook of a bare-knuckle fist fighter.

Govannon crossed the room, seeing nothing, but not needing to. The layout of his room was well known to him. He reached down to wake Bysen, but found his son's bed empty and cold. It hadn't been slept in for some time, and Govannon's anxiety grew. Bysen was missing, and in that moment, Govannon was back at

Black Fire Pass, desperately searching the infirmary tents for any sign of his boy.

He heard muffled voices from below, and reached for the knife wedged in the gap between Bysen's bed and the wall. The blade was sharp on both edges and triangular in section, meaning any wound it caused would never properly heal. It was a weapon of spite, but whoever had broken into his forge had more than earned that spite.

Govannon eased onto the stairs that led down to the forge, feeling the heat wash up from below on his skin. A blurred orange glow illuminated the lower level of the building, a glow that told Govannon his forge was burning hotter than it had ever burned before. The voices were punctuated with clangs of hammers on metal and sparks of white fire that penetrated even Govannon's limited sight. The air tasted of hot metal, burning coal and some nameless, actinic residue he couldn't identify. What in Ulric's name was going on down there?

Though he carried a knife, Govannon wasn't naïve enough to believe that he could defend himself from an intruder. Still, his forge was his domain, and anyone who thought otherwise was going to get badly hurt before they cut him down.

He counted twelve steps, made a turn to the right and then counted another ten. The heatwash from below was like nothing he had felt before, a rushing, all-enveloping fire that burned hotter than any forge he had ever known.

'Whoever you are, get out of my forge!' he bellowed, mustering as much of his warrior shout as he could. 'I swear to Ulric, I've a knife I'll stick in the neck of any bastard who tries to take me!'

Govannon saw two shapes beside the forge, one tall and hunched over, the other short and squat and swinging what looked like a short-handled sledgehammer.

White sparks flew, each like a firefly of light that cut through his blindness in staccato flashes of clarity. The knife dropped from his hands as he saw Bysen by the roaring maw of the forge, lifting a gleaming sword blade from the anvil, where one of the mountain folk stood back with a monstrously heavy-looking hammer casually slung over one shoulder.

The sight faded with the white sparks and Govannon groaned as his vision became blurred and hazy once again. He heard Bysen's voice over the roaring of the forge.

'Da, you're here!' said his son, closing the door to the firebox with an iron-reinforced boot heel. 'I didn't want to wake you, da. But the dwarf man said it didn't matter none.'

The heat in the forge dropped as the firebox door shut, though it was still hot enough to take the chill off the unnatural cold that filled Reikdorf. Refugees clamoured to take shelter in the lee of the forge, as it was one of the warmest places in the city.

'Are you all right, da?' said Bysen. 'You need to go back to sleep?'

'I'm fine,' insisted Govannon, walking toward where he had seen the dwarf with the enormous hammer.

'You are Govannon, the blind manling smith?' said a gruff voice, pitched somewhere between irritation and condescension.

'I am,' he said. 'Who are you and why are you in my forge?'

'I am Master Alaric, Runesmith to King Kurgan Ironbeard of Karaz-a-Karak, and I am here to reclaim my property. You're in a lot of trouble, manling.'

'What are you talking about? You're not making any damn sense,' said Govannon, before the identity of the dwarf hit him between the eyes. 'Wait, Master Alaric?

You're the smith who made the runefang. And Sigmar's crown.'

'Amongst other things,' grumbled Alaric in annoyance. 'I do make things other than trinkets for manlings, you know.'

'Of course, of course,' said Govannon, moving through the forge with the ease of one who had a perfect memory of its layout. 'It's a great honour to meet you. I've admired your work for years. I just wish I could have seen the Runefang Blodambana before I lost my eyes...'

'Bloodbane,' said Alaric. 'A good name well earned.'

'Bysen, fetch our guest some beer, the good stuff,' said Govannon.

'Aye, da. Right away, da,' said Bysen, moving past him. The sword blade he carried shone in the light, as clear to Govannon's sight as if he looked upon it with Cuthwin's keen eyes.

'Wait,' said Govannon, putting his hand on Bysen's arm. 'What is that?'

'It's Master Alfgeir's sword, da,' said Bysen. 'The mountain man helped me finish it.'

'He helped you...'

'Finish it,' said Bysen happily. 'Now all I need to do is take it to Master Holtwine and he can fit the handle he made for it.'

Govannon had all but forgotten about Alfgeir's sword, it had been so long since he had begun its forging. Though he had sworn to the Marshal of the Reik he would finish it before the snows, that had been an empty promise, for the work on the war machine had taken all his time and effort.

'Show me,' he ordered.

Bysen obligingly lowered the sword, and Govannon was amazed at the finished blade. Smooth beyond belief, the metal was pristine and etched with angular symbols along its centreline that sparkled with strange light. Though everything around him was as blurred as ever, the sword blade was sharp and clear, a vision of perfection that made Govannon's eyes wet with tears.

Gingerly, he tested its edges, not surprised to find that both were sharp beyond the ability of any human whetstone to grind.

He turned to Alaric. 'You did this?' he said, his voice choked.

'I came for something else, but saw that the blade needed doing,' said the dwarf. 'It's nothing, just some simple cutting and keenness runes.'

'I can see them,' said Govannon in wonderment.

'Some things are clearer than others, manling,' said the dwarf cryptically. 'Now, as to the matter I came here for. The baragdonnaz.'

'I don't know what that means,' said Govannon, finding it hard to think of anything but this perfect sword blade.

Alaric sighed, as though bored by his stupidity. 'The war machine Grindan Deeplock was returning to Prince Uldrakk of Zhufbar. The one to which you have made alterations unsanctioned by the Guild.'

'You mean the Thunder Bringer?' said Govannon, moving to the corner of the forge and removing the tarpaulin covering the war machine. Though he couldn't see it clearly, he ran his hands over its warm metal barrels. Alaric joined him and prised his hands from the metal.

'Is that what you call it?' said Alaric, shaking his head. 'Trust you manlings to call it something so bloody literal.'

'I fixed it,' said Govannon proudly. 'It took a while, but I got the metal densities in the end, though it took a lot of trial and error.'

'Fixed it? A bodge job if ever I've seen one. More errors than I'd expect from a hundred apprentices,' grunted Alaric, circling the war machine and tapping it with an iron-ringed knuckle. The dwarf listened to the sounds, grunting and harrumphing with each one, until he'd made a full circuit of the machine.

'What's he doing, da?' asked Bysen.

'I don't know,' said Govannon, angry that his finest work had been so slighted.

'I'm listening to the metal, manlings,' said Alaric. 'Which would be a damn sight easier if you two didn't keep jabbering on so.'

Govannon could contain himself no longer and declared, 'I managed to repair it, damn it, and I'll wager no other smith in the land could do what I've done. If I can just get the fire powder formula to work, then we might be able to shoot it.'

'Shoot it?' gasped Alaric. 'You want to shoot it?'

'Of course, what else would we do with it?'

'With an untested barrel made by manlings?' said Alaric, kicking the pile of iron shot stacked beside the war machine. 'And irregular shot too. Grungni and Valaya save me from manlings with ideas above their station! Even if I let you shoot the baragdonnaz, you'd likely blow yourself and anyone nearby to a thousand tiny burned pieces.'

'Now just wait a minute,' said Govannon. 'A lone Unberogen scout saved the life of the dwarf who hid this machine. Unberogen warriors found it and brought it back here. And an Unberogen smith fixed the bloody thing. The least you could be is grateful.'

'Grateful? For this?' snapped Alaric, squaring up to Govannon and planting his hands on his hips. 'Imagine your finest sword was found by a greenskin and then broken in two. Then imagine that greenskin bolted it to a rock he'd just dug out of a troll's dung pile and called it fixed. That's what this is to me.'

'Aye, well if I was surrounded by enemies I'd be grateful just to have a weapon in my hands,' snapped Govannon, weary of this dwarf's constant harping. 'In fact, I'd be damn glad of it.'

Master Alaric seemed to consider this for a moment. At last he sighed in resignation.

'You might have a point there, manling,' said Alaric. 'Very well, tradition is one thing, but an enemy at our throat is quite another. This is what I'll do, I'll make you enough black powder for a couple of volleys, but that's all. And you're to tell no other dwarfs of this.'

'So you'll help us make it work?' cried Bysen.

'I reckon I might,' said Alaric. 'Just make sure I'm nowhere nearby when you fire it.'

── NINETEEN ──

The Last Night

As IT ALWAYS was, the air was fresh and cool on Warriors Hill. The stillness that surrounded the last resting place of the honoured dead of the Unberogen was a place of solitude, where a man could wander the tombs of his forefathers and reflect on all that had gone before him and all that had made him who he was. Sigmar remembered coming here on his Dooming Day, just after he'd broken Wolfgart's arm with a smelting hammer.

His father had sent him here to walk through the dead of the tribe and listen to the whispers of the ancestors. Entering the tomb of Redmane Dregor, he'd made offerings to Morr before being plunged into darkness. Trapped within the tomb, he had prayed to Ulric and the wolf god had given him the strength to free himself from his grandfather's barrow.

Sigmar circled higher on the hill, the flag-wrapped body of Eoforth held across his chest as he carried him uphill towards his resting place. The old scholar's body weighed next to nothing, and Sigmar was ashamed he had asked so much of this man, who had already given more than enough to his tribe and his Emperor.

The priests of Morr had spoken the words of warding over Eoforth's body, but even they could not say for sure whether that would be enough to resist the sorcery of Nagash. The only sure way to keep Eoforth's remains from rising again would be to burn them, but Sigmar had balked at the idea of cremation. Eoforth would be interred within Warriors Hill, with the other heroes who had served the Unberogen.

Sigmar passed the tomb of Trinovantes and Pendrag, feeling his throat tighten and his eyes fill with tears as he thought of his lost friends. They had died in battle, and were drinking, feasting and hunting in the Halls of Ulric. No man could ask for more, yet Sigmar selfishly wished they were here beside him, fully armoured and standing ready to give battle against this dreadful foe.

At last he reached the tree-covered summit of the hill and laid Eoforth's body down on the stone slab at its centre. He unwrapped the flag, exposing Eoforth's face, and bent to kiss the old man's forehead.

'I will miss you, old friend,' said Sigmar. 'You kept me honest and true.'

Sigmar knelt and unhooked a small pouch from his belt, removing a bull's heart he had cut from the animal himself. He placed it in a bronze bowl set into the rock and poured a flask of oil across the bloody organ. Sparks from his tinderbox ignited the oil and the heart began to burn, slowly at first, for the muscular meat was tough and leathery. Eventually it caught and the heart fizzed and spat as the fire consumed it. The smell of the cooking meat filled Sigmar's nostrils.

'Father Morr, guide this soul to his final rest and watch over him as he passes from the lands of the living into the realm of the dead. Light his path through the Grey

Vaults and keep the shadow hunters from his back as he makes his way to the Halls of Ulric. Judge him worthy, for no truer son of the Unberogen has come before you. Eoforth was a warrior without a sword, but thanks to his actions the world is a safer place. His peace was won with words and wise counsel, not with blades and war. Would that we could all be so wise. Guide him to his last rest, Father Morr, and I will preserve his memory for as long as I shall live.'

The heart hissed as it was consumed, the fire flickering with a purple light. The dancing flames lit Eoforth's face, and Sigmar stood, placing a hand on his friend's chest. A tomb had been dug on the eastern face of the hill, and with the offering to Morr complete, Sigmar bent to lift Eoforth's body once again.

Cold air brushed past him, carrying the whispers of ancient voices, fleeting sighs of long dead warriors and the murmur of ghostly war shouts. Sigmar looked down, seeing that the rune-etched haft of Ghal-maraz glittered with power. The hairs on the back of Sigmar's neck stood erect and he knew he was not alone. His hand slid down to his warhammer and he spun around, bringing the weapon up to his shoulder in one smooth motion.

The hill thronged with ghostly warriors, scores of them drifting uphill from their tombs with axes and unsheathed swords. They converged on the summit, and Sigmar knew he could never fight his way through so many. Alfgeir and Wolfgart had counselled against climbing Warriors Hill alone, but Sigmar had denied any attempt to provide him with a protective escort. It felt like the right thing to do at the time, but now seemed foolish and arrogant.

The spirits closed in, crowding the summit of the hill, and Sigmar took a deep breath, flexing his fingers on the textured grip of his hammer. The dead warriors were translucent, the wavering outline of trees visible through their immaterial forms. A fearsome Unberogen war cry died on Sigmar's lips as three figures stepped from the ranks of the spirit warriors, limned in shimmering winter's light.

Armoured in the style of many years ago, some in bronze, some in iron, they wore Unberogen war helms, and carried long swords that glittered with frostlight. Wolfskin cloaks hung from their shoulders and though Sigmar knew he should be afraid, nothing of these phantoms sent any tremors of fear through him.

The largest of the three snapped up the visor of his helm and Sigmar felt himself hurled back to his childhood as the stern features of his father were revealed. King Björn looked upon his son with loving, paternal affection, his lined and bearded face alight with pride.

At his father's right stood Pendrag, resplendent in the armour he had worn in the defence of Middenheim. Even the blade he bore was a shimmering likeness of the runefang Sigmar had commanded him to wield. On Björn's left was a young man, barely old enough to ride to war, and Sigmar's heart broke to see the youthful features of Trinovantes. Twenty-five years had passed since Trinovantes's death at Astofen, the first battle they had ridden to after their Blood Night, and Sigmar was amazed to think he had ever been that young.

Tears flowed freely at the sight of these heroic warriors, friends who had stood beside him in battle and the father who had set him on the path to becoming a man. Their legacy was the Empire and their role in shaping him into the man who would build it was immeasurable. Trinovantes – Ravenna's brother and Gerreon's twin – smiled at Sigmar, and though he wanted to say how much he missed them all, how much he had loved them, he simply couldn't. The words choked him, loss and grief like a powerful hand around his throat.

His father nodded, and he knew they understood.

The spectral army moved past him and he felt their pride in his accomplishments. They watched over him from Ulric's Halls and they were at peace, knowing the lives they had lost in defence of their homelands had not been given in vain. Sigmar lowered his hammer as the spirits of the dead Unberogen lifted Eoforth's body from the rock and moved off down the hillside to his open tomb.

Björn, Pendrag and Trinovantes turned away and began moving off again, their duty to Eoforth stronger than any dark sorcery that sought to break the chains of loyalty and duty that bound the Unberogen together. Sigmar had never been so humbled in all his life. To know that the blood of these great warriors flowed in his veins was the greatest honour Sigmar could imagine.

One by one, the soul lights of the dead began to dim. Trinovantes faded back into the mists of memory, and Sigmar raised a hand in farewell. He thought he saw Trinovantes smile, but couldn't be sure. Pendrag's form grew more and more insubstantial, until he too had vanished.

Eventually only Björn remained. He and Sigmar stood in silent communion, and of all the things that mattered in this world, his father's pride was the most important. Björn looked down at Reikdorf, and Sigmar saw a wry smile tug at the corner of his mouth, feeling his proud amazement at the magnificent city that had arisen from the small settlement he had known in life. His father pointed towards the city, and turned back to Sigmar.

Know them and understand them, for it will make you mighty.

The words were not spoken, but Sigmar heard them as

clearly as though his father had been standing right next to him. King Björn nodded, knowing Sigmar had understood his message. He moved off into the darkness, and was soon lost to sight as his shade returned to the realms beyond the knowledge of mortals.

Sigmar sank to his knees, overcome with emotion. Ghal-maraz dropped to the ground and he buried his head in his hands. He wept as memories of his father and friends surged to the fore, but they were not tears shed in grief, but in remembrance of all the joy they had shared in life. At last his tears were spent, and Sigmar stood tall as he turned to look at the city below, heartened by the thousands of pinpricks of light that glittered in the darkness.

In the last month, the population had quadrupled, with thousands coming in from the countryside ahead of the rising tide of undead. Warriors, farmers and craftsmen thronged the city's streets, frightened and cold and hungry, but unwilling to give up.

Though a black host of the dead waited beyond the city walls, this island of humanity still stood inviolate. That alone was cause for hope, and as his father's last words echoed within his mind, he felt his gaze drawn up and out of his body, climbing into the sky and expanding to encompass the entirety of the Empire.

His awareness of the land was complete, and he saw the vast swathes of forests, rivers and hills. Flatlands and coastline stretched from the towering mountains of the south and east to the cliffs of the western wastelands and the frozen, ice-locked shores of the north.

Like a creeping sickness, the armies of Nagash spread throughout the Empire, hordes of the dead enslaved to the will of the ancient necromancer like war hounds on a fraying leash. Bound together by a web of dark sorcery with Nagash at its centre, the armies of the dead jealously strangled the life from the land of mortals. The southernmost reaches of the Empire were already enveloped in darkness, but across the Empire, scattered lights of resistance flared brightly against the encroaching shadow.

Sigmar saw the palisade forts of the Udose besieged by corpses of ragged flesh, while other clans were pushed into bleak highland valleys where they fought desperate battles for survival. Conn Carsten gave battle from the parapets of Wolfila's rebuilt castle, his army a patchwork of warriors from a dozen different clans. Welded together by the common foe, they fought as brothers, though they scrapped like bitter foes in times of peace.

In the east, Count Adelhard led daring hit and run attacks against the dead, riding at the head of glorious winged lancers, whooping with excitement as they charged hither and thither through the ranks of the dead with wild abandon. The Ostagoths did not build cities, their people living in settlements that could be broken down at a moment's notice and loaded onto wagons for transport. The dead had no focus for their assault, and the Ostagoth cavalry armies encircled and destroyed their enemies piecemeal.

The Cherusens and Taleutens took refuge behind the walls of their great cities. Krugar fought heroically on the spiked walls of Taalahim, the great crater city that nestled like a giant eye in the enormous expanse of the great forest. Always where the fighting was thickest, Krugar hewed the undead with glittering sweeps of Utensjarl.

Further west, Aloysis defended Hochergig with all the wild fury for which his kinsmen were famed. Forced to fight with every weapon available, many of the Cherusens chewed wildroot and drove themselves into bloody frenzies.

Atop the spire of the Fauschlag Rock, Myrsa and his

warriors hurled the dead from the walls of their soaring city. The cliff-like sides of the rock writhed with climbing horrors, yet the city still held. Myrsa's runefang shone with simple purity, and where it smote, the dead could not resist its power.

Count Otwin's lands were near empty, his people scattered by the sudden invasion of the dead from the wastelands to the north-west. Long shunned by the living, these lands had vomited forth a ravening tide of the dead that had driven the Thuringians from their lands. Many now fought in Middenheim, or had since fled to Marburg.

Jutonsryk was a city of the dead, its streets empty of life and infested with degenerate cannibal creatures. Even if this war against Nagash could be won, Jutonsryk would forever be a forsaken and damned place, where no soul would seek to live again. Its great buildings and stone walls would fall into disrepair and within the span of a lifetime, no one would know that men had once lived there.

Further south in Marburg, the dead hurled themselves at the walls of a great citadel, but the defenders here were resolute and filled with determination to hold. Here, the power of the undead seemed weakest, as though a turning point in the battle for Marburg had been reached, and mortals now had the upper hand. Sigmar scanned the walls of the citadel for Count Aldred, but could not see the ruler of the Endals. Princess Marika and Count Marius fought side by side and when Sigmar saw the shimmering blue blade of Ulfshard in the Jutone count's hand, he knew with heavy heart that Aldred was dead.

Setting aside his grief, Sigmar's awareness of the Empire shrank until he found himself staring at Reikdorf once more. Despite everything that had been lost,

Reikdorf remained. Enemies of the most terrible aspect stood poised to destroy it, but there was still hope.

Some people called hope a weakness, claiming it was foolish to trust in the world's inherent natural justice. Sigmar knew better. Hope was strength. Hope could drive men and women to the most incredible feats of heroism, from the everyday kindnesses between friends to the epic, world-changing feats of kings and warriors.

Sigmar smiled to himself, understanding that most world-changing events came about not through the actions of so called great leaders, but ordinary men and women driven to extraordinary heights of courage.

And as he had seen his land, so too he saw his people.

SIGMAR'S SIGHT TRAVELLED the streets of Reikdorf, seeing the strength that resided in every man and woman taking shelter within the city's walls. Though his body knelt atop Warriors Hill, Sigmar roamed freely through the city, flying over its thatched roofs and along its cobbled streets as though transformed into an invisible observer of life. He saw acts of tiny kindness between people who had never ventured further than the outskirts of their villages and who had been brought up to fear and mistrust outsiders; these people now shared what little food they had with those they would have fought only a few years before.

Here, an Asoborn woman offered bread to Brigundian children orphaned by the fighting, there an Unberogen family sheltered Taleutens and Endals within their home. In a silent, firelit dwelling in the northern quarter of the city, Orvin handed down his father's helmet to his son, Teon. The lad took the helmet, and even as he slid it over his head, Sigmar saw the shame that he had not been kinder to his old teacher. For his part, Orvin wished he could tell Teon how proud he was, but he didn't know how to begin. He loved his son, but a warrior's duty without a wife at his side had made them strangers. Instead, they simply sat and sharpened their swords and polished their armour in strained silence. Though there was no affection between them, both Teon and Orvin would fight for the Empire, and both would die if need be.

Sigmar passed onwards, seeing Freya coupling with Garr, the commander of the Queen's Eagles. This was the Asoborn queen's way, using sex as a means of wringing each moment dry of sensation and taking advantage of all that life had to offer. She was a passionate woman, and lived without compromise. Sigmar admired her for that, but knew she could never be his Empress. Freya would never be any one man's woman.

He did not linger on her lovemaking, but smiled as he saw Sigulf and Fridleifr practising swordplay in the other room. His heart ached to see these boys and not to know them, but to tear them from their old life for one they didn't know and wouldn't want would be a cruelty he could not inflict. These boys knew him as the Emperor, and would never know him as a father. Though it cut deeper than the sharpest sword, Sigmar knew it was the only thing that could be done.

Moving on, he saw Govannon the smith and his son, Bysen, with Master Alaric. They rolled the war machine they had been working on for weeks on end towards the eastern gates of the city. Elswyth was right, the blind smith would never willingly give up working, knowing all that would be left to him was a slow decline into death. To continue working gave him purpose, and that purpose kept him alive. Bysen was a hulking giant of a warrior, his mind left in tatters after Black Fire Pass. Both men had given so much in service of the Empire, but each was still willing to give more. Master Alaric had once again come to the aid of Sigmar's people, which spoke volumes of his character, for a dwarf's friendship was never given lightly. Sigmar was thankful every day that the irascible runesmith had seen fit to be his friend.

Alfgeir sat in the longhouse with his knights as they told bawdy tales and made proud boasts. Captain Leodan's Red Scythes drank here too. These men were eager for the coming fight, painting fire masks on their helms and images of the sun on their shields. If they were to fight in twilight, then they would bring their own light.

Leodan drank with his men, the barriers of rank broken down on this last night, but Alfgeir sat apart from his knights. He drank sparingly, bound to these fine Unberogen men, but apart from them. Thirty years separated him from the next oldest of his warriors, and where their thoughts were fixed on the battle to come, Alfgeir's were turned inwards, looking back over a life lived with honour and courage, but, ultimately, alone. In that respect, Sigmar felt more kinship with Alfgeir than any other man in Reikdorf. The Marshal of the Reik missed Eoforth, yet another thread linking him to his glorious youth cut away like a fraying rope that was on the verge of snapping. Where most men pushed thoughts of falling in battle aside, Alfgeir brooded on them – knowing his death was almost certain on the morrow.

Saddened, Sigmar flew on, passing Cuthwin and Wenyld as they drank and remembered happier times. Sigmar remembered catching the pair of them sneaking across the marketplace to spy on the Blood Night before the ride to Astofen. Neither lad had been old enough to fight, and to see them as grown men was a stark reminder of how much time had passed since then. Though it had been many years since Cuthwin and Wenyld had seen one another, they picked up where they had left off, as though it had been only a few days. Such friendships were rare, and Sigmar dearly hoped they would survive tomorrow's bloodshed.

Lastly, he moved to the large house in the south of Reikdorf where Wolfgart and Maedbh lived. Once again its walls were warm and its welcome complete. Wolfgart and Maedbh and Ulrike lay curled up together on their bed, sleeping in each other's arms and content to pass this time together. Joy touched Sigmar at this sight, a man and his wife and their child together, all pretence and antagonism forgotten as the depth of their love for one another drove out all pettiness or recriminations. This had been Sigmar's dream before the Hag Woman had cruelly disabused him of the notion that he could ever aspire to such a life.

Knowing he could never have the simple pleasures of hearth and home, wife and child, Sigmar had made his peace with knowing that the Empire was his bride. He had sworn to love it and no other, and he had kept his faith with that, sacrificing his desire for love and companionship to be the man he needed to be in order to rule. Seeing Wolfgart and Maedbh, with Ulrike nestled in the protective embrace of her father, made that sacrifice worth every moment spent alone and without Ravenna by his side.

In that moment, Sigmar vowed that when this world was done with him, when he was ready to act upon his father's words, he would honour his promise to Ravenna. When the Empire was strong enough not to need him, he would walk the wolf's road he had been promised in Ulric's fire so long ago it felt like it belonged to the story of another man's life.

Sigmar flew up and over Reikdorf, understanding that the strength in every person came from the life each one treasured. That it could be snatched away at any moment made it all the sweeter, driving men and women to chase their dreams and make them real. The dead had no dreams, no ambition and no forward momentum. If Nagash defeated Sigmar and covered the world in shadow, then it would stagnate, becoming a barren rock bereft of life and light. To cheat death and achieve immortality was one thing, but to rule over a world of grey, ashen wastelands, populated only by the shuffling, mindless dead, was no life at all. What could any man want with such a prize?

High upon Warriors Hill, Sigmar opened his eyes, feeling a swelling sense of humility as he looked down on Reikdorf with his mortal eyes once more. He rose to his feet and walked back down the hill towards his longhouse. Beyond the city was darkness, an uninterrupted sea of shadow and death. Curiously uplifted by that, Sigmar found his fear of the dead had completely vanished.

The outcome of tomorrow's battle was unimportant.

That he fought in defiance of Nagash's lifeless, empty future was enough.

Sigmar would ride out and give battle, but he would fight with all the Empire at his back.

THOUSANDS HAD GATHERED to hear the Emperor speak, filling the square at the centre of Reikdorf with a press of bodies like the crowd at an execution. Sigmar looked up to see the twin moons slung low in the sky, as though eager to witness this moment. His closest warriors gathered around him and people hung from windows and gathered on rooftops, eager to hear what the Emperor had to say as the time of battle drew near.

Freya and her Queen's Eagles formed a ring around Sigmar, who sat atop his horse beside the Oathstone. His mount was a dappled grey gelding with a bright red caparison and a mane pleated with silver cord. Armoured in his dwarf-forged plate, Sigmar was a single source of brightness in the darkness, his armour gathering all the moonlight and magnifying it tenfold. Sigmar's head was bare, his long hair unbound and spilling around his shoulders. His pale blue and green eyes swept over the thousands waiting to hear him speak, and he felt their belief in him wash over him like a tide.

People of all tribes were gathered before him. They had asked much of Sigmar over the years, and now it was his turn to ask something of them. He knew they would not refuse him.

Sigmar lifted Ghal-maraz, and the ancient heirloom of King Kurgan glimmered with runic traceries as it sensed it would soon be set loose amongst the unliving.

'People of the Empire, we are besieged by an army of the dead,' began Sigmar. 'A dread necromancer from the dawn of time has invaded our lands, murdering our people and enslaving those he kills to march in his dread legions. He comes not for plunder or any reason conquerors give, but simply to drain the land of life. He comes to our city to retrieve a powerful crown, forged by his own hand in an age forgotten by all save Nagash himself. He must not succeed, for the crown has the power to enslave all the lands of the living. I cannot stand by and let this happen, and nor will you.'

Sigmar's voice grew in power as he spoke and saw the effect his words were having. They believed him, *really* believed him. They trusted him to deliver them from this terrible foe, but this was not a battle that would be won by one man, it would need to be won by *all* the people of the Empire.

He saw they were afraid, and Sigmar remembered what his father had said before he rode to Astofen. He recognised the universal truth of these words as he said them anew, like a father passing age-won wisdom down to his son.

'I know the fear that consumes your innards like a snake, but have courage, for we are living folk of flesh and blood! Feel your heart pumping that blood around your body; it is hot and vibrant, filled with all the passions of the living. Love, hate, joy, anger, fear, sorrow, happiness, exultation! Feel them all and you will know you are alive, that your soul is free and you are a slave to no one.'

Sigmar jabbed Ghal-maraz towards the east and shouted his last demand. 'It is the dead beyond our walls that shuffle and wail, crawl and cower under the spell of their dark master who should fear us! Though the sun is shrouded by shadow, I call upon you to take up your weapons and sally forth with me to meet this foul army.'

Thousands of swords were drawn from scabbards and raised high. Axes waved and spears stabbed the air as the people gathered in Reikdorf screamed Sigmar's name. The walls shook with the deafening volume and the carrion birds perched on the roofs and garrets of the city took to the air with raucous caws of fear. The swelling roar spread through the city, taken up by every living soul in Reikdorf, even those too far away to hear Sigmar's words.

'Together we will defeat the legion of Nagash,' shouted Sigmar. 'We will send him screaming to the underworld that waits to consume him. Rally, people of the Empire! Rally to me and fight!'

SIGMAR LED THE way through the streets of Reikdorf towards the splintered wreckage of the Ostgate. Behind him marched a column of tribesmen, thousands upon thousands of warriors, men and women, old men and young, mothers, daughters, fathers and sons. Those without swords carried iron-tipped cudgels, butcher's hooks, felling axes or clubs formed from broken furniture. Sigmar's army was everyone in Reikdorf, peasant and noble-born alike. They came with him, chanting his name like a mantra or a prayer, their belief in him like a force of nature or some divine mandate stolen from the gods themselves.

His boon companions rode at his side, and though this could very well be the last day of the Empire, Sigmar faced it with pride and courage.

High Priestess Alessa was waiting for him at the Ostgate, surrounded by a hundred warriors with their heavy broadswords drawn. She carried a heavy iron box, banded with silver and secured by a lock of the same metal. Dark earth clung to the box, as though it had only recently been dug from the ground. Sigmar could feel the dark power bound to the dread artefact within, remembering the foul deeds it had driven him to before.

'You are sure about this?' said Alessa, tears streaming down her face.

'I am,' said Sigmar. 'There is no other way to face Nagash and live.'

Alessa nodded, as though she had been expecting this.

'You will need to be strong, Sigmar Heldenhammer,' she said. 'It will tempt you with all the secret things you hold deep in your heart.'

Sigmar shook his head with a derisive sneer. 'It offered me my heart's desire once before and I rejected it. There is nothing else it can show me.'

'I hope you are right,' said Alessa, opening the box. 'Or else it will not be Nagash who destroys the lands of men. It will be you.'

─═ TWENTY ═─

The Battle of the River Reik

THE ARMY OF mortals poured from the ruined gates of the city, forming a great mass of flesh and blood in the land between the two forks of the river that converged within its walls. Khaled al-Muntasir saw Sigmar at the heart of this force, a figure in shining armour to match his own. A twinge of unease flickered in the vampire's chest, as though he were watching some magnificent Nehekharan host arrayed for ritual battle instead of a pathetic, desperate horde of mortals.

Sigmar took his place at the head of maybe three hundred horsemen, each atop a powerful, armoured steed, and each bearing a mix of swords, axes and spears. As more of the Emperor's subjects marched from Reikdorf, a shape began to form of Sigmar's plan, and Khaled al-Muntasir laughed as his unease was replaced by relief.

Another block of cavalry formed up beside Sigmar's, and great wedges of infantry formed up to either side of the horsemen. Some of these were disciplined and marched like they'd been given some training, but others were little better than ragged mobs. Give them a taste of blood and death and they'd run easily enough. Yet more cavalry rode onto the northern flank of the army, their armour red-painted and bedecked with suns. A handful of chariots and painted warriors took position by the southern fork of the river, and the vampire smiled as he recognised Freya's barely-armoured form.

'Some mortals just never learn,' he said.

'What do you mean?' asked Siggurd.

'They think they can win,' said Khaled al-Muntasir. 'Even after all that's happened, they still think they can win. Hope has undone them. Hope has sent them out here to die ingloriously instead of accepting the inevitable and prospering.'

'Sigmar will always think he can win,' said Markus. 'Until the blade cleaves his heart, I'll not be too sure he's wrong.'

Khaled al-Muntasir looked over at his creation and frowned. 'You think that pathetic force can best ours?' He looked out over Sigmar's army, trying to estimate how many warriors the Emperor had. 'He has fifteen thousand men at best. We outnumber him by more than two to one. He cannot possibly defeat so many.'

Markus shrugged. 'I've heard of battles lost with better odds.'

'Impossible,' sneered Khaled al-Muntasir.

'You don't know Sigmar,' said Siggurd, his black steed pawing the ground and snorting with impatience.

Once again, the tiny ember of unease in Khaled al-Muntasir's chest was fanned, but he quashed it ruthlessly. More than numbers would decide this battle. The terrible fear of the dead would unman many of the Emperor's warriors, and for every one of them that fell, another fighter would be added to the army of the dead. Though Markus and Siggurd had not yet developed their sorcerous powers, his own were formidable. But even they were a pale shadow compared to the magic of Nagash. With a word, the necromancer could command the dead to rise, the living to wither and die, and curse the skies to bring forth elemental fury.

No, his vampire counts were simply being overly cautious, yet the thought would not leave him that this last, desperate battle was in fact a ploy to lure them into a trap. His gaze swept the mortal army as it began a slow advance, skirling war horns, trumpets and drums driving the army towards the silent host of undead. Sigmar's horsemen pulled ahead of the main battle line, riding at speed towards the centre of Nagash's army.

Khaled al-Muntasir followed the line of Sigmar's charge, seeing where it led with a derisive bark of laughter.

'What's so funny?' asked Markus.

'Sigmar wants to duel,' he said in disbelief. 'He thinks he can face Nagash.'

At the centre of the army of the dead, the pillar of terror and ice that was Nagash bellowed with rage. Black lightning surged from the necromancer, a furious, blitzing whirlwind of dark magic that consumed hundreds of revenants around him. A roaring scream of rage and bitter spite cracked the sky, and a cold rain began to fall as the wounded heavens wept over the lands of men.

Khaled al-Muntasir felt the terrible force of the necromancer's rage and, moments later, realised its source. Riding ever closer to the army of the dead, Sigmar's head was held high, and upon his brow was the glittering majesty of Nagash's crown. It pulsed with silver light, its magic unseen by mortals, but visible as a ghostly corona of light around the Emperor's head. Khaled al-Muntasir had taken it for some cheap mortal bauble, enchanted with some hedge wizard's pitiful ward charms, but the dormant power coming off it in waves told another story.

'Blood of the Ancients...' hissed Khaled al-Muntasir, angered at the sight of a mere man wearing the crown crafted by the master of the dead. The incredible power bound to its unknown metals was not for some fleshy sack of blood and meat to wear, it was for the Lord of Undeath alone. Sigmar had worn the crown once before and it had almost destroyed him, but his strength of will had been enough to resist its siren song.

A terrible thought occurred to the vampire...

Had Sigmar mastered the power of the crown?

Was that what this was, a trap to lure the army of the dead to Reikdorf just to wrest it from Nagash?

'Ride out,' commanded Khaled al-Muntasir. 'Ride out now!'

SIGMAR FELT THE awful weight of the crown at his brow, its immense power threatening to crush his skull and invade his mind with all the terrible temptations of power it had offered him before. He had had Wolfgart's help to resist it last time, now he was on his own. Black thoughts of vengeance, power and dominance filled his mind, but knowing them for what they were, he was able to push them away for now.

To march to war at the head of so great a host of men was a truly magnificent honour, but facing them was an army of nightmares. The greenskin horde at Black Fire had been larger, but so had his army. And this foe could return from the dead...

A great mass of shambling dead opposed him, a ragged, shuffling horde of corpses in numerous stages of decomposition. Many wore the garb of Empire warriors or peasants, and he kept his anger in check, lest it feed the black sorcery of the crown. Dark horsemen rode to each flank of the enemy army and ravening packs of dead wolves and ghoulish cannibals roamed the banks of the southern arm of the Reik. The Asoborns faced this scattered horde of teeth and claws, led by Garr's Queen's Eagles and Freya herself. Sigmar saw the warrior queen atop a commandeered chariot, with Sigulf acting as her rider and Fridleifr as her spear bearer. Sigmar felt a knot in his gut at the sight of those boys going into battle, but they had been blooded already and would be again if they survived this fight.

Beside Sigmar, Wolfgart stood tall in his saddle, waving towards Maedbh. Her chariot sped along beside the queen's, with Ulrike and Cuthwin in the back, each armed with bows and many quivers of arrows blessed by the priests of Taal.

Wenyld rode next to Wolfgart, holding Sigmar's banner aloft with an expression of disbelieving pride. The rippling battle flag, with its glorious beast of legend picked out in gold, represented everything this mortal army stood for and was willing to die to defend. To carry it was the greatest honour, one that had fallen to Pendrag before his death. Though Sigmar had thought Wolfgart would want to bear the banner, he had instead preferred to carry his enormous sword. Sigmar understood, and Wolfgart's battle captain had taken up the banner. Thinking back to how he had first encountered Wenyld, Sigmar was pleased the banner would be borne by someone he knew.

Looking left and right, Sigmar saw his countrymen, warriors of all different tribes and lands. Scattered among the battle-trained warriors were cheering masses of farmers, craftsmen and labourers, men who had never faced battle until now. As glad as Sigmar was to have them march out with him, he knew they could not be relied upon to stand when the fighting became close and bloody.

In the moments before battle, the priests of each temple had given their blessings to the army, but instead of retreating behind the walls, each took up a heavy hammer, mace or cudgel and joined the battle line. With the exception of the priests of Ulric, no holy men fought with the army of the Empire, but Sigmar was happy to have the help of whichever god chose to aid them this day.

Far to Sigmar's left the Red Scythes rode along the line of the northern fork of the river, Leodan leading his warriors in an attempt to flank the enemy army and put their lances and heavy swords to good use. Sigmar rode at the head of one detachment of the Great Hall Guard, while Alfgeir commanded the other. Both masses of heavy horse held the centre of the army, and Sigmar's entire strategy depended on their strength, speed and power.

Ahead of them, beyond the thousands of lurching corpses, ghostly revenants and rank upon rank of skeletal warriors, was a towering figure wreathed in black light and shimmering arcs of deathly energy. Sigmar could see Nagash clearly now, a boon from the crown no doubt, and he saw the incredible, unknowable power that seethed in his chest. Sustained by the darkest of magic, Nagash was immortal, invincible and deadly.

He felt the black gaze of the necromancer slide over him, a creeping chill that would have frozen his heart in an instant but for the power of the dwarf-forged plate that encased him. No sooner had that icy gaze felt what sat upon his brow than a hideous roar of fury shook the world and booming peals of thunder rolled across the landscape. Sheets of rain fell in cascades and brilliant traceries of lightning forked from the sky.

'Looks like you were right, old friend,' said Sigmar, thinking back to Eoforth's last words.

Even armed with that knowledge, Sigmar knew he would only get one chance to land a killing blow. He took a deep breath, whispering a prayer to Ulric.

'Is it time?' said Wolfgart.

'It's time,' said Sigmar. 'Sound the horns.'

The order was given, and all along the Unberogen line, a rippling series of horn blasts spread from the army's centre. Pipes and drums joined the crescendo, and even before the first echoes faded, the army of the Empire was on the move.

SIGMAR RAKED BACK his spurs and the gelding leapt to the charge. The ground between the forks of the river was hard-packed and flat, ideal cavalry terrain, and the sound of hoof beats was like the thunder booming in the heavens above them. Hundreds of heavily armoured horsemen kicked their mounts from a canter to a charge, yelling fearsome Unberogen war cries to banish the fear that tore at every one of them.

Wolfgart drew his heavy two-handed sword from his shoulder scabbard. The weapon was unwieldy to use from the back of a horse, but Wolfgart would sooner be defenceless than go into battle without such a blade. Wenyld held the banner high, gripping onto his horse with his thighs and stirrups as he swung the spiked ball of a great morning star in looping arcs.

Sigmar picked out the dead man he would slay, an eyeless corpse with thin, wasted arms hanging limply at its sides. His steed whinnied in fear and he lifted his hammer high.

'For Ulric!' shouted Sigmar, urging his horse to greater speed. 'For the Empire!'

Ghal-maraz slammed down and broke the corpse in two as the Unberogen cavalry struck the shambling mass of the dead in a deafening crash of iron and bone. The first ranks of the dead simply disintegrated as the unstoppable mass of horsemen crushed them with the speed and weight of their charge. Hundreds were trampled and broken apart in moments, hammers and swords and axes hacking a bloody path through the undead.

Sigmar kicked a dead man in the face, caving in the bone of his skull and backhanding his hammer into the chest of another. Ribs splintered and rotten meat sprayed from the impact. Emerald-lit eyes dulled as the corpse fell, but Sigmar was riding onward before the body had even fallen. Claws tore at his horse and his legs, but his armour was impervious to the broken nails and bony fingertips of the dead. The Great Hall Guard were the very best of the Unberogen, and these wretched specimens could not hope to halt their advance.

'Keep pushing!' shouted Sigmar. 'If we stop we are lost!'

Wenyld's morning star battered the dead from his path as he sought to keep up with Sigmar, and Wolfgart's sword clove living corpses in two with every blow. Sigmar's horse kicked out as he drove it onwards, iron-shod hooves breaking skulls and shattering rib cages as it fought as hard as its rider.

With Sigmar at their head, the Unberogen punched through the ranks of the corpse warriors, but this had been but a taster for the battle to come. These were the chaff of the dead, and served only to slow Sigmar's charge. The Great Hall Guard hacked, bludgeoned and sliced through the wall of corpses, punching through to the army beyond, where ranked up skeletal warriors marched towards them with spears lowered and shields locked together.

* * *

ALFGEIR MARVELLED AS his new sword cut through the necks of two dead men with flawless ease. It was half as light as he would have expected, yet it was perfectly balanced for his reach and strength. Wherever he swung the sword, it connected with the most vulnerable portion of his enemy, and he had left two score headless corpses in his wake. Its edge was keen beyond imagining and not a trace of grave dirt or blood befouled its surface.

Govannon had presented the sword to him as they gathered to hear Sigmar's words at the Oathstone. Together with Masters Holtwine and Alaric, Govannon had handed him the blade, hilt first, and apologised for the lack of a case.

Alfgeir had been speechless, overcome with gratitude that the smith had actually managed to fulfil his promise and finish the blade before the first fall of snow.

'If I live through this battle, I will commission a sword case from Master Holtwine,' he'd said.

'It will be my finest work,' Holtwine had said.

It was a sword of heroes, a blade that never failed to find its mark and clove to the very heart of its victim. Beyond the works of the dwarfs, no man had wielded a finer weapon. Too fine a blade to belong to one man alone; this would be the blade of the Marshal of the Reik for evermore.

Alfgeir fought with the skill and strength of a man half his age or less, showing the younger warriors how to fight like a true Unberogen. His two hundred knights fought just as hard, seeking to earn his favour with their faith and fury. While Sigmar's cavalry punched through the centre of the undead towards the necromancer, Alfgeir's riders angled their course towards the dead marching along the northern fork of the river.

Behind Alfgeir, Orvin and his son, Teon, fought the dead with crushing blows from their heavy broadswords.

Orvin was a man quick to anger, with a temper that had made him few friends in peacetime, but which served him well in battle. His son wore an old bronze helmet with a white, horsehair plume. It was dented on one side from a blow struck more than forty years ago, and Alfgeir remembered the boy's grandfather wearing the helm. The dent had come from the axe blow that had panned in his skull. Alfgeir hoped the grandson would have better luck with it.

Orvin carried the white gold banner Sigmar had presented to Alfgeir upon his coronation as Emperor, and though no words had ever been spoken to make it so, it had become a kind of unofficial talisman for the Great Hall Guard. His warriors fought all the harder when it flew above them, so Alfgeir was happy for them to count it as their own.

Alfgeir chopped the arms from a corpse seeking to drag him from his saddle and pushed his mount through the press of crushing bodies. The banner flew proudly above the knights, a beacon of light for his warriors to rally around. Though fear of this foe threatened to overcome every one of them, none would falter while the white and gold banner flew. Wolfskin cloaks streamed at their backs as they broke through the shambling dead and came face to face with rank after rank of the warriors formed from bone and iron.

'Onwards!' cried Alfgeir, urging his steed onwards. 'For Sigmar and the Empire!'

ANOTHER WOLF HOWLED as it was crushed beneath the iron-rimmed wheels of Maedbh's chariot. Its remains rotted in an instant, and Ulrike loosed an arrow through the jaws of another beast as it leapt towards them. Beside her, Cuthwin loosed with calm precision, each shaft slicing home into the body of a wolf.

'Keen eyes!' shouted Maedbh, proud to have her daughter as her spear bearer and glad to have a warrior as cool-tempered as Cuthwin next to her.

After the terror of their first battles together, Maedbh had made peace with Ulrike riding to war. Wolfgart appeared to have done likewise, though she knew neither of them would ever lose their fear of her going beyond their protection. They knew the dangers that lurked everywhere in the world, but with this invasion of the dead there were few mortals who did not. She wished she could have fought this foe alongside her husband, but the back of a chariot was no place for someone unschooled in such a demanding form of warfare.

A dozen chariots, all that had survived the battle at the river, followed Queen Freya as she led the charge towards the rabid packs of death wolves and their disgusting companions. Now fitted with spinning iron blades at their hubs, the Asoborn chariots had already torn through scores of the undead wolves, slicing them and their ghoulish brethren apart. The Queen's Eagles and hundreds of Asoborn warriors, their skin painted in the manner of the ancient queens and their hair stiffened with resin, followed in the wake of the chariots.

Maedbh hauled on the reins, sweeping her chariot in a sharp turn as a pack of pallid-skinned flesheaters ran towards her. They ran with loping, bandy-legged strides, hissing as they clawed at her chariot. Ulrike put an arrow through the nearest creature's eye, and Cuthwin put another through the throat of the one behind it. Maedbh swept up her spear and slashed it around in a wide arc, opening the top of one of the hideous cannibals' skulls.

Freya loosed an ululating Asoborn war shout and climbed onto the upper lip of her chariot's armoured frame with her ancient broadsword unsheathed. Maedbh's heart swelled with pride to see her queen fight, a fiery goddess of war sent from the violent times before the Empire, when none dared to travel in Asoborn lands for fear of the warrior women said to dwell there with sharp knives and cruel hearts. Sigulf steered the chariot with great skill, and Fridleifr killed wolf and cannibal with graceful sweeps and thrusts of his spear.

'Mother!' shouted Ulrike.

Maedbh saw the flesheater too late and felt its claws slash down her back in lines of fire. She cried out in pain as it vaulted into the chariot. Keeping one hand on the reins, Maedbh slammed her elbow into its fanged jaw. Ulrike hammered her knife up and under its ribs. It squealed horribly as it died, and Cuthwin kicked it from the back of the chariot.

'Are you hurt?' asked Ulrike.

Maedbh couldn't answer. Already she could feel filth from the creature's claws entering her body and bit the inside of her mouth bloody against the pain. Her flesh burned where she had been cut and her side was sticky with fresh blood, but Maedbh was Asoborn and this pain was nothing to one who had given birth.

'I'm fine,' she hissed through gritted teeth.

'Are you sure?'

'I'm sure,' she snapped, harsher than she meant to. 'Watch our backs…'

Ulrike nodded, and Maedbh turned back to the fighting ahead of them.

They had cut deep into the swirling mass of wolves and flesheaters, and the hideous monsters fought all around them as the Asoborn infantry caught up with the slowed chariots. To anyone but an Asoborn there was no easily discernable shape to this battle, just a confused mass of circling chariots and intertwined warriors on foot, but Maedbh knew better. She saw how close they were to being overrun. Freya should command them to withdraw, reform and charge again, but Maedbh knew the queen would never give that order.

Maedbh looked over at Freya's chariot, so proud to be a servant of this magnificent woman and glad the gods had granted her this last chance to fight alongside her. She turned her chariot around, cutting the throat of a wolf with her wheel blades and looked to see where the queen was heading.

Maedbh saw the danger before Sigulf. Years spent anticipating threats to a chariot had given her a preternatural sense for when to charge and when to evade. She saw the enormous wolf, twice as large as its brethren, as the exposed muscles on its powerful back legs bunched and hurled it through the air.

'My queen!' she screamed, but it was too late.

The giant wolf's forepaws smashed through the chariot's armour as though it was dead wood. Freya flew through the air as the chariot flipped onto its side, dragging the horses down with screams of pain as their legs shattered. The queen landed hard, cracking her skull against a rock, and lay still. Sigulf vanished amid the wreckage, but Maedbh saw Fridleifr thrown clear, the boy rolling as he hit the ground and coming to his feet like a tumbler.

'Asoborns!' ordered Maedbh. 'To the queen!'

The flesheaters surrounded the fallen queen as Maedbh whipped the reins and drove her horses on. Arrows flew from Ulrike and Cuthwin's bows as hurled javelins skewered yet more wolves and eaters of the dead. Hundreds more pressed in, scenting easy meat and knowing on some primal level that they had the chance to earn their master's favour with this prey.

LEODAN'S WARRIORS WHEELED expertly around the advancing blocks of Unberogen infantry, feeling the ground grow soft beneath their horses' feet. This close to the river, the ground was already muddy, but the cold rain was in danger of turning it into a quagmire. The Red Scythes were the elite cavalry of the Taleuten kings, and though they owed fealty to the Emperor, it felt wrong riding into battle without Count Krugar in their midst.

The mass of dead opposing them was a limping, shuffling horde of corpses, unworthy of a blade, and without skill. Yet the sheer number of them, their hunger and their mindless aggression, could drag even the noblest warrior to his doom. Leodan tried to keep that in mind as he rode towards them with his lance lowered.

He kicked his spurs back, driving his horse to charging speed, and his riders followed suit, charging in a disciplined line. To maintain cohesion in such terrain and weather was nothing short of miraculous, but the Taleutens had been masters of mounted warfare since before their earliest ancestors had been driven across the eastern mountains.

'Strike fast and ride them down!' he shouted, lowering his lance and aiming it towards the chest of a dead man with a jawbone sagging on one rotten sinew. It was a waste to use lances on such dregs, but it wasn't as though they could sling them for later use.

The Red Scythes slammed into the corpses with a wet slap of hard wood on bloated meat. Leodan's lance punched his target into the air, ripping open its chest and splintering apart with the impact. His steed slammed through the press of bodies behind the dead man, trampling them to pulp beneath its weight. In a matter of seconds, Leodan was ten deep in the mass of enemy warriors. He dropped the broken lance and unsheathed his curved cavalry sabre, slashing it through the throat of a dead man clawing at his horse's face.

He slashed left and right as the dead pressed in, cutting

off heads and lopping off rotten limbs held on by little more than glutinous tendons and scraps of gristly cartilage. His blade hewed dead flesh with ease, and his horse crushed bones with every kick. His warriors were unstoppable, riding through the mass of undead as though they were nothing more than a fleshy annoyance. The blood thundered in his ears as he destroyed these vile corpses. To ride into battle like this was to be a god, to tower over the enemy and slay them with impunity.

Leodan could imagine nothing worse than fighting on foot.

'Ulric damn you all!' whooped Leodan as the mass of corpses thinned and he knew they had broken through. This was the golden dream of every cavalryman, to break through the line before wheeling around to smash into the flanks and rear of the enemy army. He hauled on the reins and punched the air twice. Sheets of rain and the bleak darkness hid what lay beyond, but Leodan had no intention of continuing eastwards.

'Clarion! Reform and wheel right!'

A trilling trumpet blast sounded behind him and he caught a glimpse of the red banner of his troop as the rider carrying it rode alongside him. No one man ever had the singular honour of being the Red Scythes' banner bearer; it was passed between his warriors with every fight. Today it was borne by Yestyva, a man with a deadly lance and powerful sword arm.

The Red Scythes formed up with Leodan at their centre, and he snarled to see the inviting flanks of the ranked-up warriors of bone. They would roll up this line and tear the unlife from this host. To think that they had feared these creatures was ridiculous; they fell more easily than any mortal man.

Leodan kicked his spurs back and held his sabre aloft and urged his warriors onwards. The rain shifted and he heard a faint clatter of bone and jangle of trace. The trumpet blew again and his warriors went from a trot to a canter, steadily building speed as they rode to glory.

He heard the rattle of bone and iron again, louder this time. The darkness and rain lifted for the briefest moment as an arcing bolt of lightning streaked across the sky. In that moment of brightness, Leodan saw his worst nightmare.

Hundreds of skeletal horsemen, heavily armoured in shirts of black mail, black breastplates and heavy caparisons of iron. The horses were fleshless, skeletal and quite dead. Green light burned in their eyes and their chamfrons were fitted with long, barbed spikes. Each of the riders leaned low across the necks of their horses, a long black lance aimed for the hearts of the Red Scythes. Too late, Leodan saw he'd been lured into this easy attack.

Their shields were long and kite-shaped, emblazoned with skulls and images of ancient kings, their banner a ragged, torn scrap of leathery flesh with a leering jaw spread wide. They came on in a thunder, lances lowering with hideous precision.

"'Ware cavalry!' shouted Leodan, though he knew it was too late.

The black knights smashed into the Red Scythes, lances tearing through their armour and into their flesh. Men were hoisted from their saddles, screaming as the frozen iron of the enemy lances impaled them. Though seemingly fragile, the black steeds were as powerful as any mortal horse and punched into the centre of the Taleuten horsemen.

Leodan swayed aside as a lance speared past him, slashing his sword into the face of the black knight who bore it. His sword smashed the helmet from the dead warrior's skull, and sent him spinning from his horse. He wheeled as the two groups of horsemen became hopelessly entwined, a throbbing mass of warriors hacking one another from their saddles.

He plunged his sword through the neck of a dead man's horse, taking grim satisfaction as it fell apart beneath him. Leodan spun in his saddle as the clamour of battle thundered in his ears and the sky split apart with yet more lightning. Rainwater streaked his face and all he could see were flashing blades, grinning skulls beneath iron visors and blood spraying from mortal wounds. The bloody banner of the Red Scythes still flew proudly and he spurred his mount towards its glorious colours.

Before he could reach it, a thundering juggernaut of red iron and black-edged death smashed into his horse and hurled him from the saddle. He landed badly, slamming into the ground with a crack of breaking bone and the breath driven from his lungs by the fall.

Dizzy with the impact, Leodan knew at least one of his ribs was broken. He tried to stand, but pain shot up his leg and he crumpled onto one knee as the splintered ends of his shinbone ground together. Gritting his teeth, Leodan looked up and saw the enemy that had unhorsed him.

A monstrous, hulking warrior in blood-red armour towered over him, its frost-limned armour burning with a glaring rune of an ancient, bloody god. Its horned helm covered a grinning skull face with burning fire in its dead eyes.

A dread battle cry roared from the warrior, a chant and a mantra from the beginning of time, but no less potent for the vast span this champion had been dead.

Blood for the Blood God!

'Ulric save us...' wept Leodan.

* * *

THE GREAT HALL Guard smashed into the ranks of skeletal warriors and tore through their front ranks in a hammering thunder of beating iron. Alfgeir's sword sliced down through a bronze pot helmet and into the skull beneath. He wrenched the blade free and beheaded another two skeletal warriors, their armour no protection against his rune-forged weapon.

Orvin fought at his side, hacking down the dead with furious blows of his heavy broadsword. The man screamed as he slew, using his fear and turning it to anger. Teon fought at his side, his own sword arm rising and falling like a blacksmith at the anvil. The youngster had not the ferocity of his father, but he had speed and skill beyond anything Orvin could muster.

A spear jabbed at Alfgeir. He twisted in the saddle to cut the point from the shaft, following through with a lancing blow that split the dead warrior's ribcage apart. Like the shambling corpses, these dead were no match for Alfgeir, but where those first foes had little ability in battle, these dead had been warriors in life and fought with remembered skill. Swords flashed, spears thrust and the enemy plucked men from their mounts with every passing moment.

The momentum they had won from their charge was quickly spent, and every yard would now be paid for in blood. Alfgeir bellowed the name of Ulric as he fought, driving his aged body to heights of aggression and fury he had never known. The dead surrounded them, a mass of grinning faces, leering jaws and eyes filled with green balefire. Their rusted swords cut and slashed, bringing down horses and men with their unearthly magic.

He heard a wild horn blast, seeing Sigmar over to his right. The Emperor's band of horsemen crushed a path through the ranks of skeletal swordsmen. Wolfgart rode at Sigmar's side, cleaving a path with his enormous two-hander, and Alfgeir wished he could have ridden with the Emperor.

'On, damn you!' shouted Alfgeir as thunder boomed overhead and the rain beat down with ever greater force. 'The Emperor rides on and we should be with him!'

Orvin and Teon pushed next to him, fighting to clear a path through which they could match the Emperor's charge. The noise of the storm overhead sounded like a great battle was being waged in the heavens, echoing the conflict being played out in the mortal realms below. For all Alfgeir knew, that might well be the case. Perhaps they were all merely pawns of the gods, cursed to fight their wars on the face of the world while the gods were embroiled in their own nightmarish battle for survival.

'We're with you!' shouted Orvin, and Alfgeir nodded as more and more of the Great Hall Guard pushed through the mass of slashing blades, rallying for another push into the ranks of the dead. If they could recover their momentum, they could still reach Sigmar.

Orvin cried out as a black sword plunged into his stomach, a plate-clad champion of the dead driving it through his body with a powerful two-handed grip. Orvin toppled from his horse and Alfgeir cried out as the banner fell with him. He swept his sword down through the enemy warrior's blade. It shattered and the weapon-less champion turned its dead eyes upon him. Alfgeir froze as he saw death in those eyes. Not the prospect of death, but the *exact* moment his life would end. His sword arm fell to his side and his lungs failed to draw a breath. A shooting pain spiked into his left arm and he cried out as the sword fell from his grip.

The champion swept up a fallen spear and lunged towards him.

Another blade intercepted it, and Teon lanced his blade through the champion's visor. The skull broke open and the hellish green light was extinguished from its eyes. Alfgeir's breath returned with a whooshing roar in his ears, bright spots of light bursting before his eyes.

'Father!' shouted Teon, leaping from his horse and holding his father's head.

Alfgeir tried to shout at him to get back on his horse, but his throat was tight and his chest afire. The fighting swept around them, and the youngster wept as the muscles in his father's face went slack and Morr claimed his soul. Alfgeir felt their chance to counterattack slipping away, and shuddered as a deathly chill crept over him.

He had felt something similar when…

'I think you dropped this, Alfgeir,' said a voice that cut through the clash of swords and spears. 'It's very nice work. Careless of you to have lost it.'

Alfgeir turned his horse to see himself facing a warrior in midnight black plate, with a white, bloodless face and eyes red with blood-hunger. Count Markus turned Alfgeir's sword in his hand, admiring the silver runes etched along the length of the blade.

'Yes,' said Markus. 'I think I may keep this weapon after I kill you with it.'

◄ TWENTY-ONE ►

The End is Nigh

MAEDBH LEAPT FROM her chariot as it came to a halt beside Freya's body, her spear skewering a flesheater as it bent to take a bite. She swept the spear around, hurling the beast from the tip and standing over the fallen queen. Blood leaked from a wound at Freya's temple, and pooled around her mouth. Maedbh didn't have time to check if the queen was alive.

Ulrike and Cuthwin took up position next to her, loosing arrows into the mass of wolves circling them. Each shaft punched through a dead beast's side, while Fridleifr and Maedbh kept those that survived the arrows at bay with looping swings of their spears.

'Ulrike! Look to the queen!' ordered Maedbh. 'And find Sigulf!'

A wolf howled as it reared up over Maedbh, but before it could pounce, a leaf-bladed spear punched through its chest and it fell to the ground in pieces of rotten meat and mangy fur. Fridleifr pulled his spear back from the beast's body and Maedbh nodded her thanks as the monsters closed in.

'Is she dead?' asked Fridleifr, without looking down.

Ulrike shook her head, and Maedbh felt a wave of relief that almost blotted out the pain from the wound on her back. Her limbs were aching, her head thumping with a powerful headache. Her skin was clammy and cold.

She slammed the end of her spear against a flesh-eater's head, reversing it to plunge the blade into the belly of a wolf. Its weight bore her to the ground, and the haft of her spear snapped. Maedbh rolled, spying a leather-wrapped sword handle amid the wreckage of the queen's chariot. She grabbed it and spun around, swinging it two-handed to cleave a flesheater in two with one blow. Amazed, Maedbh saw she held the bronze-bladed sword of Queen Freya. It had once belonged to Eadhelm, who claimed to have looted it from a secret chamber beneath a tower of the stunted ones beyond the mountains of the east.

Maedbh rolled to her feet, the pain of her wounds forgotten as the vital energies of the sword filled her body with strength and lustful thoughts.

'Mother!' shouted Ulrike, hauling Sigulf from the wreckage. The boy was bloody, but conscious, and gripped his sword tightly.

'Can you fight?' Fridleifr asked her.

Maedbh's lip curled in anger. Of course she could fight! With this blade she could fight for a year and never get tired. Dimly she recognised this was the sword's anger and battle fury talking. Maedbh let it come, knowing she would have need of it before the day's end.

Fridleifr fought with his spear in one hand and a hammer in the other. His skill and strength were beyond compare, each powerful blow caving in a skull or opening a belly. His blond hair shone in the low light, and his features were the image of his father's. Garr and the Queen's Eagles rushed to surround their fallen queen, as yet more of the undead pressed in.

Wolves circled them and the eaters of the dead squealed and chattered as they darted in to slash with their decaying claws. Ulrike stood over Freya, wiping blood from her face and speaking to her in soft tones. Cuthwin emptied his quiver and drew his hunting knife, but Maedbh knew he'd need more than that to survive this fight.

'Can we hold them?' shouted Cuthwin.

Maedbh nodded, then saw the mass of skeletons atop iron-clad steeds riding towards them. The Asoborns were scattered and disorganised, gathered around their queen and without cohesion. A cavalry charge would ride right over them.

'Shieldwall!' shouted Fridleifr.

SIGMAR BATTERED THROUGH the ranks of the dead, his hammer clearing a path with every thunderous blow. Nothing could stand against its power, living or dead, and though every yard gained was a struggle, the Unberogen horsemen fought like heroes from the sagas beside their Emperor. He could feel the power of the crown straining at the edges of his control, pleading and begging to be allowed to help him.

Part of Sigmar wanted to let it, to use the power of its maker in the fight to defeat him, but he knew the crown's greatest strength lay in the lies it could spin. It had ensnared him atop Morath's tower with such bland-ishments, and he knew better than to trust its honeyed words.

The dead clawed at them in a frenzy, a host of biting, clawing corpses and armoured warriors of bone. His warriors fought them back with crushing blows from hammers, swords and axes, their fighting wedge pushing deep into the enemy ranks. The dead were slowing them down, but not enough to prevent them from breaking through.

At last the skeletons were smashed aside and the Unberogen circled, ready to reform and charge onwards. Sigmar reined in his horse and the rest of his warriors brought their horses to a standstill. Their horses were blown and lathered, exhausted by their ride. Sigmar's breathing was laboured, for the fight had been a hard one, and his hammer arm ached from such destruction.

Wolfgart rode alongside him, his face bloody and his mighty sword notched from the many blows he'd struck. His mail was torn and plate dented, but none of the blood coating his flesh was his own. Wenyld lifted the banner high and a roaring cheer burst from every Unberogen throat. Sigmar saw Wenyld's face was ashen, and blood streamed down his leg.

'Can you ride?' he asked the younger man.

'Aye, my lord,' said Wenyld, breathlessly. 'I was careless. Took a spear thrust a moment ago. It's nothing.'

'I've seen my share of wounds, boy,' said Wolfgart. 'That's not nothing.'

'I'll ride with you,' stated Wenyld, and there was no disagreeing with him.

'Ulric keep you,' said Sigmar, sharing a glance with Wolfgart.

Wenyld saw it and said, 'Don't worry, if I'm going to die on you I'll hand the banner over first. Can't have it falling, eh? Not now.'

'Not now,' agreed Sigmar, turning his horse and taking a moment to survey the battle. It was difficult to see much through the mass of the dead and the unnatural darkness, but he saw enough to know that they had little time to waste. The northern flank was in danger of collapsing, the Red Scythes embroiled in a furious battle with mounted black knights and a terrible avatar of destruction, while a mass of wolves and shambling corpses swept past the Asoborns towards the city walls. He couldn't see what had become of Freya, and Alfgeir's riders had become bogged down in the ranks of the skeleton warriors.

'We're on our own here,' said Wolfgart, seeing the same thing.

'Looks that way,' said Sigmar. 'But I always knew that would be how it ended.'

'Then let's finish this before I lose my nerve,' said Wolfgart, hefting his sword over his shoulder and wiping the blood from his face. 'All these men dying around us will be for nothing if we can't get through to that bony bastard.'

Sigmar nodded, searching the darkness ahead for Nagash. The necromancer was not hard to find, a towering black form atop a low hill beyond the road. Swirls of sable smoke coiled around Nagash, his undying body a black tear in the fabric of night through which all the cold of the Grey Vaults leached into the world.

Unberogen horsemen formed up on the banner, bloodied and weary after their long ride, but hungry for more.

'Our foe is within reach!' shouted Sigmar, pointing Ghal-maraz towards the hill upon which stood the necromancer.

'On! On!' cried Wolfgart in answer.

And the charge began again.

WHILE SIGMAR PUNCHED through the hordes of the dead, the people of Reikdorf marched in defence of their city.

Positioned behind the main battle line, they were thrilled and terrified, clutching makeshift weapons in the hope that they would not have to use them. It had been all too easy to follow Sigmar and his warriors through the ruined Ostgate on a wave of exhilaration, but as the rain battered down and the darkness closed in, fear returned to erode the fragile courage that had been built within the city walls.

In the centre of the mass of people gathered to the south of the gate Daegal felt his terror climb to new heights. He had fought the army of Khaled al-Muntasir by the river and terror flowed through his veins at the thought of facing the army of the dead once more. He knew it had been his cowardice that had seen the Asoborn army break, his panic that had spread to the warriors around him and caused the defeat.

Too ashamed to ride out with his fellow tribesmen, he had hidden within the city and managed to avoid any-one that knew him. Instead, he had been swept up in the borrowed courage of Reikdorf's people and found strength enough to march with them to this patch of ground before the walls.

'Please don't let me fail again,' he whispered to the gods.

KHALED AL-MUNTASIR WATCHED the battle unfold, admir-ing the strength of purpose invigorating this mortal army. He had fought for Nagash since before leaving Athel Tamara, and had been less than impressed by the skill and resilience of this northern empire. How could such a people claim to be the masters of this land?

Then he had fought the remnants of the Asoborns at the wooded hill, and the first chinks of doubt had entered his mind. Now, as Sigmar drew ever closer, Khaled al-Muntasir found himself wondering if he had grossly underestimated this barbarian Emperor. True, his people were little better than savages, but they possessed a primitive nobility that had surprised him. Individually they were weak and pathetic, but welded together by Sigmar, they were stronger than even they knew.

Khaled al-Muntasir glanced towards Nagash, wondering if he too had underestimated these mortals. It seemed absurd that he should entertain such doubts, for the host of the dead was already beginning to envelop the mortal army. Krell was butchering the warriors in the north, and the south was on the brink of collapse. The carrion eaters and corpses were already moving on the city walls, and Markus would soon end the resistance in the centre.

So why did he still feel so uneasy?

His black steed tossed its head, snorting and stamping the ground as it smelled the blood on the air. It was impatient to join the slaughter, and its hide steamed in the relentless rain cascading from the sky. Khaled al-Muntasir lifted the lank fabric of his cloak, knowing the material was ruined.

He jerked the reins of his mount, and turned his horse to the north.

Nagash's cold gaze fell upon him and he felt the necromancer's displeasure.

'The northern flank is holding out,' said Khaled al-Muntasir. 'I will take some riders and break it open.'

Nagash didn't answer, his attention firmly fixed on the glittering crown upon Sigmar's brow as the Emperor rode straight for him. Khaled al-Muntasir drew his sword and rode north, grateful to be free of that frozen, penetrating gaze.

The vampire looked to the east, to the lands already taken by the dead, and saw moonlight glittering from distant spires and forgotten castles perched high on rocky bluffs. He smiled to himself, picturing a reign of terror that could be unleashed from such a lair.

'Yes,' he said to himself. 'That would be very fine.'

ALFGEIR WATCHED AS the thing that had once been Count Markus of the Menogoths circled him, swinging the sword Govannon had forged for him. Death had erased none of the swordsman count's skill with a blade, and Alfgeir knew he could not prevail against him. Markus saw the defeat in his eyes and licked his thin, bloodless lips.

'Why don't you come down off that horse?' said the vampire. 'Make it a fair fight?'

'You have my sword,' said Alfgeir. 'How is that a fair fight?'

'True,' smiled Markus. 'Come down anyway. I can kill you just as easily on the back of your horse, but at least on foot we'll be eye to eye.'

'Fair enough,' said Alfgeir, unhitching an axe from the back of his saddle. It was a short-hafted axe, a backup weapon, and would be a poor defence against his own sword. Though the dead pressed in all around, the Great Hall Guard held them back. There was no way they could now ride to Sigmar's aid, and the bitter gall of failure tasted of ashes in his mouth.

Markus spun the sword, its glittering length moving like a snake in the vampire's grip. Alfgeir remembered fencing the Menogoth count in a friendly duel many years ago. It had been a humbling experience to be so outclassed when he rated himself highly as a swordsman.

Alfgeir faced the blood drinker, quelling his hatred for this thing that wore the face of an honourable man. He felt the ice of the vampire's nearness, gritting his teeth against its chill. Markus took up the en garde position, and Alfgeir lunged forward, the axe blade chopping for the vampire's head.

Markus stepped back, rolling the sword around Alfgeir's axe and stabbing the tip through his pauldron and into his shoulder. Alfgeir tried to shut out the pain, but it spread to his chest and he staggered. The vampire spun around Alfgeir, slashing the sword across his other shoulder and neatly slicing away his other pauldron.

'Come on,' sneered Markus. 'I remember you were better than this. Not much better, it's true, but better nonetheless.'

'That was ten years ago,' grunted Alfgeir, pushing himself upright.

'Really? You've aged badly, my friend.'

'Ulric damn you to the Grey Vaults,' hissed Alfgeir. 'You are not my friend!'

Markus came at him again, his sword dancing like a forking bolt of lightning as it whipped around Alfgeir's clumsy axe swings. Time and time again, the blade licked out and cut pieces of his armour away. Alfgeir was left bloodied and in pain with each blow.

'Kill me and be done with it!' bellowed Alfgeir, and Markus stabbed the sword an inch into the muscle of his thigh. He bled from a dozen wounds, none serious enough to kill him, but all painful enough to sap his strength with every passing second.

'Nonsense,' replied Markus. 'You haven't even begun to fight properly yet.'

Alfgeir lifted his axe again, but Markus spun around him, the sword cutting down in a blur of rune-etched silver. Agonising pain shot through Alfgeir's body, and his vision filled with white light as he reeled from the blow. His entire body was a furnace of agony. He tried to lift his arm to strike one last, desperate blow, but his body wouldn't obey him.

He saw the axe lying on the ground.

Next to the axe was his arm.

Alfgeir stared in open-mouthed shock at the neatly severed stump where his right arm had been. There was no blood, so clean and cold had the wound been cut. Horror drove him to his knees, and he fought to hold onto consciousness as the terrible nature of his maiming threatened to overwhelm him. His breath came in sharp hikes of panic.

Markus circled him, the stolen sword spinning in his grip as he looked down at Alfgeir.

'Such a shame, you would have made a fine lieutenant,' said the vampire.

'To you?' hissed Alfgeir. 'Never.'

'I suppose not,' agreed Markus, raising the sword for the deathblow.

Though the duel had been fought in isolation until now, a figure hurled itself at the vampire, one with a dented bronze helm and a heavy broadsword. Teon slashed his sword at Markus's neck, but the vampire was faster than any mortal opponent, and the tip of Teon's blade passed less than a finger's breadth from his neck.

Markus cut high with his sword and the edge slammed into the side of Teon's head.

'No!' shouted Alfgeir.

The sword bounced upwards, deflected from its decapitating course by the dent in the side of the helm to slice off the horsehair plume. Teon fell to the ground with a cry of pain, the sword spinning away and landing upright in the marshy ground. Alfgeir snatched up the fallen axe in his left hand and hurled himself at the vampire. Markus brought his sword up to block the crude attack, but Alfgeir had no intention of going blade to blade with the vampire.

He let go of the axe, and it spun through the air toward

the vampire. It struck him full in the face and Alfgeir heard bone break over Markus's shriek of pain. Instinctively, he dropped the sword as his hands flew to his face to stem the tide of dead blood. Alfgeir dropped to the ground, his strength spent in this last, futile act of defiance.

Through tear- and rain-blurred vision, he saw the handle of his sword lying in the mud at the vampire's feet. He wanted to reach out and grab it. Though it was no more than a foot away, it might as well have been a thousand yards. He closed his eyes as the world went grey and he heard the sweet sound of wolves in the distance.

A cold, winter wind blew from the north and Alfgeir felt his limbs fill with the strength of the pack. He reached out towards the sword, feeling an ice-frosted hand that was more like a clawed paw place the handle in his palm.

His fingers closed on the weapon and he opened his eyes. Snow swirled where no snow had been before and the world around him moved as though slowed to the pace of a glacier's advance. He saw droplets of blood hanging in the air, a bolt of lightning tracing a leisurely path across the heavens and the frozen breath of nearby warriors gradually expanding from their lips. Markus turned slowly towards him, his face a mask of dark blood and his red eyes filled with terrible hunger. Long fangs jutted from his jaws and his hands had become elongated claws.

Alfgeir surged to his feet, he alone able to move normally. With a roar of hatred, he sliced his sword in a sweeping arc towards the vampire. He had a moment to savour the gelid onset of fear in Markus's eyes before the blade cut into his neck and parted his head from his shoulders. No sooner had the blade connected than the normal flow of time reasserted itself. Blood spattered, lightning blazed briefly and breath vanished.

Markus collapsed to the ground, his body crumbling within his armour as decay claimed the flesh feast denied it with the blood kiss. Burning with inner embers, the vampire's body became ashes in moments, a ghostly shriek of torment exploding outwards from its demise.

Alfgeir stood on trembling legs for a second until he could stand no more. He sank to his haunches, utterly drained, and slumped over onto his back. He looked up into the sky, seeing a clear patch where the stars shone through the ghastly canopy of darkness. In the distance he heard wolves again, and smiled as the hurt of his wounds vanished.

He felt hands beneath him, lifting him upright, and the pain returned with a vengeance.

'Alfgeir!' shouted Teon. 'Ulric's bones, how did you move so fast?'

He tried to tell the lad to let him go, that Ulric was calling to him, but the sound of wolves faded into the distance and tears spilled down his cheeks.

'Ulric isn't ready for me yet,' he whispered.

'Nor me it seems,' said Teon, and Alfgeir saw how lucky the boy was to be alive. The vampire's blow had taken the plume and the top portion of the helmet, but it had missed the boy's skull by no more than the width of the blade.

'Looks like you were luckier,' said Alfgeir.

'Luckier than who?' asked Teon, tearing off his cloak and wrapping it around Alfgeir.

'Never mind...'

Teon lifted Alfgeir into his arms and he grunted in pain. He looked at the young man, seeing the grief for his fallen father, but also a strength of character his father had not possessed. Despite the pain, Alfgeir smiled, wondering if this newfound clarity was a result of his near death.

Teon looked down at him. 'Chosen by Ulric you are,' said the boy.

'What? No, I was lucky is all.'

'No,' said Teon, lifting Alfgeir onto a horse and climbing up behind him with the white gold banner tucked in the crook of his arm. 'Look at your eyes, man. You've been chosen.'

Alfgeir lifted his sword blade as Teon turned the horse back to Reikdorf. His face was gaunt and pinched with pain, his leathery skin ashen from exhaustion. He looked into his reflected eyes and a cold breath escaped him.

His eyes were pure white, the hue of northern snows.

LEODAN THREW HIMSELF to the side as the titanic warrior's black axe swept down, cleaving his fallen horse in two with one blow. Searing pain flared up his leg and he crawled away from this towering slaughterman. Its black axe came up and a hissing name burned itself into Leodan's mind, a name that was a byword for death on an undreamed of scale in ages past.

Krell…

Rivers of blood had flowed from Krell's axe, all in service to a dread god of the north, a squatting devourer of blood and skulls. Slain by one of the mountain folk thousands of years ago in an age known by some as the Time of Woes, Krell's thirst for blood and death was undiminished by the passage of uncounted centuries since his death.

Leodan fumbled for his sword, watching as five of the Red Scythes charged towards the giant warrior.

'No,' he croaked. 'Don't!'

His warning went unheeded, and Krell's axe swept out, chopping up through the horses and cleaving the riders in two. The return stroke hacked another two to the ground and before the others could strike, Krell was amongst them. One rider died with his head torn from his shoulders, the other as Krell thundered his fist into his chest and crushed his torso to a pulpy mess.

Taleuten warriors surrounded Krell, hacking at his blood-covered plate, but no blade could penetrate his damned armour. Swords scraped over his shoulder guards, axes bounced from his spiked helm and spears shattered upon his breastplate. Nothing could stand against this monstrous force of destruction, and warriors died ten at a time as Krell hacked them down, chopping bodies in two and mangling flesh with every blow from his black-bladed axe.

Leodan crawled away from Krell, weeping in pain and for the loss of his beloved Red Scythes. His leg was afire, the broken ends gouging the meat of his leg with every yard he dragged himself from the slaughter.

His world shrank to the rain-soaked ground, his muddy knuckles dragging his pain-wracked body and the sound of his men dying. Horses screamed in pain as Krell's axe butchered them too, and men cried in fear as they turned to flee. None could escape Krell's deadly blade and those terrified cries turned to death screams as the Red Scythes were cut down.

Leodan's fingers clawed the ground, the earth too sodden for him to gain a purchase. He could go no further and he rolled onto his side. His breathing was coming in shallow gasps, and he coughed blood. His broken rib had nicked his lung and few survived such a wound, least of all those in the middle of a battle with no hope of rescue.

He heard the sound of marching steps behind him, regular and perfectly in time. Metal clashed as armour moved against armour and Leodan smelled the reek of strong beer and pipe smoke. Who would be drinking and smoking in the middle of such a fight?

Someone knelt beside him and he looked up through a haze of tears and rain to see a hundred warriors of the mountain folk armed with heavy axes and hammers. The warrior beside him was armoured head to foot in plates of iron and bronze. The dwarf's breath smelled of strong beer, and a wooden pipe carved in the shape of a long cavalry horn jutted through a hole specially crafted in his helmet's visor.

'Rest easy, manling,' said Master Alaric. 'We'll handle this big fella. We killed him once before, and we can do it again.'

DAEGAL WATCHED THE black riders charge the Asoborn shieldwall and heard the crash of splintering lances, breaking shields and the clang of swords. His mouth was dry and his bladder tightened. The riders of the dead surrounded the Queen's Eagles and he couldn't see any way they could survive.

'I am a warrior of the Asoborns,' he said, repeating the words like a mantra. 'I will not fear this foe. I will not fear this foe.'

The dead streamed around the shieldwall, a host of shambling corpses and skeletal warriors marching towards the city. Scores of wolves loped alongside them, accompanied by darting packs of white-bodied flesh-eaters. Daegal could not count them, but he knew there were too many for them to handle.

Mutters of fear passed through the assembled people, the men and women of Reikdorf suddenly regretting their choice to march into this arena of warriors. Daegal could feel their fear and recognised the teetering panic that could unman them in a heartbeat. He had felt it before at the defeat by the river and knew how devastating it could be. Warriors on the brink of victory could flee a battle believing it lost if they saw their fellows running from the enemy. Sergeants said battles weren't won or lost by individuals, but Daegal knew better.

His fear had hollowed him out at the river, but as he watched the wolves and carrion eaters coming towards him, that fear was replaced by anger. These monsters had taken his honour, stripping him of the one thing he had been assured was his right and destiny as an Asoborn.

Though he had seen only twelve summers, his anger burned like an inferno in his heart.

He drew his sword as the first wolves clawed into the line of people, hurling themselves forward with fangs and claws tearing. Blood sprayed and men and women died as the wolves tore them apart. The carrion eaters came on their heels, dragging men to the ground where they were pounced upon by yet more and eaten alive as they screamed in pain.

A creature with black beads for eyes and a mouth filled with broken teeth threw itself at him, and Daegal swung his sword for its neck. It bit deep into the beast's flesh, and Daegal kicked its corpse from the blade as another came at him with its claws outstretched. He cut its hands off and stabbed it in the throat. Blood spattered him, and the reek of it drove him to even greater heights of fury. He plunged his sword blade into the flanks of a dead wolf chewing on the entrails of a man Daegal had spoken to moments before. His name had been Eoland. He had been a baker of bread, but his days of preparing loaves and sweetbreads were now over.

Daegal fought with all the courage and strength he had forgotten by the river, killing a dozen enemies with as many blows. All around him, the people of Reikdorf took heart from his steadfast courage, holding their ground in the face of these monsters. The tide of flesh-eaters and wolves broke upon the line of ordinary men and women. Blood soaked the earth, and hundreds had died in the opening moments of the fighting.

Daegal ducked the snapping jaws of a wolf and jammed his sword down its throat. Its mouth snapped shut as it died and broke the blade in two. He swept up a fallen spear, a coloured rag tied just behind its iron tip. He heard screams of pain and terror, and knew the courage of these people hung by a thread.

As it had at the river, a moment's heroism or courage would decide the outcome of this fight. Daegal raised the spear above his head, letting the chill winds catch the fabric tied to the spear. Blue and red streamed above him, not a flag, but merely two rags in the colours of Reikdorf. Though the day was grim and dark, they shone as bright as though freshly dyed and lit by the noonday sun.

The flesheaters saw him raise the makeshift banner and he saw their uncertainty.

This was his moment. This was his one and only chance to reclaim the honour these monsters had taken from him.

'People of Reikdorf, with me!' shouted Daegal.

Daegal plunged the spear into the belly of a snarling wolf and charged from the bloodied ranks of citizen warriors, an Asoborn war shout on his lips.

And the people of Reikdorf followed him.

◄ TWENTY-TWO ►

Champions of Life and Death

THE ASOBORN SHIELDWALL splintered and buckled against the charge of the black knights. Men and women were hurled from their feet by the impact of the dead riders, but more Asoborns rushed to pick up the fallen shields and plug the gap. Skeletal horsemen plunged through the shieldwall, hacking with darkly glittering swords. Garr swept his twin-bladed spear through a black rider's horse, bringing him down in a clatter of bone and plate. Maedbh's bronze blade stabbed down, plunging through the rider's helm and extinguishing the green light shimmering beyond his visor.

Garr nodded his thanks, but Maedbh was already on the move, spinning around as the thunderous sound of horsemen slamming into iron-rimmed shields boomed once more. Cuthwin now fought with a spear, wrenched from a dead man with his spine all but severed. Beside him Fridleifr rammed his own spear through a rusted gap in a dead knight's breastplate. Sigulf protected his brother's flank, holding a heavy shield and slamming it forward along with the rest of the Asoborns.

Ulrike loosed carefully aimed shafts into the dead, sending arrows through the eye sockets of those warriors whose helmets had been knocked off in the charge. Maedbh took a two-handed grip on the sword as three dead riders smashed through the shieldwall. Their defence was shrinking with every passing second, the Asoborns unable to resist the unnatural power of the black knights. One rode towards her with a curved black sword raised above its head.

Maedbh ran at the dead warrior, her own sword hungry to slay this champion of the knights. She dived forward, rolling to her feet as the rider's weapon swept over her head. She slashed her sword across the skeletal mount's rear legs, shattering the bones and toppling the rider to the ground. A host of Asoborns pounced on the dead warrior, stabbing and clubbing his bones to destruction. The second warrior rode straight for the fallen Freya, dropping from his horse and striding towards the fallen queen with murderous determination burning in his eye sockets.

Maedbh ran towards him, but the third dead rider reared up before her, his horse's bony limbs pawing the air. One hoof caught Maedbh on the shoulder and sent her spinning. She landed badly, slashing her arm open on the blade of her sword. Blood poured from the wound onto the blade and she felt a sudden sense of power and anger flow through her.

She rolled as the hooves stamped down, thrusting her sword straight up and into the horse's ribs. Like a ruptured soap bubble, something intangible broke within the steed and its form came apart in a rain of bones. Iron plates tumbled to the earth, and Maedbh rolled as the beast's rider dropped beside her.

Maedbh brought her sword around in a move of desperation. The rider's sword slammed into her own, barely a handspan from her face. Its armoured foot slammed down into her stomach and she doubled up as the rider reached down and lifted her from the ground. Its helmet slammed into her face and blood poured down her chin as she felt her nose break. The sword fell from her grip and the pain of her wounds seared her once again.

She cried out as the gouges on her back flared and the slash on her arm throbbed as though dipped in boiling water. Maedbh looked through the slit in the dead warrior's helm and into his eyes. She saw endless suffering there, a soul chained to the mortal world by dark magic and kept in enduring torment. Though nothing remained of the man this warrior had once been, his suffering was eternal and unrelenting.

The black sword drew back and Maedbh's eyes focussed on the notched tip, picturing how it would punch through her ribcage and split her heart in two. The skull's grin became wider, but before its sword could stab forward, the dead warrior's head flew from his neck and the body collapsed. Maedbh slumped to the ground, scrambling away from the warrior's remains as a glorious figure in fiery bronze stood above her with a hand outstretched.

'Thank you for looking after my sword,' said Freya, hauling Maedbh to her feet.

Ulrike and Cuthwin stood at the queen's side and her daughter held a spear out toward Maedbh.

'My queen,' gasped Maedbh. 'You're alive.'

'Never more so!' roared the queen, turning and hurling herself into the fray.

Together with Sigulf, Fridleifr, Cuthwin and Ulrike, Maedbh joined Garr's faltering shieldwall. Though

Maedbh's arm and back burned with pain, she fought like never before, unhorsing dead warriors with every thrust. Together with the Queen's Eagles they fought like the legendary heroes of old, but even with such courage there was no way the shieldwall could hold. Warriors were dying by the dozen with every passing moment and the ring of swords and spears was shrinking like a patch of snow in spring.

A black rider thundered over a shieldbearer to Maedbh's left and his steed, a black beast with skin like basalt, reared up as a powerful warrior leapt from its back. His black cloak unfolded like wings as he landed in the midst of the Asoborns. Maedbh had seen this man a handful of times only, and though he had changed beyond all mortal recognition, he still bore the features of Siggurd of the Brigundians.

The black riders charged through the gap he had broken, rampaging through the Asoborns and slaughtering them with slashing blows of their black swords. Siggurd hurled Garr to the ground, the heroic warrior's throat torn out and his head lolling on a last shred of sinew. Transformed into something evil, Siggurd's eyes blazed crimson with thirst and his fangs gleamed in the twilight as he bore Queen Freya to the ground.

Maedbh rushed to the queen's side, but a backhanded blow from the vampire count hurled her back. Ulrike sent an arrow thudding into the blooddrinker's back, and he roared in pain. His fangs bit down on Freya's neck, but before he could tear out her throat, Cuthwin leapt onto the vampire and buried his knife in his side.

Siggurd arched his back, his form blurring as though in mid transformation and he slashed a clawed hand across Cuthwin's chest. The young Unberogen fell back, his chest in tatters. Siggurd screeched in anger, his fangs bared and bloody. Fridleifr stabbed the vampire in the back with his spear, the tip punching through his belly. Siggurd spun around, wrenching the spear from Fridleifr's hands and tearing the weapon from his body. Faster than Maedbh could follow, the spear left Siggurd's hands and plunged into the boy's chest, punching through his armour and driving him to the ground.

Sigulf gave a cry of loss and anger and slashed his sword through Siggurd's arm. The vampire screeched in agony as a wash of black blood sprayed from the wound. Siggurd looked at the wound, unable to believe he had been hurt.

'That stung, little one,' hissed Siggurd, leaping forward to take hold of Freya's son.

He looked into the boy's eyes and laughed, as though at some private jest, before drawing a short-bladed dagger and ramming it into Sigulf's belly. The boy screamed, but before Siggurd could twist the knife and spill his guts, another arrow hammered the vampire's body.

Maedbh saw Ulrike standing behind the vampire, scrabbling to nock another arrow to her bowstring as Siggurd fastened his hungry gaze upon her.

'Blessed arrows,' he said, dropping the wailing Sigulf to the ground. 'Little girls shouldn't play with such dangerous things. Now I'll have to make you scream.'

The vampire stalked towards Ulrike, who fell to her knees before the terrifying figure, his form blurring as his cloak billowed around him like the wings of an enormous bat. Siggurd's eyes widened as his lower jaw distended and his fangs sprouted like daggers.

Maedbh clambered to her feet and staggered towards Ulrike, though she knew she could never reach her before Siggurd. Her pain was incredible, but she *had* to reach her daughter.

'Ulrike!' she begged, hearing a swelling roar around her. 'No, please! Don't hurt her!'

Siggurd lifted Ulrike from the ground. The young girl's face was a mask of tears. Siggurd turned back towards Maedbh. He sniffed the blood on Ulrike's face and his monstrous face broke into a horrid leer of understanding.

'Ah… this is your spawn,' said Siggurd. 'Now you will watch her die.'

Before the vampire could say another word, the roaring in Maedbh's head swelled as a mob of people charged into the black riders. There were hundreds of them, maybe even thousands. Most were without armour, dressed in the garb of farmers and ordinary men and women. They fought with the fury of Thuringian berserkers, tearing the dead riders from their saddles and breaking them apart with blows from clubs, felling axes and scythes.

Leading them was a young boy spattered in blood and with the light of battle fury in his eyes. He fought with a spear tied with blue and red rags, and Maedbh saw he knew how to use it. The boy hooked the haft around the legs of an unhorsed black rider and stabbed it down into the dead warrior's chest, twisting the blade before he withdrew it from the body. Dimly she knew she should know him, but how she could know an Unberogen boy escaped her.

The people of Reikdorf swarmed over the undead and drove them back. Siggurd threw Ulrike down as a score of howling men and women ran at him with spears and swords. Some of these, he could kill without difficulty, but all of them… Maedbh didn't think so. She ran over to Ulrike and scooped her up into her arms.

'I've got you, dear heart,' said Maedbh. 'I've got you.'

'Mother!' cried Ulrike, burying her head against Maedbh's shoulder. 'The bad man…?'

'Gone,' said Maedbh, oblivious to anything except

her daughter's weight. 'He can't hurt you now. Not ever.'

Ulrike wept into her neck, and Maedbh held her tightly, closing her eyes and willing the fear away as her body pulsed with waves of fiery pain. They stayed like that until Maedbh heard footsteps. She looked up and saw the young boy with the spear tied with the blue and red rags looking down at her.

'Is she all right?' he asked, and Maedbh caught the strong eastern accent in his words.

'Daegal?' she asked.

'Yes.'

She smiled. 'You remembered your spear training.'

He nodded, and suddenly he wasn't a blood-covered Asoborn warrior, but a boy of twelve years. She gathered Daegal to her and hugged him and Ulrike close to her chest. At last, she released them both and said, 'You were both so very brave. I can't tell you how proud I am of you. You fought like real heroes.'

Ulrike smiled through her tears, and Daegal held himself tall, as though some dreadful weight had been lifted from his shoulders. He looked back over her shoulder and Maedbh saw Freya carrying Sigulf while Fridleifr and Cuthwin had their arms around each other's shoulders to hold themselves upright. Both were bloody, but they were unbowed.

'Siggurd?' she said.

'Fled,' answered Cuthwin. 'When the people came, he took to the air and flew away.'

Maedbh nodded, looking to her queen with relief beyond words. Freya was pale and unsteady on her feet, and blood streamed from the wound at her neck. Sigulf's eyes were closed and his belly wet with crimson. His chest rose and fell, but weakly.

'He's alive?' asked Maedbh.

'Barely,' said Freya, her voice cracked and faint. 'We have to get him back to Reikdorf.'

'We *all* need to get back,' said Cuthwin. 'We've seen this lot off, but there's more of them coming this way.'

Maedbh looked to the east, and the flame of hope was smothered in her breast as she saw thousands more skeletal warriors marching in lockstep towards them. They had weathered this attack, but the dead had many more warriors to send into battle.

'Everyone back!' she shouted. 'To Reikdorf!'

KRELL'S AXE SLASHED down, but instead of cleaving through armour and flesh as it had done in his slaughter of the Red Scythes, this time his blade was halted by gromril armour and the strength of mountains. The towering monster paused in its butchery and looked down at the stout forms opposing it. The furious light in the champion's eyes burned even brighter, as though recognising the stunted forms before him from battles fought thousands of years ago.

Master Alaric felt the power of Krell's blow throughout his body, his great-grandfather's shield almost bent in two by the force. The shock reverberated through his armour and he thanked Grungni that he'd thought to strengthen himself with several firkins of beer.

'Is that the best you've got?' he sneered at the long dead champion. 'No wonder Grimbul Ironhelm was able to beat you.'

Krell roared with renewed fury, and his axe came up as a hundred dwarfs charged him. Alaric hurled himself at the ferocious champion whose name was entered countless times in the Dammaz Kron, his every transgression written in the blood of the High Kings of the age. He hammered his axe against Krell's blood-red form, feeling the star-iron of his axe bite a hair's breadth into the skull-etched plates of armour. Krell roared and slammed his axe down on a dwarf warrior's head, cleaving him from skull to groin. Blood sprayed the armour of his comrades, and they attacked with renewed fury.

Like the great pistons of Zhufbar, the dwarf axes beat the black armour of Krell, cutting shards of cursed iron away from his body, but leaving the giant, skeletal body beneath unharmed. Alaric circled behind the undead champion, rolling beneath the return swing of the black axe that left six dwarfs bisected at the waist. The ring of iron and gromril tightened around Krell, but the sheer weight of numbers only seemed to drive him to greater heights of frenzied delight.

Krell's axe swept left and right, and those it didn't kill were hurled away to land with the butchered human horsemen. An injured warrior, the one Alaric had spoken to, watched the fight in pained amazement. Alaric would sooner eat grobi dung than fail in front of a manling. The shameful life of a slayer awaited such unfortunates. That was not going to be Alaric's fate.

Yet more of the undead were moving up behind Krell, pushing forward in giant blocks of marching skeletons and lurching corpses. Hundreds of bats wheeled overhead and ghostly wisps of howling shades swirled around them. One way or another, this fight would need to end soon, for there was no way his dwarfs could hold against such numbers.

Alaric waited until Krell swung his axe in a low arc, killing another four dwarfs, before throwing aside his shield and leaping onto the dead champion's back. He wrapped his hand around a broken hunk of armour and beat his axe against Krell's shoulders.

Plates shattered under the assault, and Krell arched his back as he felt Alaric's presence. He roared and spun around, seeking to dislodge Alaric as the remaining dwarfs pressed their attack, battering his thighs with axe blows and hammer strikes. Sparks flew from the red armour, like metal fresh from the forge on an anvil. Alaric fought to hold on as he thundered his axe against the metal of Krell's armour. He felt his grip slipping and slammed his axe though a weakened plate, wedging himself in place by gripping an exposed rib within the unclean iron.

It felt like plunging his hand into an icy lake, and Alaric felt the cold of the other side seeping into his hand, a frozen touch of utter lifelessness and doom. He tried to snatch his hand back from Krell's essence, but it was stuck fast. The cold slithered through his hand, oozing through the veins and meat of his wrist. Alaric knew that when it reached his heart, he would become no better than Krell.

'Master Alaric, sir!' shouted a loud manling voice. 'Da says you got to get clear!'

Alaric knew he had only one chance to live and grimly freed his axe from the weakened plate of broken armour.

'Alaric the Mad, eh?' he said. 'Maybe they're right.'

He brought the axe down upon his wrist, the razored edge easily slicing through his flesh and bone. Alaric grunted in pain and kicked out on Krell's armour, throwing himself as far away from the champion as he could get. He landed on a dead horse and rolled behind it as he heard a series of snapping hammers being pulled back.

'Left one's out of alignment,' he grumbled, as the world filled with fire and noise.

GOVANNON PULLED THE leather firing cords, elated and terrified at the same time. He couldn't see much of the battle, which was a relief to him, yet out of the shadows one shape was terrifyingly clear. The blood red form of

Krell loomed in the darkness, a monster of nightmare come to hunt the living.

The first hammer struck the side of its brass cauldron, slowing enough to prevent the flint from sparking, and Govannon's heart sank. The hulking champion of Nagash loomed over the war machine and Govannon cursed himself for a fool in wishing to be part of this fight. Krell would kill them all; nothing could stand against this horror from an ancient age.

He cursed his naïve belief that he could repair a machine of the dwarfs, bitter that he could have spent these last weeks far more productively. Armour, swords, shields, axes, arrowheads–

The second hammer struck true, and puffs of smoke and fire frothed from the brass cauldrons at the back of the machine. The barrel erupted in a booming storm of shot and fire, another a few seconds later. Govannon's ears rang with the concussive force of the detonation and his eyes watered with the brightness of the fire erupting in thundering booms from the barrels. Then the fourth barrel fired. As the hammer slammed down in the powder cauldron of the barrel he had repaired, Bysen lifted him away as the Thunder Bringer rocked back with ferocious recoil.

The barrel held firm and erupted with a blizzard of iron shot and, clear as day, Govannon saw the towering champion fall, his blood red armour ripped to shreds by the hurricane of fire and iron. Bones were shattered and torn away, the horned helmet little more than a ragged lump of pulverised iron hanging from a torn leather chin strap.

Part of Krell's head was gone, the left side of his skull a shattered ruin. Blackness gaped within, yet the fire in Krell's right eye blazed as the dwarfs fell upon his ruined body with sharp axes and vengeful hearts.

'It worked!' shouted Govannon. 'In Ulric's name, it worked!'

'Aye, da, it worked good!' said Bysen happily. 'Big, big bang! Bysen's ears hurt!'

KHALED AL-MUNTASIR RODE at a leisurely pace towards the north, watching as the army of the dead began to fully envelop these mortals who dared to stand against Nagash. He had ridden with all speed towards where the red-armoured cavalry had fought the black knights to a standstill, but halted upon feeling Markus's death.

For a mortal, Markus was a tremendous swordsman, but enhanced with the power of undeath, he had been superlative – better even than Khaled perhaps. Yet he was dead, his soul consigned to oblivion by a mortal. The unease that had stirred in the vampire's belly all night returned, stronger this time, and he cursed himself for succumbing to such a mortal sensation.

Yet no sooner had the painful empathic horror of Markus's destruction passed than he felt Siggurd's pain as weapons blessed in the name of the god of all living things pierced his immortal flesh. He winced with each wound, unused to such pain, and felt Siggurd's anger as he was forced to flee. His two unbeatable warriors had been defeated, one destroyed, the other wounded almost to the point of dissolution.

Khaled al-Muntasir forced the anger at their incompetence aside and turned his attention to the rest of the battle, trying to regain his impregnable confidence. Thousands more dead warriors were advancing towards the city, pushing past the tiny islands of resistance that had met with some fleeting success. The battle line of mortals arrayed before the walls was fighting with admirable courage, but no hope of victory. They took backward step after backward step, and it was only a matter of time until they broke. Yet in the centre of the battle, cut off from the rest of his army, Sigmar drove for the low hillside where Nagash awaited him. Less than a hundred warriors still rode with the Emperor, yet they charged as though all of mankind were with them.

The vampire looked to the black form of Nagash, who stood with his enormous sword and twisted-snake staff in his hands. Black light flickered from the staff and blue fire wreathed the blade of his ancient sword.

'What are you waiting for?' hissed Khaled al-Muntasir. 'Just kill him and be done with it.'

Yet even as he said the words, he knew Nagash could not kill Sigmar with his black sorcery while he wore the crown. Its incredible power would protect any wearer from virtually all forms of magic.

Khaled al-Muntasir watched as Nagash raised his staff and arcing bolts of lightning forked downwards, striking the gems inset along its scaled length. A storm of dark energy surrounded the necromancer and he slammed the staff into the ground. With senses beyond those of mortals, Khaled al-Muntasir watched the energy flow from the staff and into the hillside, spreading like the roots of a poisoned tree beneath the earth.

'That's more like it,' he said.

These black roots sought the bleak places of the land, the abandoned graveyards long since paved over, the forgotten plague pits covered in quicklime and the sites of murder and mayhem. Drawn to these places like rats to a cesspit, Nagash's sorcery infused the earth with the dark magic of undeath.

And the unquiet dead rose from their ancient graves to claw their way to the world above.

THE EARTH RUMBLED with the sound of digging claws and moaning hunger, the churned grass rippling as the dead of centuries before rose to the surface. Hands long devoid of meat erupted from the earth and hauled flesh-less corpses back to the land that had consigned them to the ground. From the southern fork of the river to the city gates, a huge tear opened in the earth and a thou-sand or more dead warriors from the time before men had dwelled in cities and towns lurched unsteadily to their feet.

The Asoborns and the people of Reikdorf fleeing the onward march of the dead abandoned all pretence of an ordered retreat at the sight of this new horror. They ran for the city gates, terrified at being surrounded and cut off from their home. Even Freya, whose courage was unquestioned, fled along with her sons, Maedbh, Ulrike and Cuthwin. Daegal, with his newfound courage, formed a rearguard with the few surviving Queen's Eagles, and if any of them thought it strange to be taking orders from one so young, none remarked upon it.

Within the walls of Reikdorf, the ground broke open as the dead climbed from below, pushing their way into the half-light as Nagash's sorcery compelled their grisly remains to rise up and slay the living. Hundreds of dead things stalked the streets of the city, fighting anything warm and feasting on their flesh.

Alfgeir and Teon were trapped within a closing ring of undead, their retreat cut off by a newly emerged phalanx of the dead. They were unarmed, these dead men, but they swiftly picked up the weapons of those the Unbero-gen had already destroyed. Ragged, disorganised and freshly risen, they were formidable in their numbers if not their skill as fighters.

In the north, yet more dead arose, surrounding Gov-annon, Bysen and the dwarfs as they hacked at the indestructible corpse of Krell. Though their axes were sharper than any weapon forged by the hands of men, they could not easily undo armour worked in the forges of smiths who gave praise to the bloody gods of the north.

The mortal army was surrounded and doomed.

SIGMAR SMASHED ASIDE a pair of skeletal warriors, champions in ancient, verdigris-stained armour of a thousand years ago. Hundreds of these undying creatures surrounded him, and yet still they pushed on. Ghal-maraz flickered with silver fire and shimmering sparks flew from his every blow. Hundreds of the dead had fallen before him, but hundreds more still awaited destruction.

Beside him, Wolfgart hacked through the dead with great sweeps of his sword, each blow weaker than the last as his strength grew less and less. Where Ghal-maraz imparted a measure of its power to Sigmar, Wolfgart enjoyed no such boon. Wenyld fought mechanically, slumped low over his saddle, though Sigmar's banner still flew above the heroic warriors who rode with him.

Ghal-maraz swept out to either side, breaking the dead warriors apart with brutal cracks of shattered bone. As the last ranks of the dead were crushed beneath their horses' hooves, Sigmar's Unberogen, fifty warriors in total, rode onto the clear ground before the low hillside where Nagash awaited them. Its base was encircled by tall warriors in heavy hauberks of black iron, who carried long halberds with icy blades. A host of swirling spirits gathered in the air above the necromancer, and the darkness around him was total. Sigmar had no idea how fared the rest of his army, but knew that unless he could end this now, it would be slaughtered by morning's light.

A trail of broken bodies littered the ground behind them, and though thousands of the dead were within reach, none turned towards them, as though their presence was an irrelevance.

'Almost there,' said Wolfgart, twisting in his saddle to make sure no more of the dead were moving to attack them.

'Aye,' agreed Sigmar. 'One more push and I'll have him right where I want him.'

Wolfgart gave him a sidelong look and then burst out laughing.

'Damn me, Sigmar,' he said. 'I'm tired worse than I was at Black Fire, and that's saying something, but you can still make me smile.'

Sigmar nodded, feeling the weight of the crown at his brow grow heavier with every step his horse took towards the hillside. He felt its anger at him surge, a fury that a mere mortal dared to wield it and not partake of its power. Its maker was at hand, and it renewed its assault on his mind, battering him with dreams of pleasure, nightmares of failure and temptations of wealth, power and godhood.

None could reach Sigmar, for he had reached that place where all thoughts of self were extinguished. All that was left to him now was service to his people, and not even death could keep him from that duty. Piece by piece, Sigmar had shed all his earthly desires, putting them aside for the greater good of the Empire.

Nagash's crown had nothing left with which to tempt or intimidate him, for his entire being was dedicated to one ideal. That was something no necromancer could ever understand, the dedication of the self to a higher purpose, where the one man could make the difference between life and death, success or failure.

In this world, at this time, Sigmar was that man. He had believed that from the day he had walked amongst the tombs of his ancestors on his Dooming Day, but had *known* it when he passed through the fire of Ulric unharmed.

Everything he had done had driven him to this moment, and he knew this foe was his to face alone. Sigmar swung his leg over his saddle and dropped to the earth as a sudden stillness and silence spread outwards from the hillside. Though battle still raged beyond, Sigmar could hear nothing beyond his own laboured breathing and the distant howling of wolves.

He walked over to Wenyld and lifted his hand towards the red and gold banner.

'Time to pass it on, my friend,' said Sigmar.

Wenyld nodded, too weak from blood loss to resist as Sigmar took the banner pole from his blooded grip.

'What in Ulric's name are you doing?' demanded Wolfgart, walking his horse alongside him and dismounting. 'Get back on your horse, you fool!'

'No,' said Sigmar. 'I'm going to end this now.'

'What? You're just going to walk up to the bloody necromancer on foot?'

'That's exactly what I'm doing,' replied Sigmar, turning and making his way towards the hillside. 'And don't follow me. This is something I need to do alone.'

'Why, for the love of the gods? Tell me that at least.'

Sigmar said, 'Because this is how it has to be. You know how it goes. At the end of all the sagas, the hero always stands alone or else he's not a hero.'

'Damn the sagas,' swore Wolfgart. 'I'm not leaving you.'

'Yes you are,' said Sigmar as the ancient warriors at the base of the hill parted to allow him passage. 'Wenyld needs you.'

Wolfgart turned and caught Wenyld as he fell from his saddle. Once again the howl of wolves sounded from over forested hills and shadowed valleys, carried to Reikdorf by cold northern winds. As Wolfgart lowered the dying Wenyld to the ground, Sigmar turned and climbed the hill towards Nagash, his banner in one hand, Ghal-maraz in the other.

He heard Wolfgart shouting his name, but didn't dare look back.

━◄ TWENTY-THREE ►━

The End of All Things

EVERY STEP WAS a battle, each yard he drew nearer to the necromancer a struggle against his mortal inclination to flee this abomination. The summit of the hill was wreathed in spirits in black, ghostly revenants of lost souls doomed to attend upon Nagash from now until the end of all things. Sigmar felt the dead light of Nagash roam across his body, learning in a heartbeat how he had grown and was now edging his way to the grave.

A black miasma swirled around the base of the hill, isolating him from the mortal world beyond, and Sigmar felt his flesh recoil from the vile presence of the immortal necromancer. His armour creaked in the frozen air and webs of frost spread across his breastplate and shoulder guards. Ghal-maraz was his only warmth, the language beaten into its haft by master runesmiths glowing with fierce light beneath his grip. Sigmar held tight to its warmth, for the crown at his brow felt like an ever-tightening fist of ice.

Though it could not touch him, the crown's assault on

his mind was undiminished, taunting him for the sake of spite and hatred. Nagash's form seemed to stretch up into the darkness as Sigmar drew near, the necromancer's body growing larger and more imposing as though empowered by the very nearness of his crown.

Armoured in eldritch plates of enchanted black iron, Nagash was easily twice the height of Sigmar. His bones were suffused with a venomous green light, every crack and imperfection in his armour lambent with an internal fire that came from ancient magic woven from the myriad winds blowing from the far north. His staff was a slender length of shimmering darkness, like entwined snakes, and his sword was at least as tall as Sigmar. Cold blue flames licked along its length and it radiated a chill that touched Sigmar deep in his bones.

Nagash stared down at him, and Sigmar fought against that dread gaze, feeling his limbs fill with ice water and lead. Twin orbs of deathly green fire stared at Sigmar, eyes that had seen the world before men had walked the lands he now ruled. Thousands of years separated them, an ocean of time that Sigmar found impossible to comprehend. He could no more imagine the world of such long ago days as he could imagine the Empire in thousands of years to come.

I will show you…

The voice was like continents colliding, a deathly cadence that owed nothing to an actual voice. It was the sound of death itself. Sigmar staggered as he saw a land of forests and mountains, its people divided and the world in turmoil. Blood stained every rock, and the glint of iron weapons was everywhere. Armies of such size as to defy imagination marched all across this land, destroying everything in their path without mercy.

Bodies lay gutted by the roadside, men, women and children. Still-living captives were bound to stakes and left for the animals to devour. Sigmar saw slaughter and blood everywhere, hacked up corpses and bodies burned alive in their homes. He wept to see such destruction visited upon his people and his anger built as he sought the source of this debauchery. His gaze fell upon an army marching to a city at the confluence of many rivers. Colourful banners fluttered overhead, and the soldiers were clad in equally gaudy uniforms.

They marched in disciplined ranks, singing songs of martial pride, and Sigmar wept to see that this was no army of monsters, beasts of the undead. These were men. Worse, they were men of the Empire.

Look closer…

Though he knew it was what Nagash wanted, Sigmar could not help himself. He saw the army's banners were decorated with skulls and laurels, crossed spears and spread-winged eagles. And upon all of them were stitched scrolls, each bearing a single word.

Sigmar.

These were warriors who fought in his name. They carried weapons of unusual design, wooden staves like the thunder bows of the dwarfs, and wagons bearing unfamiliar war machines drew up the rear of the marching column. Two metal behemoths followed the supply wagons, lumbering contraptions on iron-rimmed wheels that belched steam and black smoke from square fireboxes at their rear.

This is the world you have created. This is blood that will be spilled in your name. Is it not better to leave this world and let the race of man fall into decline? Your species resurgent is one that lives only for destruction and uncertainty. It knows no other way. The dead do not squabble as this land's rulers do. The dead do not fight one another. The dead have no desires, no petty jealousies or ambitions. A world of the dead is a world at peace…

Sigmar fought against the necromancer's words, understanding that their battle would be fought in the realm of the spirit as well as that of the flesh. He closed his eyes, willing this vision away, knowing that Nagash would seek to defeat him with lies cloaked in truths.

'This may be a true vision of the future Empire,' hissed Sigmar. 'But a world of death is a world of stagnation, without the change that makes it worthwhile. What you call uncertainty, I call life itself.'

He fought down his revulsion at this vision and opened his eyes, no longer seeing the bleak vision of an Empire at war with itself, but the spirit-haunted hillside where a being of ultimate darkness opposed him.

'Show me what you will,' said Sigmar, planting his standard in the soft earth and raising Ghal-maraz over his shoulder. 'This ends with me destroying you.'

So be it.

Nagash's sword swept down and Sigmar lifted Ghal-maraz to block. Blue fire seared out from the impact and Sigmar's arms almost froze with the blow. He rolled aside as the sword slashed out again, catching him on the edge of his pauldron and lifting him from his feet. The iron froze in an instant, cracking apart in a rain of icy splinters as he landed. Cold blood streamed from Sigmar's shoulder as Nagash slipped through the air, fast as a winter squall. His sword cut into Sigmar's breastplate, shattering it like a pane of glass and piercing his chest with icy splinters.

Sigmar rolled away before the blade could penetrate deeper, swinging Ghal-maraz around to deflect yet another swift riposte. The necromancer's staff slashed down and arcing bolts of lightning leapt up from the ground. Sigmar screamed in pain as the energies enveloped him, burning his flesh with cold fire. Though it had been his bane through the entire battle, the crown now came to his aid. Its power was purest evil, but it was utterly directed in its ability to resist sorcery. Nagash's withering energy was drawn into the crown, and Sigmar felt its rage to be so abused as the searing fire vanished.

Nagash's leering skull face, too monstrous and enormous to ever have been human, swept down and Sigmar threw himself to the side as black, corrosive breath gusted from the necromancer's jaws. The hillside withered and died beneath its touch and Nagash spun around with his staff and sword raised to destroy the foolish mortal opposing him.

The necromancer's sword swung low and Sigmar leapt over it, bringing his hammer around to block a slashing blow of the staff to his body. Once again, the impact was enormous, and Sigmar knew he could not keep this up for much longer. He spun inside the necromancer's reach, but Nagash was fast and slid out of range of his strike.

Sigmar leapt towards Nagash, and the necromancer lowered his staff to block the wild blow. Ghal-maraz slammed into the entwined snakes and the runic power of the dwarfs blazed as it met the unnatural sorcery of Nehekhara. Sigmar poured every fibre of his hatred into the blow and Nagash's staff broke apart with a screaming howl of released magic. Nagash reeled from its destruction, and Sigmar saw the hand that had carried it was a shimmering metal, its surface like a silver mirror with oil smeared across it.

Nagash drew himself up to his full height, the black smoke swirling around his lower reaches spinning like an inverted whirlwind. The force of it drove Sigmar back, billowing around him and throwing up grit and sand from the summit of the hill. The hellish wind dispersed the shrieking spirits from the air, hurling them away and revealing the battle in all its horror.

See the fate of all flesh and know despair!

THE LAND BETWEEN the city and the low hill was a charnel house of blood and destruction. As Sigmar's eyes had seen into the hearts of his people the night before the battle, so now Nagash showed him the battle he had led them to. Sigmar's plan was simple, ride through the centre of the undead army and slay the necromancer. He had known that many would die to keep the dead from Reikdorf, but to see the scale of that bloodshed was shattering.

Sigmar was no stranger to battle and death. He had seen friends and loved ones slain over the course of his life, and knew the grim cost of sending men to war. He knew that his orders would see women widowed, children orphaned and lovers forever parted. He knew all this, yet to see it happening all around him, all at once, was a supreme horror.

The thousands who were fighting on this day were dying in droves. Their initial successes against the army of the dead were meaningless as the cadavers and ruined corpses rose to their feet once again. Those who had fallen in battle now returned to tear at their former sword brothers, and what had once been a magnificent host was now reduced to a few pitiful bands of survivors fighting for their last moments of life.

Even if Sigmar triumphed and slew Nagash, this day would live in infamy as a day of death and woe. There would be too many dead for it to be otherwise. Sigmar heard grating laughter as Nagash revelled in this cavalcade of slaughter. The Empire's dead would be new acolytes for his host, enslaved to reduce this world to a barren, empty wasteland.

Amid the fighting in the south, Sigmar saw Freya and Maedbh leading their children back towards Reikdorf. A multitude of skeletons climbing the walls and wading into the city via the corpse-choked river which blocked their route to safety. Unberogen and Asoborns led by a baying, blood-covered youngster defended them within a fragile shieldwall, but with dead wolves and flesh-hungry corpses closing in on them, they had minutes of life left at best.

Nagash cruelly drew his gaze onwards, and in the centre of the battlefield, Sigmar saw Teon and the Great Hall Guard enveloped by a horde of freshly-risen dead as they rode for Reikdorf's gates. Alfgeir slumped against Teon, barely conscious and near death. It broke Sigmar's heart to see the grievous wound his old friend had suffered.

Yet Nagash was not done with him.

Onwards his gaze was drawn, and Sigmar saw a host of black knights riding south towards the city, followed by hundreds of dead warriors marching in perfect lockstep. Shambling corpses in their thousands followed them, a ravening horde set to devour the living. A ring of dwarfs led by Master Alaric hacked at a fallen giant in red armour, their weapons cutting the monster apart piece by piece. It struggled as they fought it, though its body was ruined as though from a thousand heavy impacts. A wrecked machine lay on its side as a tall warrior with a heavy forge hammer stood over a fallen man in the leather apron of a blacksmith.

Sigmar recognised Master Govannon and Bysen, but pale-bellied flesheaters surrounded them. No matter how powerful Bysen's swings of the forge hammer, he would not be able to stop his father from being eaten alive. Sigmar heard the howling of many wolves and despair touched his heart to hear this choir of Ulric's chosen lamenting the death of so many brave warriors.

You see…? This is what flesh entails. Suffering. Bloodshed. Misery. Why would you seek to perpetuate this horror? What creature in my service knows fear, pain or desire? The legions of the dead want for nothing, care for nothing, love nothing. End your foolish resistance and you will be a king of death, a master of the world at my side. You will be my greatest champion and together we will end the suffering of this world!

Sigmar dropped to his knees, as the pain and anguish of every living soul upon the battlefield washed over him. What manner of man could allow such suffering? What sane individual could wish such pain on a life? To strangle a babe as it was born would be a kindness, and to end the plague of the living on this world would be an act of mercy. Sigmar's tears flowed freely and he looked up into the hungry eyes of Nagash as he loomed over him. The metallic hand reached out to him, the sharpened fingertips like silver claws as they reached for the crown.

In that moment, the sound of wolves echoed from the treeline of the northern hills, an ululating chorus that swept over the battlefield. Sigmar felt that sound lift him and fill his mind with a cold wind that had its source in the northern forests. This was a cry born in the forgotten places of ice and snow where the wolves of Ulric made their lairs. He understood that this was no lament for the fallen, but a savage affirmation of life. A war shout and cry of defiance all in one.

Sigmar rolled away from Nagash's outstretched hand, looking to the north as tens of thousands of howling men streamed over the hillside. There were few of them warriors, most dressed in rags and bearing spiked chains, spinning flails, scythes, burning brands and clanging hand bells. Blood-smeared and screaming incoherently, they had the look of madmen, a host of armed lunatics in search of a battle.

Amongst them rode two warriors in red armour and wolf-pelt cloaks. One carried a rippling banner of crimson and white, and Sigmar's heart leapt as he recognised the banner of the White Wolves.

'Redwane!' cried Sigmar, even as he realised that neither rider was the fiery warrior who commanded that elite band of horsemen. His eyes were drawn to two warriors at the forefront of this motley band of ragged madmen. Both were bearded and wore muddy tunics that were torn and stained with old blood. These men looked on the verge of death, yet charged with the ferocity of ten berserkers, seemingly oblivious to the many wounds they had cut into their own flesh. One man was unknown to him, but the other was as familiar as his own reflection. It was Redwane, but the man Sigmar had known was gone, submerged within a tortured madness that banished all thoughts of pain and fear of death.

The host of madmen struck the army of the dead and rolled right over them, crushing them beneath their bare feet and tearing them apart with their makeshift weapons. On they came in an unending tide, men and women gathered from all across the Empire, seduced by doom-laden preachings until the host that had set out from Middenheim had swollen to become this irresistible tide of crazed fanaticism.

Following behind this screaming host came painted warriors in mail shirts who marched beneath the banner of Count Otwin. Perhaps a thousand of the Berserker King's warriors came over the hills, following the deranged army led by Redwane and his unknown companion. They bayed with the voices of wolves and to see them coming to his aid gave Sigmar the strength he needed to face the necromancer.

Nagash drew himself up to his full, terrifying height, his fury at this turn of events spreading from the hillside and empowering his army with fresh hate for the living. The northern flank of the dead collapsed, smashed aside by the army of madmen and Thuringians, yet there was still a virtually inexhaustible supply of rotting flesh to replace those the mortals destroyed.

Sigmar swept Ghal-maraz around, and faced the necromancer for the last time. The crown blazed with silver light at his brow, exerting every last scrap of its power to weaken him and drain his ability to resist. As Sigmar listened to the howling of wolves, he knew it could not touch him. It had kept him safe from Nagash's magic, allowed him to smash through the ranks of the dead without pause, but now it was time to be rid of it.

He tore the crown from his brow and held it up towards Nagash.

'You want this?' he bellowed, and Nagash turned his gaze upon him. Such desire and obsession. Such aching need and devotion. Nothing else mattered to Nagash, not the defeat of Sigmar's army, not the destruction of all living things. Nothing was more important to the necromancer than this crown. Sigmar saw how much its power meant to Nagash and understood Eoforth's last message to him completely.

'You want this?' repeated Sigmar. 'Then have it!'

He threw the crown onto the withered grass of the hillside and raised Ghal-maraz to smash it asunder with one, all-powerful blow.

Nagash bellowed in horrified anger and reached for the crown with outstretched fingers, all thoughts save taking back his crown driven from his mind. Nothing else mattered, and it was the moment Sigmar had been awaiting since this fight had begun.

He leapt towards the necromancer, bringing Ghal-maraz around in a thunderous overhead sweep. The mighty hammer of the dwarfs smashed into Nagash's cuirass, breaking it into a thousand shards and powering into his chest. Green fire flared from the impact and ribs fused with dark magic thousands of years before shattered like ice as Sigmar drove his hammer into the heart of the necromancer's being.

Sigmar howled with the wolves and screamed his hatred of Nagash as the runic script on the hammer's haft shone with the purest light. Runes he had not even known existed flared to life on the hammer's head, filling Nagash's hollow existence with fiery beams of light and searing his immortal essence from within.

The necromancer shrieked as his ancient sorcery fought to resist the powerful magic of the dwarfs. Forces too titanic to be understood by mortals battled within his body, easily capable of laying waste to this entire land. Sigmar held onto Ghal-maraz as the star-iron of its head burned brighter than the sun and its grip burned his hands with its ancient fire.

'I will end you!' roared Sigmar, thrusting the hammer deeper into Nagash's body.

The necromancer gave one last shriek of horror, and his body exploded in a wash of black light and frozen fire. Dark magic and immortal energies flared upwards from his destruction like a volcanic eruption.

And the sky filled with ashes and grief.

WITH NAGASH'S DESTRUCTION, the army of the dead melted away like woodsmoke on a windy day. Warriors of bone dropped their swords and collapsed as their spirits were freed to pass on to their final rest. Undead wolves that had, moments before, been howling for blood, fell to dissolution as the magic binding their bodies to the world of mortals was undone. Spirits shrieked as their ethereal forms were drawn back to the tombs that held them, and the shambling corpses raised from their graves now slumped to the ground, reduced to nothing more than dead meat for crows.

The binding will of Nagash was absolute, and no creature that walked, drifted or flew within his host had power of its own to maintain its existence. As the necromancer's power bled away, the dead ceased their attacks on the living and returned to the realm that had first claim upon their souls. Morr's gates opened to receive them, and as each violated spirit was freed from the necromancer's iron clutches, a wave of euphoria swept over the battlefield.

Weeping men and women laughed and danced as the threat of death was lifted. They cried tears of joy, and hugged one another tight. The nearness of death had reawakened every mortal heart's appreciation of the gift of life. Though that would fade in time, for now it was a glorious moment that would never be forgotten.

Nor was Nagash's influence confined to the dead at Reikdorf, for the black strands of his web of control stretched all across the Empire. The dead at Marburg dropped to the ground as the will driving them over the citadel walls faded into nothingness, while those clawing their way into Middenheim fell from the causeway and tumbled from the sheer sides of the Fauschlag Rock. The Udose watched in amazement as the dead ceased their attacks into their hidden valleys and crumbled to dust around the walls of Conn Carsten's clifftop fortress.

Count Aloysis stood atop the ramparts of Hochergig and waved a Cherusen banner as the dead melted away from his walls, while Count Krugar rode through the gates of Taalahim in triumph. In the eastern reaches of the Empire, Count Adelhard rallied his warriors in a krug around the Bechahorst, a spire of dark stone in the northern marches of his lands, and drank *koumiss* to toast the end of this fight.

The lands of the south were silent, for their people were already dead. Alone among the southern tribal homelands, the Merogens had endured. Count Henroth led his warriors from within their great castles of stone, blinking in the new light and disbelieving that such a miracle could have saved his people.

Nagash's legions were no more, and the living had endured.

The long dark night of the dead was over.

KHALED AL-MUNTASIR CLIMBED to the top of the hillside, his bones aching and his flesh scoured by the incomprehensible destruction of Nagash. The vampire's armour was in tatters, his white cloak torn and burned by the fire that had threatened to consume him. The necromancer's doom had threatened to drag him to destruction as well, but his blood was of a higher calibre than that of the ancient priest king of Nehekhara.

Siggurd crawled by his side, the newly-sired vampire's body wracked with pain. The Asoborns had almost destroyed him, and in his weakened state, his immortal flesh had all but succumbed to the same destruction as had vanquished the army of the dead. Only his superior pedigree had saved him, but it would take dozens of bodies' worth of blood to restore him. His whimpering cries were repugnant to Khaled al-Muntasir's ears, but he was of his blood and could not be abandoned to the savage mercies of the mortals.

Nothing lived on the hillside, every blade of grass withered and every inch of soil barren. His footsteps left prints in ashen sand as he climbed to the top, where he saw the architect of the necromancer's demise.

Sigmar stood with his back to Khaled al-Muntasir, his softly glowing hammer at his side and the crown of Nagash lying at his feet. The crown shone with a dull light, and Khaled al-Muntasir wondered what glories he might achieve were he to take it. The Emperor's flesh was a mass of bruised blood, frostburn and suffering. The vampire licked his lips, seeing that the mortal was at the very end of his endurance. Easy meat.

'You have destroyed that which could not be destroyed,' said Khaled al-Muntasir.

'I told you that you were not welcome in my lands,' said Sigmar, without turning. 'I told you that I would kill you if I saw you again.'

'An empty threat,' said the vampire, taking a step towards Sigmar. Siggurd moaned in hunger and pain, the smell of blood drawing his broken gaze.

'Is it?' said Sigmar, turning to face him. 'Test it, and I will send you to join your master.'

'You are weak,' said the vampire. 'Spent. I could kill you and drink your blood before you could raise a hand to stop me. The crown will be mine and all you have achieved here will have been for nothing.'

'Then come at me,' said Sigmar, lifting Ghal-maraz.

Khaled al-Muntasir laughed, but the sound died in his throat as he saw the hatred in Sigmar's eyes. There was strength and power there beyond anything men should know, a cold fire that came not from mortal realms, but from a place long forsaken that did not belong on this world. Its winter fire hailed from a place of gods and monsters, a realm of power beyond imagining and where the laws of nature held no sway. All this power and more burned in Sigmar's eyes, though he knew it not.

In that instant of connection, Khaled al-Muntasir knew that if he took another step his undying existence would be ended. For the first time since he had awoken as an immortal blood drinker, Khaled al-Muntasir knew the meaning of fear. His limbs trembled. The thought of oblivion and the bleak emptiness that awaited him robbed him of all his courage.

Siggurd pawed at the ground, desperate for blood and unable to comprehend why his master hesitated to end this upstart mortal. His senses dulled and broken by his pain, Siggurd could not feel the terrible danger Sigmar represented to him and all his kind. The Emperor's hate of the blood drinkers was a force all of its own, a force that transcended time and all notions of mortality.

Khaled al-Muntasir backed away from Sigmar, dragging the wretched vampire count he had sired back down the hillside. Terror of Sigmar's inner power burned into their damned souls with unending torment as his voice chased them from the battlefield.

'Hear now the word of Sigmar Heldenhammer,' shouted the Emperor. 'I curse you and all your kind to be my enemies for all time!'

The vampires fled into the shadows.

SIGMAR WATCHED THE vampires run, thankful that his killing boast had not been put to the test. His body was a mass of pain, his heart heavy with the mourning yet to come, and his soul was sickened to see what might yet become of his beloved Empire. The air around him was thick with foetid vapours, unclean fumes that lingered in the wake of the necromancer's destruction. Yet even as he waited, a fresh wind was building, blowing from the west with clean air and the promise of new beginnings.

He took a deep breath, savouring the sweetness of that air. It had been so long since he had tasted air untainted with the ashen reek of grave dust and death that he had almost forgotten what it was like. Freed from the necromancer's magic, the land was already beginning to heal, purging the foulness of dark magic from its soil and wind.

Soon the desolation of Nagash would be little more than a memory, for the world was more resilient than people knew. It would outlast mankind, and its mountains, forests and rivers would see them dead and buried before it would even blink. Mortals were a flicker in the life of this world, yet even that was worth holding onto.

Sigmar opened his eyes as he saw a host of men and women gathering around the desolate hillside, warriors from his army, people from his city and allies from across the land. They were weeping tears of hope and mourning, loss and relief.

The battle was over and they were alive.

Sigmar dropped to one knee before his people, giving homage to them as they had given homage to him. The sky above the battlefield began to lighten as the perpetual twilight of Nagash was banished. Its sullen gloom had gripped the Empire for so long that its people had forgotten the feel of sunlight on their skin. Its radiance spread across the land, a bounteous illumination that banished evil to the shadows and chased away the darkness.

Sigmar smiled and turned his face to the sun.

'People of the Empire,' he said. 'A new day is upon us.'

◄ EPILOGUE ►

IN THE AFTERMATH of the battle, the bodies of the dead were gathered and taken to the blasted hilltop where Sigmar had defeated Nagash. Nothing would ever grow there again, and the priests of Morr declared it a fitting place for the dead to be given their final rest. Night after night, the priests of all the gods spoke prayers for the dead, and scattered the ashes into the river Reik, where they were carried downstream to Marburg and the open ocean.

Count Marius and Princess Marika were married a month after Nagash's defeat, the ceremony attended by Sigmar, Krugar, Aloysis, Otwin, and Myrsa. Claiming the injuries she had suffered at Siggurd's hands still pained her, Freya and her wounded sons returned to Three Hills to rebuild what the dead had destroyed. Though many people muttered darkly as to what the union of Jutones and Endals might mean for the Empire, Sigmar had blessed the marriage and gifted the couple with a pair of golden sceptres from his treasure vaults.

Wolfgart and Maedbh remained in Reikdorf with

Ulrike, though they decided that they would split their time between Sigmar's city and Three Hills. Never again would they allow anger to get the better of them, and never again would they allow themselves to be parted with bitter words between them. Within days of the wedding at Marburg, Maedbh announced to Wolfgart and Ulrike that she was with child, and the celebration that accompanied the news was more raucous than the wedding feast of Marius and Marika.

Redwane left Reikdorf within a day of the victory, leading his ravaged, self-mortifying band of madmen into the forests of the Empire. Less than a thousand of them remained, their headlong charge into the undead costing the majority of them their lives. Sigmar had caught Redwane as he prepared to lead his march of doom, but no words could reach the younger man; his hope had been crushed and life now held no meaning for him. Otwin told Sigmar how the crazed Redwane and Torbrecan had broken the siege of his castle and whipped the people of the Empire along the route of his march south into a morbid frenzy. Taking up a hook-knotted rope, Redwane wished the Emperor well and set off into the shadowed forest with Torbrecan, leaving his heartbroken White Wolves behind.

Master Alaric and his dwarf warriors had sought to destroy Krell after the fire of the repaired Thunder Bringer had brought him low, but Nagash's will was not the only force empowering the dread champion's unlife. The monstrous warrior had fought his way clear of the dwarfs' vengeance, and fled into the north. Too blooded to pursue, the dwarfs had watched in bitter impotence as Krell escaped the clutches of their blades. Yet more entries were noted for the Dammaz Kron, the names of all the dwarfs Krell had slain.

Govannon and Bysen both survived the Battle of the

River Reik, as it was becoming known, and returned to their forge. The Thunder Bringer had been crushed in the fighting raging around Krell, but its remains had been salvaged and brought back within the city walls while the dwarfs grieved their fallen brothers. Though it was smashed beyond all hope of repair, Govannon immediately set about working out how to make newer and bigger machines. A scrap of fire powder from the misfiring barrel had been recovered from the wreckage, and the near-blind smith was optimistic he would be able to replicate it.

If Master Alaric knew of this, he gave no sign, and after meeting privately with Sigmar in his longhouse, led his warriors in solemn procession to the east. The loss of his hand affected him deeply, and as Sigmar watched the mountain folk return to their homeland, he sensed a great melancholy within Alaric.

Sigmar returned Nagash's crown to High Priestess Alessa, and bade her take it far from the Empire, somewhere its evil power would be unable to corrupt men's souls. With a group of iron-willed warriors, Alessa left Reikdorf and rode into the east, never to return.

Of all the warriors who had fought for Sigmar, Alfgeir carried the burden of victory more than most. Though many men and women had been dreadfully wounded in the fighting, the loss of his arm cut the Marshal of the Reik far deeper than the flesh. His eyes never regained their normal colour and no fire could warm his skin. Six months to the day after the battle's end, Alfgeir rode a white horse into the north toward a frozen lake, where he met a fur-cloaked warrior with two wolves at his side.

Wenyld and Sigmar watched him go, and the Emperor knew that a stronger compulsion than duty to Reikdorf called to his old friend. As Alfgeir vanished over the hillside, Sigmar bade Wenyld farewell and made his way into the depths of the frozen forest to the west of Reik-dorf.

The cathedral of evergreen trees was a shimmering winter garden of glistening icicles and stillness. Walking paths he had not taken in years, he made his way to a peaceful hollow where weeping willows drooped with the weight of snow and ice on their branches. A gurgling waterfall spilled into a wide pool, and a simple head-stone was set at its edge.

He touched the headstone and looked to the east.

'Soon, my love,' said Sigmar. 'Soon.'

ABOUT THE AUTHOR

Hailing from Scotland, Graham McNeill worked for over six years as a Games Developer in Games Workshop's Design Studio before taking the plunge to become a full-time writer. In addition to twenty novels for the Black Library, Graham's written a host of SF and Fantasy stories and comics, as well as a number of side projects that keep him busy and (mostly) out of trouble. His Horus Heresy novel, *A Thousand Sons*, was a New York Times bestseller and his Time of Legends novel, *Empire*, won the 2010 David Gemmell Legend Award. Graham lives and works in Nottingham and you can keep up to date with where he'll be and what he's working on by visiting his website.

Join the ranks of the 4th Company at
www.graham-mcneill.com

An Exclusive Interview with
Graham McNeill

BL: What attracted you to writing for the Time of Legends series, and the Sigmar character in particular?

GM: If you're going to write about anybody historical in the Old World, as far as human characters go, it's got to be Sigmar. He's the character who casts his shadow the longest over the Empire. Everything he's done is legendary, so it fits the Time of Legends series perfectly. Telling his deeds and humanising them without reducing them was a real challenge. Sigmar's story had to be epic, but he had to be a real character that wasn't just going to steam through everything in the way that a Space Marine would. He was human, he was fallible, he didn't win all the time, he was wounded and bled, but his story still had to be suitably grand-scale.

BL: This trilogy is your first Warhammer Fantasy fiction for some time – how did it feel returning to that setting?

GM: I was really looking forward to it – I love writing fantasy. I don't get to do as much of it as I would like. I was really excited about it, even though this series is very different to writing Warhammer, because the Warhammer World as we know it from contemporary books just doesn't exist yet. This is very much a proto-Empire; we're seeing a land of barbarians and tribesmen change from one state of affairs to another, albeit slowly, taking their first steps towards the Empire as we know it.

I've always loved writing fantasy books – axes swinging, cavalry charges, that's the kind of stuff I enjoy the most. I write it a lot quicker than I write 40k and Horus Heresy – I find those require a much more meticulous approach, and they need more reworkings along the way before I am happy to hand the manuscript in. Fantasy novels tend to flow a lot quicker and I am much more pleased with the initial output. It feels more natural because you can relate to the characters much more easily than in 40k. They still want much the same things that we do – a roof over your head, companionship, family. In 40k characters are more worried about not being crushed by daemons or orks invading your home world. In Warhammer you still have concerns of beastmen and ogres and orcs, of course, but the characters' immediate homely concerns are much more familiar to us. That's probably why it's easier to write, but that also presents its own challenges, because you still want to make it feel like a different world, not just a historical setting.

BL: As you say, Sigmar casts a long shadow in the history of the Empire. How do you approach writing about a character that is so well-known within the Games Workshop background?

GM: You need to make sure he gets plenty of 'wow' moments in the books – flying through the air to smash a dragon ogre in the face with Ghal-maraz, fighting Nagash, any number of big moments. You also give him enough humanity to make sure he has the strength, the understanding and the wisdom to be better than everyone else. There's no getting away from it – Sigmar is the greatest of the Empire, the one who has the vision to see beyond the petty in-fighting and tribal wars. He can see that the race will either live together or die alone. Therefore he needs to come across as the kind of person people would follow into battle, or listen to when he speaks and change their lives based on his words. That comes with his charisma, but all sorts of things go into making a character charismatic. You're trying to capture a somewhat indefinable characteristic there.

Essentially I tried to cherry-pick the personality traits I wanted to give him that were interesting and fun and heroic but also making sure he wasn't *all* that – he wasn't all square-jawed, Sgt. Rock, leading from the front. He did suffer loss, he wasn't infallible, he did go off at the deep end – he is an Unberogen tribesman barbarian warrior at the end of the day, not a gentleman soldier! The key to making him work was to give him a rounded personality.

BL: How about approaching those events that are detailed in the background? How do you go about making those tense and dramatic, even though the outcome is already known?

GM: Taking events people know and put a surprising twist on them has always been the writer's challenge with this series and the Horus Heresy. We know Sigmar wins at Black Fire Pass, that's a given, and I'm not going to try and subvert Warhammer history by saying he didn't! But still, making it tough for the hero is important. I often use the Bruce Willis/Steven Seagal dichotomy – in *Die Hard* John McClane was always beaten up by the end; he was bloodied, his feet were in tatters, his vest was covered in dirt – you could tell he'd been through the wars. You watch something like *Under Siege* and at the end Steven Seagal has hardly broken sweat. You never really felt he was in danger, whereas with John McClane, while you always knew he was going to win, you didn't know what kind of state he was going to be in.

And that's exactly it for these books. Even though you know someone will make it, you can beat the hell out of them along the way, both mentally and physically. Also, if you build up the characters that surround your hero, they can serve as a means of hurting the main character through their loss. That way your readers feel that, though a victory has been won, a terrible price has been paid to get it. If you create good enough characters, you become attached to them along the way. If some people are lost, you feel there has been tension and things for you to worry about, and you still wonder who is going to live and who is going to die.

BL: There are some epic battles throughout this trilogy, and none more so than in *God King*. How do you go about capturing the full glory – and horror – of warfare?

GM: I often draw sketches of the battle and scenes that are going to happen, picking out the key moments pivotal to the flow. Keeping things coherent, so that the reader can follow what's going in, is important. But it also needs to be ragged enough that you feel the confusion that people in the battle suffer – they can only see what's happening for a few yards around them, their immediate vicinity. They can be fighting and think they are kicking ass, not knowing that the rest of the army has collapsed and is running back to the wall! Or they can be winning, but see a few folk running and think the battle's lost.

It's essentially a mix of camera distances – sometimes you pull out and show the shape of the battle, the flanking and the manoeuvres, the strategic elements; sometimes you're right in the thick of it, and sometimes you're with a couple of units charging through... varying that allows you to show the progress of the battle as well as the nitty-gritty of it. As much as any student of historical warfare or writer of battles might say 'I'd love to see a battle', you really wouldn't! It would just be the most horrifying slaughter you can ever imagine, and trying to remember that is important. You want those moments of glory; you want the cavalrymen breaking the enemy line and surging through and the feeling of exultation that comes with it. But you also have to remind people that we're not glorifying in this – the fact remains that thousands of people are going to die and be maimed for life. It's bloody and it's real and it can be glorious, but it's also horrible.

BL: The second book of the Sigmar trilogy, *Empire*, claimed an unprecedented success when it won the David Gemmell Legend Award recently. How did it feel to win, and what has it done for your career?

GM: It was an awesome moment. Being a huge fan of David Gemmell, to win an award bearing his name was a real affirmation, and proved to me that tie-in fiction is just as legitimate a form of writing as any other. People were voting for the book that they liked, and, although I didn't know David Gemmell, I suspect that's the sort of thing he might have approved of. It was very unexpected given the competition that was there that night – I never thought we would win it. I'm still pretty *'wow'* about it, because *we* did that – my website, the BL website, readers and friends and fans around the world really joined forces to make it happen. I've no idea what margin we won by – and I don't want to know if it was by one vote or a million votes – but either way it was an amazing effort from everyone who banded together.

As far as changes to my career, it's a bit soon to tell, but I've got an axe above my computer now, so that's certainly good!

BL: And what can we expect from Sigmar next?

GM: Well, the biggest challenges (that we know of…) have been met and overcome in these three books, so I'm pretty much free to take the story wherever I want now. I've sown some seeds in the trilogy – particularly the last one – for future stories, ones that will allow me to explore the time of Sigmar in new ways, and tell quite different stories, not just Big Bad arises and We Must Defeat It stories. There's moments of awesome still to come, just not how you might expect them…